Dangerous Connections by

Pierre Choderlos de Laclos

PREFACE.

This Work, or rather Collection, which the Public will, perhaps, still find too voluminous, contains but a small part of the correspondence from which it is extracted. Being appointed to arrange it by the persons in whose possession it was, and who, I knew, intended it for publication, I asked, for my sole recompence, the liberty to reject every thing that appeared to me useless, and I have endeavoured to preserve only the letters which appeared necessary to illustrate the events, or to unfold the characters. If to this inconsiderable share in the work be added an arrangement of those letters which I have preserved, with a strict attention to dates, and some short annotations, calculated, for the most part, to point out some citations, or to explain some retrenchments I have made, the Public will see the extent of my labours, and the part I have taken in this publication.

I have also changed, or suppressed, the names of the personages, and if, among those I have substituted, any resemblance may be found which might give offence, I beg it may be looked on as an unintentional error.

I proposed farther alterations, as to purity of style and diction, in both which many faults will be found. I could also have wished to have been authorised to shorten some long letters, several of which treat separately, and almost without transition, of objects totally foreign to one another. This liberty, in which I was not indulged, would not have been sufficient to give merit to the work, but would have corrected part of its defects.

It was objected to me, that the intention was to publish the letters themselves, and not a work compiled from the letters; that it would be as distant from probability as truth, that eight or ten persons, who were concerned in this correspondence, should have wrote with equal purity of style: — And on my representing that there was not one which did not abound with essential faults, and was not very open to criticism, I was answered, that every reasonable reader would undoubtedly expect to find faults in a collection of letters of private persons, since among all those hitherto published by authors of the highest reputation, and even some academicians, there are none totally exempt from censure. Those reasons have not convinced me; and I am still of opinion they are easier to give than likely to obtain assent; but I had not my option, and submitted, reserving only the liberty of entering my protest, and declaring my dissent, as I now do.

As to the merit of this work, perhaps it does not become me to touch upon it; my opinion neither can, or ought, to influence any one. However, as some wish to know something of a book before they take it in hand, those who are so disposed will proceed with this preface — the rest will do better to pass on to the work itself.

Though inclined to publish those letters, I am yet far from thinking they will meet success; and let not this sincere declaration be construed into the affected modesty of an author: for I declare, with the same frankness, that if I had thought this collection an unworthy offering to the Public, it should not have taken up any part of my time. — Let us try to reconcile this apparent contradiction.

The merit of a work consists in its utility, or its agreeableness, and even in both, when it admits of both. But success, which is not always the criterion of merit, often arises more from a choice of subject than the execution, more from the aggregate of the objects presented than the manner of treating them: such a collection as the title announces this to be, being the letters of a whole circle, and containing a diversity of interests, is not likely to fix the attention of the reader. Besides, the sentiments they contain being feigned or dissembled, can only excite an interest of curiosity, always infinitely inferior to that of sentiment, and less disposed to indulgence, as well as more apt to be struck with defects in the narrative, as they are constantly in opposition to the only desire curiosity seeks to gratify. These defects are, perhaps, partly compensated by the quality of the work; I mean the variety of style — A merit which an author seldom attains, but which here presents itself, and prevents, at least, a dull uniformity. Perhaps merit may also be allowed to many observations, either new or little known, which are interspersed through those letters: and this, to pass the most favourable judgment on them, will be found to constitute their best pretension to pleasing.

The utility of the work, which will, perhaps, be more strongly contested, appears more easy to establish: it is at least useful to morality, to lay open the means used by the wicked to seduce the innocent; and those letters will efficaciously concur for so salutary a purpose. There will also be found in them the proof and example of two important truths, which one would be apt to think unknown, seeing how little they are practised: the one, that every woman who admits a bad man to her society, ends with becoming his victim; the other, that every mother is at least imprudent, that suffers any but herself to gain possession of her daughter's confidence.

Young persons, of both sexes, may also here learn, that the friendship so readily held out to them by people of bad morals, is ever a dangerous snare, equally fatal to their happiness and virtue; yet, abuse or evil always unhappily confining too nearly on good, appears so much to be dreaded in this respect, that far from recommending the perusal of works of this kind to youth, I think it of the utmost importance to keep all such very far from their reach. The time when productions of the nature of the present may be no longer dangerous, but begin to be useful, was fixed by a lady of great good understanding. "I think," said she to me, after having read the manuscript of this correspondence, "I should render my daughter an essential service in putting this book in her hands on her wedding-day." Should all mothers think thus, I shall congratulate myself on having published it.

Yet I shall leave this flattering supposition at a distance; and I still think this collection will please but few. — Men and women of depraved minds will take an interest in discountenancing a work that may injure them; and as they are never wasting in ingenuity, they may bring over the whole class of rigorists, who will be alarmed at the picture we have dared to present of profligacy.

The pretenders to free thinking will take no concern in the fate of a devout woman, whom, for that reason, they will not fail to pronounce weak, whilst the devotee will be displeased to see virtue sink under misfortune, and will complain that religion does not sufficiently display its power. On the other hand, persons of a delicate taste will be disgusted with the simplicity and defective style of many of the letters, whilst the generality of readers, led away with the idea that every thing that appears in print is a work of labour, will think he sees in some of the other letters the laboured style of an author sufficiently apparent, notwithstanding the disguise he has assumed.

To conclude; it will be pretty generally said, that a thing is little worth out of its place; and that if the too correct style of authors takes off from the gracefulness of miscellaneous letters, negligences in these become real faults, and make them insupportable when consigned to the press.

I sincerely own that those reproaches may have some foundation. I believe also, I might possibly be able to answer them, even without exceeding the length of a preface: but it is clear, that were I to attempt to answer every thing, I could do nothing else; and that if I had deemed it requisite to do so, I should at once have suppressed both preface and book.

EXTRACT

FROM THE

CORRESPONDENCE

ON WHAT CONCERNS THE

[No. III.]

THE UTILITY OF NOVELS.

THE NOVEL OF

DANGEROUS CONNECTIONS.

Are novels useful, or are they prejudicial to the morals? is a question long agitated, and not yet resolved; for the reasons on both sides are equally plausible. Undoubtedly Richardson, who is read and cited every where, though prolix and diffuse, has not a little contributed to the practice of pure morality; and yet, on the other hand, what mischiefs have been produced by the immense multitude of novels of all sorts with which France and all Europe have been overrun for some years past; and, as if the evil done by these temporary plagues was not sufficiently accomplished during their short existence, it is prolonged by reviving them in eternal collections. A novel, the morality of which is equivocal, is a very dangerous poison; a novel that only possesses mediocrity, is at best useless. Even a good novel is but aliment for a child, or some weak being, to whom morality unadorned is a disgusting object. Hence we may conclude, that every thinking man will take care to banish this kind of works from his library.

He will then likewise proscribe that novel, now so much prized, called *Dangerous Connections, or Letters collected in a Society, and published for the Instruction of other Societies.*

After having read a few pages of this work, one is almost led to think this title a piece of pleasantry; the letters of Madame de Merteuil, and of the Viscount de Valmont, *published* truly *for the instruction of society.* Is it in order to form people to the detestable art of seduction, or to inspire them with a horror of it? and yet this work has been censured, and approved; has had all the honours of war, while so many other useful works are like the manes of the ancients, to whom a sepulchre was denied, and who were forced to wander upon the gloomy banks of the Styx, and admitted only by stealth. *O cæcas hominum mentes!*

I am far from a wish to calumniate the author, who, I am assured, is a military man of the highest character for wit and good conduct; but his work, which seems to have a moral end in view, is in reality very dangerous. It has been said to be a picture of the manners of a certain class in society; and, if it was not a resemblance, where would be its utility? Must monsters be created to cause in us an aversion of ordinary vices? If it is true, it ought to have been concealed; there are shocking nudities which our minds revolt at rather than receive any instruction from. The veil that covers the Tiberiuses and the Messalinas, ought not to be wholly lifted up.

Young men will find in this novel easy means of seduction; young women will here see portraits of embellished vice; and old libertines will be amused by the exploits of Valmont. But what a monster is Valmont, if such a character exists; and those who know that class of society, assure us, they have met with many such. If there really are such beings, ought not their society to be avoided carefully? It is a forest filled with robbers: to enter it we should be well armed. It is a road full of great precipices, to avoid falling into which, we must be very circumspect.

What a character is the Marchioness de Merteuil! Sometimes she is a Medea, sometimes a Messalina. Read the tenth letter: vice is to be drawn; but should it be drawn in such seducing colours? Are there many young people who will prefer the character of a virtuous man to the brilliant and lively one of the profligate Valmont? Are there many who will not blush at the awkwardness of Cecilia? And when one blushes at being ridiculed, they are not very far from the vice that exempts them from it. In France, ridicule is too much dreaded; they would rather be vicious; and this book will rather assist that taste.

The style of romances may serve to lead us to the knowledge of the morals of ages and nations. Thus the country, which has lately produced the natural and moving *Henrietta of Gerstenfeld*, is far from the state of depravity of Paris and London. I form my opinion from the book. In the last age the French novels were full of gallantry and virtuous love, because then they were gallant and respectful. In this age, they have substituted wit to love, and the novels are stuffed with an unintelligible jargon of metaphysics. Of this they grew tired, and libertinism succeeded to it. From thence so many licentious romances. The immense quantity that are produced is a complete proof of the corruption of the age; the rapidity with which they are bought, the rage with which they are devoured, farther prove this depravation.

Doing justice to the zeal that seems to animate the author of those observations, we may be permitted, I hope, to make some farther remarks on the manner he has presented his? Before we begin to examine the degree of moral utility contained in the novel of *Dangerous Connections*, the author of the correspondence first begs leave to ask whether novels in general are useful or prejudicial to morals? This method is the most prudent; but is it not singular, that, acknowledging the indecision of this question, because the reasons for and against are equally seducing, he is still so bold to condemn, indiscriminately, all novels, without assigning any new reasons in justification of this definitive sentence? On the contrary, the author asserts, Richardson's novels have been useful to morality, to preserve them in their purity and in the same breath advises all thinking men to banish them from their libraries! Are the consequences suitable to the premises? Is not that confounding the genus with the species? But if it was even true, that the best novel is only food for infancy, or a weak being, for whom unadorned morality is a terrifying object, would the author's decision be the more justifiable? I will not determine; but I would ask what he means by those *thinking* men, for whom unadorned morality is not terrifying? It would be, perhaps, those declaiming misanthropes, who censure and despise every thing that does not bear a resemblance to their savage and austere way of thinking? I have sometimes had a good opinion of their understanding, but been ever diffident of their hearts; were we to attend to them, we should also banish from our libraries the divine poem of Telemachus, which is the first of novels, which modest qualification does not hinder it from being, if one may venture to call it, the first of our books; not only by the grandeur of the business it treats, but also by the manner in which it is treated. We should also banish from our libraries even the works of the *Correspondence*, the morality of which is become very interesting, by an ornamented, pure and elegant style; if, notwithstanding those qualities, this work has its opposers, would it find many readers if it was divested of them? God forbid I should ever intend making a general apology for all novels! that would be the idea of a Demoniac; I only mean to justify useful novels. If any one makes a bad use of this kind of writing, I most willingly acquiesce in their condemnation. Let us now examine whether the author of *Dangerous Connections* deserves to suffer.

What is a novel? A correct picture of morals put in motion. — What should be the aim of a novel? To blend instruction with amusement. — When the morals of the actors are corrupt, is it allowable, with deference to decency, to draw them in their proper shades and colours? Undoubtedly it is; but with the greatest caution, lest by giving vice, whose contagion must be dreaded, its true, though seducing and agreeable aspect, without resisting, diminishing, or rendering useless, the effect it may produce by the contrast of gentleness, peace, and happiness, which virtue secures. The author of the *Errors of the Heart and Mind*, and the other of the *Confessions of the Count of — —*, have gone wide of this mark; yet their characters are drawn after nature; the Meilcourts are still the ornament of the Bon Ton societies. But should irregularities be drawn without inflicting their punishment? Should vice, with impunity, applaud its infamous triumphs? Should innocence weep without being avenged? Certainly not. Those novels deserve the severest censure of the author of the Correspondence; those are the books which should be carefully concealed from the busy curiosity of young people. Let any one take the trouble to compare the works I have now quoted, and similar ones, with the novel of *Dangerous Connections*, shall we not always feel a certain aversion, a kind of antipathy for Valmont and the Marchioness de Merteuil, notwithstanding the brilliant cast he has given two performers. Let some attention be paid to the skill with which he has contrasted them in the gentle, sensible, and generous Madame de Rosemonde; how moving, how unaffected her virtue. The following letter, wrote to the victim of the profligate Valmont, is, in my opinion, alone sufficient to counterbalance, at least, the impression this same Valmont, and the infamous accomplice in his crimes, could make.

LETTER CXXX.

Madame de Rosemonde, *to the Presidente de* Tourvel.

"Why, my lovely dear, will you no longer be my daughter? Why do you seem to announce that our correspondence is to cease?[1] Is it to punish me for not guessing at what was improbable; or do you suspect me of creating you affliction designedly? I know your heart too well, to imagine you would entertain such an opinion of mine. — The distress your letter plunges me in is much less on my own account than yours. Oh! my young friend, with grief I tell you, you are too worthy of being beloved ever to be happy in love. Where is there a truly delicate and sensible woman, who has not met unhappiness where she expected bliss? Do men know how to rate the women they possess?

"Not but many of them are virtuous in their addresses, and constant in their affections — but even among those, how few that know how to put themselves in unison with our hearts. I do not imagine, my dear child, their affection is like ours. They experience the same transport often with more violence, but they are strangers to that uneasy officiousness, that delicate solicitude, that produces in us those continual tender cares, whose sole aim is the beloved object. Man enjoys the happiness he feels, woman that she gives.

"This difference, so essential, and so seldom observed, influences, in a very sensible manner, the totality of their respective conduct. The pleasure of the one is to gratify desires; but that of the other is to create them. To know to please is in man the means of success; and in woman it is success itself.

"And do not imagine the exceptions, be they more or less numerous, that may be quoted, can be successfully opposed to those general truths, which the voice of the public has guarantied, with the only distinction as to men of infidelity from inconstancy; a distinction of which they avail themselves, and of which they should be ashamed; which never has been adopted by any of our sex but those of abandoned characters, who are a scandal to us, and to whom all methods are acceptable which they think may deliver them from the painful sensation of their own meanness.

"I thought, my lovely dear, those reflections might be of use to you, in order to oppose the chimerical ideas of perfect happiness, with which love never fails to amuse our imagination. Deceitful hope! to which we are still attached, even when we find ourselves under the necessity of abandoning it—whose loss multiplies and irritates our already too real sorrows, inseparable from an ardent passion. This task of alleviating your trouble, or diminishing their number, is the only one I will or can now fulfil. In disorders which are without remedy, no other advice can be given, than as to the regimen to be observed. The only thing I wish you to remember is, that to pity is not to blame a patient. Alas! who are we, that we dare blame one another? Let us leave the right of judging to the Searcher of hearts; and I will even venture to believe, that in his paternal sight, a crowd of virtues may compensate a single weakness.

"But I conjure you, above all things, my dear friend, to guard against violent resolutions, which are less the effects of fortitude than despondency: do not forget, that although you have made another possessor of your existence (to use your own expression) you had it not in your power to deprive your friends of the share they were before possessed of, and which they will always claim.

"Adieu, my dear child! Think sometimes on your tender mother; and be assured you always will be, above every thing, the dearest object of her thoughts.

"*Castle of — —.*"

If the openness of the little Volanges, or her ignorance, should seem ridiculous to those of her own age, the unhappy consequences that resulted from it, will be an useful lesson to mothers to be cautious in what hands they intrust the education of their children. But can a young girl, who has once imbibed this bad education, avoid the consequences I mention, without any other guide but her timidity and absolute ignorance of vice? Is it in a corrupt world, in which she is just entering, that she will receive the fatal knowledge? Does not the author of the Correspondence himself say, "To enter it, we should be well armed; it is a road full of precipices: to avoid falling into which, we must be very circumspect." This is all well—But if, unfortunately, I am blind, or without a guide, who is to restore me sight, or lead me? I conclude, then, that a young person, who would be pleased, at first, with the brilliant character of the Marchioness de Merteuil, would soon change her opinion, and not be tempted to imitate her, when she would see the dreadful and examplary punishment inflicted on this guilty woman. She will shudder at the thought of the miseries to which one single fault condemned Cecilia Volanges. Valmont perishing in the bloom of life, by a violent death, loaded with the contempt and disgrace of all men of worth, disowned even by the wicked, will deter all those, whose vanity and a desire to shine might induce them to copy such a character, from attempting to imitate him.

(By the ABBÉ KENTZINGER.)

[1] See Letter cxxviii.

DANGEROUS CONNECTIONS.

LETTER I.

CECILIA VOLANGES *to* SOPHIA CARNAY, *at the Convent of the Ursulines of* – –.

You see, my dear friend, I keep my word, and that dress does not totally take up all my time; I shall ever have some left for you. In this single day I have seen more finery of attire, than in the four years we have spent together; and I believe the haughty Tanville[1] will be more mortified at my first visit, when I shall certainly desire to see her, than she used to be every time she came to see us *in fiochi*. Mamma advises with me in every thing; she behaves to me no longer as a boarder in a convent. I have a chamber-maid to myself; a chamber and a closet of my own, and a very pretty scrutoire, of which I keep the key, and where I can lock up every thing. My Mamma has told me, I must be with her every morning at her levee; that it would be sufficient to have my head dressed by dinner, because we should always be alone, and that then she would each day tell me what time I should come to her apartment in the evening. The remainder of my time is at my own disposal; I have my harpsichord, my drawings, and books, just as in the convent, only that the mother abbess is not here to scold. And I may always be idle, if I please: but as I have not my dear Sophy to chat and laugh with, I am as well pleased with some occupation. It is not yet five, and I am not to go to Mamma till seven: what a deal of time, if I had any thing to tell you! but nothing has been yet mentioned to me of any consequence: and if it were not for the preparation I see making, and the number of women employed for me, I should be apt to think they have no notion of my nuptials, and that it was one of old Josephine's[2] tales. Yet Mamma having so often told me, that a young lady should remain in a convent, until she was on the point of marriage, and having now brought me home, I am apt to think Josephine right.

A coach has just stopped at our door, and Mamma has sent for me. If it should be my intended!–I am not dressed, and am all in agitation; my heart flutters. I asked my maid, if she knew who was with my Mamma? "Why," says she, laughing, "it is Mr. C– –." I really believe it is he. I will certainly return and write you the whole; however, that's his name. I must not make them wait. Adieu, for a moment!

How you will laugh at your poor Cecilia, my dear Sophy! I'm quite ashamed! But you would have been deceived as well as I. On entering Mamma's room, I saw a gentleman in black, standing close by her, I saluted him as well as I could, and remained motionless. You may guess, I examined him from head to foot. "Madam," said he to Mamma, "this is a most charming young lady, and I am extremely sensible of your goodness." So positive a declaration made me tremble all over; and not being able to support me, I threw myself in an armed chair, quite red and disconcerted. In an instant he was at my knees, and then you may judge how poor Cecilia's head was bewildered; I instantly started up and shrieked, just as on the day of the great thunder. Mamma burst out laughing, saying, "Well, what's the matter? Sit down, and give Mr. – – your foot." Thus, my dear friend, Mr. – – turns out to be my shoemaker. You can't conceive how much I was ashamed; happily, there was no one but Mamma present. I am, however, resolved when I am married he shall not be my shoemaker. Well! am I not now much the wiser? Farewell! it is almost six, and my maid says it is time to dress. Adieu! my dear Sophy; I love you as much as I did at the convent.

P. S. I don't know whom to send with this, and shall wait till Josephine calls.
Paris, Aug. 3, 17 — .
[1] A boarder in the same convent.
[2] Josephine was the portress of the convent.

LETTER II.

The MARCHIONESS DE MERTEUIL *to the* VISCOUNT VALMONT, *at the Castle of* — — .

Return, my dear Viscount, return! How can you think of idling your days with an old aunt, whose fortune is already settled on you! Set out the moment you receive this letter, for I want you much. A most enchanting idea has just struck me, and I wish to confide the execution of it to you.

This hint should be sufficient, and you should think yourself so highly honoured by my choice, as to fly to receive my orders on your knees: but my favours are thrown away on one who no longer sets a value on them; and you presume upon my kindness, where the alternative must be eternal hatred, or excessive indulgence. I will acquaint you with my scheme; but you, like a true knight errant, must first swear to undertake no other adventure until this is achieved. It is worthy a hero. You will at once satiate love and revenge. It will be an additional exploit to your memoirs; yes, your memoirs, for I will have them published, and I will undertake the task. But to return to what more immediately concerns us. Madame de Volanges intends to marry her daughter: it is yet a secret; but she yesterday informed me of it. And whom do you think she has chosen for her son-in-law? Count Gercourt. Who could have thought I should have been allied to Gercourt? I am provoked beyond expression at your stupidity! Well, don't you guess yet? Oh, thou essence of dulness! What, have you then pardoned him the affair of Madame the Intendante? And I, monster![1] have I not more reason for revenge? But I shall resume my temper; the prospect of retaliation, recalls my serenity.

You and I have been often tormented with the important idea framed by Gercourt, of the lady he intended honour with his hand, and his ridiculous presumption of being exempt from the unavoidable fate of married men. You know his foolish prepossessions in favour of conventual education, and his still more weak prejudices for women of a fair complexion: and I really believe, notwithstanding Volanges' sixty thousand livres a year, he never would have thought of this girl, had she not been black eyed, or not educated in a convent.

Let us convince him, he is a most egregious fool, as one day or other he must be: but that's not the business; the jest will be, should he act upon so absurd an opinion. How we should be diverted the next day with his boasts! for boast he will: and if once you properly form this little girl, it will be astonishing if Gercourt does not become, like so many others, the standing ridicule of Paris. The heroine of this new romance merits all your attention; she is really handsome, just turn'd of fifteen, and a perfect rose-bud; awkward as you could wish, and totally unpolished: but you men don't mind such trifles; a certain languishing air, which promises a great deal, added to my recommendation of her, leaves only to you to thank me and obey. You will receive this letter to-morrow morning: I require to see you at seven in the evening. I shall not be visible to any one else till eight, not even to my chevalier, who happens to be my reigning favourite for the present; he has not a head for such great affairs. You see I am not blinded by love. I shall set you at liberty at eight, and you'll return to sup with the charming girl at ten, for the mother and daughter sup with me. Farewell! it is past noon. Now for other objects.

Paris, Aug. 4, 17—.

[1] To understand this passage, it must be remarked, that the Count de Gercourt had quitted the Marchioness de Merteuil for the Intendante de — —, who had on his account abandoned the Viscount de Valmont, and that then the attachment of the Marchioness to the Viscount commenced. As that adventure was long antecedent to the events which are the subject of these letters, it has been thought better to suppress the whole of that correspondence.

LETTER III.

CECILIA VOLANGES *to* SOPHIA CARNAY.

I have yet no news for my dear friend. Mamma had a great deal of company at supper last night. Notwithstanding the strong inclination I had to make my observations, especially among the men, I was far from being entertained. The whole company could not keep their eyes from me; they whispered; I could observe plainly they were speaking of me, and that made me blush; I could not help it: I wish I could; for I observed when any one looked at the other ladies they did not blush, or the rouge they put on prevented their blushes from being seen. It must be very difficult not to change countenance when a man fixes his eyes on you.

What gave me the most uneasiness was, not to know what they thought of me; however, I think I heard the word pretty two or three times: but I'm sure I very distinctly heard that of awkward; and that must be very true, for she that said so is a relation, and an intimate friend of Mamma's. She seems even to have taken a sudden liking to me. She was the only person who took a little notice of me the whole evening. I also heard a man after supper, who I am sure was speaking of me, say to another, "We must let it ripen, we shall see this winter." Perhaps he is to be my husband; but if so, I have still to wait four months! I wish I knew how it is to be.

Here's Josephine, and she says she is in haste. I must, however, tell you one of my awkward tricks—Oh, I believe that lady was right.

After supper, they all sat down to cards. I sat next Mamma. I don't know how it happened, but I fell asleep immediately. A loud laugh awoke me. I don't know whether I was the object of it; but I believe I was. Mamma gave me leave to retire, which pleas'd me much. Only think, it was then past eleven! Adieu, my dear Sophy! continue to love thy Cecilia, I assure you the world is not so pleasing as we used to think it.

Paris, Aug. 4, 17—.

LETTER IV.

The VISCOUNT DE VALMONT *to the* MARCHIONESS DE MERTEUIL.

Your orders are enchanting, and your manner of giving them still more delightful; you would even make one in love with despotism. It is not the first time, you know, that I regret I am no longer your slave; and yet, monster as you style me, I recall with rapture the time when you honoured me with softer names. I have often even wish'd again to deserve them, and to terminate, by giving along with you an example of constancy to the world. But matters of greater moment call us forth; conquest is our destiny, and we must follow it: we may, perhaps, meet again at the end of our career; for permit me to say, without putting you out of temper, my beautiful Marchioness! you follow me with a pretty equal pace; and since, for the happiness of the world, we have separated to preach the faith, I am inclined to think, that in this mission of love, you have made more proselytes than I. I am well convinced of your zeal and fervour; and if the God of Love judged us according to our works, you would be the patron saint of some great city, whilst your friend would be at most a common village saint. This language no doubt will surprise you; but you must know, that for these eight days I hear and speak no other; and to make myself perfect in it, I am obliged to disobey you.

Don't be angry, and hear me. As you are the depository of all the secrets of my heart, I will intrust you with the greatest project I ever formed. What do you propose to me? To seduce a young girl, who has seen nothing, knows nothing, and would in a manner give herself up without making the least defence, intoxicated with the first homage paid to her charms, and perhaps incited rather by curiosity than love; there twenty others may be as successful as I. Not so with the enterprise that engrosses my mind; its success insures me as much glory as pleasure; and even almighty Love, who prepares my crown, hesitates between the myrtle and laurel, or will rather unite them to honour my triumph. Even you yourself, my charming friend, will be struck with a holy respect, and in a fit of enthusiasm, will exclaim, This is the man after my own heart!

You know the Presidente Tourvel, her devout life, her conjugal love, and the austerity of her principles; that is the object I attack; that is the enemy worthy of me; that is the point I intend to carry. I must tell you, the President is in Burgundy, prosecuting a considerable suit, (I hope to make him lose one of greater importance,) his inconsolable partner is to remain here the whole time of this afflicting widowhood. A mass each day, a few visits to the neighbouring poor, prayers morning and evening, a few solitary walks, pious conferences with my old aunt, and sometimes a melancholy game at whist, are her only amusements: but I am preparing some of a more efficacious nature for her. My guardian angel led me here for our mutual happiness. Fool that I was! I used to regret the time that I sacrificed to the customary ceremonies. How should I now be punished, by being obliged to return to Paris! Fortunately there must be four to make a whist party; and as there is no one here but the curate of the place, my eternal aunt has pressed me much to sacrifice a few days to her; you may judge, I did not refuse her. You can't conceive how much she caresses me ever since; and above all, how much she is edified by seeing me so regular at mass and at prayers. But little does she imagine the divinity I adore there.

Thus, in the space of four days, have I given myself up to a violent passion. You are no stranger to the impetuosity of my desires, and how readily all obstacles fly before me: but I'll tell you what you don't know, that solitude adds immensely to the ardour of desire. I have but one idea; I cherish it by day, and dream on't by night. I must possess this woman, lest I should be so ridiculous as to be in love; for whither may we not be led by frustrated desire? Oh, delicious enjoyment! I implore thee for my happiness, and, above all, for my repose. How happy it is for us, that the women make so weak a defence! Were it otherwise, we should be but their cowardly slaves. I feel myself at this moment penetrated with gratitude towards complaisant ladies, which, naturally leads me to you, at whose feet I prostrate myself to obtain my pardon, and finish this already too long letter. Adieu, my charming friend!

Castle of – –, Aug. 3, 17 – .

LETTER V.

The MARCHIONESS DE MERTEUIL, *to the* VISCOUNT VALMONT.

Do you know, Viscount, your letter is wonderfully insolent, and has almost made me angry? But it plainly proves that you have lost your reason; and that consideration alone suppresses my indignation. Like a tender and generous friend, I forget my own injury, and am wholly taken up with your danger; and irksome as it is to enter into argument, I yield to the necessity of it at this time.

You possess the Presidente Tourvel! What a ridiculous extravagance! I here plainly perceive your downright folly, whose nature is to desire that you cannot obtain. But let's examine this woman. She has regular features, it's true, but a total want of expression; a tolerable shape, but without the least elegance; dresses most horridly, with a bundle of ruffs about her neck, and her stays up to her chin. I tell you as a friend, two such women would be quite sufficient to ruin your reputation. Do you remember the day she collected for the poor at St. Roch, when you thank'd me so much for the view of so curious an exhibition. I think I see her still giving her hand to that great looby with the long hair, ready to fall at each step with her calash of four ells over every one's head, and blushing at every courtesy. Who then would have dared to tell you, you will sigh for this woman? For shame, Viscount! Blush yourself, and return to reason. I'll promise to keep this matter secret.

Let us now examine the disagreeable consequences that await you. What rival have you to encounter? A husband. Don't you feel yourself humiliated at that name? What a shame if you fail! and if you succeed, where is the glory?—I go farther: pleasure is out of the question; for who ever had any with a prude? I mean, with a sincere one: reserv'd in the very bosom of pleasure, they give you but half enjoyments. The entirely devoting one's self, that delirium of voluptuousness, where pleasure is refined by excess—all those gifts of love are strangers to them. I'll prognosticate for you: suppose your summit of happiness, you'll find your Presidente will think she has done enough in treating you as a husband; and, be assured, that in the most tender conjugal tête-à-tête, the numerical distinction *two* is always apparent. But in this case it is much worse; your prude is a devotee, and of that sort you are in a perpetual state of childhood; perhaps you may get over this obstacle: but don't flatter yourself that you'll annihilate it. Should you conquer the love of God, you'll not be able to dispel the fear of the devil; and though in holding your charmer in your arms, you may feel her heart palpitate, it will be from fear, not love. You might, perhaps, had you known this woman sooner, have made something of her; but she is now two-and-twenty, and has been married almost two years. Believe me, Viscount, when a woman is so far incrusted, she must be left to her fate; she will never be any thing more than an undistinguishable individual of a species.

And for such a curious object you refuse to obey me; you bury yourself in your aunt's sepulchre; you abandon a most delicious adventure that is marked out for the advancement of your reputation. By what fatality is it, that Gercourt must always have the advantage of you?

I declare I am not out of temper: but at this instant I am inclined to think you don't deserve the reputation you possess; and I consider your conduct with such a degree of indignation, as tempts me to withdraw my confidence from you. No, I never can bring myself to make Madame de Tourvel's lover the confidant of my secret designs.

I will tell you, however, that the little Volanges has made a conquest. Young Danceny is distracted for her. He has sung with her, and she really sings better than belongs to a convent boarder. They have yet many duos to rehearse together, and I am much mistaken if she would not readily get into unison with him; it is true, Danceny is but a boy yet, who will waste his time in making love, but never will come to the point. Little Volanges is wild enough; but at all events, it will never be so pleasing as you could have made it. I am out of temper with you, and shall most certainly fall out with the Chevalier when he comes home. I would advise him to be mild, for at this time I should feel no difficulty to break with him.

I am certain that if I had sense enough to break off with him now, he would be a prey to the most violent despair; yet nothing diverts me more than an enraged lover. He, perhaps, would call me perfidious, and that word has ever pleased me; it is, after the epithet cruel, the sweetest to a woman's ear, and the least painful to deserve. I will seriously ruminate on this rupture. You are the cause of all this—I shall leave it on your conscience. Adieu! recommend me to your Presidente in her prayers.

Paris, Aug. 7, 17—.

LETTER VI.

VISCOUNT DE VALMONT *to the* MARCHIONESS DE MERTEUIL.

There is then no woman that does not abuse the empire she has gained; and you, whom I have so often called my indulgent friend, are no longer so, you are not afraid to attack me even in the very object of my affections. What a picture have you drawn of Madame de Tourvel! What man would not have forfeited his life by so daring an act of insolence? And what woman but you would not, at least, have determined me to blast her reputation? For heaven's sake! never put me to such rude trials again. I will not be answerable for the consequence. In the name of friendship, have patience till I have this woman, if you must slander her. Don't you know, that the time for its causing any impression on me will be after I have enjoyed her? But where do I wander? Does Madame de Tourvel, in order to inspire a passion, need any deception? No; to be adorable, 'tis enough she is herself. You find fault with her dress: you are right; all ornaments are prejudicial to her; every thing that hides her lovely form is hurtful. It is in unaffected negligence she is truly ravishing. Thanks to the suffocating heat of the season, a deshabille of plain lawn adorns her charming, easy shape. A thin muslin handkerchief covers her bosom; and my stolen, but penetrating glances, have already seized its enchanting form. You say her figure has no expression. What should it express, when nothing speaks to her heart? No, indubitably, she has not, like our coquettes, those false looks, which sometimes seduce, but ever deceive. She knows not how to fill up a void of phrase by an affected smile; and though she has the finest teeth in the world, she only laughs at what pleases her. But she is particularly admirable in the most trifling amusements, where she gives the picture of the frankest and most natural gaiety. In visiting a wretched being that she hastens to relieve, her looks declare the unsullied joy and compassionate bounty of her heart. At the most trifling expression of praise or flattery, the tender embarrassment of unaffected modesty is suffused over her celestial figure. She is a prude and devotee, and thence you conclude, she is cold and inanimate. I think quite otherwise. What astonishing sensibility must she not have, to diffuse it as far as her husband, and to love a being always absent! What stronger proof can you require? I found out a method, however, to obtain another; I directed our walk in such a manner that we had a ditch to leap over, and although very active, she is still more timid—you may very well judge a prude dreads taking a leap. She was obliged to trust herself to me. I raised this modest woman in my arms. Our preparations, and the skip of my old aunt, made our sprightly devotee laugh most immoderately: but as soon as I seized on her, by a dexterous awkwardness, our arms were mutually entwined in each other; I pressed her bosom against mine, and in this short interval I felt her heart palpitate more quickly; a lovely blush covered her face, and her modest embarrassment informed me her heart beat with love and not with fear. My aunt was deceived as you had been, and said, "The child is frightened;" but the charming candour of this child would not permit her to countenance a lie, and she ingenuously answered, "Oh, no; but—" That word alone has cleared up my doubts. From this instant, sweet hope has banished cruel inquietude. I will have this woman. I will take her from a husband who does not deserve her. I'll even snatch her from the god she adores.

How delicious to be by turns the object and conqueror of her remorse! Far be from me the idea of curing her of her prejudices! they will add to my glory and happiness. Let her rely on her virtue, and sacrifice it. Let her crime terrify her, without being able to resist its impulse; and, alarmed with a thousand terrors, let her neither be able to forget or conquer them but in my embraces.

Then I'll consent to her saying, "I adore thee." She, of all your sex, will be the only one worthy to pronounce that word. Then shall I truly be the god of her idolatry. Confess ingenuously to me, that in our arrangements, as indifferent as they are free, what we style happiness scarce deserves the name of pleasure. I'll freely acknowledge, I imagined my heart withered, and incapable only of sensual gratification; I began to deplore my prematurely advanced age; Madame de Tourvel has restored me to the illusive charms of youth. With her, actual enjoyment is not necessary to my happiness. The only thing that alarms me is the time this adventure will take up; for I am resolved to risk nothing. In vain do I bring to remembrance my successful acts of temerity on many occasions; I can't think of attempting them now. To crown my bliss, she must give herself up, and that's not an easy matter to accomplish.

I am confident even you must approve my discretion, for as yet I have not mentioned the word love; but we are already got as far as those of friendship and confidence. In order to deceive her as little as possible, and, above all, to guard against any thing that may come to her knowledge which might shock her, I have myself related to her, by way of self-accusation, some of my most remarkable adventures. You would be delighted to see how innocently she catechises me. She says she is determined to make a convert of me: but has not the least suspicion how much the purchase will cost her. She does not think, that her becoming advocate, to use her own words, *for the many I have undone*, she is beforehand pleading her own cause.

This idea struck me yesterday, in the midst of one of her little sermons, and I could not resist the pleasure of interrupting her, to tell her that she spoke like a prophet. Adieu, my lovely friend! you see I am not totally lost.

P. S. But what's become of our poor Chevalier? Has he destroyed himself in a fit of despair? Indeed you are a million of times worse than I; and if I was vain, you'd mortify me to be so much outdone.

From the Castle of — —,
Aug. 9, 17 —.

LETTER VII.

CECILIA VOLANGES *to* SOPHIA CARNAY.[1]

If I have not said any thing to you as yet of my marriage, it is because I am as ignorant of the matter as the first day I came home. I begin to accustom myself not to think about it, and I am very happy as I am. I practice my harpsichord and singing much; and I am fonder of them than when I had a master, or rather now I have got a better one. The Chevalier Danceny, the gentleman I mentioned to you before, with whom I sang at Madame Merteuil's, is so obliging to come every day to sing with me for hours together. He is exceedingly agreeable. He sings like an angel, and sets the words of his own composition to very pretty music. It is a great pity he is a Knight of Malta! I think, were he to embark in wedlock, his wife would be very happy. He is the sweetest creature breathing. Without the affectation of complaisance, every thing he does is endearing. He always chides me about music, or some other trifle; but he blends with his censures so much concern and good nature, that one can't help being pleased. His very looks seem to speak obliging things. And with all this, he is the most complaisant man possible: for instance; yesterday he was asked to a private concert, but spent the evening at Mamma's, which gratified me exceedingly; for, when he is absent, I have no one to speak to, and am quite stupid: but, when he is with us, we chat and sing together, and he always has something to say to me. Madame de Merteuil and he are the only two amiable persons I yet know. Adieu, my dear friend! I promised to be perfect to-day in a little air, with a very difficult accompaniment, and I must keep my word. I must set about practising it against his return.

From − −, Aug. 7, 17−.

[1] Not to tire the reader's patience, we suppress many of the letters of this daily correspondence, and give only them we think necessary for unfolding the events of this society. For the same reason we suppress all those of Sophia Carnay, and several of those of the actors in this piece.

LETTER VIII.

Presidente DE TOURVEL *to* MADAME DE VOLANGES.

Permit me, Madam, to assure you, no one can be more sensible of the confidence you repose in me, nor have more at heart the happy establishment of Mademoiselle de Volanges than I have. With my whole soul I wish her that felicity which I am confident she merits, and which I have no doubt she will obtain through your prudence. I have not the honour of knowing Count Gercourt, but conceive the most favourable opinion of him, as he is your choice. I limit my good wishes to the hope that this match may be as happy as mine, which was also one of your making, and which gratitude daily calls to my remembrance. May the happiness of Mademoiselle de Volanges be the reward of that I enjoy, and may the best of friends be also the happiest of mothers!

I am really mortified that I am not at present able, personally, to assure you of the grateful sentiments of my heart, and to accomplish what I wish for much, an acquaintance with Mademoiselle de Volanges.

After having experienced your maternal fondness, I think I am entitled to the tender friendship of a sister from her. I entreat you, Madam, to claim it for me, until I have it in my power to deserve it. I propose residing in the country during Mr. de Tourvel's absence. I now enjoy and improve in the respectable company of Madame Rosemonde. This lady is ever delightful; her great age has not the least impaired her gaiety or memory; her body may be eighty-four, but her understanding is only twenty. Our retirement is enlivened by the Viscount Valmont, her nephew, who has condescended to spend a few days with us. I only knew him by character, which gave me an unfavourable opinion of him, that now I don't think he deserves. Here, where the bustle of the world does not affect him, he is very agreeable, and owns his failings with great candour. He converses with me very confidentially, and I sometimes sermonize him with asperity; you, who know him well, will, I dare say, think such a conversion worth attempting: but I am afraid, notwithstanding all his promises, eight days in Paris will destroy all my labours; however, his residence here will be so much gained from his general course of life, and I am clear, that the best thing he can do will be to remain in inactivity. He knows that I am now writing to you, and begs leave to present his most respectful compliments. I beg you'll also accept mine with that condescension you have ever had for me, and be assured of the sincerity of the sentiments with which I have the honour to be, &c.

From the Castle of — —,

Aug. 9, 17—.

LETTER IX.

MADAME DE VOLANGES *to the* Presidente DE TOURVEL.

I never yet doubted, my young and charming friend, of your friendship for me, nor of the interest you take in all my concerns. It is not to clear up this point, on which I hope we are for ever agreed, that I reply to your answer; but I think myself obliged to say a word or two relative to Viscount Valmont.

I must own, I did not expect to meet such a name in a letter from you. How is it possible there can be any communication between you and him? You do not know that man. Where did you find the idea you have imbibed of the heart of a libertine? You tell me of his uncommon candour; yes, truly, Valmont's candour is very uncommon. He is yet more false and dangerous than he is lovely and seducing: never since his earliest youth, has he taken a step, or spoke a word, without a design; and never formed a design that was not criminal or improper. My dear friend, you know me; you know that of all the virtues I endeavour to acquire, indulgence is the one I cherish most; and if Valmont had been hurried away by the impetuosity of his passions, or if, like a thousand more at his time of life, he had been seduced by the errors of youth, I would have compassionated his person, blamed his conduct, and have patiently waited until time, the happy maturer of green years, should have made him fit for the society and esteem of worthy people: but that's not Valmont's case; his conduct is the result of principle; he calculates how far a man can proceed in villainy without risking reputation, and has chosen women for his victims, that his sacrifices may be wicked and cruel without danger. I shall not dwell on the numbers he has seduced; but how many has he not utterly undone? Those scandalous anecdotes never come within the sphere of your retired and regular course of life. I could, however, relate you some that would make you shudder; but your mind, pure as your soul, would be defiled with such descriptions: convinced, as I am, that Valmont will never be an object of danger to you, such armour is unnecessary to guard you. I can't, however, refrain telling you, that successful or not, no woman he ever yet dangled after, but had reason to repent her folly. The only exception to this general rule is the Marchioness de Merteuil; she alone has been capable not only of resisting, but of completely defeating his wickedness.

I must acknowledge, this trait in her character strikes me the most forcibly; and has amply justified her to the world for some trifling indiscretions in the outset of her widowhood.[1] However, my charming friend, authorised as I am, by age, experience, and much more by friendship, I am obliged to inform you, the world take notice of Valmont's absence; and that if they come to know that he has for any time formed a trio with you and his aunt, your reputation will be at his mercy, which is the greatest misfortune that can happen to a woman. I therefore advise you to prevail on his aunt not to detain him longer; and if he should still determine to remain, I think you should not hesitate a moment on quitting the place. But why should he remain? How does he employ himself in the country? I am certain, if his motions were watched, you would discover that he has only taken up his residence in that commodious retreat for the accomplishment of some act of villainy he meditates in the neighbourhood.

When it is not in our power to prevent an evil, let us at least take care to preserve ourselves from its consequences. Adieu! my lovely friend. An accident retards my daughter's marriage for some little time. Count Gercourt, whom we daily expected, informs me his regiment is ordered for Corsica; and as the military operations are not yet over, it will be impossible for him to return before winter: this disconcerts me; however, it gives me hope we shall have your company at the wedding; and I was vexed it should take place without you. Adieu! I am as free from compliment as reserve, entirely yours.

P. S. Bring me back to the recollection of Madame de Rosemonde, whom I shall always love for her great merit.

[1] Madame de Volanges' error informs us, that Valmont, like most profligate wretches, did not impeach his accomplices.

LETTER X.

The MARCHIONESS DE MERTEUIL, to VISCOUNT VALMONT.

Are you out of temper with me, Viscount, or are you dead, or, which is pretty much the same, do you live no longer but for your Presidente? This woman, who has restored you to the *illusive charms of youth*, will also soon restore you to its ridiculous follies. You are already a timid slave; you may as well be in love at once. You renounce your *happy acts of temerity on many occasions;* and thus, without any principle to direct you, give yourself up to caprice, or rather chance. Do you know, that love is like physic, *only the art of assisting nature?* You see I fight you on your own ground, but it shall not excite any vanity in me; for there is no great honour in engaging a vanquished enemy. *She must give herself up*, you tell me; without doubt she must, and will, as others, but with this difference, that she'll do it awkwardly. But that it may terminate in her giving herself up, the true method is to begin by taking her. What a ridiculous distinction, what nonsense in a love matter; I say love; for you really are in love. To speak otherwise would be deceiving you, would be concealing your disorder from you. Tell me, then, my dear sighing swain, of the different women you have had, do you think you gained any of them by force? Whatever inclination we may have to yield, however we feel our compliance unavoidable, still must there be a pretence; and can there be a more commodious one for us, than that which gives us the appearance of being overcome by force? For my part, I own nothing charms me to much as a brisk lively attack, where every thing is carried on with regularity, but with rapidity; which never puts us to the painful dilemma of being ourselves constrained to remedy an awkwardness which, on the contrary, we should convert to our advantage; and which keeps up the appearance of violence, even when we yield, and dexterously flatters our two favourite passions, the glory of a defence, and the pleasure of a defeat. I must own that this talent, which is more uncommon than one would imagine, always pleased me, even when it did not guide me, and that it has sometimes happened that I have only surrendered from gratitude: thus, in our tournaments of old, beauty gave the prize to valour and address.

But you, you who are no longer yourself, you proceed as if you dreaded success. And pray how long is it since you have fallen into the method of travelling so gently, and in such bye-roads? Believe me, when one has a mind to arrive, post-horses and the high road is the only method.

But let us drop this subject; it the more puts me out of temper, as it deprives me of the pleasure of seeing you. At least, write me oftener than you do, and acquaint me with your progress. You seem to forget that this ridiculous piece of business has already taken up a fortnight of your time, and that you neglect every body.

Now I mention neglect, you resemble those who send regularly to inquire of the state of health of their sick friends, and who never concern themselves about the answer. You finish your last letter by asking whether the Chevalier is dead. I make no reply, and you are no farther concerned about the matter; have you forgot my lover is your sworn friend? But comfort yourself; he is not dead; or if he was, it would be from excess of pleasure. This poor Chevalier, how tender! How formed for love! How sensibly he affects one! He distracts me. Seriously, then, his happiness in being loved by me, inspires me with a true affection for him.

The very day I wrote you that I was taken up in contriving our rupture, how happy did I not make him! And yet I was in earnest engaged how I should make him desperate when he appeared. Whether whim or inclination, he never appeared to so much advantage. However, I received him coolly; he expected to spend a couple of hours with me before my time of seeing company. I told him I was going abroad, he begg'd to know where; I refused to tell him. He insisted to know; *where you will not be,* I replied with some tartness. Happily for him he was petrified at my answer; for had he pronounced a syllable, a scene would have ensued which would infallibly have brought on the intended rupture. Astonished at his silence, I cast a look at him, with no other design, I swear, but to observe his countenance; I was instantly struck with the deep and tender sadness that covered this charming figure, which you have owned it is so difficult to resist. The same cause produced the same effect; I was a second time overcome; from that instant I endeavoured to prevent his having any reason to complain. I am going out on business, said I, in a milder tone, and the business relates to you; ask no more questions. I shall sup at home; at your return you'll know all: he then recovered his speech; but I would not suffer him to go on. I'm in great haste, continued I. Leave me until night. He kissed my hand and departed. In order to make him, or perhaps myself, amends, I immediately resolved to show him my villa, of which he had not the least suspicion; I called my faithful maid, Victoire. I am seized with my dizziness, said I; let all my servants know I am gone to bed; when alone, I desired her to put on a footman's dress, and metamorphosed myself into a chamber-maid.

She ordered a hackney-coach to my garden-door, and we instantly set out; Being arrived at this temple dedicated to love, I put on my genteelest deshabille; a most delicious one, and of my own invention: it leaves nothing exposed, but every thing for fancy to imagine. I promise you the pattern for your Presidente, when you shall have rendered her worthy of wearing it.

After those preparations, whilst Victoire was taken up with other matters, I read a chapter of the Sopha, a letter of the New Eloisa, and two of La Fontaine's Tales, to rehearse the different characters I intended to assume. In the mean time, my Chevalier came to my house, with his usual eagerness. My porter refused him admittance, and informing him I was indisposed, delivered him a note from me, but not of my writing; according to my usual discretion. He opens, and finds in Victoire's writing;—"At nine precisely, at the Boulevard, opposite the coffee-houses."

Thither he proceeds, and a little footman whom he does not know, or at least thinks he does not know, for it was Victoire, tells him he must send back his carriage and follow him. All this romantic proceeding heated his imagination, and on such occasions a heated imagination is useful. At last he arrives, and love and astonishment produced in him the effect of a real enchantment. In order to give him time to recover from his surprise, we walked a while in the grove; I then brought him back to the house. The first thing which presented itself to his view, was a table with two covers, and a bed prepared. From thence we went into the cabinet, which was most elegantly decorated. There, in suspense, between reflection and sentiment, I flung my arms around him, and letting myself fall at his knees—"Alas! my dear friend," said I, "what reproaches do I not deserve, for having, for a moment, given you uneasiness by an affected ill-humour, in order to enhance the pleasure and surprise of this moment, for having concealed my heart from your tenderness! Forgive me; I will expiate my crime with the most ardent love." You may guess what was the effect of this sentimental declaration. The happy Chevalier raised me, and my pardon was sealed on the same sopha where you and I, in a similar way, so cheerfully sealed our eternal rupture.

As we had six hours to pass together, and that I was determined the whole time should be devoted to delight him, I moderated his transports, and called lovely coquetry to the aid of tenderness. I don't know I ever took so much pains to please, or ever, in my own opinion, succeeded so well. After supper, by turns, childish and rational, wanton and tender, sometimes even libertine. I took pleasure in considering him as a Sultan, in the midst of his Seraglio, to whom I alternately supplied the places of different favourites; and indeed, his reiterated offerings, though always received by the same woman, were received as by a new mistress.

At length, when day appeared, it was necessary to part; and notwithstanding all he said, and even what he did, to prove the contrary, there was, on his part, as much necessity for it, as want of inclination. At the instant of parting, for a last adieu, I delivered him the key of this happy mansion: I had it for you alone, said I, and it is fit you should be the master of it; it is but right the high priest should dispose of the temple. By this artifice, I anticipated any reflections which might arise in his mind relative to the propriety of a villa, which is ever matter of suspicion. I know him so well, that I'm certain he will never make use on't but for me; and if I should have a fancy to go there without him, I have another key. He by all means would make an appointment for another day; but I as yet love him too much, to wear him out soon; the true maxim is, not give into excess, but with those one wishes to be rid of. This he is a stranger to; but, happily for him, I know it for us both.

I perceive it is now three in the morning, and that I have wrote a volume, though I intended but a short letter. Such are the charms of confidential friendship; it is that confidential friendship that renders you the object I love most; but indeed the Chevalier is the object that pleases me most.

From — —, Aug. 12, 17—.

LETTER XI.

The Presidente DE TOURVEL *to* MADAME VOLANGES.

The severity of your letter would have terrified me strangely, dear madam, if I had not here stronger reasons to think myself perfectly safe, than those you give me for apprehension. The formidable Mr. de Valmont, the terror of our sex, seems to have laid aside his murderous arms, before he entered this castle. Far from having formed any design, he did not even appear to have brought any claims; and the accomplishments of an amiable man, which his enemies even give to him, almost vanish to give place to the character of good-natured creature. Probably it is the country air has wrought this miracle; one thing I can assure you, tho' incessantly with me, even seemingly pleased with my company, not a word that has the least tendency to love has escaped him, not even one of those phrases that most men assume, without having, like him, any thing to plead in their justification. Never does he put one under the necessity of flying for shelter to that reservedness to which a woman, who will maintain her dignity, is obliged to have recourse now-a-days, to keep the men within bounds. He does not abuse the gaiety he inspires. Perhaps he flatters a little too much; but it is with so much delicacy, that he would reconcile even modesty to praise. To conclude, had I a brother, I would wish him to be what Mr. de Valmont is here. There are many women, perhaps, would wish him to have a more *pointed* gallantry; and I own I am greatly obliged to him for the good opinion he entertains, by not confounding me with them.

This description undoubtedly differs very much from that you have given me; and yet they may both carry a resemblance, if we ascertain our times. He himself agrees he has done many wrong things, and, perhaps, the world has imputed many more to him. But I have seldom met with men who spoke more respectfully of women of character, almost to enthusiasm.

In this point, at least, you inform me he is not a deceiver. I rest the proof on his conduct to Madame de Merteuil. He often speaks of her; and always so much in her praise, and with the appearance of so much affection, that I imagined, until I received your letter, that what he had called friendship was really love. I condemn myself for my rash opinion, in which I am the more blameable, as he himself has frequently spoke in her justification; and I own his honest sincerity I looked on as artifice. I don't know, but it appears to me, that the man who is capable of so constant a friendship for a deserving woman, cannot be an abandoned libertine; but whether we are to attribute his prudent conduct here to any scheme in this neighbourhood, as you suppose, is a question. There are some few agreeable women around us; however, he seldom goes abroad except in the morning, and then he says he goes a shooting; he seldom brings home any game, it is true, but he tells us he is a bad shot. However, what he does out of doors, concerns me but little; and if I wished to be informed, it would be only to have one more reason to come into your opinion, or to bring you over to mine.

As to what you propose, that I should endeavour to shorten the time of Mr. de Valmont's residence here, it appears to me a matter of some difficulty, to desire an aunt not to have her nephew with her; and a nephew for whom she has the greatest affection. However, I promise you, through deference only, and not that I see any necessity for it, to take the first opportunity to make this request either to him or her. As to myself, Mr. de Tourvel is acquainted with my intention of remaining here until his return, and he would, with reason, be astonished at my levity. Thus, Madam, I have given you a long explanation; but I thought a justification of Mr. de Valmont to you, where it appears very necessary, a debt to truth. I am not the less sensible of the friendship which suggested your advice. I am also indebted to it for the obliging manner in which you acquaint me of the delay of Madame de Volanges' nuptials, for which accept my most sincere thanks; but whatever pleasure I might expect on that occasion in your company, would be willingly sacrificed to the satisfaction of knowing M. de Volanges' happiness sooner completed, if, after all, she can be more so than with a mother, every way deserving her respect and tenderness. I partake with her those sentiments which attach me to you, and beg you'll receive this assurance of them with your usual goodness.

I have the honour to be, &c.

From − −, *Aug.* 13, 17−.

LETTER XII.

CECILIA VOLANGES *to the* MARCHIONESS DE MERTEUIL.

Madam,

My Mamma is indisposed; she will not go out to-day, and I must keep her company: thus I am deprived the honour of attending you to the opera. I assure you I regret more the loss of your company than the performance. I hope you are persuaded of this, for I have a great affection for you. Be so good to tell the Chevalier Danceny, I have not yet got the collection which he mentioned, and that if he can bring it himself to-morrow, I shall be obliged to him. If he comes to-day, he will be told we are not at home; but the reason is, Mamma sees no company. I hope she will be better to-morrow.

I have the honour, &c.

From − −, *Aug.* 13, 17−.

LETTER XIII.

The MARCHIONESS DE MERTEUIL *to* CECILIA VOLANGES.

I am much concerned, my charming girl, to be deprived of the pleasure of seeing you, as well as for the cause; I hope we shall find another opportunity. I performed your commission with the Chevalier Danceny, who will certainly be very sorry to hear of your Mamma's indisposition; if she'll admit me to-morrow, I'll wait on her. She and I will attack the Chevalier de Belleroche at piquet[1]; and in winning his money, we shall have the double pleasure of hearing you sing with your amiable master, to whom I shall propose it. If it be agreeable to your Mamma and you, I will answer for my two Knights and myself. Adieu, my lovely girl! My compliments to Madame de Volanges. I embrace you most affectionately.

From – –, Aug. 13, 17–.

[1] This is the same who is mentioned in Madame de Merteuil's letters.

LETTER XIV.

CECILIA VOLANGES *to* SOPHIA CARNAY.

I did not write to you yesterday, my dear Sophy; but I assure you it was not pleasure that prevented me. My Mamma was indisposed, and I did not quit her the whole day. At night, when I retired, I had not spirits to do any thing; and I went to bed very early, in order to terminate the day: never did I pass so long a one. It is not but I love Mamma very much; but I don't know how it was. I was to have gone to the opera with Madame de Merteuil; the Chevalier Danceny was to have been there. You know they are the two I love most. When the hour of the opera arrived, my heart was oppressed in spite of me; every thing displeased me, and I wept involuntarily. Fortunately Mamma was in bed, and could not see me. I am sure Chevalier Danceny must have been chagrined as well as I; but the company and performance must have amused him: I am very differently situated. But Mamma is better to-day, and Madame de Merteuil, Chevalier Danceny, and another gentleman, will be with us. Madame de Merteuil comes late, and it's very tiresome to be so long alone. It is only eleven, yet I must practise my harpsichord, it is true; and then my toilet will take me up some time, for I will have my head well dressed to-day. I really believe our mother Abbess was right, that one becomes a coquet on entering into life. I never had so strong a desire to be handsome, as for some days past, and I think I am not so handsome as I thought; in women's company that paint, one looks much worse; for example, all the men think Madame de Merteuil handsomer than me; that does not vex me much, because she loves me: and then she assures me the Chevalier Danceny thinks me handsomer than her. It is very good natured of her to tell me so; she even seemed to be glad of it. Now I don't conceive how that can be. It is because she loves me so much! And he too! Oh that gives me infinite pleasure! I really think, barely looking at him makes me appear handsome. I would always be looking at him, if I was not afraid of meeting his eyes: for as often as that happens, it disconcerts me, and gives me uneasiness; but that signifies nothing. Adieu, my dear Sophy! I am going to dress.

Paris, Aug. 14, 17–.

LETTER XV.

VISCOUNT VALMONT *to the* MARCHIONESS DE MERTEUIL.

Indeed you are very kind not to abandon me to my melancholy fate: the life I lead here is really fatiguing, from excess of repose and insipid uniformity. Reading your letter with the particulars of your delightful excursion, I was tempted twenty times to pretend business, fly to your feet, and beg of you to commit, in my favour, an infidelity to your Chevalier, who really does not deserve his bliss. Do you know you have roused my jealousy? Why tell me of an eternal rupture? I recant an oath taken in a fit of frenzy. We should not have been entitled to so solemn a privilege, had we seriously intended to keep it. Ah, may I be one day revenged in your embraces, for the vexation the Chevalier's happiness gives me! I am all indignation I own, to think that a man who has scarce common sense, without taking the least trouble, and only simply following the instinct of his heart, should find a happiness I can't attain. Oh, I will disturb him: promise me I shall disturb him! But have you not humiliated yourself? You take the trouble to deceive him, and he is happier than you. You think you have him in your toils, but you are in his. He sleeps quietly, whilst you wake for his pleasures. What could his slaves do more?

Hark ye, my lovely friend, while you divide yourself among many, I am not in the least jealous; I then look down on your lovers as on Alexander's successors; incapable of preserving among them that empire where I reigned sole monarch; but that you should give yourself up entirely to one of them, that another should exist as happy as me, I will not suffer; don't expect I'll bear it! Either take me again, or take another; and do not, by any exclusive caprice, betray the inviolable friendship we have sworn to each other.

Is it not curious, that I should have reason to complain of love? You see I give into your ideas, and confess my errors. If not to be able to exist without the possession of what we desire, if to sacrifice time, pleasure, and life for it, then am I really in love; and I have made no progress. I should not even have a word to say to you on the subject, but for an accident that racks my imagination, and leaves me in suspense between hope and fear.

You know my huntsman; a treasure of intrigue, and a true valet as ever dramatic pen drew. You may conceive he had it in his instructions to be in love with the waiting-maid, and make the servants drunk.

The rascal is happier than his master; he has already succeeded; and has just discovered that Madame de Tourvel has appointed one of her people to observe me, and even to follow me in my morning excursions, as much as possible, without being perceived.

What does this woman mean? Thus, then, the most virtuous of them will venture to do things, that one of us would not dare think on! Well, I swear—but before I think of being revenged for this female artifice, I will endeavour to convert it to my advantage. Hitherto those suspected excursions had no view; I must give them one. This deserves my utmost attention, and I quit you to reflect on it. Adieu, my charming friend!

Always from the Castle of ――,
Aug. 15, 17―.

LETTER XVI.

CECILIA VOLANGES *to* SOPHIA CARNAY.

Ah, Sophia, I have a deal of news! But may be I should not tell you: I must tell it, however, to somebody, I can't keep it. Chevalier Danceny — I'm in such trouble, I can't write; I don't know where to begin. Since the agreeable evening that I related to you I spent at Mamma's[1], with him and Madame de Merteuil, I said no more of him: that was because I resolved not to say any more of him to any one; but I was always thinking of him notwithstanding. Since that, he is become so melancholy, that it makes me uneasy; and when I asked him the reason, he answered me he was not so, but I could plainly see he was. He was yesterday more so than usual; that did not, however, prevent him from singing with his usual complaisance; but every time he looked at me, my heart was ready to break. After we had done singing, he locked up my harpsichord; and bringing me the key, begged I would play again in the evening when I was alone. I had no suspicion of any thing; I even refused him: but he insisted so much, that I promised I would. He had his reasons for it. When I retired to my room, and my maid was gone, I went to my harpsichord. I found hid among the strings an unsealed letter from him. Ah, if you did but know all he writes! Since I read his letter, I am in such raptures I can think of nothing else. I read it over four times running, and then locked it in my desk. I got it by heart; and when I laid down I repeated it so often, I could not think of sleeping; as soon as I shut my eyes, I thought I saw him, telling me every thing I had just read. I did not sleep till very late; and, as soon as I awoke, (though it was very early,) I got up for the letter, to read it at my leisure; I took it into bed, and began to kiss it; as if — — but may be I did wrong to kiss a letter thus, but I could not help it.

Now, my dear friend, if I am very well pleased, I am also very much troubled; for certainly I must not answer it. I know that must not be, and yet he urges it; and if I don't answer it, I am certain he will be again melancholy. It is a great pity; what would you advise me to? But you know no more than I. I have a great mind to tell Madame de Merteuil, who has a great affection for me. I wish I could console him; but I would not do any thing wrong. We are taught good-nature, and yet we are forbid to follow its dictates, when a man is in question. That I can't understand. Is not a man our neighbour as well as a woman, and still more so? For have we not a father as well as a mother, a brother as well as a sister, and there is the husband besides? Yet if I was to do any thing that was not right, perhaps Mr. Danceny himself would no longer have a good opinion of me! Oh, then I would rather he should be melancholy! And I shall still be time enough; though he wrote yesterday, I am not obliged to write to-day; and I shall see Madame de Merteuil this evening, and if I can have so much resolution, I will tell her all. Following her advice, I shall have nothing to reproach myself; and may be she may tell me I may give him a few words of answer, that he may not be melancholy. I'm in great uneasiness! Adieu! Be sure tell me what you think I ought to do.

Aug. 13, 17 — .

[1] The letter that is mentioned here was not found; but there is reason to believe that it is that Madame de Merteuil mentions in her letter which Cecilia Volanges refers to.

LETTER XVII.

The CHEVALIER DANCENY *to* CECILIA VOLANGES.

Before I give way, Miss, whether shall I call it, to the pleasure or necessity of writing to you, I begin by entreating you to hear me: I am sensible I stand in need of your indulgence, in daring to declare my sentiments for you; if they wanted only vindication, indulgence would be useless. Yet, after all, what am I about to do, but exhibit your own productions? I have nothing to say that my looks, my confusion, my conduct, and even my silence, have not already told you! Why should you be displeased with sentiments to which you have given birth? Proceeding from you, they certainly should be offered you; if they are as inflamed as my heart, they are as chaste as your own. Where is the crime to have discovered how to set a proper value on your charms, your bewitching qualifications, your enchanting graces, and that affecting ingenuousness which so much enhances such valuable accomplishments? No; undoubtedly there is not: but one may be unhappy, without being guilty, which must be my fate, should you refuse to accept a homage, the first my heart ever made. Were it not for you, I should still have been, if not happy, yet undisturbed. I saw you, and tranquillity fled my soul, and left my happiness uncertain!

And yet you seem to wonder at my grief, and demand the cause; I have even sometimes thought it gave you uneasiness. Ah, speak but the word, and my felicity will be complete! But before you pronounce it, remember it may also overwhelm me in misery. Be the arbitress of my fate, you can make me happy or miserable for ever; into what dearer hands can I commit such a trust? I shall finish as I began, by imploring your indulgence; I have entreated you to hear me; I shall farther presume to beg an answer. If refused, I shall think you are offended; though my heart is witness, my respect equals my love.

P. S. If you indulge me with an answer, you can convey it in the same way through which manner you receive this: it is both safe and commodious.

Aug. 18, 17—.

LETTER XVIII.

CECILIA VOLANGES *to* SOPHIA CARNAY.

What, my Sophia, you blame beforehand the step I intend to take! I had uneasiness enough already, but you add considerably to it. You say, I certainly ought not to answer his letter; you are quite, at your ease, and can give advice; but you know not how I am circumstanced, and are not able, not being on the spot, to give an opinion. Sure I am, were you so situated, you would act as I do. Certainly, according to etiquette, I should not answer his letter; and by my letter of yesterday, you may perceive my intention was not to reply; but I don't think any one was ever so circumstanced as I am.

And, then, to be left to my own discretion! For Madame de Merteuil, whom I depended on seeing in the evening, did not come. Every thing is against me; she is the cause of my knowing him. In her company, it has almost always been, that I have seen and spoke to him. It is not that I have any ill-will towards her for it—but I'm left to myself when I want her advice most. Well, I'm greatly to be pitied! Only think, yesterday he came as usual. I was so confused I could not look at him; he could not speak to me, for Mamma was with us. I knew he would be vexed when he found I had not wrote to him; I did not know how to appear. He immediately asked me if I had a mind he should bring my harpsichord. My heart beat so I could scarcely say yes. When he returned it was much worse. I just glanced at him. He did not see me, but looked as if he was ill; that made me very unhappy. He tuned my harpsichord, and said, with a sigh, Ah, Miss! He spoke but those two words; and in such a tone as threw me into the greatest confusion. I struck a few chords without knowing what I did: Mamma asked him to sing; he excused himself, saying, he was not well; but I had no excuse, and was forced to sing. I then wished I had no voice; and chose, on purpose, a song that I did not know; for I was certain I could not sing any one, and some notice would have been taken.

Fortunately a visitor came; and as soon as I heard a coach coming, I stopped, and begged he would put up my harpsichord. I was much afraid he would then go away, but he returned. Whilst Mamma and the lady, who came, were chatting together, I wished to look at him for a moment; I met his eyes, and I could not turn mine from him. That instant I saw his tears flow, and he was obliged to turn his head aside to hide them. I found I could not withstand it; and that I was also ready to weep. I retired, and instantly wrote with a pencil on a slip of paper, "I beg you'll not be so dejected; I promise to answer your letter."—Surely you can't say there was any harm in this; I could not help it. I put my note in the strings of my harpsichord, as his was, and returned to the saloon. I found myself much easier, and was impatient until the lady went away. She was on her visits, and soon retired. As soon as she was gone, I said I would again play on my harpsichord, and begged he would bring it. I saw by his looks he suspected nothing; but when he returned, oh, he was so pleased! In laying the instrument before me, he placed himself in such a manner that Mamma could not see, and squeezed my hand—but it was but for a moment: I can't express the pleasure I received; I drew it away however; so that I have nothing to reproach myself with.

Now, my dear friend, you see I can't avoid writing to him, since I have promised; and I will not chagrin him any more I am determined; for I suffer more than he does. Certainly, as to any thing bad, I would not be guilty of it, but what harm can there be in writing, when it is to prevent one from being unhappy? What puzzles me is, that I shall not know what to say; but that signifies nothing; and I am certain its coming from me will be quite sufficient.

Adieu, my dear friend! If you think me wrong, tell me; but I don't believe I am. As the time draws near to write to him, my heart beats strangely; however, it must be so, as I have promised it.

From — —, Aug. 20, 17—.

LETTER XIX.

CECILIA VOLANGES *to* CHEVALIER DANCENY.

You was so pensive, Sir, yesterday, and it gave me so much uneasiness to see you so, that I could not avoid promising to answer the letter you wrote me. I now think it unbecoming; yet, as I promised, I will not break my word, a proof of the friendship I have for you. Now I have made this acknowledgment, I hope you will never more ask me to write to you again, or ever let any one know I have wrote to you; for I should most certainly be blamed, and it might occasion me a deal of uneasiness. But above all, I hope you will not have a bad opinion of me, which would give me the greatest concern; for I assure you, I could not have been induced to do this by any one else. I wish much you would not be so melancholy as you have been, lately, as it deprives me of all the satisfaction I have in your company. You see, Sir, I speak very sincerely to you. I wish much that our friendship may be lasting; but I beg you'll write to me no more.

I have the honour to be,
CECILIA VOLANGES.
Aug. 20, 17 — .

LETTER XX.

The MARCHIONESS DE MERTEUIL *to* VISCOUNT VALMONT.

So, knave, you begin to wheedle, lest I should laugh at you! Well, I forgive you. You say so many ridiculous things, that I must pardon you, the trammels you are kept in by your Presidente; however, my Chevalier would be apt not to be so indulgent, and not to approve the renewal of our contract; neither would he find any thing very entertaining in your foolish whim. I laughed, however, exceedingly at it, and was truly sorry I was obliged to laugh alone. Had you been here, I don't know how far my good humour might have led me; but reflection came to my aid, and I armed myself with severity. It is not that I have determined to break off for ever; but I am resolved to delay for some time, and I have my reasons. Perhaps some vanity might arise in the case, and *that* once roused, one does not know whither it may lead. I should be inclined to enslave you again, and oblige you to give up your Presidente; but if a person of my unworthiness should give you a disgust for virtue itself, in a human shape, what a scandal! To avoid this danger, these are my stipulations.

As soon as you have obtain'd your lovely devotee, and that you can produce your proofs, come, I am yours. But I suppose it unnecessary to inform you that, in important matters, none but written proofs are admitted. By this arrangement I shall, on the one hand, become a reward instead of a consolation, and this idea pleases me most: on the other hand, your success will be more brilliant, by becoming in the same moment the cause of an infidelity. Come then, come speedily, and bring the pledge of your triumph; like our valiant knights of old, who deposited, at their ladies' feet, the trophies of their victories. I am really curious to know what a prude can say after such an adventure; what covering she can give her words after having uncovered her person. You are to judge whether I rate myself too high; but I must assure you beforehand, I will abate nothing. Till then, my dear Viscount, you must not be angry that I should be constant to my Chevalier; and that I should amuse myself in making him happy, although it may give you a little uneasiness.

If I was not so strict a moralist, I believe at this instant he would have a most dangerous rival in the little Volanges. I am bewitched with this little girl: it is a real passion. I am much mistaken, or she will be one day or other one of our most fashionable women. I can see her little heart expanding; and it is a most ravishing sight!—She already loves her Danceny to distraction, yet knows nothing of it; and he, though deeply smitten, has that youthful timidity, that frightens him from declaring his passion. They are both in a state of mutual adoration before me: the girl has a great mind to disburden her heart, especially for some days past; and I should have done her immense service in assisting her a little; but she is yet a child, and I must not commit myself. Danceny has spoke plainer; but I will have nothing to do with him. As to the girl, I am often tempted to make her my pupil; it is a piece of service I'm inclined to do Gercourt. He gives me time enough, as he must remain in Corsica until October. I have in contemplation to employ that time effectually, and to give him a well trained wife, instead of an innocent convent pensioner. The insolent security of this man is surprising, who dares sleep quietly whilst a woman he has used ill is unrevenged! If the little thing was now here, I do not know what I might say to her.

Adieu, Viscount—good night, and good success; but, for God's sake, dispatch. Remember, if you let this woman slip, the others will blush at having been unconnected with you.

Aug. 20, 17—.

LETTER XXI.

From VISCOUNT VALMONT *to the* MARCHIONESS DE MERTEUIL.

I have at length, my dear friend, made an advance, and one of such importance, that though it has not led to the full completion of my wishes, convinces me I am in the right road, and dispels my dread of having gone astray. I have at last made my declaration of love; and although the most obstinate silence was preserved, I have obtained an answer of the most flattering, unequivocal nature; yet, not to anticipate matters, but to recur to their origin: you may remember a spy was appointed over my proceedings; well, I determined this shameful treatment should be converted into the means of public edification; and I laid my plan thus: I ordered my confident to look out for some distressed person in the neighbourhood, who wanted relief. This you know was not a very difficult discovery. Yesterday evening he informed me that the effects of a whole family were to be seized on as this morning, for payment of taxes. I first took care to be certain that there was neither woman nor girl in the house, whose age or appearance could raise any suspicion of my intended scheme. When I was satisfied of this, I mentioned at supper that I intended going a shooting next day. Here I must do my Presidente justice; she certainly felt some remorse for the orders she had given; and not being able to overcome her curiosity, she determined to oppose my design. It would be exceedingly hot; I should probably injure my health; I should kill nothing, and fatigue myself in vain; and during this conversation, her eyes, which spoke a plainer language than she perhaps intended, told me she wished those simple reasons should pass current. You may guess I did not assent to them, and even was proof against a smart invective upon shooting and sportsmen; I held my ground even against a little cloud of discontent that covered her celestial face during the rest of the evening. I was at one time afraid she had revoked her orders, and that her delicacy would mar all. I did not reflect sufficiently on the strength of woman's curiosity, and was mistaken; my huntsman cleared up my doubts however that night, and I went to bed quite satisfied.

At daylight I rose, and set out. I was scarcely fifty yards from the castle, when I perceived my spy at my heels. I began to beat about, directing my course across the fields towards the village I had in view; my amusement on the way was making the fellow scamper; who, not daring to quit the high road, was often obliged to run over treble the ground I went. My exertions to give him exercise enough, put me in a violent heat, and I seated myself at the foot of a tree. And would you believe it, he had the insolence to slide behind a thicket not twenty yards from, me, and seat himself also. I once had a great inclination to send him the contents of my piece, which, though only loaded with small shot, would have cured his curiosity; but I recollected he was not only useful, but even necessary to my designs, and that saved him. On my arrival at the village, all was bustle; I went on, and inquired what was the matter, which was immediately related to me. I ordered the collector to be sent for; and, giving way to my generous compassion, I nobly paid down fifty-six livres, for which five poor creatures were going to be reduced to straw and misery. On this trifling act, you can't conceive the chorus of blessings the bystanders joined in around me—what grateful tears flowed from the venerable father of the family, and embellished this patriarchal figure, which a moment before was hideously disfigured with the wild stamp of despair! While contemplating this scene, a younger man, leading a woman with two children, advancing hastily towards me, said to to them, "Let us fall on our knees before this image of God;" and I was instantly surrounded by the whole family prostrate at my feet.

I must acknowledge my weakness; my eyes were full, and I felt within me an involuntary but exquisite emotion. I was amazed at the pleasure that is felt in doing a benevolent act; and I'm inclined to think, those we call virtuous people, have not so much merit as is ascribed to them. Be that as it may, I thought it fit to pay those poor people for the heart-felt satisfaction I had received. I had ten louis-d'ors in my purse, which I gave them; here acknowledgments were repeated, but not equally pathetic: the relief of want had produced the grand, the true effect; the rest was the mere consequence of gratitude and surprise for a superfluous gift.

In the midst of the unmerited benedictions of this family, I had some resemblance to the hero of a drama in the *denouement* of a play. Remark that the faithful spy was observable in the crowd. My end was answered: I disengaged myself from them, and returned to the castle.

Every thing considered, I applaud myself for my invention. This woman is well worth all my solicitude; and it will one day or other prove to be my title to her: having, as I may say, thus paid for her beforehand, I shall have a right to dispose of her at my will, without having any thing to reproach myself with.

I had almost forgot to tell you, that, to make the most of every thing, I begged the good people to pray for the success of my undertakings. You shall now see whether their prayers have not already been in some measure efficacious. But I'm called to supper, and I should be too late for the post, if I did not now conclude. I am sorry for it, as the sequel is the best. Adieu, my lovely friend! You rob me a moment of the pleasure of seeing her.

Aug. 20, 17—.

LETTER XXII.

The Presidente DE TOURVEL *to* MADAME DE VOLANGES.

You will, I doubt not, Madam, be desirous to be informed of an incident in the life of Mr. de Valmont, which seems to me to form a striking contrast to all those that have been related to you. Nothing can be more painful than to think disadvantageously of any one, or so grievous as to find those who have every qualification to inspire the love of virtue, replete with vice; besides, you are so inclined to the exercise of the virtue of indulgence, that I think I can't please you more, than in furnishing you motives for reconsidering any judgment you may have formed, that may be justly accused of rigour. Mr. Valmont now seems entitled to this favour, I may almost say to this act of justice, for the following reason:

This morning he went on one of those excursions, which might have given room to imagine a scheme in the neighbourhood; a supposition which, I must own, I too hastily adopted.

Happily for him, and still more happily for us, since it preserves us from an act of injustice, one of my people had occasion to go the same way;[1] and thus my fortunate, but censurable curiosity was satisfied. He acquainted us that Mr. de Valmont, having found at the village of ----, an unhappy family whose effects were on the point of being sold for payment of taxes, not only discharged the debt for the poor people, but even gave them a pretty considerable sum besides. My servant was witness to this virtuous act; and informs me that the country people, in conversation, told him, that a servant, whom they described, and who mine believes to belong to Mr. de Valmont, had been yesterday at the village to make inquiry after objects of charity. This was not a transitory fit of compassion; it must have proceeded from determined benevolence, the noblest virtue of the noblest minds; but be it chance or design, you must allow, it is a worthy and laudable act; the bare recital of it melted me to tears! I will add also still farther, to do him justice, that when I mentioned this transaction, of which he had not given the least hint, he begin by denying it to be founded; and even when he acquiesced, seemed to lay so little stress on it, that his modesty redoubled its merit. Now tell me, most venerable friend, if M. de Valmont is an irretrievable debauchee? If he is so, and behaves thus, where are we to look for men of principle? Is it possible that the wicked should participate with the good the extatic pleasures of benevolence? Would the Almighty permit that a virtuous poor family should receive aid from the hand of an abandoned wretch, and return thanks for it to his Divine Providence? And is it possible to imagine the Creator would think himself honoured in hearing pure hearts pouring blessings on a reprobate? No; I am rather inclined to think that errors, although they may have been of some duration, are not eternal; and I cannot bring myself to think, that the man who acts well, is an enemy to virtue. Mr. de Valmont is only, perhaps, another example of the dangerous effects of connections. I embrace this idea, and it gratifies me. If, on the one hand, it clears up his character in your mind, it will, on the other, enhance the value of the tender friendship that unites me to you for life.

I am, &c.

P. S. Madame de Rosemonde and I are just going to see the poor honest family, and add our assistance to Mr. de Valmont's. We take him with us, and shall give those good people the pleasure of again seeing their benefactor; which, I fancy, is all he has left us to do.

Aug. 20, 17 —.

[1] Madame de Tourvel does not venture to say it is done by her order.

The VISCOUNT DE VALMONT *to the* MARCHIONESS DE MERTEUIL.

I broke off at our return to the castle. Now to my narrative: I had scarce time to dress and return to the saloon, where my charmer was making tapestry, whilst the curate read the gazette to my old aunt. I placed myself near the frame. Softer looks than usual, almost bordering on fondness, soon informed me the spy had made a report of his business; and, in fact, the lovely woman could no longer keep the secret; being under no apprehension of interrupting the good pastor, whose utterance was perfectly in the pulpit style. I have also some news to tell, said she, and immediately related my adventure with an exactitude that did honour to her historian's accuracy. You may guess how my modesty displayed itself; but who can stop a woman's tongue, who unconsciously praises the man she loves? I determined to let her go on. One would have imagined she was preaching the panegyric of some saint, whilst I, not without a degree of hope, attentively observed every circumstance that bore an appearance propitious to love: her animated look, free action, and above all, the tone of her voice, which, by a sensible alteration, betrayed the emotion of her soul. She had scarcely finished, when Madame de Rosemonde said, "Come, my dear nephew, let me embrace you." I soon concluded the lovely panegyrist could not offer an objection to my saluting her in turn. She attempted to fly; but I soon seized her in my arms; and far from being able to resist, she had scarce power to support herself. The more I contemplate this woman, the more amiable she is. She hastened back to her frame, with every appearance of resuming her work, but in such confusion, that her hand shook, and at length obliged her to throw it aside.

After dinner, the ladies would visit the objects of my unaffected charity; I accompanied them; but I shall spare you the unentertaining narrative of this second scene of gratitude. My anxious heart, panting with the delightful remembrance of what had passed, made me hasten our return to the Castle. On the road, my lovely Presidente, more pensive than usual, spoke not a word; and I, entirely absorbed in the means of employing the events of the day to advantage, was also silent. Madame de Rosemonde alone spoke, and could receive but few and short answers. We must have tired her out, which was my design, and it succeeded to my wish. When we alighted she retired to her apartment, and left my fair one and me tête-à-tête in a saloon, poorly lighted: gentle darkness, thou encourager of timid love!

I had not much trouble to direct our conversation to my object. The fervour of my lovely preacher was more useful than my own skill. "When the heart is so inclined to good," said she, glancing a most enchanting look, "how is it possible it should at the same time be prone to vice?" "I don't deserve," replied I, "either this praise or censure; and I can't conceive how, with so much good sense as you possess, you have not yet discovered my character. Were my candour even to hurt me in your opinion, you are still too deserving to with-hold my confidence from you. You'll find all my errors proceed from an unfortunate easiness of disposition. Surrounded by profligates, I contracted their vices; I have, perhaps, even had a vanity in excelling them. Here too the sport of example, impelled by the model of your virtues, and without hope of ever attaining them, I have however endeavoured to follow you: and, perhaps, the act you value so highly to-day would lose its merit, if you knew the motive!" (You see, my charming friend, how nearly I approached to the truth.) "It is not to me those unfortunate people are obliged, for the relief they have experienced. Where you imagined you saw a laudable act, I only sought the means to please. I was only, if I must so say, the feeble agent of the divinity I adore!" (Here she would have interrupted me, but I did not give her time.) "Even at this instant," added I, "it is weakness alone extracts this secret from me. I had resolved not to acquaint you of it; I had placed my happiness in paying to your virtues, as well as your charms, a pure and undiscoverable homage. But, incapable of deceit, with such an example of candour before me, I will not have to reproach myself with any vile dissimulation. Imagine not that I dare offend you by a criminal presumption. I know I shall be miserable; but I shall cherish my sufferings: they are the proofs of the ardour of my love:—at your feet, in your bosom, I will deposit my grievances; there will I gather strength to bear up against new sufferings; there I shall meet compassion, mixed with goodness and consolation; for I know you'll pity me. O thou whom I adore! hear me, pity me, help me." All this time was I on my knees, squeezing her hands in mine; but she, disengaging them suddenly, and covering her eyes with them, exclaimed, "What a miserable wretch am I!" and burst into tears. Luckily I had worked myself up to such a degree that I wept also; and taking her hands again, I bathed them with my tears. This precaution was very necessary; for she was so much engaged with her own anguish, that she would not have taken notice of mine, if I had not discovered this expedient to impress her with it. This also gave me leisure to contemplate her charming form—her attractions received additional embellishment from her tears. My imagination began to be fired, and I was so overpowered, that I was tempted to seize the opportunity!

How weak we are, how much governed by circumstances! since I myself, forgetful of my ultimate design, risked losing, by an untimely triumph, the charms of a long conflict, and the pleasing struggles that precede a difficult defeat; and hurried away by an impetuosity excusable only in a raw youth, was near reducing Madame de Tourvel's conqueror to the paltry triumph of one woman more on his list. My purpose is, that she should yield, yet combat; that without having sufficient force to conquer, she should have enough to make a resistance; let her feel her weakness, and be compelled to own her defeat. The sorry poacher takes aim at the game he has surprised—the true huntsman runs it fairly down. Is not this an exalted idea? But perhaps by this time I should have only had the regret of not having followed it, if chance had not seconded my prudence.

A noise of some one coming towards the saloon struck us. Madame de Tourvel started in a fright, took a candle, and went out. There was no opposing her. It was only a servant. When I was certain who it was, I followed her. I had gone but a few steps, when, whether her fears or her discovering me made her quicken her pace, she flung herself into, rather than entered, her apartment, and immediately locked the door. Seeing the key inside, I did not think proper to knock; that would have been giving her an opportunity of too easy resistance. The happy simple thought of looking through the key-hole struck me, and I beheld this adorable woman bathed in tears, on her knees, praying most fervently. What deity dared she invoke? Is there one so powerful as the god of love? In vain does she now seek for foreign aid; I am henceforward the arbiter of her fate.

Thinking I had done enough for one day, I retired to my apartment, and sat down to write to you. I had hopes of seeing her again at supper; but she sent word she was gone to bed indisposed. Madame de Rosemonde proposed to go to see her in her room; but the arch invalid pretended a head-ach, that prevented her from seeing any one. You may guess I did not sit up long after supper, and had my head-ach also. After I withdrew, I wrote her a long letter, complaining of her rigour, and went to bed, resolved to deliver it this morning. I slept badly, as you perceive by the date of this letter. I rose and read my epistle over again, which does not please me: it expresses more ardour than love, and more chagrin than grief. It must be altered when I return to a sufficient degree of composure.

It is now dawn of day, and I hope the freshness of the morning will bring on a little sleep. I return to bed; and whatever ascendant this woman may have over me, I promise you never to be so much taken up with her, as not to dedicate much of my thoughts to you. Adieu, my lovely friend.

Aug. 21, 17—, four o'clock in the morning.

LETTER XXIV.

VISCOUNT VALMONT *to the* Presidente DE TOURVEL.

From mere compassion, Madam, vouchsafe to calm my perturbed soul; deign to inform me what I have to hope or fear. When placed between the extremes of happiness and misery, suspense is a most insupportable torment. Alas! why did I ever speak to you? Why did I not endeavour to resist the dominion of your charms that have taken possession of my imagination? Had I been content with silently adoring you, I should at least have the pleasure that ever attends even secretly harbouring that passion; and this pure sentiment, which was then untroubled by the poignant reflections that have arisen from my knowledge of your sorrow, was enough for my felicity: but the source of my happiness is become that of my despair, since I saw those precious tears; since I heard that cruel exclamation, *Ah! miserable wretch that I am.* Those words, Madam, will for a long time wring my heart. By what fatality happens it, that the softest passion produces only horror to you! Whence proceed these fears? Ah! they do not arise from an inclination of sharing in the passion. Your heart I have much mistaken; it is not made for love: mine, which you incessantly slander, is yet the only one of sensibility; yours is even divested of pity—were it not, you could have afforded a wretched being, who only related his sufferings, one word of consolation; you would not have deprived him of your presence, when his sole delight is in seeing you; you would not have made a cruel mockery of his disquietude, by acquainting him you were indisposed, without giving him liberty to make any inquiries on the state of your health; you would have known, that a night that brought you twelve hours rest, was to him an age of torment.

Tell me, how have I deserved this afflicting rigour? I am not afraid even to appeal to yourself: what have I done, but yielded to an involuntary sensation, inspired by beauty, and justified by virtue, always kept within due limits by respect, the innocent avowal of which proceeded from hopeless confidence? and will you betray that confidence that you seemed to countenance, and to which I unreservedly gave way? No, I will not believe it; that would be supposing you capable of an injustice, and I never can entertain, even for a moment, such an idea: I recant my reproaches; I may have been led to write them, but never seriously believed them. Ah, let me believe you all perfection; it is the only satisfaction now left me! Convince me you are so, by extending your generous care to me; of the many you have relieved, is there a wretch wants it so much as I do? Do not abandon me to the distraction you have plunged me into: assist me with your reason, since you have deprived me of mine; and as you have reformed me, complete your work by enlightening me.

I will not deceive you; it will be impossible for you to conquer my love, but you may teach me how to regulate it: by guiding my steps, by prescribing to me my conversation, you will, at least, preserve me from the most dreadful of all misfortunes, that of incurring your displeasure. Dispel, at least, my desponding fears; tell me you pity and forgive me; promise me your indulgence; you never will afford me that extent of it I wish; but I call for so much of it as is absolutely necessary to me: will you refuse it?

Adieu, Madam! Accept, graciously, the homage of my feelings, to which my respect is inseparably united.

Aug. 20, 17—.

LETTER XXV.

VISCOUNT VALMONT *to the* MARCHIONESS DE MERTEUIL.

I now transmit to you the proceedings of yesterday: at eleven I went to Madame de Rosemonde's, and under her auspices, was introduced to the fair pretended invalid, who was still in bed. Her eyes seemed very heavy; I hope she slept as badly as I did. I seized an opportunity, whilst Madame de Rosemonde was at a distance, to present my letter; it was refused, but I left it on the bed, and very politely approached my old aunt's easy chair, who would be near *her dear child*, to whom it now became necessary to put up the letter to avoid scandal. She indiscreetly said, she believed she had a little fever. Madame de Rosemonde desired I would feel her pulse, praising, at the same time, my skill in physic: thus my enchantress experienced a double mortification, to be obliged to give me her arm, and to find her little artifice would be detected. I took her by the hand, which I squeezed in one of mine, whilst, with the other, I ran over her smooth delicate arm; the sly being would not answer a single one of my inquiries, which made me say, as I retired, "I could not feel even the slightest emotion." I suspected her looks would be rather severe; in order to disappoint her, I did not look at her: a little after she said she was desirous to rise, and we left her alone. She appeared at dinner, which was rather gloomy, and informed us she would not go out to walk, which was telling me I should not have an opportunity of speaking to her. It then became necessary, and I felt this to be the fit place, to fetch a sigh and assume a melancholy look; she undoubtedly expected it, for it was the first time, that day, our eyes met. With all her discretion, she has her little artifices as well as others. I found an opportunity to ask her *if she had decided my fate?* I was not a little astonished to hear her reply, *Yes, Sir, I have wrote to you.* I was very anxious to see this letter; but whether it was design, awkwardness, or timidity, she did not deliver it until night, when she retired to her apartment. I send it you, as also the rough copy of mine; read and give your opinion; observe with what egregious falsity she protests she is not in love, when I am certain of the contrary; and she'll complain, if I deceive her afterwards, and yet is not afraid to deceive me beforehand! — My lovely friend, the most artful man is barely on a level with the most inexperienced woman. I must, however, give in to all this nonsense, and fatigue myself to death with despair, because Madam is pleased to play a severe character. — How is it possible not to resolve to avenge such indignities, — but patience! Adieu, I have still a great deal to write.

Now I think on't, send me back the inhuman woman's letter; it is possible that hereafter she may expect to find a great value set upon such wretched stuff, and one must be regular.

I say nothing of little Volanges, she shall be our subject the first opportunity.

Aug. 22, 17 — .

LETTER XXVI.

The Presidente DE TOURVEL *to* VISCOUNT VALMONT.

You certainly, Sir, would not receive a letter from me, if my foolish conduct, last night, did not put me under the necessity of coming to an explanation. I wept I own; and the words you cite may have escaped me; tears, words, and every thing you have carefully noted; it is then necessary to explain all:

Being accustomed to inspire only becoming sentiments, and habituated only to conversations that I might attend to without a blush, and consequently to possess a degree of confidence, which, I flatter myself, I have a right to, I am a stranger to dissimulation, and know not how to suppress the sensations which I experience. The astonishment and confusion your behaviour threw me into, an unaccountable dread, from a situation not at all suited to me, and perhaps the shocking thought of seeing myself confounded with the women you despise, and treated with the same levity; all these reasons united, provoked my tears, and may have made me, and I think with reason, say, I was miserable.

This expression, which you think so pointed, would be still certainly too weak, if my tears and words had another motive; if instead of disapproving sentiments that ought to offend me, I had the slightest apprehension of participating them.

No, Sir, I have no such apprehensions; if I had, I should fly a hundred leagues from you; I would fly to some desert, there to bewail the misfortune of having known you. Notwithstanding my certainty of not having, or ever having, an affection for you, perhaps I should have acted more properly, in following the advice of my friends, in never permitting you to approach me.

I thought, and that is my only error, that you would have had some respect for a woman of character, whose wish was to find you deserve a similar appellation, and to do you justice, and who pleaded in your vindication, whilst you were insulting her by your criminal designs: no, Sir, you do not know me, or you would not thus presume, upon your own injustice, and because you have dared to speak a language I should not have listened to, you would not have thought, yourself, to write me a letter I ought not to read; and you desire I should *guide your steps, and prescribe your conversation!* Well, Sir, silence and oblivion is the only advice that is suitable for me to give, and you to follow; then, only, will you have a title to pardon: you might even obtain some title to my gratitude — but no, I shall make no request to a man who has lost all respect for me; I will not repose confidence in one who has already abused it. You oblige me to fear, nay, perhaps, to hate you, which was not my wish; I hoped to see in you the nephew of my most respectable friend; I opposed the voice of friendship to that of the public that accused you: you have destroyed all; and I foresee you will not be disposed to regain any thing.

I shall content myself with informing you, Sir, your sentiments offend me; that your declaration of them is an insult, and far from ever thinking to partake of them, you'll oblige me never to see you more, if you don't observe, on this subject, a silence, which I think I have a right not only to expect, but to require. I enclose you the letter you wrote me, and I hope you will, in the same manner, return me this: I should be extremely mortified that any traces should remain, of an event which ought never to have existed.

I have the honour,
Aug. 21, 17 — .

LETTER XXVII.

CECILIA VOLANGES *to the* MARCHIONESS DE MERTEUIL.

How shall I thank you, dear Madam, for your goodness: you judged well that it would be easier for me to write than speak; what I have to tell you is not an easy matter; but you are my friend! Yes, you are my very good friend! And I'll endeavour not to be afraid; and then I have so much occasion for your advice! — I am in great grief; I think every one guesses my thoughts, especially when he is present; I redden up as soon as any one looks at me. Yesterday, when you saw me crying, it was because I wanted to speak to you, and I don't know what hindered me; when you asked me what ailed me, the tears came into my eyes in spite of me. I could not have spoke a word. If it had not been for you, Mamma would have taken notice of it; and then what would have become of me? This is the way I spend my time for these four days: that day, Madam, I will out with it, on that day Chevalier Danceny wrote to me; I assure you, when I received his letter, I did not know what it was; but to tell the truth, I read it with great pleasure. I would have suffered any thing all my lifetime, rather than he should not have wrote it to me; however, I know very well I must not tell him so; and I can even assure you, that I told him I was very angry; but he says it gets the better of him, and I believe him; for I had resolved not to answer him, and yet I could not avoid it. I wrote him but once, it was partly even to tell him not to write to me any more; yet he is continually writing; and as I don't answer him, I see plainly he is very melancholy, and that afflicts me greatly: so that I do not know what to do, nor what will become of me: I am much to be pitied!

I beg, Madam, you'll tell me, would there be any great harm in writing an answer to him now and then, only until he can prevail on himself to write me no more, and to be as we used to be before? For myself, if it continues this way, I don't know what I shall do. I assure you, on reading his last letter, I could not forbear crying all the time; and I am very certain, that if I do not answer him again, it will make us both very uneasy.

I will enclose you his letter, or a copy of it, and you'll see he does not ask any harm. However, if you think it is not proper, I promise you I will not give way to my inclination; but I believe you'll think as I do, that there's no harm in it.

And now that I am upon it, give me leave to put you a question: I have been often told it was very wrong to be in love with any body, but why so? What makes me ask you, is this; the Chevalier Danceny insists there's no harm at all in it, and that almost every body is; if that's the case, I don't know why I should be the only one should be hindered; or is it that it is only wrong for young ladies? For I heard Mamma herself say, that Madam de D — — loved M. M — —, and she did not speak as if it was so bad a thing; and yet I am sure she would be very angry with me, if she had the least suspicion of my affection for M. Danceny. She behaves to me always as if I was a child, and never tells me any thing at all. I thought, when she took me from the convent, I was to be married; but now I think not. It is not that I care much about it, I assure you; but you who are so intimate with her, you, perhaps, know something about it; and if you do, I hope you will tell me.

This is a very long letter, Madam; but since you was so good to give me leave to write to you, I made use of it to tell you every thing, and I depend on your friendship.

I have the honour, &c.

Paris, Aug. 23, 17 — .

LETTER XXVIII.

CHEVALIER DANCENY *to* CECILIA VOLANGES.

You still, Miss, refuse to answer my letters. Will nothing move you? and must every day banish the hopes it brings! What sort of friendship is it that you consent shall subsist between us? If it is not powerful enough even to make you sensible of my anguish; if you can coolly, and unmoved, look on me, while I suffer, the victim of a flame which I cannot extinguish; if, instead of inspiring you with a confidence in me, my sufferings can hardly move your compassion. — Heavens! your friend suffers, and you will do nothing to assist him. He requests only one word, and you refuse it him! And you desire him to be satisfied with a sentiment so feeble, that you even dread to repeat it. Yesterday you said you would not be ungrateful. Believe me, Miss, when a person repays love only with friendship, it arises not from a fear of being ungrateful: the fear then is only for the appearance of ingratitude. But I no longer dare converse with you on a subject which must be troublesome to you, as it does not interest you; I must, at all events, confine it within myself, and endeavour to learn to conquer it. I feel the difficulty of the task; I know I must call forth my utmost exertions: there is one however will wring my heart most, that is, often to repeat, yours is insensible.

I will even endeavour to see you less frequently; and I am already busied in finding out a plausible pretence. Must I then forego the pleasing circumstance of daily seeing you; I will at least never cease regretting it. Perpetual anguish is to be the reward of the tenderest affection; and by your desire, and your decree, I am conscious I never shall again find the happiness I lose this day. You alone were formed for my heart. With what pleasure shall I not take the oath to live only for you! But you will not receive it. Your silence sufficiently informs me that your heart suggests nothing to you in my favour; that is at once the most certain proof of your indifference, and the most cruel manner of communicating it. Farewell, Miss.

I no longer dare flatter myself with receiving an answer; love would have wrote it with eagerness, friendship with pleasure, and even pity with complacency; but pity, friendship, and love, are equally strangers to your heart.

Paris, Aug. 23, 17 — .

LETTER XXIX.

CECILIA VOLANGES *to* SOPHIA CARNAY.

It is certain, Sophy, that I told you, one might in some cases write to an admirer; and I assure you, I am very angry with myself for having followed your advice, which has been the cause of so much uneasiness to the Chevalier Danceny and me; and what proves I was right, is, that Madame de Merteuil, who is a woman that ought to know those things perfectly, has at length come to think as I do. I owned every thing to her: at first she thought as you did; but when I had explained every thing to her, she was sensible it was a different case: she requires only that I should show her all my letters, and those of Chevalier Danceny, to be certain I should say nothing but what I ought; so now I am pretty easy. Lord! how I do love Madame de Merteuil; she is a good woman, and a very respectable one; so that her advice may be safely followed. Oh! how I shall write to M. Danceny, and how well satisfied he'll be; he will be more so than he thinks; for, till now, I only mentioned friendship to him, and he wanted me always to call it love. I believe it was pretty much the same; but I was afraid—that was the fact. I told Madame de Merteuil of it; she told me I was in the right; and that an avowal of love ought only to be made when one could no longer help it: now I'm sure I cannot help it much longer; after all, it is all one, and it will please him most.

Madame de Merteuil told me also, that she would lend me some books, which treat that subject very fully, and would teach me how to conduct myself, and also to write better than I do: for she tells me all my faults, and that is a proof she loves me; she charged me only to say nothing to Mamma of those books, because it would look as if she had neglected my education, and that might displease her. I will engage I shall say nothing of it.

It is, however, very extraordinary, that a woman, who is but a very distant relation, should take more care of me than my mother! I am very happy to be acquainted with her.

She has asked my Mamma leave to take me to the opera, to her own box, the day after to-morrow; she told me we should be by ourselves, and would chat all the while, without danger of being overheard.—I like that a great deal better than the opera. My marriage will be, in part, the subject of our conversation, I hope; for she told me it was very certain I was to be married; but we had not an opportunity to say any more. Is it not very strange Mamma says nothing at all to me about it.

Adieu, my dear Sophy; I am going to write to Chevalier Danceny. I am quite happy.
Aug. 24, 17—.

LETTER XXX.

CECILIA VOLANGES *to the* CHEVALIER DANCENY.

At last, Sir, I consent to write to you, to assure you of my friendship, of my *love* even, since without that you must be unhappy. You say I have not a tender heart: I assure you you are much mistaken; and I hope you now doubt it no longer. If you were uneasy because I did not write to you, do you think it did not give me a great deal of concern too? The reason was, I would not, for all the world, do any thing that was wrong; and I should not even have owned my affection for you, if I could have helped it; but your grief gave me too much uneasiness. I hope now you will be so no longer, and that we shall be very happy.

I expect to have the pleasure of seeing you this evening, and that you will come early; it will not be as much so as I wish. Mamma sups at home, and I believe she will ask you to stay. I hope you will not be engaged, as you was the day before yesterday. Surely the company you went to sup with must have been very pleasing, for you went very soon; but let us talk no more of that. Now that you know I love you, I hope you will be with me as often as you can; for I am never pleased but when with you; and I wish, with all my heart, you were the same.

I am very sorry you should still be melancholy; but it is not my fault. I shall desire to play on the harpsichord as soon as you come, that you may have my letter immediately. I think that is the best thing I can do.

Farewell, Sir; I love you with all my heart; the oftener I tell you so, the more happy I feel. I hope you will be so too.

Aug. 24, 17 — .

LETTER XXXI.

CHEVALIER DANCENY *to* CECILIA VOLANGES.

Yes, certainly, we shall be very happy. My happiness is secure, since I am beloved by you. Yours will never end, if it lasts as long as my love. And do you love me, and no longer dread telling me so? *The oftener you tell me so, the more happy you feel.* After having read the enchanting *I love you,* wrote with your hand, I heard your lovely mouth repeat the avowal. I figured to me those charming eyes, rendered still more so by the expression of tenderness fixed on me. I have received your vows to live for me alone. Oh receive mine, to devote my life to your happiness, and be assured I never will deceive you!

What a happy day was yesterday! Why has not Madame de Merteuil always secrets to impart to your Mamma? Why must the idea of the restraint that attends us, be mixed with the delicious remembrance that fills my soul? Why can't I for ever squeeze that lovely hand, that wrote *I love you,* imprint it with my kisses, and be thus revenged for your refusal of a greater favour?

Tell me, then, my Cecilia, when your Mamma came back, when, by her presence, we were constrained to behave with indifference to each other, when you could no longer console me by assurances of love, for the refusal of proof, did not you feel some sorrow? did not you say to yourself, one kiss would have made him completely happy, and refused it? Promise me, my lovely charmer, that you'll be not so rigorous the first opportunity. Such a promise will enable me to bear up against the disappointments that I foresee are preparing for us, and the crosses I shall meet, will at least be softened by the certainty that you share them.

Adieu, my adorable Cecilia! The hour is come that I am to be with you. It would be impossible for me to leave off, if it was not to go to you. Adieu, once more, my dearest love!

Aug. 25, 17 — .

LETTER XXXII.

MADAME DE VOLANGES *to the* Presidente DE TOURVEL.

You wish then, Madam, that I should form a good opinion of the virtue of Monsieur de Valmont? I own I cannot bring myself to it; and that I should have as much difficulty to think so from the simple fact you relate, as to believe a man of acknowledged worth to be vicious for the commission of one fault. Human nature is not perfect in any shape, neither in good nor evil. The profligate wretch has his virtues as well as the virtuous man his weaknesses. This truth is so much the more necessary to be believed, because, from thence arises the necessity of indulgence for the wicked as well as the good; and that it preserves these from pride, and those from being discouraged. You will, without doubt, think that I don't now practise the doctrine I speak; but it appears to me a most dangerous weakness, to put the man of virtue and the profligate on an equality.

I will not take upon me to scrutinize the motives of Mr. Valmont's action; I'll even think it in itself laudable; but nevertheless, has he not, all his life, been employed in spreading trouble, dishonour, and scandal in families? Listen, if you will, to the voice of the unhappy people he has relieved: but let not that prevent you from attending to the cries of a hundred victims that he has sacrificed. If, as you say, he was only one example of the danger of connections, would he be the less a dangerous connection? You suppose him capable of a happy reformation: let us go farther, suppose this miracle completed; would not the public opinion be still against him, and ought not that to be sufficient to regulate your conduct? God alone can absolve at the moment of repentance; he is the searcher of hearts; but men can judge only by actions; and no one, after having lost the esteem of the world, has a right to complain of diffidence, which makes this loss so difficult to be repaired. I would have you think above all, my dear young friend, that to lose this esteem, it is sometimes enough to seem to set little value upon it, and do not tax this severity with injustice; for as the world has a right to think that no one renounces this precious jewel, who has good pretensions to it, whoever is not restrained by this consideration, is on the brink of danger. Such, however, would be the aspect, an intimate connection with Mr. de Valmont would carry with it, were it ever so innocent.

Alarmed with the warmth with which you defend him, I hasten to anticipate the objections I foresee you'll make. You'll quote Madame de Merteuil, whose connection with him has escaped censure; you'll perhaps ask me why I admit him to my house? You will tell me, that far from being rejected by the worthy part of society, he is admitted, even sought for, by what is called good company: I can, I believe, answer to all.

Madame de Merteuil, who is really a very valuable woman, has, perhaps, no other defect but that of too much confidence in her own strength; she is a dexterous guide, who delights in driving her chariot between rocks and precipices, in which her success alone justifies her: it is right to praise her, but it would be imprudent to follow her; she herself is convinced, and condemns herself for it, and as she grows in experience, her conduct is more reserved; and I can confidently assure you, we are both of the same opinion.

As to what relates to myself, I will not excuse it more than in others; I admit Mr. de Valmont: without doubt he is received every where; that is an inconsequence to be added to the many others that govern society. You know as well as me, that we spend our lives in remarking, complaining, and giving ourselves up to them. Mr. de Valmont, with a pompous title, a great fortune, many amiable qualities, saw early, that to gain an ascendant in society, it was sufficient to know how to manage with equal address, praise, and ridicule. No one, like him, possesses this double talent; with the one he seduces, with the other he makes himself dreaded: he is not esteemed, but flattered. Such is his existence in the midst of a world, that, more prudent than bold, would rather keep on good terms with him than combat him.

But neither Madame de Merteuil nor any other woman would venture to shut herself up in the country, almost tête-à-tête, with such a man. It was reserved for the most discreet, and the most virtuous among them, to set an example of such an inconsequence; pardon the expression, it slipped from me through friendship. My charming friend, even your virtue betrays you, by the security it inspires you with. Think, then, on the one hand, that you will have for judges frivolous people, who will not believe in a virtue, the model of which they cannot find among themselves; and on the other, profligates, who will feign not to believe in it to punish you. Consider you are now doing what many men would be afraid to risk; for among the young men of fashion, to whom Mr. de Valmont is now become the oracle, the most prudent seem to dread appearing too intimately connected with him; and you are under no apprehensions; ah, return, I conjure you! If my reasons are not sufficient to persuade you, at least give way to my friendship; it is it that makes me renew my instances, it is it must justify them. You will think it severe, and I wish it may be useless; but I would much rather you should have reason to complain of its solicitude, than its negligence.

Aug. 24, 17—.

LETTER XXXIII.

The MARCHIONESS DE MERTEUIL *to the* VISCOUNT DE VALMONT.

Now that you dread succeeding, my dear Viscount, now that your scheme is to furnish arms against yourself, and that you wish more to fight than conquer, I have nothing more to say. Your conduct is certainly a masterpiece of prudence; in a contrary supposition, it would be the highest act of folly; and to tell you my sentiments freely, I fear your project is entirely chimerical.

I do not reproach you for having let slip the opportunity; for I really cannot see that you had it in your power; and I know well, whatever others may say, that an opportunity lost may be found again, and that a rash step is irrecoverable.

But I admire your wisdom in commencing a correspondence, and I defy you to foresee how it will end. You perhaps hope to prove to this woman, that she should give herself up? And that seems to me a truth of opinion, more than of demonstration; and that to make it be relished, you soften, and not argue; but what purpose would it answer to soften by letter, since you would not be on the spot to benefit by it? If all your fine phrases should even produce the intoxication of love, do you flatter yourself that it would be of so long a duration that reflection would not come time enough to prevent its consequences? Think, then, how much it will take to write a letter, and how much before it can be delivered; and then consider if a woman, of the principles of your devotee, can think so long on what she endeavours never at all to think of: this proceeding may do very well with children, who while they write, I love you, do not know they say I give myself up to you; but Madame de Tourvel's reasoning virtue makes her know the value of the terms. This appears very plain; for notwithstanding the advantage you had over her in your conversation, she foils you in her letter; and what will be the consequence? That by long debating, you will not bring to compliance; that by dint of searching for good reasons, she will find them, will give them, and stick to them; not so much because they are good in themselves, as not to act inconsistently.

Moreover, a remark I am astonished you have not made, is, that nothing is so difficult in love, as to write what one does not feel. I mean to write with the appearance of truth; it is not but the same phrases are used; they are not arranged in the same manner; or rather, they are arranged with too much perspicuity, and that is worse.

Read over your letter again; it displays so much regularity that you are discovered in every phrase. I am inclined to think your Presidente is so unfashionable as not to perceive it; but what is that to the purpose? the consequence will be still the same; that is the defect of romance; the author racks his brain, heats his imagination, and the reader is unmoved. Heloise is the only exception I know; and notwithstanding the great talents of the author, from this observation alone, I have ever been of opinion, that the work is grounded in truth; not so in speaking; the custom of conversation gives it an air of tenderness, to which the facility of tears still greatly adds; expressive desires blend themselves with the languishing look, and, at last, incoherent speeches more readily bring on that turbulence of passion, which is the true eloquence of love; but above all, the presence of the beloved object banishes reflection, and makes us wish to be overcome.

Believe me, my dear Viscount, she does not desire you should write any more; retrieve your error, and wait for the opportunity of speaking to her. This woman has more fortitude than I expected; her defence is good, and were it not for the length of her letter, and the pretence she gives you for a replication in her grateful phrase, she would not at all have betrayed herself.

And what, I think, ought to ascertain your success is, she exhausts all her strength at once; and I foresee she will persist in it, for the defence of a word, and will have none left for the crisis.

I send you back your two letters, and, if you are prudent, they should be the last till after the happy moment. It is too late to say any thing of the little Volanges, who comes on very well, and gives me great satisfaction. I believe I shall have done before you, which ought to make you very happy. Farewell for to-day!

Aug. 24, 17 — .

LETTER XXXIV.

VISCOUNT VALMONT *to the* MARCHIONESS DE MERTEUIL.

You write enchantingly, my charming friend; but why take so much trouble to prove a position which all the world knows, that to make a quick progress in love matters, it is better to speak than write? This, I believe, is the full contents of your letter; and is it not the first elements of the art of seduction? I will only remark, that you make but one exception to this principle, and that there are two: with children, who take this step through timidity, and give themselves up through ignorance, you must add the women of genius, who are dupes to self-love and vanity, which leads them into the snare. For example; I am very certain that the Countess de B——-, who answered, without hesitating, my first letter, had then no more affection for me, than I had for her; and that in this connection she had no other view, than being engaged with a person whom she imagined would do her honour.

However, a lawyer will tell you, that the maxim is not applicable to the question; for you suppose that it is at my option to write or speak, which is not the case. Since the affair of the 20th, my cruel charmer, who keeps on the defensive, has studiously avoided meeting me, a piece of address which totally disconcerts me: so that if it should continue, she will oblige me to think seriously on the means of regaining this advantage; as I most assuredly will not be baffled by her in this manner; even my letters are the occasion of a little warfare: not satisfied with giving no reply, she even refuses receiving them, and I am under the necessity of a new stratagem for each, which does not always succeed.

You may recollect in what a simple manner I delivered the first; the second was not more difficult. She required I should return her letter; I gave her mine instead of it, without her having the least suspicion. But whether from vexation to have been duped, whether through capriciousness or virtue, for she will oblige me to believe she is virtuous, she has obstinately refused the third. I expect, however, from the embarrassment that this refusal had like to put her in, she will in future be more cautious.

However, I was not much astonished that she would not receive that letter, which I offered her in a very plain manner—that would have been granting something—and I expect a longer defence. After this effort, which was only an essay by way of trial, I put a cover over my letter, and taking the opportunity when she was at her toilette, when Madame de Rosemonde and her waiting-maid were present, I sent it her by my huntsman, ordering him to tell her that it was the paper she asked me for. I rightly judged that she would dread a scandalous explanation, which a refusal would necessarily have brought on; and indeed she took the letter. My ambassador, who had orders to observe her countenance diligently, and who is a shrewd fellow, perceived only a slight blush, with more embarrassment than anger.

I applauded myself, being very certain that she would either keep this letter, or, if she meant to return it, she must take an opportunity when we were alone, and then could not avoid a conference. About an hour after, one of her people came into my room, from his mistress, and delivered me a packet, folded in another form than my own, on the cover of which I immediately perceived the long-wished-for characters. I broke the seal with rapture—Behold! it was my own letter, unsealed, and doubled down.—I suspect she dreaded I was not so scrupulous as she, on the score of scandal, which made her invent this diabolical stratagem. You know me well—I have no occasion to describe the rage this put me into. However, I was obliged to be calm, and to think of other means—and this is the only one I could think of:—

Every morning there is a man sent for the letters from this to the post office, which is about three quarters of a league; for this purpose a small box, in the shape of a trunk, is made use of; the master of the post office keeps one key, and Madame de Rosemonde the other. Every one puts in their letters when they think proper, and they are carried at night to the post office: in the morning the messenger goes back for those that arrive. All the servants, strangers and others, take it in turn. It was not my servant's turn; but he offered to go, on pretence that he had business there.

I wrote my letter. I disguised the superscription in a feigned hand, and counterfeited tolerably, on the cover, the post mark of *Dijon*. I chose this town in a gay humour, as I wished for the same rites as the husband; I also wrote from the same place; and likewise because my fair one had been all day expressing her wish to receive letters from Dijon, I thought it but right to give her that satisfaction.

Those precautions taken, it was a matter of no difficulty to mix this letter with the others; and I still had it in view to be witness to its reception; for the custom is to assemble together at breakfast, and wait the arrival of the letters before we separate. At length they arrived.

Madame de Rosemonde opened the box. "From Dijon," said she, giving the letter to Madame de Tourvel. "It is not my husband's writing," replied the other, in some confusion, breaking open the seal immediately. The first glance informed her who it came from, and made such a change in her countenance, that Madame de Rosemonde took notice of it, and said, "What ails you?" I immediately drew near, saying, "This letter must be very dreadful indeed!" The timorous devotee did not lift up her eyes, nor speak a syllable; and to conceal her embarrassment, feigned to run over the letter, which she was scarce able to read. I enjoyed her uneasiness; and wishing to push it a little farther. — "Your easy air," replied I, "makes me hope that this letter has been the occasion of more astonishment than grief." Her anger then overpowered her prudence. "It contains," replied she, "things that offend me much; and that I am astonished any one would dare write to me." And "who then can it be?" replied Madame de Rosemonde. "It is not signed," replied the angry fair; "but the letter and its author I equally despise: and I shall take it as a favour to say no more about it." So saying, she tore the audacious epistle, put the scraps in her pocket, rose, and went out.

Notwithstanding all this anger, she nevertheless has my letter; and I depend upon her curiosity that she will read it.

The circumstances of this day would lead me too far. I enclose you the rough draft of my two letters, which will acquaint you with every thing. If you wish to know the course of this correspondence, you must accustom yourself to decypher my minutes; for I would not for the world take the trouble of copying them. Adieu, my lovely friend!

Aug. 25, 17 — .

LETTER XXXV.

VISCOUNT VALMONT *to the* Presidente DE TOURVEL.

You must be obeyed, Madam; and I must convince you, that, notwithstanding all the faults you are pleased to think me guilty of, I have yet at least so much delicacy as not to suffer a single reproach to escape my lips, and sufficient resolution to impose on myself the most painful sacrifice. You command me to be silent, and to forget you. Well, I shall constrain my love to be silent, and, if possible, I shall forget the cruel manner in which it has been received. Undoubtedly my wish to please gave me no right to it; and I must farther acknowledge, that the necessity I was under of having your indulgence, was not a sufficient title to obtain it: but you consider my love as an atrocious affront; you forget that if it is a fault, you are at once both the cause and the apology for it. You forget also, that accustomed as I was to lay open my soul to you, even when that confidence might be detrimental to me, it was no longer possible for me to hide the sentiments with which I was affected; and what is the result of sincerity, you look upon as the effect of arrogance; and in recompence of the most tender, the most respectful, and the most sincere love, you drive me far from you. You even threaten me with your hatred. Where is the man who would not complain to be so treated? But I submit, and suffer all without murmuring. You strike, and I adore! The inconceivable ascendant you have obtained over me, has rendered you sole mistress of my sentiments; and if my love alone disobeys, if you cannot destroy it, it is because it is your own work, not mine.

I ask no return; that I never flattered myself with: I don't even implore that pity which the concern you seem to take for me flattered me with the hope of; but I believe, I own, I have a right to claim your justice.

You inform me, Madam, that some persons have endeavoured to prejudice me in your esteem. If you had given credit to the advice of your friends, you would not have even suffered me to approach you. Those are your terms; who then are those officious friends? Certainly those people of such severe morals, and such rigid virtue, will have no objection to give up their names; they certainly would not take shelter behind the same screen with the vilest of slanderers; and I shall then be no longer ignorant of their name and their charge. Consider, Madam, I have a right to know both one and the other, since you judge me from their report. A criminal is never condemned without being told his crime, and naming his accusers. I ask no other favour; and I, beforehand, engage to make good my justification, and to compel them to retract.

If I have, perhaps, too much despised the empty clamours of the public, which I set little value on, it is not so with your esteem; and when I consecrate my whole life to merit it, it shall not be ravished from me with impunity. It becomes so much the more precious to me, as I shall, without doubt, owe to it the request you fear to make me, and which, you say, would give me a right to your gratitude. Ah! far from requiring any, I shall think myself highly indebted to you, if you can assist me with an opportunity of being agreeable to you.

Begin then by doing me more justice, and let me be no longer ignorant of what you wish me to do; if I could guess at it, I would save you the trouble of telling it me. To the pleasure of seeing you, add the happiness of serving you, and I shall extol your indulgence. What then can prevent you; it is not, I hope, the dread of a refusal? That, I feel, I should never be able to pardon you. It is not one not to return you your letter. I wish more than you that it may no longer be necessary to me; but accustomed as I am to believe you so soft a disposition, it is in this letter only that I can find you such as you wish to appear. When I form the vow of endeavouring to make you sensible to my flame, I feel that you would fly a hundred leagues from me, rather than consent; when your accomplishments justify and augment my passion, it still tells me that it insults you; and when in your presence this passion is my supreme good, I feel that it is my greatest torment. You may now conceive that my greatest happiness would be to return you this fatal letter: to ask it again would give me a kind of authority to believe its contents. After this, I hope you will not doubt of my readiness to return it.

Aug. 21, 17—.

LETTER XXXVI.

VISCOUNT VALMONT *to the* Presidente DE TOURVEL.

(Post mark from Dijon.)

Your severity, Madam, increases daily; and permit me to say, you seem to dread more being indulgent than unjust. After passing judgment on me without giving me a hearing, you must certainly be sensible it was less difficult not to read my reasons than to answer them. You obstinately refuse to receive my letters; you return them contemptuously; and you force me to use artifice at the very instant that my sole object is to convince you of my integrity. The obligation you lay me under of defending myself, will, I hope, apologize for the means I am constrained to use. Moreover, as I am convinced, that to be justified in your mind, it will be sufficient that the sincerity of my sentiments should be laid open to you, I thought this innocent stratagem might be forgiven. I will, then, dare hope that you will forgive it; and that you will not be much surprised that love is more industrious to show itself than indifference is to banish it.

Permit me then, Madam, to lay my heart entirely open to you. It is yours, and it is but right you should know it.

When I arrived at Madame de Rosemonde's, I little imagined the fate that awaited me. I knew not you was here; and I must add with the sincerity that characterises me, had I known it, my repose would not have been disturbed: not but that I should have rendered that homage to your beauty it so justly requires; but being long accustomed to experience only desires, to surrender only to those where my hopes flattered success, I knew nothing of the torments of love. You was witness to the pressing instances of Madame de Rosemonde, to detain me some time. I had already spent one day with you: at length I acquiesced, or rather thought I acquiesced, to the pleasure so natural and reasonable, of paying a proper regard to so respectable a relation.

The manner of living here undoubtedly differed widely from that I had been accustomed to; yet I perceived no difficulty in conforming to it, and without ever thinking of diving into the cause of so sudden a change, I attributed it solely to that easiness of temper, which, I believe, I have already mentioned to you.

Unfortunately (but why must it be a misfortune?) knowing you more, I soon discovered that that enchanting form, which alone had raised my admiration, was the smallest of your attractions; your celestial soul astonished and seduced mine; I admired your beauty, but adored your virtue. Without a thought of obtaining you, I was resolved to deserve you; seeing your indulgence for my past follies, I was ambitious to merit your approbation for the future.

I sought it in your conversation, I watched for it in your looks; in those looks which diffused a poison so much more dangerous, as it spread without design, and was received without diffidence.

Then I knew what was love; but far from complaining, resolved to bury it in eternal silence. I gave way without dread or reserve to this most delicious sentiment. Each day augmented its power; and soon the pleasure of seeing you became a necessity. Were you absent a moment, my heart was oppressed; at the noise of your approach it fluttered with joy. I no longer existed but by you and for you; and yet I call on yourself to witness, if ever in the gaiety of rural amusements, or in the more serious conversations, a word ever escaped from me that could betray the secret of my heart.

At length the day arrived which gave birth to my misfortune; and by an inconceivable fatality, a worthy action gave the signal. Yes, Madam, it was in the midst of the poor wretches I had delivered, that giving way to that precious sensibility that embellishes beauty itself, and enhances virtue, you led a heart astray which was already too much intoxicated by love.

You may, perhaps, recollect, what a gloom spread over me at my return. Alas, I was totally employed in combating a passion which I found was overpowering me!

It was after having exhausted all my strength and reason in this unequal combat, that an accident I could not have foreseen, left us alone; then I own I was overcome. My full heart could neither command my words or tears; but is it then a crime? And if it be one, is it not sufficiently punished by the racking torments to which I am devoted?

Consumed by a hopeless love, I implore your pity, and you return me hate: no other happiness in view but that of gazing on you, my unconscious eyes seek you, and I tremble to meet your looks. In the deplorable state to which you have reduced me, I pass my days in concealing my sorrows, and my nights in cherishing them; whilst you, tranquil and peaceful, only know them by having been the cause, and enjoying it; and yet it is you that complain, and I excuse myself.

This is, notwithstanding, a true recital of what you call injuries, which rather deserve to be called misfortunes. A pure and sincere love, a profound respect, and an entire submission, are the sentiments with which you have inspired me. I should not dread to present such homage even to the Divinity. Oh thou, who art one of his most beautiful works, imitate his mercy, think on my cruel torments; above all, think that as you have put me between the supremest felicity and despair, the first word you pronounce will for ever decide my fate!

Aug. 23 ,17 — .

LETTER XXXVII.

The Presidente DE TOURVEL *to* MADAME DE VOLANGES.

I submit, Madam, to the sympathetic voice of friendship. Long accustomed to have a deference to your advice, I am led to believe it always founded in reason. I will even acknowledge that Mr. de Valmont must be exceedingly dangerous indeed, if he can assume the character he puts on here, and be the man you represent him. However, since you require it, I will do all in my power to remove him hence if possible; for it often happens that things, very simple in themselves, become extremely embarrassing through forms.

It appears, however, totally impracticable to make this requisition to his aunt; it would be equally revolting to both. I would not, without great reluctance, even determine to quit this place; for besides the reasons I already wrote you relative to Mr. de Tourvel, if my departure should be contrary to Mr. de Valmont's wishes, as is not impossible, could he not readily follow me to Paris? And his return, of which I should be, or, at least, appear to be, the object, would it not seem much more extraordinary than an accidental meeting in the country, at a lady's who is known to be his relation, and my particular friend?

I have, then, no other resource left but to prevail on him to leave this place. I am aware of the difficulties I have to encounter in such a proposal; yet as he seems to make it a point to convince me, that he is not the unprincipled character he has been represented to me, I hope to succeed. I shall even be glad of an opportunity to be satisfied whether (to use his own words) the truly virtuous females ever had, or ever will have occasion to complain of his conduct. If he goes, as I hope he will, it will certainly be in deference to my request; for I have no manner of doubt of his intention to spend a great part of the autumn here; but if, on the contrary, he should obstinately refuse me, it will be time enough for me to depart, which I promise you I will do.

This I believe, Madam, is all your friendship requires of me: I shall eagerly gratify it, and convince you, that notwithstanding *the warmth* with which I have defended Mr. de Valmont, I am nevertheless disposed not only to hear, but also to follow the advice of my friends.

From – –, Aug. 25, 17–.

LETTER XXXVIII.

The MARCHIONESS DE MERTEUIL *to* VISCOUNT VALMONT.

My dear Viscount, I this moment received your enormous packet. If the date is right, I should have had it twenty-four hours sooner; however, was I to take the time to read it, I should not have any to answer it; therefore, I prefer owning its receipt, and let us chat on other matters. It is not that I have any thing to say relative to myself; for the autumn has left nothing in Paris scarce that bears the human form, and for this month past, my prudence and discretion are truly amazing; any other than my Chevalier would be tired out with my constancy. Having no other amusement, I divert myself with the little Volanges, who shall be the subject of this epistle.

Do you know you have lost more than you can imagine, in not taking this child under your tuition? She is really delightful; she has neither disposition or motive; you may then guess her conversation is mild and easy. I do not think she will ever shine in the sentimental line; but every thing announces the most lively sensations. Without wit or artifice, she has, notwithstanding, a certain kind of natural duplicity, if one may speak so, which sometimes astonishes me, and will be much more successful, as her figure exhibits the picture of candour and openness. She is naturally very caressing, and she sometimes entertains me: her imagination is surprisingly lively; and she is the more agreeable, as she is totally ignorant, and longs to know every thing. Sometimes she takes fits of impatience that are truly comic; she laughs, she frets, she cries, and then begs of me to instruct her, with a most seducing innocence. I am almost jealous of whoever that pleasure is reserved for.

I do not know whether I wrote you, that for four or five days past I had the honour to be her confident. You may guess at first I affected an appearance of severity; but when I observe that she imagined I was convinced with her bad reasons, I let them pass current; and she is fully persuaded it is entirely owing to her eloquence: this precaution was necessary, lest I should be exposed. I gave her leave to write and say, *I love*; and the same day, without her having any suspicion, I contrived a tête-à-tête for her with her Danceny. But only think, he is such a fool, he has not yet obtained a single kiss from her. However, the boy makes pretty verses. Lord, what stupid creatures those wits are! He is so much so, that he makes me uneasy; for I am resolved not to have any thing to do with him.

Now is the time you might be very useful to me. You are enough acquainted with Danceny to gain his confidence; and if he once gave it you, we should go on at a great rate. Make haste with your Presidente, for I am determined Gercourt shall not escape. I spoke to the little thing yesterday about him, and painted him in such colours, that she could not hate him more were she married to him for ten years. However, I gave her a long lesson on conjugal fidelity; nothing is equal to my severity on this point. By this means I establish my reputation for virtue, which too great a condescension might destroy; and increase the hatred with which I mean to gratify her husband. And, lastly, I hope, by making her think it is not lawful to indulge in a love matter only during the short time she is unmarried, she will come to a decision more expeditiously to lose no time.

Adieu, Viscount! I shall read your volume at my toilette.
Aug. 27, 17—.

LETTER XXXIX.

CECILIA VOLANGES *to* SOPHIA CARNAY.

My dear Sophia, I am very melancholy and uneasy. I have wept almost the whole night. Not but that at present I am very happy; but I foresee it will not last long.

I was at the opera last night with Madame de Merteuil; we chatted a good deal of my match; I am not much pleased with the husband she announces to me. She tells me I am to be married next October, to the Count de Gercourt: he is of a noble family, rich, and colonel of the regiment of — —; that is all very well. But, on the other hand, he is old—he is almost six and thirty. Madame de Merteuil says he is morose and ill-tempered; and she dreads much I shall not be happy with him. I even perceived plainly she spoke as if she was certain of it, though she would not speak out, for fear of giving me uneasiness. She dwelt almost the whole evening on the duties of wives to their husbands: she acknowledges Mr. de Gercourt is not at all amiable, and yet, she says, I must love him. She has even told me that when I am married, I must not love Chevalier Danceny, as if that was in my power! I assure you I shall ever love him; or rather would never be married at all. Let Mr. de Gercourt take the consequence—he is not the man of my choice. He is now in Corsica—a great distance. I wish with all my heart he may stay there these ten years. If I was not afraid of being sent back to the convent, I would tell mamma that he is not agreeable to me; but to do that might be still worse. I don't know how to act. I never loved Mr. de Danceny as much as I do now; and when I think I have only one month more to be as I am, the tears burst into my eyes immediately. I have no consolation but in Madame de Merteuil's friendship; she is so tender hearted, she unites with me in all my sorrows; and then she is so amiable, that when I am in her company, I think no more of them; besides, she is very useful to me, for she has taught me what little I know; and she is so good natured, I can tell her every thing I think of, without being at all ashamed. When she thinks it not right, she sometimes chides me, but always very gently: whenever that happens I spare no endeavours to appease her. She, at least, I may love as much as I will, and there is no harm in that; which gives me great pleasure. However, we have agreed that I must not appear so fond of her before every one, and especially before mamma, lest she should entertain any suspicion on the score of the Chevalier Danceny. I assure you, if I could always live as I now do, I should think myself very happy. Nothing torments me but this horrid Gercourt! But I shall say no more of him: I find if I did, I should be melancholy. I will go write to Chevalier Danceny, and will only talk to him of my love, and will not touch any subject that may distress him.

Adieu, my dear friend. You now find you are wrong in complaining of my silence; and that notwithstanding *the busy life I lead*, as you call it, I have still time to love and write to you.[1]

Aug. 27, 17—.

[1] We shall hereafter suppress Cecilia Volanges and Chevalier Danceny's letters, being uninteresting.

LETTER XL.

The VISCOUNT DE VALMONT to the MARCHIONESS DE MERTEUIL.

My inhuman mistress not content with declining an answer to my letters, and even refusing to receive them, she endeavours to deprive me of the pleasure of seeing her, and insists I should quit this place. What will surprise you more is, that I have acquiesced in every thing. You will, no doubt, blame me. Yet I thought I should not let slip the opportunity of receiving her commands; being, on the one hand, convinced, that whosoever commands is responsible, and on the other, that the imaginary air of authority we give the women, is the most difficult snare for them to escape: besides, the precautions she has taken not to be with me alone, put me in a very dangerous situation, which I thought it prudent to be extricated from at all events: for being incessantly with her, without being able to direct her attention to the subject of love, it was the more to be dreaded she would become accustomed to see me with indifference—a disposition of mind which you very well know is seldom overcome.

You may judge I did not acquiesce without making conditions. I even took care to stipulate for one impossible to be performed; not only that I may be at liberty to keep or break my word, but engage in a discussion, either verbally or in writing, whenever my fair one might be more satisfied with me, or feel the necessity of relaxing. I should have ill managed indeed, if I did not obtain an equivalent for giving up my pretensions, though they are not of a justifiable nature.

Having laid before you my reasons in this long exordium, I begin the history of the two last days. I shall annex, as proofs, my fair one's letter with my answer. You will agree with me few historians are more exact than I am.

You may recollect the effect my letter from Dijon had the day before yesterday. The remainder of that day was rather tempestuous. The pretty prude did not make her appearance until dinner was on the table, and informed us she had got a bad head-ach; a pretence for concealing the most violent ill humour that ever possessed woman. Her countenance was totally altered; the enchanting softness of her tone was changed to a moroseness that added new beauty to her. I shall make a good use of this discovery in future; and convert the tender mistress into the passionate one.

I foresaw the evening would be dull; to avoid which, I pretended to have letters to write, and retired to my apartment. I returned about six to the Saloon; Madame de Rosemonde proposed an airing, which was agreed to. But the instant the carriage was ready, the pretended sick lady, by an act of infernal malice, pretended, in her turn, or, perhaps to be revenged of me for my absence, feigned her head-ach much worse, and forced me to undergo a tête-à-tête with my old aunt. I don't know whether my imprecations against this female demon had their effect; but she was in bed at our return.

Next morning, at breakfast, she was no more the same woman: her natural sweetness had returned, and I had reason to think my pardon sealed. Breakfast being over, the lovely woman arose with an easy air, and walked towards the park; I soon followed her, as you may imagine. "Whence arises this inclination for a walk?" said I, accosting her. "I have wrote a great deal this morning," she replied, "and my head is a little fatigued." — "I am not so happy," replied I, "as to have to reproach myself with being the cause of that fatigue." — "I have wrote you," said she, "but I hesitate to deliver my letter: — it contains a request, and I fear I must not flatter myself with success." — "I swear if it be possible." — "Nothing more easy," replied she; "and though perhaps you ought to grant it from a motive of justice, I will consent even to obtaining it as a favour." She then delivered me her letter, which I took, as also her hand, which she drew back, without anger, and more confusion than vivacity. "The heat is more intense than I imagined," said she; "I must return." In vain did I strive to persuade her to continue our walk; — she returned to the Castle; — and were it not for the dread of being seen, I would have used other means as well as my eloquence. She returned without uttering a syllable; and I plainly saw this pretended walk had no other object than to deliver me her letter. She retired to her apartment, and I to mine, to read her epistle. I beg you will read that, and my answer, before you go farther.

LETTER XLI.

The Presidente DE TOURVEL *to* VISCOUNT VALMONT.

Your behaviour towards me, Sir, has the appearance of your seeking opportunities to give me more reason to complain of your conduct than I hitherto have had. Your obstinacy in teasing me incessantly with a subject that I neither will or ought to attend to; the ill use you have made of my candour, or timidity, to convey your letters to me; but, above all, the indelicate manner you imagined to hand me the last, without having paid the least attention to the consequences of a surprise which might have exposed me, would authorise me to reproach you in terms as severe as merited. But I am inclined, instead of renewing my complaint, to bury all in oblivion, provided you agree to a request as simple as it is just.

You yourself have told me, Sir, I ought not to apprehend a denial; although, from an inconsistency which is peculiar to you, this phrase was even followed by the only refusal you had in your power to give,[1] I am still disposed to think you will, on this occasion, keep a promise you so formally and so lately made.

I require, therefore, you would retire from hence, and leave me, as your residence here any longer will expose me to the censure of the public, which is ever ready to paint things in the worst colours, and a public whom you have long habituated to watching such women as have admitted you into their society.

Though my friends have for some time given me notice of this danger, I did not pay proper attention to it; I even combated their advice whilst your behaviour to me gave me reason to think you did not confound me with the crowd of women who have reason to lament their acquaintance with you. Now that you treat me in the same manner, and that I can no longer mistake, it is a duty I owe to the public, my friends, and myself, to take the necessary resolution. I might also add, that a denial would avail little, as I am determined, in case of a refusal, to leave this place immediately.

I do not seek to lessen the obligation your complaisance will lay me under; and will not conceal from you, that if you lay me under the necessity of leaving this, you will put me to inconvenience. Convince me then, Sir, as you have often told me, that a woman of virtue will never have reason to complain of you: show me, at least, that if you have ill treated such a woman, you are disposed to atone for the injury you have done her.

Did I think my request required any justification in your sight, it would be enough, I think, to tell you the whole conduct of your life makes it necessary; it is not my fault a reformation has not taken place. But I will not recall events that I wish to forget, and which would lead me to pass a severe sentence on you at the time I am offering you an opportunity of deserving my utmost gratitude. Farewell, Sir. Your determination will tell me in what light I am to behold you for life.

Your most humble, &c.

Aug. 25, 17 —.

[1] See Letter the 35th.

LETTER XLII.

VISCOUNT DE VALMONT *to the* Presidente DE TOURVEL.

Though the conditions you impose on me, Madam, are severe indeed, I shall not refuse to comply; for I perceive it is impossible for me to oppose any of your wishes. As we are agreed on this point, I dare flatter myself that, in return, you will permit me to make some requests, much easier to be granted than yours, and which, notwithstanding, I don't wish to obtain but through a perfect resignation to your will.

The one, which I hope your justice will suggest, is, to name my accusers; I think the injury they have done me authorises me to demand who they are: the other request, for which I crave your indulgence, is, to permit me sometimes to renew the homage of a passion, which now, more than ever, will deserve your pity.

Reflect, Madam, that I am earnest to obey you, even at the expence of my happiness; I will go farther, notwithstanding my conviction, that you only wish my absence to rid you of the painful sight of the victim of your injustice.

Be ingenuous, Madam; you dread less the public censure, too long used to reverence you, to dare to harbour a disadvantageous opinion of you, than to be made uneasy by the presence of a man, whom it is easier to punish than to blame. You banish me on the same principle that people turn their eyes from the miserable wretches they do not choose to relieve.

And then absence will redouble my torments; to whom but you can I relate my grievances? From what other person am I to expect that consolation, which will become so necessary in my affliction? Will you, who are the cause, refuse me that consolation?

Be not surprised, neither that before my departure, I should endeavour to justify my sentiments for you, nor that I shall not have the resolution to set out, until I receive the order from your own mouth.

Those reasons oblige me to request a moment's interview. It would be in vain to think that a correspondence by letter would answer the end. Volumes often cannot explain what a quarter of an hour's conversation will do. You will readily find time to grant me this favour; for, notwithstanding my eagerness to obey you, as Madame de Rosemonde is well apprised of my design to spend a part of the autumn with her, I must, at all events, wait the return of the post, to pretend a letter of business obliging me to return.

Farewell, Madam; never till now did I experience the force of this expression, which recalls to me the idea of my separation from you. If you could conceive how distressingly it affects me, my obedience would find me some favour in your sight. Receive, however, with more indulgence, the homage of the most tender and respectful passion.

Aug. 26,17 — .

Sequel to the Fortieth Letter.

From the VISCOUNT DE VALMONT *to the* MARCHIONESS DE MERTEUIL.

Now, my lovely friend, let us discuss this affair a little. You readily conceive, that the virtuous, the scrupulous Madame de Tourvel, cannot grant the first of my requests — that of informing me who my accusers are, without a breach of friendship: thus, by promising every thing on that condition, I am not at all committed; and you must be very sensible, that the negative she must give me, will give me a title to all my other objects; so that, by leaving this place, I shall obtain the advantage of a regular correspondence, with her own consent; for I don't set great value upon the interview that I ask, by which I mean no more than to accustom her beforehand not to refuse other personal applications to her, when I shall have real occasion for them.

The only thing that remains to be done before my departure is, to know who are those that take the trouble to prejudice me in her opinion.

I presume it is that pedantic scoundrel her husband; I wish it may; for, as a conjugal prohibition is a spur to desire, I should be certain that from the moment of gaining her consent to write to me, I should have nothing more to fear from the husband, because she would then find herself under the necessity of deceiving him.

And if she has a confidential friend, and that friend should be against me, I think it will be necessary to raise a cause of misunderstanding between them, in which I hope to succeed: but, in the first place, I must see my way clear.

I imagined yesterday I had attained that necessary preliminary; but this woman does not act like any other. We were in her apartment when dinner was announced. She had just time to finish her toilet; and from her hurry, and making apologies, I observed her leave the key in her bureau; and she always leaves the key in her chamber door. My mind was full of this during dinner. When I heard her waiting-maid coming down stairs, I instantly feigned a bleeding at the nose, and went out. I flew to the bureau, found all the drawers open, but not a single paper; yet there is no occasion to burn them, situated as she is. What can she do with the letters she receives? and she receives a great many. I left nothing unexamined; all was open, and I searched every where; so that I am convinced this precious deposit is confided only to her pocket.

How they are to be got at, my mind has been fruitlessly employed ever since yesterday in contriving means: I cannot conquer my inclination to gain possession of them. I often regret that I have not the talent of a pickpocket. Don't you think it ought to be made a part of the education of a man of intrigue? Would it not be humorous enough to steal a letter or a portrait of a rival, or to extract from the pocket of a prude, materials to unmask her? But our forefathers had no ideas: it is in vain for me to rack my brains; for it only convinces me of my own inability, without furnishing me any remedy.

I returned to dinner very dissatisfied: my fair one however brought me into good humour, by her anxious enquiries on my feigned indisposition: I did not fail to assure her that I had for some short time, violent agitations, which impaired my health. As she is persuaded the cause proceeded from her, ought she not in conscience endeavour to calm them? Although a devotee, she has very little charity; she refuses any compliance to supplications of love; and this refusal appears to me sufficient to authorise any theft to obtain the object. But adieu; for although I am writing to you, my mind is taken up with those cursed letters.

Aug. 27, 17—.

LETTER XLIII.

The Presidente DE TOURVEL *to the* VISCOUNT DE VALMONT.

Why, Sir, do you endeavour at a diminution of my gratitude to you? Why obey me only by halves, and in some measure make a bargain of a simple, genteel act? It is not, then, sufficient that I am sensible of its value! You not only ask a great deal of me, but you demand what it is impossible to grant. If my friends have talked of you to me, they could only do so from regard for me: should they even be mistaken, their intention was not the less good; and yet you require that I should repay this proof of their esteem, by giving you up their names. I must own I have been very wrong in acquainting you of it; and I now feel it in a very sensible manner. What would have been only candour with any one else, becomes imprudence with you, and would be a crime was I to attend to your request. I appeal to yourself, to your honour; how could you think me capable of such a proceeding? Ought you even to have made me such a proposition? No, certainly; and I am sure, when you reflect, you will desist from this request.

The other you make of writing to me is little easier to grant; and if you will think a moment, you cannot in justice blame me. I do not mean to offend you; but after the character you have required, and which you yourself confess to have partly merited, what woman can avow holding a correspondence with you? And what virtuous woman could resolve to do that which she would be obliged to conceal?

If I was even certain that your letters would be such as would give me no cause of discontent, and that I could always be conscious I was sufficiently justified in receiving them, then, perhaps, the desire of proving to you that reason, not hatred, guided me, would make me surmount those powerful considerations, and cause me to do what I ought not, in giving you sometimes permission to write to me; and if, indeed, you wish it as much as you express, you will readily submit to the only condition that can possibly make me consent to it: and if you have any gratitude for this condescension, you will not delay your departure a moment.

Give me leave to make one observation on this occasion: you received a letter this morning, and you did not make use of that opportunity to acquaint Madame de Rosemonde of your intended departure as you promised me; I now hope that nothing will prevent you from keeping your word. I hope much that you will not wait for the interview you ask, which I absolutely will not agree to; and that, instead of the order that you pretend to be so necessary, you will be satisfied with my request, which I again renew to you. Farewell, Sir!

Aug. 27, 17—.

LETTER XLIV.

VISCOUNT DE VALMONT *to the* MARCHIONESS DE MERTEUIL.

Share in my joy, my charming friend; I am loved; I have at length triumphed over that rebellious heart. In vain does she still dissemble; my happy address has discovered the secret. Thanks to my unremitting efforts, I know all that interests me: since last night, that propitious night, I am again myself; I have discovered a double mystery of love and iniquity; I shall enjoy the one, and be revenged of the other; I shall fly from pleasure to pleasure. The bare idea of it transports me almost beyond the bounds of prudence; and yet I shall have occasion for some of it, to enable me to put any proper order in my narrative; but let us try:

Yesterday, after I had wrote my letter, I received one from the celestial devotee; I send it enclosed; you will observe she with less awkwardness than might be expected, gives me leave to write to her; yet presses my departure, which I well knew I could not defer without prejudice to myself. However, tempted by a curiosity to know who had wrote against me, I was still undetermined how to act. I attempted to bribe her chamber-maid, to induce her to give me her mistress's pockets, which she could easily do at night, and replace them the next morning, without giving the least suspicion. I offered ten louis d'ors for this trifling service; but I found her a hesitating, scrupulous, or timid creature, whom neither my eloquence nor money could bring over. I was using farther solicitations, when the bell rung for supper. I was then obliged to break off; and thought myself very happy in obtaining from her a promise to keep my secret, on which, however, you may believe I placed little dependence.

I never was more out of humour. I found I had committed myself, and reproached myself much for the imprudent step I had taken.

After I retired in great anxiety, I spoke to my huntsman, who was entitled, as a successful lover, to some share of credit. I desired he would prevail on this girl to do what I required, or at least to insure secrecy: he, who in general makes no doubt of success in any thing he undertakes, appeared dubious of this negociation, and made a reflection, the depth of which astonished me: "You certainly know better than I can tell you, Sir," said he, "that to kiss a girl is nothing more than to indulge her in a fancy of her own, and that, there is a wide difference often between that and making her act according to our wishes; and I have so much less dependence on her, as I have much reason to think she has another swain, and that I only owe my good fortune to her want of occupation in the country; and had it not been for my zeal for your service, Sir, I should not have sought it more than once (this lad is a treasure). As to the secret," added he, "what purpose will it answer to make her promise, since she will risk nothing in deceiving us? To speak of it again, would only make her think it of greater importance, and make her more anxious to insinuate herself into her mistress's favour, by divulging it." The justness of these reflections added to my embarrassment. Fortunately the fellow was in a talking mood; and as I had occasion for him, I let him go on: while relating his adventures with this girl, he informed me the room she slept in was only separated from the apartment of her mistress by a single partition, and as the least noise would be heard, they met every night in his room. I instantly formed my plan, which I communicated to him, and we executed it successfully.

I awaited until the clock struck two, and then, as was agreed, went to the rendezvous, with a lighted candle in my hand, and under pretence of having several times in vain rung the bell. My confidant, who plays his part to admiration, performed a little scene of surprise, despair, and confusion, which I put a stop to, by sending him to warm me some water, which I pretended to have occasion for; the scrupulous waiting-maid was the more disconcerted, as the fellow, who had improved on my scheme, had made her make a toilet very suitable to the heat of the season, but which it by no means apologised for.

Being sensible the more this girl was humbled, the less trouble I should have to bring her to my designs, I did not suffer her to change either her situation or dress; and having ordered my servant to wait for me in my room, I sat by her bed-side, which was in much disorder, and began a conversation. It was necessary to keep the ascendant I had obtained, and I therefore preserved a *sang froid* that would have done honour to the continence of Scipio; and without taking the smallest liberty with her, which her ruddy countenance, and the opportunity, perhaps, gave her a right to hope; I talked to her of business with as much indifference, as I would have done with an attorney.

My conditions were, that I would would observe the strictest secrecy, provided the day following, at the same hour, she put me in possession of her mistress's pockets, and my offer of ten louis-d'ors. I now confirm I will not take any advantage of your situation. Every thing was granted, as you may believe; I then retired, and left the happy couple to repair their lost time.

I employed mine in sleep: and in the morning, wanting a pretence not to answer my fair one's letter before I had examined her papers, which could not be till the night following, I resolved to go a-hunting, which took up the greatest part of the day.

At my return I was received very coolly. I have reason to believe she was a little piqued at my want of eagerness to make good use of the time that remained, especially after the softer letter which she wrote me. I formed this conjecture, because, on Madame de Rosemonde's having reproached me on my long absence, the fair one replied with some acrimony, "Oh, let us not reproach Mr. de Valmont for his attachment to the only pleasure he can find here." I complained that they did not do me justice, and took the opportunity to assure them I was so well pleased with their company, that I sacrificed to it a very interesting letter that I had to write; adding, that not having been able to sleep several nights, I endeavoured to try if fatigue would not bring me my usual rest; my looks sufficiently explained the subject of my letter, and the cause of my want of rest. I took care to affect, during the whole evening, a melancholy softness, which succeeded tolerably well, and under which I disguised my impatience for the hour which was to give me up the secret she so obstinately persisted in concealing. At length we retired; and soon after the faithful waiting-maid brought me the stipulated price of my discretion: when in possession of this treasure, I proceeded with my usual prudence to arranging them; for it was of the utmost importance to replace every thing in order.

I first hit upon two letters from the husband, indigested stuff, a mixture of uninteresting details of law-suits, and unmeaning protestations of conjugal love, which I had the patience to read through; but not a syllable in either concerning me. I put them in their place with some disgust; but that vanished on finding, in my hand-writing, the scraps of my famous letter from Dijon, carefully collected. Fortunately it came into my head to run them over. You may guess the excess of my raptures, when I distinctly perceived the traces of my adorable devotee's tears. I must own I gave way to a puerile emotion, and kissed this letter with a transport that I did not think myself susceptible of. I continued the happy search; I found all my letters in order according to their dates; and what still surprised me more agreeably was, to find the first of them, that which I thought had been returned to me by my ungrateful fair one, faithfully copied in her own hand-writing, but in an altered and trembling manner, which sufficiently testified the soft agitation of her heart during the time she was employed at it.

So far I was entirely occupied with love; but soon gave way to the greatest rage. Who think you it is that wants to destroy me, with this woman I adore? What fury do you suppose wicked enough to form so diabolical a plan! You know her: it's your friend, your relation; it is Madame de Volanges. You cannot conceive what a string of horrible stories the infernal Megera has wrote against me. It is she, and she alone, has disturbed the peace of this angelic woman; it is by her counsels, by her pernicious advice, that I find myself obliged to retire; I am sacrificed to her! Certainly her daughter shall be seduced; but that is not sufficient, she shall be ruined; and since the age of this accursed woman shelters her from my blows, I must strike at her in the object of her affections.

She will then force me to return to Paris; she obliges me to it! Be it so; I will return; but she shall have reason to lament my return. I am sorry Danceny is to be the hero of this adventure; he has a fund of honour that will be a restraint upon us; but he is in love, and we are often together: I may turn him to account. My anger overcomes me, and I forget that I am to give you the recital of what has passed to-day.

This morning I saw my lovely prude; she never appeared so charming; that was of course; it is the most powerful moment with a woman, that shall produce an intoxication of soul, which is so often spoke of, and so rarely felt, when, though certain of their affections, we have not yet possessed their favours; which is precisely my case. Perhaps the idea, also, of being deprived of the pleasure of seeing her, served to embellish her. At length the post arrived, and brought me your letter of the 27th; and whilst I was reading it, I hesitated whether I should keep my word or not; but I met my fair one's eyes, and I found it impossible to refuse her any thing.

I therefore announced my departure immediately after Madame de Rosemonde left us: I was four paces distant from the austere lovely one, when she started with a frightened air, "leave me, leave me, Sir," said she; "for the love of God, leave me!" This fervent prayer, which discovered her emotion, animated me the more; I was now close to her, and took hold of her hands, which she had joined together with the most moving, affecting expressiveness. I then began my tender complaints, when some evil genius brought back Madame de Rosemonde. The timid devotee, who has in reality some reason to be apprehensive, seized the opportunity, and retired.

I notwithstanding offered her my hand, which she accepted; and judging favourably of this kindness, which she had not shown for so long a time, and again renewing my complaints, I endeavoured to squeeze hers. She at first endeavoured to draw it back; but upon a more pressing instance, she gave it up with a good grace, although without either answering this emotion or my discourse. Being come to the door of her apartment, I wanted to kiss that hand before I left her: she struggled, but an *ah! think I am going to part*, pronounced with great tenderness, made her awkward and defenceless; the kiss was scarcely given, when the hand recovered its strength to escape, and the fair one entered her apartment where the waiting-maid was: here ends my tale.

As I presume you will be to-morrow at the Lady Marechale's de — —, where, certainly, I shall not go to look for you; and as at our first interview we shall have a great many things to talk over, especially that of the little Volanges, which I do not lose sight of; I have determined to send this letter before me; and although it is so long, I will not close it until the moment I am going to send it to the post; for I am so circumstanced, that a great deal may depend on an opportunity; and I leave you to watch for it.

P. S. Eight o'clock at night.

Nothing new; not the least moment of liberty; even the greatest care employed to avoid it. Yet as much grief as decency would permit, for the least another event, which may not be a matter of indifference, as Madame de Rosemonde has commanded me to give an invitation to Madame de Volanges, to come and spend a few days in the country.

Adieu, my lovely friend, until to-morrow, or the day after at farthest!
Aug. 28, 17—.

LETTER XLV.

The Presidente DE TOURVEL *to* MADAME DE VOLANGES.

Mr. de Valmont is gone this morning, Madam: you seemed so anxiously to wish for this event, that I have thought it my duty to impart it to you. Madame de Rosemonde is inconsolable for the loss of her nephew, whose company was really very pleasing: she spent the whole morning in talking to me of him with her usual sensibility; she was inexhaustible in his praise. I thought myself bound to attend to it without interruption; and indeed I must own she was right on many heads; besides, I was sensible I was the cause of this separation, and have no prospect of making her amends for the pleasure of which I have deprived her. You know I am not naturally inclined to gaiety, and our manner of life here will not contribute much to increase it.

Had I not been following your advice, I should have been inclined to think I had acted too precipitately; for I was really hurt at the grief I had caused my respectable friend; I was so much moved, that I could have mingled my tears with hers.

We now live on the hope that you will accept the invitation that Mr. de Valmont will give you from Madame de Rosemonde, to come and pass a little time with her. I hope you have no doubt of the great satisfaction your compliance will give me; and indeed you should make us amends. I shall be happy in this opportunity of having the pleasure of being sooner acquainted with Mademoiselle de Volanges, and to be near you, to assure you more and more of the respectful sentiments with which I am, &c.

Aug. 29, 17—.

LETTER XLVI.

The CHEVALIER DANCENY *to* CECILIA VOLANGES.

What then has happened to you, my adorable Cecilia! What can have caused so sudden, so cruel a change in you? What are become of your vows of eternal constancy? Even yesterday you renewed them with so much pleasure: what! can to-day make you forget them? In vain do I examine—I can't find any reason given by myself; and it afflicts me much to have to seek the cause in you. Ah, no! you are neither fickle or deceitful; and even in this moment of despair, no unworthy suspicion shall disgrace my heart; and yet, from what fatality are you no longer the same? No, cruel creature, you are not! The tender Cecilia, the Cecilia I adore! whose constancy is pledged to me, would not have shunned my tender looks; would not have thwarted the happy accident that placed me near her; or, if any reason that I can't conceive, had forced her treat to me with so much rigour, she would at least have condescended to have informed me of it.

Ah! you don't know, you never can know, what you have made me suffer at this day, what I shall suffer at this instant! Do you then think I can live without your love? Yet, when I begged but a word, a single word, to dispel my fears, instead of making a reply, you feigned a dread of being overheard; and this obstacle, which then had no existence, you gave birth to by the place yon fixed on in the circle. When forced to leave you, and I asked what hour I should see you to-morrow, you feigned not to know; and to Madame de Volanges was I obliged for telling me. Thus the moment hitherto so much panted for, of being with you to-morrow, will bring me only distress and grief; and the pleasure of seeing you, as yet the greatest my heart could experience, must now give way to the dread of being troublesome.

I already feel this: my fears prevent me from talking to you of my passion. Though *I love you*, that enchanting sound, which I so much delighted in repeating, when I could hear it, in my turn; that sweet word which sufficed for my felicity, no longer offers me, if you are altered, but eternal despair. I cannot however think that this talisman of love has lost all its effect, and I still strive to make use of it. Yes, my Cecilia, *I love you*[1]. Repeat then this happy expression with me. Remember you have accustomed me to it; and now to deprive me of it, would be to condemn me to torments, which, like my love, will only end with my life.

    Aug. 29, 17—.

[1] Those who have not sometimes had occasion to feel the value of a word, of an expression consecrated by love, will not find any sense in this phrase.

LETTER XLVII.

The VISCOUNT DE VALMONT *to the* MARCHIONESS DE MERTEUIL.

I shall not see you to-day, my charming friend; and I will give you my reasons, which I hope you will accept with your usual good nature.

Instead of returning directly to town yesterday, I stopped at the Countess de — —'s, whose country seat was almost in my road; where I dined, and did not arrive in Paris till near seven o'clock, and alighted at the opera, where I thought you might be.

When the opera was over, I went into the green room to see my old acquaintances; there I found my old friend Emily in the midst of a numerous circle, male and female, who were engaged to sup with her that night at P— — —. I no sooner came among them, but, by the unanimous voice, I was entreated to be of the party. One, a short, thick figure, who stammered out his invitation in Dutch French, I immediately recognised to be the master of the feast. I yielded.

I learned, on our way there, that the house we were going to was the price agreed on for Emily's condescension to this grotesque figure, and that this supper was in fact a wedding feast. The little man could not contain himself for joy, in expectation of the happiness that awaited him; and I saw him so enraptured with it, that I felt a strong inclination to disturb it; which I effected.

The only difficulty was to bring Emily to consent, in whom the burgomaster's riches had raised some scruples: however, after some solicitation, I brought her at length to consent to my scheme, which was, to fill this little beer hogshead with wine, and thus get rid of him.

The sublime idea we entertained of a drunken Dutchman, made us exert ourselves. We succeeded so well, that by the time the dessert was brought on the table, he was not able to hold his glass, whilst the tender Emily and I plied him incessantly, till, at length, he fell under the table so drunk, that it must have lasted at least eight days. We then determined to send him back to Paris; and as he had not kept his carriage, I ordered him to be packed into mine, and I remained in his room. I then received the compliments of the company, who retired soon after, and left me master of the field of battle. This frolic, and perhaps my long retirement, made Emily so desirable, that I promised to remain with her until the resurrection of the Dutchman.

This condescension is a return for that she has just had for me, in submitting to serve me as a desk to write to my lovely devotee, to whom it struck me as a pleasant thought, to write in bed with, and almost in the arms of, a girl, where I was interrupted by a complete infidelity. In this letter I give her an exact account of my conduct and situation. Emily, who read the epistle, laughed immoderately, and I expect it will make you laugh also.

As my letter must be marked at the Paris post-office, I leave it open for you, enclosed. Read it, seal it, and send it there. But, pray, do not use your own seal, nor even any amorous emblem—an antique head only. Adieu, my lovely friend!

P. S. I open my letter to acquaint you, I have determined Emily to go to the Italian opera; and will take that opportunity to visit you. I shall be with you at six the latest; and if agreeable to you, I will accompany you to Madame de Volanges' at seven. It would not be decent to defer longer acquainting her with Madame de Rosemonde's invitation; besides, I shall be glad to see the little Volanges.

Adieu, fair lady! I hope so much pleasure will attend my embracing you, that the Chevalier may be jealous of it.

From P – – –, Aug. 30, 17—.

LETTER XLVIII.

The VISCOUNT DE VALMONT *to the* Presidente DE TOURVEL.

(Post-mark, Paris.)

It is after a very stormy night, during which I have not closed my eyes; it is after having been in incessant agitations, both from uncommon ardour, and entire annihilation of all the faculties of my soul, I come to you, madam, to seek the calm I so much stand in need of, and which I cannot yet hope to enjoy; for the situation I now write of, convinces me more than ever of the irresistible power of love: I can hardly preserve command over myself, to arrange my ideas in any order; and I already foresee that I shall not be able to finish this letter, without being obliged to break off. What! cannot I then hope that you will one day experience the emotions I do at this moment! I may venture, however, to assert, that if you thoroughly experienced such emotions, you could not be totally insensible to them. Believe me, Madam, settled tranquillity, the sleep of the soul, that image of death, does not lead to happiness; the active passions alone lead the way; and notwithstanding the torments you make me suffer, I may, I think, assure myself, that I am this moment happier than you. In vain do you overwhelm me with your afflicting severities; they do not prevent me from giving a loose to my love, and forgetting, in the delirium it causes me, the despair to which you abandon me: thus I revenge myself of the exile to which you have condemned me. Never did I before experience so much pleasure in writing to you. Never did I feel in this pleasing employment so sweet, so lively an emotion! Every thing conspires to raise my transports! The very air I breathe wafts me luxurious pleasure; even the table I write on, now, for the first time, consecrated by me to that use, becomes to me a sacred altar of love; how much more lustre will it not hence derive in my eyes! I will have engraven on it my oath ever to love you! Forgive, I beseech you, my disordered senses. I ought, perhaps, to moderate transports you do not share in. I must leave you a moment to dissipate a frenzy which I find growing upon me: I find it too strong for me.

I return to you, Madam, and certainly return always with the same eagerness; but the sentiment of happiness has fled from me, and gives place to the most cruel state of privation. What does it avail me to talk to you of my sentiments, if it is only in vain that I seek means of convincing you? After so many repeated efforts, my confidence and my strength both abandon me at once. If I recall to my mind the pleasures of love, that only produces a more lively sense of regret at being deprived of them. I see no resource but in your indulgence, and I too well experience at this moment how much I want it, to hope to obtain it. Yet my passion was never more respectful, or ought to give you less offence: it is such, I can venture to say, as the strictest virtue would have no reason to dread; but I am afraid any longer to take up your time with the pains I experience, certain as I am that the object who causes them, does not share them. I must not, at least, presume too far on goodness, which I should do by dwelling on this melancholy picture; I shall only implore you to give me a reply, and never to doubt the veracity of my sentiments.

Wrote from P – – –, dated at Paris,
Aug. 30, 17 –.

LETTER XLIX.

CECILIA VOLANGES *to the* CHEVALIER DANCENY.

Without being either fickle or deceitful, it is sufficient, Sir, to account for my conduct, to know there is a necessity for an alteration in it: I have promised myself a sacrifice to God, until I can offer him also the sacrifice of my sentiments for you, which the religious state you are in renders doubly criminal. – I well know it will give me a great deal of uneasiness, and I will not conceal from you that, since the day before yesterday, I have continually wept when I thought on you; but I hope God will grant me the necessary strength to forget you, which I constantly beg of him night and morning. I even expect, from your friendship and good breeding, that you will not endeavour to interfere with me in the good resolutions that I have been inspired with; and which I endeavour to cherish. I therefore request that you will not write to me any more, as I assure you I shall give no answer; and it would oblige me to acquaint my mamma of every thing that happens, which would entirely deprive me the pleasure of seeing you.

I shall, notwithstanding, have all the attachment for you, that one can have, consistently with innocence; and from my soul I wish you all manner of happiness. I know very well you will love me no longer, and, perhaps, you will soon love another better than me; but this will be an additional penance for the fault I committed in giving you my heart, which I ought to have reserved for God and my husband, when I shall have one. I hope the divine mercy will pity my weakness, and not afflict me with misfortunes that I shall not be able to bear.

Farewell, Sir! I can assure you, that if it was lawful for me to love any one, I should never love any but you; but that is all I can say, and perhaps more than I ought.

Aug. 31, 17 –.

LETTER L.

The Presidente DE TOURVEL *to the* VISCOUNT DE VALMONT.

Is it thus, then, Sir, you fulfil the conditions on which I consented to receive your letters sometimes? And have I not reason to complain, when you mention a sentiment which I should dread to harbour, even were it not inconsistent with every idea of my duty.

If there was a necessity of fresh arguments to preserve this salutary fear, I think I may find sufficient in your last letter; for really, at the time you think to apologise for your passion, you, on the contrary, convince me of its multiplied horrors, for who would wish to purchase pleasure at the expence of reason? Pleasures so transitory, and that are always followed by regret, and often by remorse.

Even yourself, in whom the habitude of this dangerous delirium ought to diminish the effect, are notwithstanding obliged to agree, that it often becomes too strong for you, and you are the first to complain of the involuntary disturbance it causes in you. What horrible ravages would it not then make in an unexperienced and sensible heart, which would augment its force by the greatness of the sacrifices it would be obliged to make?

You believe, or feign to believe, Sir, that love leads to happiness; but I am fully persuaded that it would make me so totally miserable, that I wish never to hear the word mentioned. I think that even speaking of it hurts tranquillity; and it is as much from inclination as duty, that I beseech you to be hereafter silent on that subject: this requisition you may very easily grant at this time. You are now returned to Paris, where you will find opportunities enough to forget a sentiment which probably owed its birth to the habit you have of making this your whole employment; and the strength of your present passion, is probably to be ascribed to your want of other objects in the country. Are you not now in that place where you often saw me with indifference? Can you take a step there without meeting an example of your mutability? Are you not there surrounded by women, who, all more amiable than me, have a greater right to your homage? I have not the vanity with which my sex is reproached; I have still less of that false modesty, which is nothing less than a refinement of pride; and it is with sincerity I assure you, that I am not conscious of possessing attractions: had I the greatest, I should not think them sufficient to fix you. To request of you, then, to think no more of me is only to beg of you to do now what you did before, and what you certainly would do in a very short time, were I even to make a contrary request.

This truth, which I do not lose sight of, would be alone a sufficient reason to listen to you no longer. I have a thousand other reasons; but without entering into long discussion, I shall once more entreat, as I have already done, that you will not write to me more upon a sentiment to which I ought not to listen, much less make any return.

Sept. 1, 17—.

END OF THE FIRST VOLUME.

DANGEROUS

CONNECTIONS:

A SERIES OF

LETTERS,

SELECTED FROM THE CORRESPONDENCE

OF

A PRIVATE CIRCLE;

AND PUBLISHED FOR THE INSTRUCTION

OF SOCIETY.

---

*BY M. C**** de L***.*

"I have observed the Manners of the Times, and have wrote those Letters."

J. J. Rousseau, Pref. to the New Eloise.

SECOND EDITION.

IN FOUR VOLUMES.

VOL. II.

London:

PRINTED FOR J. EBERS, OLD BOND STREET.

1812.

LETTER LI.

The MARCHIONESS DE MERTEUIL *to* VISCOUNT VALMONT.

Upon my word, Viscount, you are intolerable; you treat me with as little ceremony as if I was your mistress. Do you know you will make me angry, and that I am this instant in a most horrible passion? so you are to meet Danceny to-morrow morning? you know how important it is I should see you before that interview; yet, without giving yourself any farther trouble, you make me wait the whole day, while you run about I know not where. You are the cause of my having been *indecently* late at Madame de Volanges', which all the old women thought *exceedingly strange;* I was under the necessity of amusing them the rest of the evening, to keep them in temper; for one must be on good terms with old women; they decide on the reputation of the young ones.

Now it is one o'clock; and instead of going to bed as I ought, I must sit up to write you a long letter, which will add to my drowsiness by its disagreeable subject. You are very lucky that I have not time to scold you. Do not imagine, however, I forgive you: you have only to thank my hurry. Hear me, then: with a little address, you may, to-morrow, obtain Danceny's confidence. The opportunity is favourable: it is that of distress. The little girl has been at confession, has told all like a child, and has been since so terrified with the fear of hell, that she is absolutely determined on a rupture. She related to me all her little scruples in a manner that I am confident her head is turned. She showed me that letter, declaring her breaking off, which is in the true style of fanatical absurdity. She prattled for an hour to me without a word of common sense, and yet she embarrassed me; for you will conceive I could not risk to open my mind to such an idiot.

I observe, however, amidst all this nonsense, that she is not the less in love with her Danceny; I even took notice of one of those resources which love always supplies, and to which the girl is curiously enough a dupe. Tormented with the thoughts of her lover, and the fear of being damned for those thoughts, she has taken it into her head to pray to God to make her forget him; and as she renews this prayer every hour in the day, she is thus incessantly thinking of him.

To any one more *formed* than Danceny, this little circumstance would be more favourable than impropitious; but the youth is such a Celadon, that unless we assist him, it will take him so much time to conquer the slightest obstacles, that we shall not have time enough to carry our project into effect.

You are quite right, it is a pity, and I am as sorry as you that he should be the hero of this adventure; but what can be done? What is past is not to be recalled, and it's all your fault. I desired to see his answer; it was wretched stuff. He gives her numberless reasons to prove that an involuntary passion is not criminal; as if it became involuntary in the moment of desiring to resist it. This idea is so simple, that it even struck the girl herself. He laments his misfortune in a manner somewhat pathetic; but his grief is so cold, and yet bears the appearance of being so fixed and sincere, I think it impossible that a woman, who has an opportunity of driving a man to despair with so small a risk, should not gratify the whim. He informs her he is not a monk, as the little one imagined; and that is certainly the best part of his letter: for, were a woman absurd enough to be seized with a propensity to monastic love, the gentlemen who are Knights of Malta would not deserve the preference.

However, instead of throwing away time in arguments which would have committed me, and perhaps without persuasion, I approved the scheme of breaking off; but told her in such cases it was more genteel to declare the reasons in conversation, than write them; that it was also usual to return the letters and other trifles that might have been received; and thus seeming to enter into her views, I determined her to give Danceny a meeting. We immediately concluded the method of bringing it about; and I undertook to prevail upon her mother to go on a visit without her; and to-morrow evening is the decisive hour of our meeting. Danceny is apprised of it. For God's sake, if you possibly can, prevail on this lovely swain to be less languid; and tell him, since he must be told every thing, that the true method of overcoming scruples, is to leave nothing to lose, to those who are subject to scruples: that this ridiculous scene may not be renewed, I did not omit raising doubts in her mind, on the discretion of confessors; and I assure you she repays me the fright she put me into, by her present apprehensions, lest her confessor should tell her mother all. I hope, after I have had one or two more conferences with her on this subject, she will not be so ridiculous to tell her foolish nonsense to the first comer[1].

Adieu, Viscount! Seize on Danceny, give him his lesson; it would be shameful we should not do as we pleased with two children. If we meet more difficulty than we first imagined in this business, let us reflect to animate our zeal; you, that your object is Madame de Volanges' daughter; and I, that she is intended to be Gercourt's bride. Adieu!

Sept. 2, 17—.

[1] The reader must have long since observed, from Madame de Merteuil's manners, that she paid little regard to religion. All this detail would have been suppressed; but it was thought, that to show effects, it was necessary to touch upon the causes of them.

LETTER LII.

VISCOUNT DE VALMONT *to the* Presidente DE TOURVEL.

You forbid me, Madam, to talk to you of my love: but where shall I find courage to obey you? Entirely engrossed by a passion, which ought to be of an agreeable nature, and which your obduracy renders so tormenting; languishing in the exile to which you have condemned me; existing only in a state of privation and sorrow, a prey to the most cruel reflections, which incessantly recall to my mind your indifference; must I then lose my only remaining consolation? Can I have any other, than sometimes to bare to you a heart overwhelmed by you with anguish and bitterness? Will you turn aside, not to see the tears you cause to flow? Will you refuse even the acknowledgment of the sacrifices you require? Would it not then be more consonant to your soft tender disposition, to pity a wretch you have made miserable, than to aggravate his sorrows by a prohibition equally unjust and rigorous?

You affect to fear the passion of love, and yet you will not see that you alone cause the evils you reproach to it. Most indubitably it must be a painful sensation when the object that inspires it does not participate in it: but where is happiness to be found, if reciprocal love does not produce it? A tender friendship, a sweet confidence, that confidence which is the only untinctured with reserve, care softened, pleasure augmented, enchanting hopes, delicious reflections; where are they to be found but in love? You calumniate it, who to share all its blessings have only to cherish it; and I, forgetful of the torments it causes, am only anxious to defend it. You oblige me also to defend myself: for whilst I devote my life to adore you, yours is employed in searching out new faults in me. Already do you suppose me volatile and deceitful; and taking advantage of a few trivial errors which I ingenuously confessed, you are pleased to confound what I then was, with what I now am. Not satisfied with having delivered me up to the torments of living at a distance from you, you add to it a cruel mockery of pleasures to which you have made me too sensible. You neither credit my promises nor oaths. Well! there is one pledge yet left me to offer, of which you can have no doubt; I mean yourself. I only beg of you to ask yourself with sincerity, if you don't believe I love you sincerely? Whether you have the least doubt of your empire over my heart? Whether you are not even certain of having fixed this, as yet, I most own, too inconstant heart? I will consent to suffer for this error. I shall lament, but shall not appeal. If, on the other hand, and just to us both, you should be obliged to acknowledge, that you now have not, nor ever will have, a rival, do not oblige me to combat chimeras. Leave me, at least, the consolation to believe, you no longer doubt a sentiment which never will, never can end but with my life. Permit me, Madam, to beseech you to answer positively this part of my letter.

Should I even give up that epoch of my life, which, it seems, has hurt me so much in your opinion, it is not that I want reasons to defend it: for, after all, what is my crime? Why, not to be able to resist the torrent in which I was plunged, launched into the world young and inexperienced. Bandied, as it were, from one to another, by a number of women, who all hastened, by their facility, to prevent a reflection that they knew would be unfavourable to them, was it for me to set the example of a resistance that was not opposed to me? Or should I have punished myself for a momentary error by an useless constancy, which would only have exposed me to ridicule? And what other method but a speedy rupture can justify a shameful choice?

But I can truly say, that this intoxication of the senses, or, perhaps, this delirium of vanity, never reached my heart. Born, as it were, for love, intrigue could only distract it; but was not sufficient to take possession of it. Surrounded by seducing, but despicable objects, none went to my soul. Pleasures offered, but I sought virtues; and I even thought myself inconstant, because I was delicate, and had feelings.

When I saw you, I began to be enlightened. I soon perceived that the charms of love were attached to the qualities of the soul; that they alone could produce an excess and justification of love. I instantly felt, that it would be as impossible not to love you, as it would be to love any other but you.

Such, Madam, is the heart which you dread to yield to, and whose fate you are to determine: but be it as it will, you will never be able to alter the sentiments that attached it to you; they are as unalterable as the virtues which gave them birth.

Sept. 3, 17 — .

LETTER LIII.

VISCOUNT DE VALMONT *to the* MARCHIONESS DE MERTEUIL.

I saw Danceny, and only obtained a half-confidence from him; he is tenacious in concealing the name of the little Volanges, and spoke of her as of a very discreet person, and something inclined to devotion. As to the rest, he related his adventure with tolerable propriety, especially the last event. I heated his imagination as much as I could, and ridiculed his scrupulous delicacy; but he is still the same, and I cannot depend upon him: I shall be able to tell you more of him after to-morrow. We go to-morrow to Versailles, and shall endeavour to dive into him by the way.

The interview that was to take place to-day gives me some hopes: perhaps every thing succeeded to our wishes; and perhaps nothing now remains but to extract the confession, and gather the proofs. This business will be easier for you to perform than me, for the little thing is more open, or, which is the same thing, more silly then her discreet lover; notwithstanding, I'll do my best.

Adieu, my lovely friend! I have a great deal of employment on my hands. I will neither see you this night nor to-morrow: but if you come to the knowledge of any thing, let me have a line at my return. I shall certainly sleep in Paris.

Sept. 3, 17 — .

LETTER LIV.

The MARCHIONESS DE MERTEUIL *to the* VISCOUNT DE VALMONT.

Yes, to be sure, Danceny is a very proper person to get any thing out of. If he has said any thing to you, he is a braggart. I do not know such a fool in love matters, and I reproach myself more and more for the pains we take for him. Do you know, I had like to be exposed on his account, and for no purpose whatever? Oh! I shall be revenged, I assure him.

When I called yesterday on Madame de Volanges, she had altered her mind; she would not go out; she said she was indisposed, and I was forced to make use of all my eloquence to bring her to a resolution; and the moment was drawing near that Danceny would have arrived before we set out; which would have been so much the more awkward, as Madame de Volanges had told him the evening before, she would not be at home: her daughter and I were upon thorns.

At length we set out; and the little thing squeezed my hand so affectionately, bidding me adieu, that in spite of her project for a rupture, which she was seriously engaged in, I prognosticated wonders from the evening's amusement.

But my uneasiness was not to end thus. We were scarcely half an hour at Madame de — —'s, when Madame de Volanges was really taken ill, and wanted to return home: but I, who was afraid that we should surprise the young people, as there was every reason to dread, took the resolution to alarm her on the score of her health, which fortunately is not very difficult, and detained her an hour and a half without consenting to bring her back, lest the motion of the carriage should be prejudicial to her. At length we returned at the hour agreed on. By the bashful look I observed at our arrival, I own I thought that, at least, our labour was not lost.

The strong inclination that I had to be satisfied, made me remain with Madame de Volanges, who immediately went to bed; and after having supped by her bedside, we came away soon, in order to leave her to her repose, and went into her daughter's apartment. She, on her part, did every thing I expected from her; scruples fled, new oaths of constancy, &c. &c. but that blockhead Danceny did not advance a step farther than he was before. One can quarrel with him safely, for the reconciliation would not be difficult; the little thing, however, says, that he wanted farther advantages, but she knew how to defend herself: I would venture, however, to lay a wager, that she brags, or, at least, excuses him, and I am even almost certain of it. I took it into my head, to know what defence she was capable of making; and from question to question, I warmed her imagination to such a degree — in short, you may believe me, there never was a person more susceptible of a sensitive surprise than she is. This little dear creature is truly amiable; she deserves a better lover; she, at least, shall have a good friend, for I am most sincerely attached to her. I have promised to model her, and I believe I'll keep my word. I have often perceived the want of a female confident, and I would rather have her than any other; but I can't make any thing of her, until she is — what she must be; that is one more reason for being angry with Danceny.

Farewell, Viscount; do not come to my house to-morrow, unless it be in the morning. I have acquiesced to the pressing invitations of the Chevalier for a night at the villa.

Sept. 4, 17 — .

LETTER LV.

CECILIA VOLANGES *to* SOPHIA CARNAY.

You were in the right, my dear Sophy; thy prophesies are more successful than thy advice. Danceny, as you predicted, has been stronger than my confessor, than you, or even myself; we are just as we were before. I am not sorry for it; and if thou art, and that you scorn me, it is because you are a stranger to the pleasure I have in loving Danceny. It is easy to lay down rules how we should act; but if you had ever experienced the distress we feel for those we love, how we participate in his joys, how difficult it is to say no, when we wish to say yes, you would no longer be astonished: I who have already sensibly felt it, cannot as yet conceive it. Now, can you believe that I can see Danceny cry, without crying myself? That, I assure you, is impossible; and when he is pleased, I am happy; it is in vain to talk about it; what is, must be, and I am sure it is so.

I wish you were in my room;—but that is not what I mean to say; for certainly I would not give place to any one: but I wish you were in love with somebody; it is not only that you should understand me better, but that you should have less reason to find fault; but also that you should be happier, or, rather, that you should begin to taste of happiness.

Our amusements, our trifles, and all that, is folly; but in love, a word, a look only, is the summit of happiness. When I see Danceny, I wish for nothing more: when he is from me, I wish for nothing but him. I cannot account for it: but I imagine that every thing that pleases me, bears a resemblance to him. When he is absent from me, I dream of him; and when I can think of him without being disturbed, that is, when I am alone, I am happy. When I close my eyes, I think I see him; I recall his conversation, and I think I hear him speak; then I sigh—I feel myself agitated in a strange manner—it is a kind of sensation; I don't know what to call it; but it is inexpressibly delightful.

I am apt to think, that when one is in love, it diffuses itself to our friendship: that I have for thee, has never altered; it is always the same as it was at the convent; but that I experience with Madame de Merteuil, is more like the affection I have for Danceny than that I have for thee; and I sometimes wish she was a man; that is, perhaps, because it is not a childish friendship like ours; or else, that I see them so often together. But this I am sure of, between them both they make me very happy. After all, I don't think there is any great harm in what I do. I wish I was to remain as I am; for there is nothing gives me uneasiness but the thoughts of my marriage. And if Mr. de Gercourt is so disagreeable as he is described to me, which I have no doubt of, I don't know what will become of me. Adieu, my dear Sophy; I love thee most affectionately.

Sept. 4, 17—.

LETTER LVI.

The Presidente DE TOURVEL *to the* VISCOUNT DE VALMONT.

What purpose would it answer, Sir, to give a reply to your request? For to agree with your opinions would be a stronger motive to beware of them; and without either attacking or defending their sincerity, it is enough for me, and ought to be so for you also, to know, that I neither ought or will answer them.

Let us suppose for a moment, that you may have a sincere affection for me, (and it is only that we may have done with this subject, that I admit this supposition), would the obstacles that separate us be the less insurmountable; and ought not my wishes to be still the same, that you should overcome this passion, and every effort of mine employed to assist you, by hastening to deprive you of all manner of hope? You agree that this *idea must hurt, when the object that inspires it does not share it.* You are sufficiently convinced that it is impossible for me to share it; and if even I experienced such a misfortune, I should be the more to be pitied, without adding in the least to your happiness. I hope I have such a share in your esteem, that you will not call what I now say in question. Cease, then, I conjure you, cease to disturb a heart to which tranquillity is so necessary; do not oblige me to regret my acquaintance with you.

Beloved and esteemed by a husband, who I love and respect, my duty and pleasure are united in the same object; I am happy; I ought to be so. If there are more lively pleasures existing, I wish them not; I will not be acquainted with them. Can any be so pleasing as to be at peace with oneself, to enjoy days of serenity, to sleep without disturbance, and to awake without remorse? What you call happiness, is the tumult of the senses, the storm of passions, the aspect of which is dreadful, even viewing it from the shore; and who then would encounter such storms? Who would dare embark upon a sea spread with thousands and thousands of wrecks, and with whom? No, Sir, I will remain upon land; I cherish the links with which I am attached; I would not break them if I could; and if even I was not bound, I would speedily wear them.

Why do you pursue my steps? Why do you obstinately follow me? Your letters, which were to be but seldom, succeed each other with rapidity; they were to be discreet, and you entertain me with nothing but your mad passion. You surround me with your ideas, more than you did with your person; put away under one form, you again appear under another. The things I desire you to be silent upon, you say over again in another manner. You take a pleasure in perplexing me, by captious reasons, and you evade mine. I will not reply to you any more: — how you treat the women you have seduced! how contemptibly do you speak of them! I will readily believe some of them deserve it; but are they all then so contemptible? Ah, doubtless they are, since they have relinquished virtue, to give themselves up to a criminal passion; in that moment they lost all, even the esteem of him to whom they sacrificed every thing! This punishment is just; but the idea alone is enough to make one shudder; but what is all this to me? Why should I trouble myself about you or them; what right have you to disturb my peace? Leave me. See me no more; write me no more, I beseech you; I even require it. This letter shall be the last you will ever receive from me.

Sept. 5, 17 — .

LETTER LVII.

VISCOUNT DE VALMONT *to the* MARCHIONESS DE MERTEUIL.

I received your letter yesterday at my return. Your anger is enchanting. You could not have felt Danceny's errors in a more lively manner, if they had even affected yourself. It is undoubtedly for the sake of revenge, that you accustom his mistress to commit little infidelities: you are a mischievous creature. How delightful you are! and I am not astonished that one can resist you less than Danceny. At length I have gained the confidence of this hero of romance. He has no longer any secrets with me. I much extolled the supreme happiness attendant on an honourable passion; proved that one such passion was infinitely superior to ten intrigues; and that even I am but a timid lover. He was so pleased with this way of thinking, it being so conformable to his own, and enchanted with my candour, that he poured out his whole soul, and vowed an everlasting friendship without reserve; however, our project is not more advanced.

At first he seemed of opinion, that a young lady should be treated more cautiously than a woman, as having more to lose. He is particularly persuaded, that a man is unjustifiable, who reduces a girl to the necessity of marrying him, or living dishonoured, when the girl is in much more affluent circumstances than the man, as is his present case. The mother's confidences, the daughter's candour; every thing intimidates and restrains him. The difficulty lies not in over-ruling his arguments, however just. With the assistance of his passion, and a little address, they might soon be overturned, being so open to ridicule, and so opposite to fashion. But the obstacle to this having the effect upon him is, that he thinks himself happy as he is. First amours appear, in general, more honourable, or, as it is called, more chaste, because they are slower, and not, as is imagined, from delicacy or timidity: in those, the heart, astonished by an insensible instinct, stops, as it were, to enjoy the delight it feels; and this powerful delight takes such strong possession of a young mind, as absorbs it, and renders it callous to every other kind of enjoyment. This axiom is so true, that a libertine when in love, if such a being exists, becomes from that moment less anxious of enjoyment; and to sum up all, between the behaviour of Danceny and the little Volanges, and mine with the prude, Madame de Tourvel, the difference is only in degree. A few well-timed obstacles thrown in the young man's way, might have been serviceable; for obstacles, accompanied with mystery, have a wonderful effect in inspiring boldness. I am apprehensive you have hurt our scheme by being too useful to him; your conduct would have been excellent with an experienced *man*, who had no view beyond desire: but you might have foreseen, that a youth of honourable dispositions, and immersed in love, the greatest value of favours, is to be proof against love; and consequently, the more certain he might be of being beloved, the less enterprising he would be. What is to do now, I know not; but I am of opinion, the girl cannot be caught before marriage, and that our labour will be lost. I am very sorry for it, but there is no remedy.

Whilst I am writing a dissertation on this business, you are better employed with your Chevalier. That recalls to my memory your promise to commit an infidelity in my favour; I have it in writing, and I don't intend it should be waste paper. I will allow, the time of payment is not expired: it would be a generous act in you not to wait the day fixed for discharging it; on my part, I would acknowledge myself your debtor for the interest. What say you, my lovely friend; are not you tired of your constancy? This Chevalier is a wonderful fellow, it seems. But I am determined to compel you to acknowledge, that if you found any merit in him, it arose from your having forgot me.

Adieu, my dear friend! I embrace you as ardently as I desire to possess you. I defy all the Chevalier's embraces to attain to an equal degree of ardour.

Sept. 5, 17—.

VISCOUNT DE VALMONT *to the* Presidente DE TOURVEL.

How is it I deserved the reproaches you make me, and the indignation you express against me? The most violent, and yet the most respectful attachment, the most absolute submission to your will, is, in a few words, the history of my conduct and sentiments towards you. Sinking under the weight of an unhappy passion, the only consolation left was to see you; you ordered me to depart, and I obeyed without murmuring. For this sacrifice you permitted me to write to you, and now I am to be deprived of this only satisfaction. But shall I then have it torn from me without a struggle? No, certainly; it is too dear: it is the only one that remains, and I hold it from you.

You say my letters are too frequent. I beg you will reflect, that for these ten days that I have been exiled from you, a single moment has not passed that was not taken up in thinking of you, and yet I have wrote you but two letters. *I entertain you with nothing but my mad passion.* Ah! what can I say but what I think? All I could do, was to soften the expression; and I hope you will believe me when I assure you, I have only let you see what I could not hide. At length you threaten to answer me no more. And thus the man who prefers you to every thing, and whose respect is still greater than his love, you are not content to treat with the utmost severity, but add to it contempt. But why all those threats and this wrath? What occasion for them, when you are certain to be obeyed, even in your unjust orders? Is it then possible for me to contradict your wishes; and have I not already proved it? But will you abuse your power over me? After having made me miserable, after all your injustice, will it be an easy matter for you to enjoy that tranquillity that you say is so necessary to you? Will you never tell yourself—he made me arbitress of his fate, and I made him miserable; he implored my aid, and I did not even give him a compassionate glance—Do you know how far despair may drive me? No.

To sooth my cares, you should know the extent of my passion, and you do not know my heart.

But to what am I made a sacrifice? To chimerical fears. Who inspired them? The man who adores you; a man over whom you will ever have an absolute sway. What do you dread, what can you dread, from a sentiment that you will always have the power to direct at your pleasure? Your imagination creates monsters, and the fears they raise you attribute to love. With a little confidence those fears will vanish.

A learned writer has said, that in order to dispel one's fears, it would be almost always sufficient to search the cause[1]. It is to love, above all others, that this truth is applicable. Love and your apprehensions will subside. In the room of terrifying objects, you will find a tender submissive lover, and a delicious sentiment; your days will be marked with bliss; and the only regret you will have, will be to have lost so much time in indifference. Myself even, since I have abandoned my errors, exist no longer but for love. I regret the time spent in pleasure; and I feel it is from you alone my happiness must proceed. But let me entreat you, that the pleasure I have in writing to you may not be interrupted by the dread of offending. I will not disobey you; but lay myself at your feet, and there reclaim the happiness you want to deprive me of; the only one that is left me. I call on you; hear my prayers, and behold my tears. Ah, Madam! will you refuse me?

Sept. 7, 17 — .

[1] It is imagined Rousseau in his Emily; but the citation is not exact, and the application that Valmont makes is false; and, perhaps, Madame de Tourvel had not read Emily.

LETTER LIX.

VISCOUNT DE VALMONT *to the* MARCHIONESS DE MERTEUIL.

Pray inform me, if you can, what is all this nonsense of Danceny. What has happened, and what has he lost? His fair one, perhaps, is angry at his constant respect; and really one would be vexed at a smaller matter. What shall I say to him to-night at the rendezvous he requested, and which I have given him at all events. I shall most certainly lose my time to attend his doleful ditty, if it does not lead us to something. Passionate complaints are supportable only in a recitative obligato, or in grand airs. Give me your directions then about this business, and what I am to do; otherwise I shall desert, to avoid the dulness I foresee. Could I have a little chat with you this morning? If you are *busy*, at least give me a line, and the catchword for the part I am to act.

Where was you yesterday? I can never now have the pleasure of seeing you. At this rate, it was not worth while to keep me in Paris in the month of September. Take some resolution, however; for I have just received a most pressing invitation from the Countess de B— —, to go see her in the country; and she writes very humorously, "that her husband has the finest wood in the world, which he preserves carefully for the amusement of his friends;" and you know I have some kind of right to that wood. I will go see it again, if you have no employment for me. Adieu! Remember Danceny is to be with me at four o'clock.

Sept. 8, 17 — .

LETTER LX.

CHEVALIER DANCENY *to the* VISCOUNT DE VALMONT.

(Enclosed in the preceding.)

Ah, Sir! I am in a state of desperation; all is lost. I dare not confide to paper the cause of my troubles; but want to pour them forth in the bosom of some faithful friend. At what hour can I see you, to seek consolation and advice from you? I was so happy the day I opened my mind to you; now, what an alteration! every thing is adverse to me. What I suffer upon my own account is the least part of my torments; my uneasiness for a much dearer object is what I cannot support. You, who are happier than me, can see her; and I expect from your friendship that you will not refuse me: but I must speak to you, and give you your instructions. I know you will pity and assist me. In you my hopes are centered. You are sensible; you know what love is, and you are the only one in whom I can confide: do not refuse me your assistance.

Adieu, Sir! the only relief I experience in my sorrow, is to think I have still such a friend as you left. Pray inform me, at what hour I can find you at home; if it is not this morning, I beg it may be early in the afternoon.

Sept. 8, 17 —.

LETTER LXI.

CECILIA VOLANGES *to* SOPHIA CARNAY.

My dear Sophy, pity thy poor Cecilia; she is very unhappy. Mamma knows all. I cannot conceive how she had any suspicion; and yet she has discovered every thing. Last night mamma appeared to be a little out of temper; but I did not take any notice of it; and whilst she was at cards, I chatted very agreeably with Madame de Merteuil, who supped with us. We had a great deal of talk about Danceny; and yet I believe we were not overheard. She went away, and I retired to my apartment.

I was undressing when mamma came in, and ordered my waiting maid to retire; she demanded the key of my escrutoire. The tone in which she made this requisition threw me all in a flutter, so that I could scarcely support myself; I made believe I could not find it: but at length I was obliged to obey. The first drawer she opened was the very one where all Chevalier Danceny's letters were. I was so perplexed, that when she asked me what they were, I could give her no other answer, but that it was nothing at all; but when I saw she began to read the first that offered, I had scarce time to fall into a chair, when I fainted. As soon as I recovered, my mother, who had called in the waiting maid, retired, desiring me to go to bed. She carried off all Danceny's letters. I shudder every time I think that I must appear before her again. I have done nothing but cry all night.

It is but just daylight, and I write to you, in hopes that Josephine will come. If I can speak to her alone, I shall beg of her to leave a note, that I shall write, with Madame de Merteuil; and if I cannot, I will put it in your letter, and you will be so good as to send it, as from yourself. It is from her alone that I can receive any consolation. We will, at least, speak of him, for I never hope to see him more. I am very unhappy. She perhaps will be kind enough to deliver a letter to Danceny. I dare not confide in Josephine, and still less in my waiting maid; for it is, perhaps, she that told my mother that I had letters in my desk.

I will not write to you any more now, because I must have time to write to Madame de Merteuil and Danceny, and to have all my letters ready, if she will take charge of them; after that, I will go to bed again, that they may find me in bed when they come into my room. I will say I am ill, to prevent my being called to mamma. I shall not tell a great lie; for I surely suffer as much as if I had a fever. My eyes are inflamed with crying; and I have a weight at my stomach, which prevents me from breathing. When I think I never shall see Danceny more, I wish I was dead. Farewell, my dear Sophy. I can't write any more; my tears suffocate me.

Sept. 7, 17 —.

LETTER LXII.

MADAME DE VOLANGES *to* CHEVALIER DANCENY.

You will certainly not be surprised, Sir, after having so grossly abused the confidence of a mother, and the innocence of a child, to be no longer admitted into a house where you have repaid the sincerest friendship with the blackest ingratitude. I prefer desiring you never more to appear here, rather than giving orders to my servants to refuse you admittance, which would affect us all, by the remarks that would infallibly be made. I have a right to expect you will not put me under the necessity of taking this step. I must also acquaint you, that if you should hereafter make the least attempt to keep up a correspondence with my daughter, a severe and everlasting confinement shall withdraw her from your solicitations. I leave it then to yourself, Sir, to determine whether you will be the cause of her misery, as you have attempted to be that of her dishonour. As to myself, my resolution is fixed, and she's informed of it.

I send you, enclosed, all your letters; and I expect you will send me back those of my daughter; and that you will concur in leaving no mark of an event, the remembrance of which fills me with indignation; her with shame, as it should you with remorse.

I have the honour, &c.

Sept. 7, 17 —.

LETTER LXIII.

MARCHIONESS DE MERTEUIL *to* VISCOUNT DE VALMONT.

Yes, certainly, I can explain Danceny's letter to you. The incident that gave birth to it is my work, and I think it a master-piece. I lost no time since I received your last letter; and, in the words of the Athenian architect, "What he has said, I will perform."

There must be obstacles then for our hero of romance; and his happiness lulls him. Oh! leave that to me, I will cut out work for him; and I am much mistaken if he sleeps so quietly hereafter. It was necessary to make him sensible of his folly; and I flatter myself that he now regrets the opportunity he has let slip. You say also, that is necessary there should be a little mystery in the business: well, take my word for it, that shall not be wanting. I have this good quality, that if I am but told my faults, I am not at rest till I amend them. Now to inform you what I have done—at my return the day before yesterday, in the morning I received your letter, which is truly admirable. Being fully satisfied that you had very well pointed out the cause of the disorder, I set about finding the method of cure. But first I lay down; for the indefatigable Chevalier did not suffer me to take the least repose; and I thought I should sleep: but no; totally taken up with the thoughts of rousing Danceny from his lethargy, or punishing him for it, I could not close my eyes; and it was not until after I had well digested my plan, I got two hours repose.

I went that same evening to see Madame de Volanges; and told her, in pursuance of my scheme, in a very confidential manner, I was very certain there subsisted between her daughter and Danceny a dangerous connection. This woman, so penetrating in your business, was blinded to such a degree, that at first she replied, I certainly was mistaken; her daughter was but a child, &c. &c. I could not venture to tell her all I knew: but quoted looks, words, *which much alarmed my friendship and virtue*. I spoke almost as well as a devotee: to give the finishing blow to my intelligence, I told her I thought I saw a letter given and received. That I also recollected she one day opened a drawer in her bureau, in which I observed several papers, which she doubtless carefully preserves. "Do you know any one she corresponds with frequently?" At that question Madame de Volanges' countenance changed, and I observed some tears drop from her. "I thank you, my worthy friend," said she, squeezing my hand; "I shall inquire into it."

After this conversation, which was too short to cause any suspicion, I joined company with the little thing. I left her soon after, to beg of the mother not to discover to her daughter what I had told; which she promised me the more readily, as I observed what a happy thing it was that this child had placed such a confidence in me as to open her heart, which gave me an opportunity of assisting her *with my good advice*. I am the more satisfied that she will keep her promise, as no doubt she will plume herself on her penetration with her daughter. Thus I am authorised to keep up the ton of friendship with the little one, without giving umbrage to Madame de Volanges, which must be avoided. I shall moreover by this means have opportunities of conversing as long and as secretly as I please with the daughter, without alarming the mother.

This I put in practice that same evening; for after my party at cards was ended, I took the young one into a corner, and began upon the subject of Danceny, which never fatigues her; and diverted myself in heating her imagination with the pleasure she would have in seeing him the next day: there is no sort of extravagance but what she came into; it was necessary to pay her in hope, what I took from her in reality; moreover, this will make the blow the more sensible; and am confident that the more she suffers, the more ready she will be to make herself amends at the first opportunity. We ought to accustom those we intend for great adventures, to great events.

After all, she may afford a few tears, for the pleasure of having her Danceny. She is distracted about him! Well, she shall have him; and perhaps the sooner for this little storm. It is a troublesome dream which will be most delicious at waking; and, take every thing together, I think she ought to be grateful. But to the point: I retired very well satisfied with myself. Either Danceny, said I, animated by obstacles, will redouble his affection, and then I will serve him to the utmost; or, if he is the booby I am sometimes inclined to think him, he will be desperate, and think himself undone: even then, I shall be revenged of him as much as in my power; I shall have increased the mother's esteem for me, the daughter's friendship, and the confidence of both. As to Gercourt, who is the first object of my care, I shall be very unfortunate, or very awkward indeed, if, having such an ascendant over his wife's mind as I already have, and shall still have more, I did not find means of making him what I wish. I laid down with those pleasing ideas, slept very well, and did not awake till it was late.

In the morning I found two letters, one from the mother, and the other from the daughter; and could not help laughing to find in both literally this phrase,—"*It is from you alone I expect any consolation.*" And indeed it is pleasant enough to console for and against, and to be the sole agent of two interests so directly opposite. Thus I am like the Divinity, receiving the opposite vows of blind mortals, without altering my immutable decrees. However, I have quitted this grand roll, to take on me that of the consoling angel; and I went, according to the precept, to visit my two friends in their affliction.

I began with the mother, who I found in a very melancholy situation, which partly revenges you, for the obstacles you have experienced from your charming prude. Every thing succeeded wonderfully; my only uneasiness was, lest Madame de Volanges should seize this opportunity of gaining her daughter's confidence, which would have been a very easy matter, if she had used mild and friendly admonitions; and giving to the advice of reason the tone and air of indulgent tenderness. Fortunately she armed herself with severity; and behaved so badly, that nothing was left for me but to applaud. It is true she had like to have overthrown my plan entirely, by the resolution she had taken to shut up her daughter in the convent; but I warded the blow, and prevailed on her only to threaten it, in case Danceny should continue his pursuit, in order to oblige them both to a circumspection which I think so necessary for my success.

From thence I went to the daughter: you cannot conceive how much grief embellished her: if I can only infuse a little coquetry into her, I will engage she will cry often: but now she wept sincerely.—Struck with this new charm, which I knew not before, and which I was very glad to observe, at first I gave her a few awkward consolations, which rather augment than relieve distress; and by this means led her to almost a state of suffocation. She cried no longer, and I really began to fear she would fall into convulsions. I advised her to go to bed, which she agreed to, and was her waiting maid: she had not dressed her head, her hair all loose upon her shoulders; her neck quite bare; I embraced her, she fell back in my arms, and her tears flowed again. Ye gods, how lovely she was! If the Magdalen was thus, she was much more dangerous as a penitent, than as a sinner.

When the lovely girl was in bed, I began really to comfort her in good earnest. I dispelled her fears of the convent, and raised her hopes of seeing Danceny privately; and sitting by the bedside, "If he was here now!" said I.—Enlarging on the subject, I led her from thought to fancy, so that she soon forgot her affliction. We should have parted perfectly satisfied with each other, had she not wanted to prevail on me to deliver a letter to Danceny, which I absolutely refused. I dare say my reasons will meet your approbation.

First, it would be running a risk with Danceny; but had that been the only reason I could have alleged with the girl, there are a great many others I must impart to you. Would it not be risking the fruits of all my labours, to give our young people so easy a method, and so speedily of putting a period to their distress? Moreover, I should not be sorry to oblige them employ a domestic in this adventure; for if it has a happy issue, as I hope it will, she must feel her consequence immediately after marriage; and I know no means so certain of spreading her fame; or if they did not speak, which would be miraculous indeed, we could speak for them, and it would be more convenient the indiscretion should lay with them.

You must then infuse this idea into Danceny to-day; as I cannot depend on the little Volanges' waiting maid, whom she seems diffident of, you may point out my faithful Victoire. I shall take care to ensure success: this idea pleases me much, as the secret will be useful to us, and not to them; for I am not yet at the end of my story.

Whilst I excused myself from taking her letter, I every moment dreaded she would have mentioned the penny-post, which I scarcely could have refused. Fortunately, through ignorance or distress, or that she was more anxious for the answer than the letter, which she could not have had by the same means, she never mentioned it; but to be guarded against this idea, if it should happen, or at least she should not have an idea of making use of it, I returned to her mother, and induced her to take her daughter to the country for a short time;—and where do you think? Does not your heart leap for joy? Why, to your old aunt's, Madame de Rosemonde. She is to acquaint her of it this day: thus you are authorised to go to your beloved devotee, who can no longer object to the scandal of a tête-à-tête; and thanks to my industry, Madame de Volanges shall herself repair all the mischief she has done you.

But hark ye, I must insist you are not to be so taken up with your own affairs as to neglect this; remember how much I am interested in it. I wish you to be not only the correspondent, but the confidant, of the two young ones; acquaint Danceny, then, of this journey, and make him a tender of your services. Remove every difficulty, but that of delivering your credentials to his fair one; and remove that obstacle, instantly, in pointing out the medium of my chamber-maid. Doubtless he will embrace it, and for your reward you will be the confidant of a young heart, which is ever of consequence. The poor little thing, how she will blush when she gives you her first letter! I cannot help thinking the character of a confidant, against which so many prejudices are formed, appears to be a tolerable relaxation, when one has other employment upon their hands, which is your case.

The denouement of this intrigue depends entirely upon you. You must watch the moment when you are to reunite your actors. The country offers a thousand opportunities, and Danceny will be ready to fly at your first signal; a night, a disguise, a window;—but if the little thing comes back as she goes, it is your fault; if you think she should want any assistance from me, let me know. I think I have given her a tolerable lesson on the danger of keeping letters, so I may now venture to write to her; and I am still determined to make her my pupil.

I believe I forgot to tell you her suspicions, in regard to her correspondent, at first fell upon the waiting maid; but I turned them off to the confessor; that is killing two birds with one stone.

Adieu, Viscount! This letter has taken me a long time, and my dinner has been put back; but friendship and self-love dictated it.

You will receive it at three, that will be time enough.

Complain of me now if you dare; and go, if you are inclined, to the Comte de B— —'s wood: you say he keeps it for the amusement of his friends; that man is the friend of the world; but adieu! I am hungry.

Sept. 9, 17—.

LETTER LXIV.

The CHEVALIER DANCENY *to* MADAME DE VOLANGES.

(Annexed to the 66th Letter, from the Viscount to the Marchioness.)

Without seeking, Madam, to justify my conduct, and without the least cause of complaint of yours, I can only lament the unhappiness of three persons all worthy of a better fate. I beg leave to assure you, my chagrin, on this occasion, proceeds more from being the cause than the victim. Since yesterday, I have often endeavoured to do myself the honour of answering your letter, without being able to perform my resolution; yet I have so many things to say, that I must overcome every other consideration; and if this letter is incoherent, you may very well imagine that I stand in great need of your indulgence in my present painful situation.

Permit me, therefore, Madam, to demur against the first position of your letter. I venture to assure you, I have neither abused your confidence, nor Mademoiselle de Volanges' innocence: I have paid a proper respect to one and the other, they alone depend on me; and were you to make me responsible for an involuntary sentiment, I shall not be afraid to declare, that the one Mademoiselle your daughter inspired me with, may perhaps displease, but ought by no means to offend you. This motive, which I feel more than I can express, I leave you and my letters to determine on.

You forbid me to come to your house in future, and I most certainly will submit to your pleasure on this occasion; but give me leave to remonstrate, that such an abrupt absence will give as much cause to remarks you wish to avoid, as the orders you have declined giving, for the same reason, would create; and I think this consideration more important on Mademoiselle de Volanges' account than my own. I therefore beseech you to weigh attentively those things, and not suffer your severity to get the better of your prudence. I am confident that the interest of your daughter alone will govern your resolutions; I shall therefore wait your farther commands.

Yet, if you should think proper to permit me to wait upon you sometimes, I engage myself, Madam, (and you may depend upon my promise), I shall not attempt to abuse your condescension, by presuming to speak in private to Mademoiselle de Volanges, or convey any letter to her. The dread of doing any thing that might affect her reputation, influences me to this sacrifice; and the happiness of some time seeing her would be a sufficient recompence.

This part of my letter is the only answer I can make to the fate you intend for Mademoiselle de Volanges, and which you mean to be dependent on my conduct. It would be deceiving you to promise more. A vile seducer may make his projects subservient to circumstances, and calculate them to events; but the passion with which I am inspired admits of only two sentiments, courage and constancy.

What me, Madam! me consent to be forgotten by Mademoiselle de Volanges, and I to forget her? No, never! I will be constant to her; she has received my vows, and I now again renew them. Forgive me, Madam; I am going astray; I must resume my reason.

One thing more remains to be mentioned, in reply to the letters you require. I am really unhappy to be obliged to add a refusal to the wrongs you already charge me with: but I beseech you to attend to my reasons, and vouchsafe to remember to enhance their value: that the only consolation I have left for the loss of your friendship, is the hope of preserving your esteem.

Mademoiselle de Volanges' letters, ever precious to me, become more so at this moment. They are my only felicity; they bring back to my remembrance the only charm of my life! Yet, I beg you will believe me, I would not hesitate a moment to sacrifice them to you; and the regret of being deprived of them, would give way to my strong desire of proving my most respectful obedience to your orders; but, very powerful considerations, which I am confident you yourself will not blame, prevent me.

It is true you have got the secret from Mademoiselle de Volanges; but permit me to say, and I believe I am authorised, that it is the effect of surprise, and not of confidence. I do not pretend to blame the step you have taken, which may be sanctioned by your maternal care. I respect your right; but that will not dispense me from doing my duty. The most sacred of all, I conceive, is not to betray the confidence reposed in us. I should therefore be in the highest degree guilty, were I to expose to the eyes of another the secrets of a heart, which has been disclosed to me alone. If Mademoiselle your daughter consents they should be given up to you, let her speak—her letters are useless to you: if, on the contrary, she should think proper to keep her secrets to herself, you certainly will not expect, Madam, that I should disclose them.

As to the secrecy in which you wish this event may remain, rest satisfied, Madam, that in every thing that concerns Mademoiselle de Volanges, I may even set the heart of a mother at defiance. But to take away all manner of uneasiness from you, I have provided against every accident. This precious deposit, which formerly was superscribed, *Papers to be burnt*, is endorsed at present, *Papers belonging to Madame de Volanges*. This resolution may sufficiently convince you that my refusal is not influenced by any dread that you should find in those letters, a single sentiment that you should have any personal cause to complain of.

This, Madam, is a very long letter. It would yet, however, be too short, if it left you room for the least doubt of the honour of my sentiments, the sincere regret I am under of having displeased you, and the profound respect with which I have the honour to be, &c.

Sept. 7, 17—.

LETTER LXV.

CHEVALIER DANCENY *to* CECILIA VOLANGES.

(*Sent open to the Marchioness de Merteuil, in the 66th Letter of the Viscount.*)

Ah, my Cecilia! what will become of us? What will save us from the miseries that hang over us? Love, at least, can give us resolution to support them. I cannot express my astonishment, my distraction, on seeing my letters, and reading Madame de Volanges'. Who is it can have betrayed us? On whom do your suspicions fall? Is it by any imprudent act of your own? How do you employ your time? What has been said to you? I wish to know all, and am ignorant of every thing. Perhaps you are in the same situation.

I enclose you your mamma's letter, with a copy of my answer to it. I hope you will approve of what I wrote: and I want much to be satisfied whether you will approve of the steps I have taken since this fatal discovery, which all tend to hear from you, and to be able to write to you; and, who knows, perhaps to see you again with more freedom than ever.

I can't express the joy, my Cecilia, I conceive at the prospect of seeing you once more; renewing my vows of eternal love, and receiving yours. Who would not bear torments to enjoy so much happiness! I have this prospect in view; and the methods I mean to take, are what I beseech you to approve. I am indebted for them to the anxiety of a worthy friend; and I only ask that you will permit my friend to be also yours.

But, perhaps, I ought not to have engaged your confidence without your consent; misfortunes and necessity must plead in my favour. It is love led me on; it is love solicits your indulgence; implores you to forgive so necessary a confidence, without which we should be for ever separated.[1] You know the friend I mean; he is also the friend of the woman you love best—the Viscount Valmont.

My design was, to engage him first to prevail on Madame de Merteuil to deliver you a letter. He was of opinion this scheme would not succeed; but he will answer for her waiting-maid, who lays under some obligations to him. She will then deliver you this letter, and you may trust her with your answer.

This means will be of very little use, if, as Mr. de Valmont tells me, you are to set out immediately for the country: but in that case he will be our friend. The lady, to whose house you are going, is his near relation. He will make use of this pretence to go there at the same time that you do; and we can carry on our correspondence through him. He even assures me, if you leave the management to him, he will provide us the means of seeing each other, without danger of a discovery.

Now, my dear Cecilia, if you love me, if you compassionate my misfortunes, if, as I hope, you partake my sorrows, you will not refuse your confidence to a man who will be our guardian angel. Were it not for his assistance, I should be reduced even to despair of being able to soften the distresses I have caused you: I hope they will soon be at an end. But, my dearest life, promise me not to give way to them; neither suffer yourself to be too much dejected. The idea of your grief is an insupportable torment to me. I would cheerfully die to make you happy; you know it well. May the certainty of being adored, bring some small consolation to your soul. Let me be assured you pardon the evils my love has made you suffer, for my consolation.

Adieu, my dear Cecilia!

Sept. 9, 17—.

[1] Mr. Danceny is wrong; for he had already made a confidant of Mons. de Valmont. See Letter the 57th.

LETTER LXVI.

The VISCOUNT DE VALMONT *to the* MARCHIONESS DE MERTEUIL.

When you have read the two enclosed letters, you will be able to judge, my charming friend, whether I have fulfilled your commission. Although they are both dated to-day, they were wrote yesterday, at my house, and under my inspection; that to the girl is every thing we could wish. I am humbled by the depth of your wisdom, if one may judge by the success of your proceedings. Danceny is all on fire; and you may be certain, that at the first opportunity, you will have nothing to reproach him with. If his fair one will be but tractable, every thing will terminate as we wish in a little time after her arrival in the country. I am provided with sufficient schemes; thanks to your care. I am now decidedly Danceny's friend.

This same Danceny is yet very young. Would you believe it? I have never yet been able to prevail on him to promise the mother to renounce his love; as if there was any difficulty in promising, when one is determined not to keep one's word. It would be deceitful, says he incessantly. Is not this a most edifying scruple, especially when he is about seducing the daughter? This is the true picture of mankind; all equally profligate in their projects: if any weakness happens in the execution, they call it probity.

It is now your business to hinder Madame de Volanges from being startled at what little indiscretions he may have let fall in his letter; keep us out of the convent; endeavour to make her relinquish her demand of the little one's letters: for he will not give them up, and I am of opinion he ought not: here love and sound sense agree. I have read those letters; I could hardly bear it; however, they may hereafter be useful.

Notwithstanding all our discretion, something may blaze abroad, which might break off the marriage, and render abortive all our Gercourt schemes: but as I must be revenged of the mother, for my own satisfaction, in that case, I must reserve to myself the debauching of the daughter. In selecting those letters, and only producing a part, the little Volanges would appear to have made the first advances, and have absolutely given herself up: and some of the letters might even entangle the mother, or, at least, make her appear guilty of an unpardonable negligence. I readily conceive, that the scrupulous Danceny would at first be startled; but as he would be personally attacked, I believe he might be brought to. It is a thousand to one, that it does not happen so; but we must provide against everything.

Adieu, my lovely friend! I would be glad you could sup to-morrow at the Marechale de — —; I could not be off.

I think it unnecessary to recommend secrecy with Madame Volanges, about my country jaunt: she would soon take it into her head to remain in town; but when once arrived, she will not go back the next day; and if she only gives us eight days, I will answer for every thing.

Sept.. 9, 17—.

LETTER LXVII.

The Presidente DE TOURVEL *to the* VISCOUNT DE VALMONT.

I was determined not to answer you any more, Sir, and, perhaps, the embarrassment I now experience, is the strongest proof that I ought not. Notwithstanding, I will leave you no cause of complaint against me; and will convince you that I have done every thing I ought.

I gave you leave to write to me, you say? I admit it; but when you put me in mind of this permission, do you think I forget the conditions on which it was granted? If I had adhered to them as strictly as you have disregarded them, you would not have received a single line from me; yet this is now the third, and whilst you are doing every thing you possibly can to oblige me to break off this correspondence, I am employed in the means of keeping it up. There is one, and it is the only one, which, if you refuse, will be sufficient proof, say what you will, how little you esteem it:

Give over, then, a language that I neither can nor will hear; renounce a passion that terrifies and offends me; and which, perhaps, you should be the less attached to, as it is the only obstacle that separates us. Is this passion, then, the only one that you are capable of? is it so powerful as to exclude friendship? and could you possibly not wish to have her for a friend, whom you would wish to inspire with more tender sentiments? I cannot believe it: this humiliating idea would turn me against you for ever!

Thus offering you my friendship, Sir, I give you every thing that belongs to me; every thing that is at my disposal; what can you wish for more? To this proposition, so pleasing to my mind, I shall expect your consent; as also, your word of honour, that this friendship will constitute your happiness. I shall forget every thing that has been related to me, and I will depend upon your care to justify my choice.

You see how frankly I deal with you, which ought to be a proof of my confidence in you; it rests with you to increase it still more; but I must inform you, that the first expression of love will for ever destroy it, and will bring back all my fears: it will be the first signal of an eternal silence from me to you.

If, as you say, *you have abandoned your errors,* would you not rather be the object of friendship of a virtuous woman, than that of the remorse of a guilty one? Adieu, Sir! You may conceive that having said thus much, I can say nothing more that you have not already answered.

Sept. 9, 17—.

LETTER LXVIII.

VISCOUNT DE VALMONT *to the* Presidente DE TOURVEL.

How is it possible, Madam, to answer your last letter; how shall I dare speak truth, when my sincerity may ruin me with you? Yet I must; I often tell myself, I would rather deserve than obtain you; and were you for ever to refuse me a happiness I incessantly wish for, I will at least make you acknowledge, that my heart is worthy of it.

What a pity it is, as you say, *that I have abandoned my errors*, with what transport should I not have read that letter which I tremble to answer to-day? You deal *frankly* with me; you testify your *confidence*. You even offer me your friendship: how bountiful are you, Madam, and how much I regret I cannot benefit by them. Why am I no longer the same!

For if I really was, if I had but a common passion for you, that slight desire, the child of seduction and pleasure, which is yet now called love, I would speedily take advantage of every thing I could obtain, without being much concerned about the delicacy of the measures, provided they ensured success. I would flatter your frankness, in order to dive into you; I would endeavour to gain your confidence, with an intention to betray it; I would accept your friendship in the hope of leading you astray. — This picture, no doubt, alarms you, Madam; — but it would be the true portrait of myself, if I was to tell you that I consented to be your friend only.

What! Should I consent to share with another a sentiment proceeding from your soul? If I should ever tell you so, do not believe me. From that moment I would seek to deceive you; I might still have desires, but I certainly would love you no longer.

Not but your amiable frankness, your charming confidence, and your pleasing friendship, are immensely valuable to me; — but love, sincere love, such as you have inspired me with, reuniting all those sentiments, by giving them more energy, cannot, as they do, be satisfied with that tranquillity, that ease of mind, which will allow of comparisons, and even sometimes of preferences. No, Madam, I will not be your friend, I will love you with the most ardent and tender affection, and yet the most respectful. You may deprive it of hope, but you cannot annihilate it.

What right have you to pretend to dispose of a heart, whose homage you refuse? By what refinement of cruelty do you envy me the happiness of my love? It belongs to me; and is independent of you; and I know how to preserve it. If it is the source, it is also the remedy of my misfortunes. Once more no, persist in your cruel resolutions; but leave me love. You enjoy the pleasure of my misery; be it so, endeavour to tire out my perseverance, I shall at least know how to oblige you to decide my fate; and you may, perhaps, one day do me justice. Not that I ever hope to make you sensible of my pain, but you shall be convinced, though not persuaded; and you shall say I have judged him too severely.

But you are unjust to yourself: to see you without loving you, to love you without being constant, are both equally impossible; and, notwithstanding the modesty that adorns you, it must be easier for you to lament, than be astonished at the sentiments you gave birth to. But as for me, whose only merit is to have discovered their value, I will not lose it; and far from agreeing to your insidious offers, I again renew, at your feet, the oaths I have made to love you eternally.

Sept. 10, 17 — .

LETTER LXIX.

CECILIA VOLANGES *to the* CHEVALIER DANCENY.

(*Wrote with a pencil, and re-copied by Danceny.*)

You desire to know how I spend my time? I love you, and am always crying. My mother speaks to me no longer; she has taken away my paper, pens, and ink; I now make use of a pencil, which I fortunately had in my pocket, and I write this on the back of your letter. I must certainly approve of whatever you have done; I love you too well, not to use every means to hear from you, and give you some account of myself. I did not use to love Mr. de Valmont; I did not think him to be so much your friend; I will endeavour to accustom myself to him, and I will love him on your account. I cannot tell who betrayed us; it must be either my waiting-maid or my confessor. I am very unhappy: to-morrow we set out for the country, and I do not know for how long a time. Good God, not to see you any more! I have no more room, adieu! Endeavour to read this. Those letters, wrote with a pencil, will, perhaps, rub out; but the sentiments engraved on my heart never will.

Sept.. 10, 17—.

LETTER LXX.

VISCOUNT DE VALMONT *to the* MARCHIONESS DE MERTEUIL.

My dear friend, I have a most important piece of news for you: last night I supped, as you know, at the Marechale de — —, where you were spoke of; I said not all the good that I think, but all that I did not think of you. Every one seemed to be of my opinion, and the conversation languished, as it always happens when people talk well of their neighbours; when at length Prevan spoke, "God forbid," said he, rising up, "that I should have the least doubt of the virtue of Madame de Merteuil; but I dare say, that she owes it more to levity than principle. It is, perhaps, easier to please her, than follow her; and as one seldom fails in running after a woman, to meet others in one's way, those may be as much, if not more, valuable than she; some are dissipated by a new taste, others stop through lassitude; and she is, perhaps, one of the women who has had the least opportunity of making a resistance, of any of Paris; for my part," said he, (encouraged by the smiles of some of the women), "I will not credit Madame de Merteuil's virtue, until I have killed six horses in her service."

This scurvy jest succeeded, as all those do that are replete with scandal; and whilst the laugh went round, Prevan seated himself, and the conversation became general; but the two Countesses de B— —, near whom the incredulous Prevan seated himself, began a particular conversation which I overheard.

The challenge that was given to bring you to compliance was accepted; and the promise of telling all was exchanged; of all those which passed in this conversation, that will be the most religiously observed: but now you have timely notice; and you know the the old proverb.

I have only to tell you, moreover, that this Prevan, who you do not know, is amazingly amiable, and still more subtle. If you have sometimes heard me say the contrary, it is only because I don't like him, and that I delight in contradicting his successes; for I am not ignorant how my opinion weighs with some thirty of our women à-la-mode.

And really I have, for a long time, prevented him by this means, of making a figure in what is called the grand theatre. He worked prodigies without advancing his reputation. But the eclat of his triple adventure, by fixing every one's eyes on him, has given him a certain air of confidence that he, until then, wanted, and has made him truly formidable. He is, perhaps, at this time, the only man I dread meeting in my way; and, your interests apart, you will do me the greatest service in making him ridiculous. I leave him in good hands; and I hope at my return he will be a lost man.

In recompence, I promise you to bring the adventure of your pupil to a good issue, and to employ my time as much for her as my lovely prude.

She has just now sent me a plan of capitulation. Her whole letter announces a wish to be deceived. It is impossible to offer any means more commodious, or more stale. She will have me to be her friend. But I, who am fond of new and difficult methods, will not let her off so easily; for certainly I have not taken so much pains about her, to terminate by the ordinary methods of seduction.

On the contrary, my design is, that she should feel the value, and the extent, of every one of the sacrifices she shall make; not to lead her on so fast, but that remorse may follow every step; to make her virtue expire in a slow agony; to fix her attention incessantly on that mortifying spectacle, and not to grant her the happiness of having me in her arms, till I have forced her to no longer dissemble her desire: for I am worth little indeed, if I am not worth the trouble of asking. Then I shall be revenged of a haughty woman, who seems to blush to own she adores.

I have then refused this precious friendship, and hold to my title of lover. As I am not ignorant that this title, which at first appears but trifling, is, notwithstanding, of real importance to be obtained, I took peculiar care of my style, and endeavoured to scatter through my letter that kind of disorder which only can display sentiment, and talked as much nonsense as possible; for, without that, there is no tenderness: that, I believe, is the reason that women excel us so much in love letters.

I finished mine by a soothing sentence; that is another consequence of my profound observations. After a woman's heart has been some time kept in exercise, it wants rest: and I have often remarked, that a flattery is, for all of them, the softest pillow we can offer.

Adieu, my lovely friend. I set out to-morrow. If you have any orders to give me for the Countess de − −, I shall stop with her to dinner. I am sorry to set out without seeing you. Forward me your sublime instructions, and assist me with your wise counsels in the decisive moment.

Above all, beware of Prevan; and may I one day indemnify you for this sacrifice. Adieu!
Sept. 11, 17−.

LETTER LXXI.

VISCOUNT DE VALMONT *to the* MARCHIONESS DE MERTEUIL.

My blundering huntsman has left my letter-case at Paris. My fair one's letters, Danceny's for the little Volanges, all is left behind; and I want them all. He is just going to set off to repair his folly; and while he saddles his horse, I take the opportunity to give you a detail of my night's adventure; for I hope you will believe I don't lose time.

It is in itself but trifling; being nothing more than another heat with the Viscountess de M———. The detail however is interesting. I am moreover pleased to let you know, that if I have the talent of ruining the women, I am no less clever in saving them when I am inclined. The most lively, or most difficult side, is what I always choose; and I never reproach myself with doing a good act, provided it entertains and amuses me.

I found the Viscountess here; and as she was very pressing with the other solicitations, that I should sleep here, "Well, I agree," said I, "on condition I sleep with you." — "That is impossible," said she; "Vressac is here." Until then I only meant to pass a joke; but the word *impossible* roused me as usual. I was humbled to be sacrificed to Vressac; I determined not to bear it, and insisted on it.

The circumstances were not favourable for me. Vressac has been foolish enough to give umbrage to the Viscount; so that she cannot see him any longer at home: and this journey to the good Countess was concerted between them, to endeavour to steal a few nights. The Viscount seemed to be out of temper at meeting Vressac here; but as his passion for hunting is stronger than his jealousy, he has remained, notwithstanding the Countess, whom you well know, having fixed the wife in an apartment in the great gallery; placed the husband on one side, and the lover on the other, and left them to settle the matter between themselves. Their evil genius would have it that I should be lodged opposite to them.

Yesterday Vressac, who, as you may believe, humours the Viscount, hunted with him, notwithstanding it is a diversion he is not fond of, and reckoned he would be consoled at night in the embraces of the wife, for the chagrin the husband gave him that day: but as I imagined he would have occasion for repose, I resolved to prevail on his mistress to give him time to take it.

I succeeded, and induced her to pick a quarrel with him about this hunting match, which he evidently agreed to only for her sake. A worse pretence never could have been hit on: but no woman knows better than the Viscountess how to employ that usual talent of all, to affect ill temper instead of reason, and to be never so difficult to be appeased as when they are in the wrong. Besides, it was not a convenient time for explanations; and as I only wished for one night with her, I consented they should make it up the next day.

Vressac was then huffed at his return. He wanted to know the reason she quarrelled with him; he endeavoured to justify himself; the husband, who was present, was the apology for breaking off the conversation; he however attempted to seize the opportunity, when the husband was absent, to beg he might be heard at night. Then the Viscountess was sublime: she was exasperated at the audacity of men, who, because they have experienced a woman's affection, think themselves entitled to abuse it; when, at the same time, the woman has every cause to be offended; and having changed her argument, she spoke so well, on delicacy and sentiment, that Vressac was mute and confounded; and I even thought she was right: for you must know, as a friend to both, I made up the trio.

She at length declared positively she would not increase the fatigues of the chase by the additional ones of love, and that she could not think of disturbing such pleasing amusements. The husband returned. The unhappy Vressac, who could no longer reply, addressing himself to me; after relating, with much circumlocution, his reasons, which I was as well satisfied with as he could be, requested I would speak to the Viscountess, which I promised him: and I did; but it was to thank her, and settle the hour and method of meeting.

She informed me, that, being situated between her husband and lover, she thought it more prudent to go to Vressac, than to receive him in her apartment; and that as I was fixed opposite to her, she thought it would be better to come to my room; that she would come the moment her maid left her; only to leave my door open, and wait for her.

Every thing was done as agreed on; and she came to me about one.

Not being much inclined to vanity, I shall not enter into particulars: however, you know me well; I was well pleased with myself.

At dawn of day we were forced to part. Here the tale begins. The giddy creature thought she had left her door half open; we found it shut, and the key withinside. You can't conceive the distraction of the Viscountess. "Ah! I am undone," she exclaimed. I must own it would have been whimsical to have left her so; but was it possible to think a woman should be ruined for me, that was not ruined by me? And should I, as the generality of men do, be overcome by an accident? A lucky thought occurred, and thus I settled the business.

I soon perceived the door might be broke upon, but not without some noise. With some difficulty I prevailed on the Viscountess to cry out, Robbers, murder, thieves, &c. &c. We had so settled it, that, at the first alarm, I should burst open the door, and she should fly to her bed. Yon can't imagine how difficult it was to make her resolve, even after she had consented. She was, however, obliged to comply; and at the first burst the door flew open.

The Viscountess was right not to lose a moment; for instantly the Viscount and Vressac were in the gallery, and the waiting maid in her mistress's chamber.

I alone was cool, and overturned a watch light that was burning; for it would have been ridiculous to have feigned such a panic, having a light in the room. I scolded the husband and lover for their drowsiness, confidently insisting that her cries, and my efforts to burst open the door, had lasted at least five minutes.

The Viscountess, who recovered her courage in bed, seconded me tolerably well, and strenuously insisted there was a robber in her room; but with something more sincerity she declared she never had been more frightened in her life. We searched every where, but found nothing; at last I made them observe the watch light overturned: we concluded a rat had given us this fright and disturbance. My opinion was unanimously adopted. After some stale jests on rats, the Viscount returned to bed, begging she would in future choose more peaceable rats.

Vressac drew near the Viscountess, and passionately told her, Love revenged him; to which she replied, fixing her eyes on me, "He must then have been very angry indeed: for he has had ample satisfaction; but I am much fatigued, and want rest."

I was very well pleased. Before we parted, I pleaded so powerfully for Vressac, that I brought about a reconciliation. The lovers embraced, and I also received theirs. I was indifferent to the Viscountess's kisses; but I own I was pleased with Vressac's. We left her; after having received his thanks, we returned to our beds.

If the tale diverts you, I don't mean to bind you to secrecy. Now I have had my amusement, it is right the public should also have their share. For this time you have only the history; hereafter we shall talk of the heroine.

Adieu. My huntsman has been in waiting an hour. I particularly recommend it to you to be on your guard against Prevan.

From the Castle of — —,
Sept. 15, 17 —.

LETTER LXXII.

CHEVALIER DANCENY *to* CECILIA VOLANGES.

(Delivered only the 14th.)

Oh, my Cecilia! How much I envy Valmont's good fortune; to-morrow he will see you. He will deliver you this letter; whilst I, languishing far from you, will lead a wretched lingering life. Between regret and misery, my life, my dearest life, pity me not only for my own misfortunes, but also for yours; for it is they that deprive me of my resolution.

How dreadful the reflection, to be the cause of your misery! Had it not been for me, you would have been happy; will you forgive me? Speak! Say you forgive me; tell me you love me; that you will love me ever, which is the only consolation that is now left me. Not that I doubt it; but it relieves my anguish; you love me then? Yes, you love me with your whole heart. I do not forget it was the last word you spoke: it is treasured in mine; it is there deeply engraved. With what transports did my heart answer it!

Alas, in that happy moment, I was far from foreseeing the dreadful fate that awaited us! Let us seek for means to soften it. If I am to believe my friend, it will be enough that you should have the confidence in him he deserves. I was chagrined, I must own, at the disadvantageous idea you had of him. I knew the bad opinion your mamma had imbibed, and in submission to that opinion, I had, for some time, neglected a truly amiable man, who now is ready to serve me; who endeavours to reunite us, whilst your mamma has cruelly torn you from me. I conjure you, my love, to have a more favourable opinion of him; remember he is my friend, and wishes to be yours; that he can procure me the happiness of seeing you. If those reasons do not convince you, my Cecilia, you do not love me as much as I love you; you no longer love me as you did. Ah! if you should ever love me less, — but no, Cecilia's heart is mine: I have it for life; and if I must feel the torments of an unsuccessful passion, her constancy, at least, will insure me the inexpressible joy of a permanent affection.

Adieu, my lovely dear! Do not forget that I suffer; it will be your fault if I am not perfectly happy; attend to the vows of my heart, and receive the tender kisses of love.

Sept. 11, 17—.

LETTER LXXIII.

VISCOUNT DE VALMONT *to* CECILIA VOLANGES.

(Annexed to the foregoing.)

The friend who takes upon him to assist you, knows that you have not materials to write with, therefore has provided them for you. You will find in the anti-chamber of your apartment, under the great clothes press on the left hand, paper, pens, and ink, which he will renew whenever you please, and which, he thinks, you may leave in the same place, if you cannot find a better.

He requests you will not be offended, if he seems to take little notice of you in company, and only to treat you as a child. This behaviour appears necessary to him, to avoid suspicion, and to be able more effectually to bring about your and his friend's happiness. He will endeavour to get opportunities to speak to you, when he has any thing to say or to give you; and hopes to be able to accomplish it, if, on your part, you will second him.

He also advises you to give him the letters you will receive, after you have read them, in order to avoid all bad consequences.

He finishes his letter by assuring you, if you confide in him, he will employ his utmost endeavours to soften the persecution that a cruel mother makes two persons undergo; one of which is his best friend, and the other seems to him to deserve his tenderest concern.

Castle of − −, Sept. 14, 17−.

LETTER LXXIV.

MARCHIONESS DE MERTEUIL *to* VISCOUNT DE VALMONT.

You are very soon alarmed, my dear friend: this Prevan must be formidable indeed, but what a simple modest creature am I, who have often met this haughty conqueror, and have scarce ever looked at him; nothing less than your letter would have made me pay the least attention to him. I corrected my error yesterday; he was at the Opera, almost opposite to me; I was captivated with him. He is not only handsome, but very handsome; fine delicate features, and must improve on a clearer inspection. You say, he wants to have me, he certainly will do me a great deal of honour and pleasure; but seriously, I have taken a fancy to him, and tell you, in confidence, I have taken the first step towards an advance. I do not know whether I shall succeed, but this is fact.

He was at a very little distance from me, coming out of the Opera, and I gave a rendezvous to the Marquis de − − −, to sup on Friday at the Lady Marechale's, so loud that he might hear, which, I believe, is the only house I can meet him in; and have not the least doubt but he heard me. If the ungrateful wretch should not come − Tell me sincerely, do you think he will? I protest if he does not, I shall be out of temper the whole evening. You see he will not find so much *difficulty in following me;* and what will surprise you more is, he will find less, in *pleasing me..* He says he will kill six horses in paying his addresses to me; oh! the poor animals shall not die. I should never have patience to wait so long. You know it is not my principle to make any one languish, when once I am decided in their favour, as I really am in his.

Now, you must agree, there is some pleasure in talking rationally to me, has not your *important advice* had great success; but what can I do? I vegetate for a long time; it is more than six weeks since I have permitted myself a gaiety; this is the first, how can I refuse it? Is not the subject worth the trouble? Can there be any one more agreeable in every sense of the word?

You are obliged to do him justice; you do more than praise him; you are jealous of him. Well, I shall judge between you both, but first I must take informations, and that is what I mean to do. Be assured I shall be an upright judge; you shall be both weighed in the same scale; for your part, I have already received your memorial, am entirely acquainted with your affairs. Is it not reasonable that I should also know your adversary's case? Come, go through your business with a good grace, and to begin, inform me, I beg of you, this triple adventure, of which he is the hero. You talk to me as if I knew the whole matter, who never heard a word of it. Probably it happened during the time of my journey to Geneva, and your jealousy prevented you from giving me an account of it. Repair this fault immediately; remember *that every thing that* interests him, *is of consequence to me.* I think it was spoke of at my return; but I was so taken up with other matters, I rarely pay attention to any thing of this kind that is not new.

If what I require should be even contrary to your inclination, remember how much you are indebted to me for the cares and solicitude I have had upon your account. Is it not to them you are indebted for being now with your Presidente, when your own folly drove you from her? Have I not put it in your power to be revenged of Madame de Volanges, for her acrimonious zeal against you? How often have you deplored the time you lost in search of adventures, now you have them at command? Love, hatred, make your choice, they are under the same roof with you; by doubling your existence, you can caress with the one hand, and strike with the other.

It is to me even you are indebted, for the adventure of the Viscountess—It pleases me. I agree with you it must be published, for if the opportunity influenced you, as I am apt to think, to prefer mystery to rumour; at that time must acknowledge, notwithstanding, this woman does not deserve so handsome a procedure.

Moreover, I have reason to dislike her; the Chevalier de Belleroche thinks her handsomer than me, and for several reasons I would be glad to break off with her; there is none more plausible than to have a story to relate, one cannot keep company with her after.

Farewell, Viscount! Remember that as you are situated, time is precious: I will employ mine in thinking how to make Prevan happy.

Sept. 15, 17—.

LETTER LXXV.

CECILIA VOLANGES *to* SOPHIA CARNAY.

[In this Letter, Cecilia Volanges gives a most circumstantial account of every thing that relates to herself, in the events which the reader has seen at the end of the first volume, the 59th Letter, and the following; for this reason a repetition was thought unnecessary; at last she speaks of Viscount de Valmont, and thus expresses herself:]

I assure you he is a very extraordinary man: my mamma speaks very ill of him, but the Chevalier Danceny is enamoured with him, and I believe he is in the right. I never saw a man so artful; when he gave me Danceny's letter, it was amongst a good deal of company, and no one knew any thing of the matter. It is true I was very much frightened, because I had no notion of any such thing, but hereafter I shall be on the watch. I conceive, already, how he would have me return the answer; it is very easy to understand him, for he has an eye tells one every thing; I do not know how he contrives: he told me in the note which I mentioned to you, he would not seem to take any notice of me before mamma; really one would imagine he never thinks of it, and yet every time I want to look at him, I am sure to meet his eyes fixed upon me.

There is a lady here, also an intimate friend of mamma's, I did not know, who appears to me not to like Mr. de Valmont. Although he seems to be all attention to her, I am afraid he will soon grow tired of this life, and return to Paris; that would be dreadful indeed! He must be an exceeding good-natured man, to come here on purpose to serve his friend and me. I wish to know how I could testify my gratitude; but I don't know how to speak to him; and if I even had the opportunity, I should be so ashamed I should not know what to say.

I cannot speak to any body freely, about my love affair, but Madame de Merteuil; perhaps even with thee, to whom I tell every thing, if it was in a chatting way, I should be abashed. Even with Danceny himself, I have often felt, as it were, against my inclination, a kind of fear, which prevented me from saying every thing I could wish. I am very sorry for it now, and I would give any thing in the world for a moment, to tell him only once how much I love him. Mr. de Valmont has promised him, if I will be ruled by him, he will find an opportunity for us to see each other. I am very well inclined to do whatever he would have me; but I can't conceive how it is possible.

Farewell, my dear friend: I have no more room.[1]
From the Castle of − −, *Sept.* 14, 17−.

[1] Mademoiselle de Volanges having a little time after changed her confidant, as will be seen in the following Letters, there will no more be given in this collection of those she continued to write to her friend in the convent.

LETTER LXXVI.

VISCOUNT DE VALMONT *to the* MARCHIONESS DE MERTEUIL.

I cannot comprehend you; you were either in a whimsical mood, or, when you wrote, in a very dangerous fit of madness. If I did not know you very well, my charming friend, I should be really alarmed; and, colour it as you will, I should have a great deal of reason.

Vainly do I read, and read again, your letter. I can't conceive you; for it is impossible to take your letter in the style it is couched; what did you then mean to say? Did you only mean there was no occasion to give oneself so much trouble against so despicable an enemy: if so, you are wrong. Prevan is really amiable; he is more so than you imagine; and has, in a peculiar manner, that happy talent of interesting one much about love affairs, which he introduces on every occasion, and in all companies. Few women can avoid the snare of replication, because, as they all have pretensions to artifice, none will lose the opportunity of displaying it. And I need not tell you that a woman, who consents to talk of love, commonly ends with being entrapped, or, at least, acts as if she was. He refines on this method, which he has even brought to a science, by often introducing the women themselves as witnesses of their own defeat: this I aver, and can prove.

I was let into the secret only at second hand; for I never was intimate with Prevan. We were six in company: the Countess de P− −, thinking herself amazingly fine, and even possessing the talent of keeping up a general conversation well, related to us minutely the manner she had surrendered to Prevan, with all circumstances. She gave the recital with so much composure, that she was not even disconcerted at a smile which escaped us all at the same time. I shall never forget, one of us, to excuse himself, feigned to doubt what she said, or rather what she related; she gravely answered, that none of us could be so well informed as she; and she was not even afraid to call upon Prevan, and ask him whether she had omitted a single circumstance.

This I think sufficient to call him a very dangerous man: but is it not enough for you, Marchioness, he is *handsome, very handsome,* as you say? Or that he should make on you *one of those attacks that you are sometimes fond of rewarding, for no other motive, but because you think it well carried on?* Or that you would think it pleasing to surrender for any reason whatever? Or — but it is impossible for me to guess the infinity of whims which rule the minds of women, and by which alone you resemble your sex. Now you are informed of the danger, I have no doubt; but you may easily avoid it; and yet it was necessary to put you on your guard. I return to my text; what do you mean to say?

If it is not a banter on Prevan, besides its being very long, it is not to me it can be useful; it is in the face of the world you must make him ridiculous; and I renew my instances to you on that subject.

Ah! I believe I have discovered the enigma. Your letter is a prophecy; not what you will do, but what he will believe you ready to do, at the moment of his disgrace. I approve this project well enough; however, it requires great management. You know, as well as I do, it is absolutely the same thing to the public, whether you are connected with a man, or receive his addresses, unless the man is a fool, which Prevan is not by any means; if he can only save appearances, he will brag, and every thing will be greedily swallowed. Fools will believe him, others will seem to believe him; and then what becomes of your resources? I am really alarmed; not that I have any doubt of your abilities; but the best swimmers are often drowned.

I think myself no novice in the ways of debauchery. I have discovered a hundred, nay, a thousand. My mind is often engaged in thinking how a woman could escape me, and I never could find out the possibility. Even yourself, my charming friend, whose conduct is a masterpiece; I have often thought your success was more owing to good fortune than good management.

After all, I am, perhaps, seeking a reason where there is none; and I am astonished I have been for this hour past treating seriously a subject that you certainly mean as a jest. How you will laugh at me! but be it so; let us talk of something else. I am wrong; it must be the same subject; always of women to be had or ruined, and often of both.

I have here wherewithal, as you justly remark, to give me employment in both capacities, but not with equal facility. I foresee revenge will outstrip love. The little Volanges is ready, I will answer for her; all now depends upon the opportunity which I take upon me to provide: but not so with Madame de Tourvel; this woman distracts me. I have no conception of her. I have a hundred proofs of her love; but I have also a thousand of her resistance. Upon my word, I am afraid she will escape me.

The first effect that my return produced gave me more flattering expectations. You may guess, I was willing to judge for myself; and to be certain of seeing her first emotions, I took care not to be announced by any formality, calculating my journey so as to arrive while they were at dinner, and fell from the clouds like an opera divinity.

Having made a sufficient noise coming in to draw their attention to me, I could observe with the same glance my old aunt's joy, Madame de Volanges' vexation, and the confused pleasure of her daughter. My fair one sat with her back to the door. Being employed at that instant cutting up something, she did not even turn her head. I addressed myself to Madame de Rosemonde; and at the first word, the tender devotee hearing my voice, gave a scream, in which I thought there was more of love than surprise or terror. I was then got so far into the room as to be able to observe her countenance; the tumult of her soul, the struggle of ideas and sentiments, were strongly depicted in twenty different forms on it. I seated myself at table close by her; she did not know what she said or did. She endeavoured to keep on eating; but it was in vain. At length, in less than a quarter of an hour, her pleasure and her embarrassment overpowering her, she thought it best to beg leave to retire from table, under a pretence of wanting a little air. Madame de Volanges wanted to accompany her; the tender prude would not permit it: too happy, doubtless, to find a pretence to be alone, and give herself up without restraint to the soft emotions of her heart.

I dispatched my dinner as soon as possible. The dessert was scarcely served, when the infernal Volanges, probably with a design to prejudice me, got up to follow the charming woman. I foresaw this project, but disappointed her. I feigned to take this particular motion for a general one; and rising at the same time, the little Volanges and the curate of the place followed our example, so that Madame de Rosemonde was left at table with the old Commander de T—, who both also took the resolution to follow us. We all went then to join my fair one, whom we found in the arbour near the castle; and as she wanted solitude more than a walk, she chose rather to return with us, than to oblige us to stay with her. As soon as I was certain that Madame de Volanges would not have an opportunity of speaking to her alone, I began to think of executing your orders, and exert myself for the interest of your pupil. When coffee was over, I went up to my apartment, entered the other's to reconnoitre the ground, and formed my dispositions to ensure the correspondence of the little one. After this first step, I wrote a few words to inform her of it; and to demand her confidence, I tacked my note to Danceny's letter; returned to the saloon, where I found my fair one stretched upon a sofa at full length, in a most delicious abandonment.

This sight rousing my desires, animated my looks. I knew they should be tender, yet urgent; and placed myself in such a manner, as to be able to employ them successfully. Their first essay obliged my celestial prude to cast down her beautiful modest eyes. I viewed for some time this angelic figure; then running over her whole frame, amused myself with considering the outlines and forms of her person through the light dress she wore. After gazing on her from head to foot, my eyes went back from the feet to the head—my charming friend, the soft look was fixed on me, but she instantly cast her eyes down again; being desirous of bringing them back, I turned my eyes from her. Then was established between us that silent convention, the first treaty of timid lovers, who to satisfy the mutual want of seeing each other, permit soft looks to succeed until they mingle together.

Fully satisfied that my charmer was entirely taken up with this new delight, I took upon me to watch for our mutual safety: but when I was assured that a pretty lively conversation took off the attention of the company, I endeavoured to make the eyes freely speak their own language. At first I darted some glances, but with so much reserve, that modesty itself could not be alarmed at it; and to make the lovely timid woman easier, I appeared as much embarrassed as she; by little and little, our eyes accustomed to meet, fixed themselves a little longer, and at length did not quit each other; I perceived in hers that soft languishing air, happy presage to love and desire: but it was only for a moment; and she soon recovered herself; she changed her looks and position with some confusion.

As I determined she should have no doubt of my remarking her different emotions, I started suddenly, asking her, with a frightened look, if she was indisposed. Immediately the company assembled round her. I let them all pass before me; and as the little Volanges, who was working tapestry near a window, took some time in quitting her frame, I seized the opportunity to give her Danceny's letter.

I was a little distance from her, and threw the letter in her lap. She really did not know what to do. You would have laughed to see her surprise and embarrassment; yet I did not laugh, lest so much awkwardness should betray us: but a glance and a frown, made her comprehend that she was to put it in her pocket.

The remainder of the day had nothing interesting. What has happened since, will, perhaps, bring on events that will please you, at least, as to what regards your pupil; but it is better to employ one's time in executing than in relating them: moreover, this is the eighth page I have written, and I am a good deal fatigued; so adieu.

It will be unnecessary to tell you, that the little thing has answered Danceny.[1] I have also had a letter from my fair one, to whom I wrote the day after my arrival. I send you both letters. You will read them, or let it alone; for those perpetual tiresome repetitions, of which I begin to be disgusted, must be very insipid for a person unconcerned.

Once more, adieu! I still love you much: but I beg, if you speak again of Prevan, that it may be in intelligible language.

From the Castle of − −, Sept. 17, 17−.

[1] This letter was not found.

LETTER LXXVII.

VISCOUNT DE VALMONT *to the* Presidente DE TOURVEL.

From whence proceeds, Madam, the cruel care you take to avoid me? How does it happen, that the most tender eagerness on my part, can only obtain from you an indifference, that one could scarcely justify to a man who had even done one an injury? When love recalls me to your feet, and a happy accident places me beside you, you would rather feign an indisposition, and alarm your friends, than consent to remain near me. How often yesterday did you turn away your eyes from me, to deprive me of the pleasure of a look; and if, for an instant, I could observe less severity in them, it seemed as if you intended not that I should enjoy it, but that I should feel my loss in being deprived of it.

This is, I dare say, a treatment not consistent with love, nor can it be permitted to friendship; and yet you know that one of those sentiments animates me, and I thought myself authorised to believe you would not refuse me the other. This precious friendship, which you undoubtedly thought me worthy of, as you condescended to offer it, what have I since done to forfeit? Have I prejudiced myself by my frankness; and will you punish me for my candour? Are you not, at least, afraid of offending the one or the other? For is it not in the bosom of my friend I deposit the secrets of my heart? Is it not to her alone I thought myself obliged to refuse conditions which, had I accepted, would give me an opportunity of breaking them, and, perhaps, of successfully abusing them? Or would you force me to believe, by so undeserved a rigour, if I had deceived you, I should have gained more indulgence?

I do not repent of a conduct I owe to you and myself: but by what fatality is it, that every laudable action of mine becomes the signal of a new misfortune to me?

And after having, by my obedience, merited the only praise you have vouchsafed to bestow on my conduct, I now, for the first time, lament the misfortune of displeasing you. After giving you proofs of my entire submission, by depriving myself of the happiness of seeing you, to please your delicacy, you want to break off your correspondence with me, and take away this feeble amends of a sacrifice you exacted, to deprive me of my love, which alone could have given you that right. In fine, it is after speaking to you with a sincerity which even my love could not weaken, you fly from me to-day as a dangerous seductor, whose perfidiousness was fully proved.

Will you then never cease being unjust? Inform me, at least, what new wrongs I have committed, that could cause so much severity; and do not refuse to prescribe the orders you would have me follow. Surely it is not too much to desire to know, when I engage to execute them.

Sept. 15, 17—.

LETTER LXXVIII.

The Presidente DE TOURVEL *to the* VISCOUNT DE VALMONT.

You seem surprised, Sir, at my behaviour; and, indeed, your style falls little short of calling me to account, as if you were authorised to blame it. I really think I have much more reason for astonishment and complaint; but since the refusal contained in your last answer, I have taken my resolution to behave with an indifference that may not give any occasion for remarks or reproaches; yet as you ask some eclaircissements which, I thank heaven, I find no difficulty in giving, I will once more explain myself.

Any person who should read your letters would think me either unjust or fantastical. I don't think I deserve that character; but I am of opinion, you above all the rest of mankind would be the readiest to catch at it. You must be sensible, that in putting me under the necessity of a justification, you oblige me to recall every thing that has passed between us. You imagined you would gain by the scrutiny: I am inclined to think, I may even stand the test in your opinion; and perhaps it is the only way to discover which of us has a right to complain.

To begin, Sir, from the day of your arrival at this castle. You will acknowledge, I hope, your character authorised me at least to be upon the reserve, and I might, without apprehending the imputation of an excess of prudery, have restricted myself to exact politeness. You yourself would have behaved to me with deference, and only thought it strange, that a plain woman, so unacquainted with the ways of the world, had not sufficient penetration to appreciate your merit; that would have been certainly the most prudent method, and which I was so much inclined to follow, that I will freely own, when Madame de Rosemonde came to inform me of your arrival, I had occasion to recollect my friendship for her, and hers for you, to conceal my uneasiness at the unwelcome news.

I will freely own, at first you exhibited a behaviour much more favourable to you than what I had conceived: but you must also allow, it lasted but a very short time; and that you soon grew tired of a constraint, for which you did not think yourself sufficiently indemnified by the advantageous idea I had of you.

Then taking advantage of my candour and tranquillity, you did not scruple cherishing sentiments which you could not have the least doubt but would offend me; and whilst you was every day multiplying and aggravating the wrongs you did me, I endeavoured to forget them, and even offered you an opportunity, in some measure, of redressing them. My requisition was so fair, that you even thought you could not refuse it, but asserting a right from my indulgence, you made use of it to demand a permission, which doubtless I ought not to have granted, and which yet you obtained. The conditions annexed to it you did not observe; your correspondence was such, that each letter made it a duty to answer you no more. Even at the very time when your obstinacy obliged me to insist on your going away, that by a blameable condescension I sought the only means which, consistent with duty, was allowed me not to break entirely with you. But an humble sentiment has no value in your eyes. You despise friendship; and in your mad intoxication, ridiculing misery and shame, you seek nothing but victims and pleasure.

As fickle in your proceedings, as contrary to your own principles in your charges, you forget your promises, or you make a jest of violating them; and after consenting to depart from me, you come back without being recalled, without paying the least regard to my solicitations or my reasons, without even the decency of a notice. You ventured to expose me to a surprise, which, although very simple in itself, might have been interpreted very unfavourably for me by the persons who were present, and, far from endeavouring to dissipate this moment of embarrassment you gave birth to, you carefully sought to augment it. At table you chose precisely to place yourself beside me. A slight indisposition obliged me to go out before any of the company; and instead of paying any respect to my solitude, you bring them all to disturb me. Being returned again into the saloon, if I move, you follow me; if I speak, you always reply to me. The most indifferent word is a pretence for you to bring on a conversation, which I do not wish to hear, and which often may bring my name in question; for notwithstanding all your address, Sir, I believe others can see as well as me.

Thus, then, reduced to a state of inaction and silence, you nevertheless continue to pursue me. I cannot lift my eyes without meeting yours. I am incessantly obliged to turn my looks from you; and by an inconsequence, you fix the eyes of the whole company on me, at a time when I could even wish to hide myself from my own.

Yet you complain of my behaviour, and are astonished at my anxiety to fly from you. Blame rather my indulgence, and be astonished I did not set out the moment you arrived. I ought to have done it; perhaps you will yet oblige me to this violent, though necessary measure, if you do not cease your offensive pursuits. No; I never will forget what I owe to myself, what I owe to the obligations I have taken, which I respect and cherish. Be assured, if I should ever be reduced to the unhappy choice of sacrificing myself or them, I would not hesitate a moment.

Sept. 16, 17—.

LETTER LXXIX.

The VISCOUNT DE VALMONT *to the* MARCHIONESS DE MERTEUIL.

I thought to have gone a-hunting this morning, but it is most horrible weather. I have no book to read but a new romance that would tire a boarding-school girl. We shall not breakfast these two hours; therefore, notwithstanding my long letter of yesterday, I will still chat with you, and am confident you will not think me tedious, for I will entertain you concerning *the very handsome Prevan.*

So you know nothing at all about this famous adventure which separated the *inseparables.* I would venture to lay a wager, you will recollect it at the first word. I will give it you, however, since you desire it.

You may remember all Paris was astonished, three women equally handsome, equally possessing the same talents, and having the same pretensions, should remain so intimately connected since the time of their appearance in the world. At first it was imagined it proceeded from their great timidity; but soon surrounded by a number of gallants, whose homages they shared, they soon began to feel their consequence, by the eagerness and assiduity with which they were followed. Still their union became the stronger. One would have imagined the triumph of one was also that of the other two; however, every one flattered himself that love would cause a rivalship. Those fair ones contended for the honour of the apple of discord; and I myself would have been a competitor, if the high reputation the Countess de — — was in at that time would have permitted me to have committed an infidelity before I had obtained the consummation of my desires.

However, our three beauties that same carnival made their choice, as if in concert; and far from exciting any disturbance, it rendered their friendship more interesting by the charms of confidence.

The crowd of unfortunate pretenders coalesced with the envious women, and this scandalous constancy was submitted to public censure. Some promulgated, that in this society of *the inseparables*, so called at that time, the fundamental law was, that every thing should be in common, that love even was subservient to the same law. Others asserted, that the three lovers were not exempt from rivals. Others went so far as to say, they had only been admitted for decency sake, and had only obtained a sinecure title.

These reports, whether true or false, had not their wished-for effect; the three couple perceived plainly they were undone if they separated at this period, therefore resolved to stem the torrent. The public, who soon tire of every thing, shortly gave up a fruitless scandal. Carried away by their natural levity, they were engaged in other pursuits. Returning again to this, with their usual inconsequence, they changed their criticisms to commendations. As every thing is here fashionable, the enthusiasm gained ground, and became a perfect rage, when Prevan undertook to verify those prodigies, and to fix the public opinion and his own on them.

He then laid himself out for those models of perfection. Being easily admitted into their society, from thence he drew a favourable omen; he very well knew, those who lived in a happy state were not so accessible; and soon perceived the so-much-boasted happiness, like that of kings, was more envied than desirable. He observed among those pretended inseparables, they began to seek for pleasures abroad, they were often absent; from thence he concluded, the ties of love or friendship were already relaxed or broken; that those of self-love and habit still preserved some kind of strength.

Still the women, whom necessity kept together, preserved the same appearance of intimacy among themselves: but the men, more free in their proceedings, found duties to fulfil, or business to do, which they always lamented, but nevertheless did not neglect; their meetings were thus scarcely ever complete.

This behaviour was very useful to the assiduous Prevan, who being, in course, at liberty with the widow of the day, alternately found an opportunity of offering the same homage to the three friends. He readily saw, if he made a choice, it would be his destruction; the shame of being discovered to be the first transgressor would deter the one who had the preference, and the vanity of the two others would render them mortal enemies of the new lover; they would not fail to display all their resentment against him, and jealousy would certainly recall a rival, who, perhaps, might be troublesome. Thus every thing was attended with difficulty: but in his triple project, every thing was made easy; each woman was indulgent, because she was interested, and each man, because he thought he was not.

Prevan was engaged to only one woman at that time. Fortunately for him, the sacrifice was not very difficult, as she became celebrated. The addresses of a great prince, which had been dexterously rejected, together with her being a foreigner, had drawn the attention of the court and town upon her. Her lover shared the honour, and made a very good use of it with his new mistresses; the only difficulty was, to carry on those three intrigues in front, whose march should be regulated by the movements of the slowest: and I have been assured by one of his confidents, that his greatest trouble was to retard one of them who was ripe a fortnight before the others.

At length the expected day came. Prevan, who had obtained the consent of them all, regulated their motions in the following manner: One of the husbands was absent, another was to go on a journey early the next morning, the third remained in town. The inseparable friends had agreed to sup with the future widow; but the new master would not suffer any of the old servants to be invited. The morning of the same day, he divided into three lots the fair foreigner's letters. In the one he enclosed her picture; in the second, an amorous cypher she herself had drawn; the third enclosed a lock of her hair. Each received her share of sacrifice, and, in return, consented to send to their discarded lovers, letters of dismission.

That was doing a great deal; but yet was not enough. She whose husband was in town, was at liberty during the day only; and it was agreed, that a feigned indisposition should prevent her from supping with her friend, but the evening should be dedicated to Prevan; the night was granted by her whose husband was out of town; and day-light, the time the third husband was to set off, was the happy moment allotted for the other.

Prevan, who neglects nothing, flies to the fair foreigner's in an ill humour, which soon spread, and leaves her, after an altercation which brought on a quarrel that ensured him leave of absence for twenty-four hours at least. His dispositions thus made, he returned home, to take some repose; but other affairs awaited him.

The letters of dismission had opened the eyes of the discarded lovers; none of them had the least doubt but that he was sacrificed to Prevan: and the vexation of being tricked, with the mortification of being discarded, they all three, as if in concert, but without communicating with each other, resolved to have satisfaction, and demanded it accordingly of their fortunate rival.

So that at his arrival he found three challenges, which he nobly accepted: but unwilling to lose the pleasure or reputation of this adventure, he fixed the meeting for the next morning, all three at the same hour and place, at one of the gates of the wood of Boulogne.

Night being come, he run his triple career with equal success; at least, he has since vaunted, that each of his new mistresses had received three times the pledges of his love. Here, as you may well imagine, the proofs are deficient. All that can be required from the impartial historian is to request the incredulous reader to remark, that vanity, and an exalted imagination can bring forth prodigies. Moreover, the, morning that was to follow so brilliant a night, seemed to excuse circumspection for the events of the day. The following facts have, however, a greater degree of certainty.

Prevan came punctually to the place appointed, where he found his three rivals, who were a little surprised at meeting each other, and perhaps, partly consoled on seeing the companions of their misfortunes. He accosted them with an affable and cavalier air, and made them the following speech, which has been faithfully related to me:

"Gentlemen," said he, "meeting here together, you certainly guess that you have all the same subject of complaint against me. I am ready to give you satisfaction: but let chance decide between you, which of you three will be the first to require a satisfaction that you have all an equal right to. I have brought neither witness nor second. I had not any in the commission of the offence: I do not require any in the reparation." Then, agreeable to his character of a gamester, "I know," says he, "one seldom holds in three hands running; but be my fate what it will, the man has lived long enough who has gained the love of the women and the esteem of the men."

Whilst his adversaries, astonished, silently looked on each other, and, perhaps, hurt at the indelicacy of this triple combat, which made the party very unequal, Prevan resumed, "I will not conceal from you, that last night has been a very fatiguing one. It would be but generous to give me time to recruit. I have given order to prepare a breakfast; do me the honour to accept of it. Let us breakfast together with good humour. One may fight for such trifles; but I don't think it should have any effect on our spirits."

The breakfast was accepted. It is said, Prevan never shone more. He not only had the address not to mortify his rivals, but even to persuade them, they all would have easily had the same success; and made them agree, that none would have let slip the opportunity no more than himself. Those facts being acknowledged, the matter was entirely settled; and before breakfast was over, they often repeated, that such women did not deserve that men of honour should quarrel about them. This idea brought on cordiality; the wine strengthened it; so that in a short time afterwards, an unreserved friendship succeeded rancour.

Prevan, who doubtless liked this denouement as well as the other, would not, however, lose his celebrity; and dexterously forming his projects to circumstances, "Really," says he, "it is not of me, but of your faithless mistresses you should be revenged, and I will give you the opportunity. I already feel, as you do, an injury, which I shall soon share with you; for if neither of you have been able to fix the constancy of one, how can I expect that I can fix them all? Your quarrel then becomes my own. If you will sup with me to-night at my villa, I hope to give you your revenge." They desired an explanation: but he answered with that tone of superiority, which the circumstances authorised him to take, "Gentlemen, I think I have already sufficiently shown you, that I know how to conduct matters; leave every thing to me." They all agreed; and having took leave of their new friend, separated until evening, to wait the effect of his promises.

He returned immediately to Paris, and, according to custom, waited on his new conquests; obtained a promise from each to take a tête-à-tête supper with him at his villa. Two of them started some small difficulties, but nothing was to be refused after such a night. He made his appointments at an hour's distance from each other, to give him the time necessary for the maturing his scheme. After these preparations, he gave notice to the other conspirators, and they all impatiently expected their victims.

The first being arrived, Prevan alone received her, and with a seeming eagerness led her to the sanctuary, of which she imagined herself the goddess; then retiring on some slight pretence, was immediately replaced by the insulted lover.

You may guess the confusion. A woman who was not accustomed to adventures of this sort, rendered the triumph very easy. Every reproach that was omitted, was looked on as a favour; and the fugitive slave, again delivered to her first master, thought herself happy in the hope of pardon on resuming her chains. The treaty of peace was ratified in a more solitary place; and the void scene was alternately replaced by the other actors in pretty much the same manner, but with the same finale.

Still each of the women thought herself *sola* in this play. Their astonishment is not to be described, when, called to supper, the three couple reunited: but their confusion was at the summit, when Prevan made his appearance, and had the barbarity to make apologies to the ladies, which, by disclosing their secrets, convinced them fully how much they had been tricked.

They sat down, however, to table, and recovering from their confusion, the men gave themselves up to mirth, and the women yielded. It is true, their hearts were all full of rancour; but yet the conversation was nevertheless amorous; gaiety kindled desire, which brought additional charms; and this astonishing revel lasted till morning. At parting, the women had reason to think themselves forgiven: but the men, who preserved their resentment, entirely broke off the connection the next day; and not satisfied with having abandoned their fickle ladies, in revenge, published the adventure. Since, one has been shut up in a convent, and the other two are exiled to their estates in the country.

Thus you have heard Prevan's history. And now I leave you to determine whether you will add to his fame, and be yoked to his triumphal chariot Your letter has made me really uneasy; and I wait with the utmost impatience a more explicit and prudent answer to my last.

Adieu, my lovely friend! Be diffident of whimsical or pleasing ideas, which you are rather apt to be readily seduced by. Remember, that in the course you run, wit alone is not sufficient: that one single imprudent step becomes an irremediable evil: and permit prudent friendship to sometimes guide your pleasures.

Adieu! I love you notwithstanding, as much as if you was rational.
Sept. 18, 17 —.

LETTER LXXX.

CHEVALIER DANCENY *to* CECILIA VOLANGES.

Cecilia, my dear Cecilia! when shall we see each other again? How shall I live without you? Where shall I find strength or resolution? No, never, never, shall I be able to bear this cruel absence. Each day adds to my misery, without the least prospect of its having an end. Valmont, who had promised me assistance and consolation; Valmont neglects, and, perhaps, forgets me. He is with his love, and no longer acquainted with the sufferings of absence. He has not wrote to me, although he forwarded me the last letter; and yet it is on him I depend to know when and by what means I shall have the happiness to see you. He, then, can say nothing. You even do not mention a syllable about it. Surely it cannot be, that you no longer wish for it. Ah, my Cecilia! I am very unhappy. I love you more than ever: but this passion, which was the delight of my life, is now become my torment.

No, I will no longer live thus. I must see you, if it was but for a moment. When I rise, I say to myself I shall see her no more. Going to bed, I say, I have not seen her: and notwithstanding the length of the days, not a moment of happiness for me. All is grief, all is despair; and all those miseries arrive from whence I expected all my joys. You will have an idea of my situation, if you add to all this, my uneasiness on your account. I am incessantly thinking of you; and ever with grief. If I see you unhappy and afflicted, I bear a part in your misfortunes; if I see you in tranquillity and consoled, my griefs are redoubled. Everywhere and in every circumstance am I miserable.

Ah! it was not thus when you were here; every thing was then delight: the certainty of seeing you made absence supportable. You knew how I employed my time. If I fulfilled any duties, they rendered me more worthy of you; if I cultivated any science, it was in hopes to be more pleasing to you, whenever the distractions of the world drew me from you. At the opera, I sought to discover what would please you. A concert recalled to my mind your talents, and our pleasing occupations in company. In my walks, I eagerly sought the most slight resemblance of you. I compared you to all wherever you had the advantage. Every moment of the day was distinguished by a new homage, and each evening laid the tribute at your feet.

What is now left me? Melancholy grief, and the slight hope which Valmont's silence diminishes, and yours converts into uneasiness. Ten leagues only separate us: and yet this short space becomes an insurmountable obstacle to me; and when I implore the assistance of my friend and of my love, both are cold and silent; far from assisting, they will not even answer me.

What, then, is become of the active friendship of Valmont? But what is become of the tender sentiments which inspired you with that readiness of finding out means of daily seeing each other? I remember, sometimes I found myself obliged to sacrifice them to considerations and to duties. What did you then not say to me? By how many pretexts did you not combat my reasons? I beg you will remember, my Cecilia, that my reasons always gave way to your wishes. I do not pretend to make any merit of it. What you wished to obtain, I was impatient to grant; but I, in turn, now make a request; and what is that request? Only to see you a moment; to renew, to receive the assurance of eternal love. Is it not, then, any longer your happiness as well as mine? I reject this desponding idea, which is the summit of misery. You love me; yes, you will always love me. I believe it; I am sure of it; and I shall never doubt it: but my situation is dreadful, and I can no longer support it. Adieu, Cecilia!.

Sept. 18, 17 — .

LETTER LXXXI.

The MARCHIONESS DE MERTEUIL *to the* VISCOUNT DE VALMONT.

How your fears raise my compassion! How much they convince me of my superiority over you! So you want to teach me how to conduct myself! Ah, my poor Valmont! what a distance there is still between you and me! No; all the pride of your sex would not be sufficient to fill up the interval that is between us. Because you are not able to execute my schemes, you look upon them as impossible. It well becomes you, who are both proud and weak, to attempt to decide on my measures, and give your opinion of my resources. Upon my word, Viscount, your advice has put me out of temper. I cannot conceal it.

That to hide your incredible awkwardness with your Presidente, you should display as a triumph the having disconcerted for a moment this weak woman who loves you, I am not displeased. That you should have obtained from her a look, I smile, and pass over. That feeling, in spite of you, the insignificancy of your conduct, you should hope to deceive my attention, by flattering me with the sublime effort you have made to bring together two children, who are eager to see each other, and who, I will take upon me to say, are indebted to me only for this eagerness; that I will also pass over. That, lastly, you should plume yourself on those brilliant acts, to tell me in a magisterial tone, that *it is better employ one's time in executing their projects than in relating them;* that vanity hurts me not; I forgive it. But that you should take upon you to imagine I stand in need of your prudence; I should go astray, if I did not pay a proper regard to your advice; that I ought to sacrifice a whim, or a pleasure, to it: upon my word, Viscount, that would be raising your pride too much for the confidence which I have condescended to place in you.

What have you then done, that I have not surpassed by a million of degrees? You have seduced, ruined several women: but what difficulties had you to encounter? What obstacles to surmount? Where is the merit that may be truly called yours? A handsome figure, the effect of mere chance; a gracefulness, which custom generally gives; some wit, it's true, but which nonsense would upon occasion supply as well; a tolerable share of impudence, which is solely owing to the facility of your first successes. Those, I believe, are all your abilities, if I am not mistaken; for as to the celebrity which you have acquired, you will not insist, I presume, that I should set any great value on the art of publishing or seizing an opportunity of scandal.

As to your prudence and cunning, I do not speak of myself, but where is the woman that has not more of it than you? Your very Presidente leads you like a babe.

Believe me, Viscount, one seldom acquires the qualities one thinks unnecessary. As you engage without danger, you should act without precaution. As for you men, your defeats are only a success the less. In this unequal struggle, our good fortune is not to be losers; and your misfortune, not to be gainers. When I would even grant you equal talents with us, how much more must we surpass you by the necessity we are under of employing them continually?

Let us suppose, that you make use of as much address to overcome us, as we do to defend ourselves, or to surrender; you will, at least, agree with me, it becomes useless after you succeed. Entirely taken up with some new inclination, you give way to it without fear, without reserve; its duration is a matter of no consequence to you.

And really those reciprocal attachments, given and received, to speak in the love cant, you alone have it in your power to keep or break. Happy yet do the women think themselves, when in your fickleness you prefer secrecy to scandal, or are satisfied with a mortifying abandonment, and that you do not make the idol of to-day the victim of to-morrow.

But if an unfortunate woman should first feel the weight of her chains, what risks does she not run if she attempts to extricate herself from them, if she should dare to struggle against them? She trembling strives to put away the man her heart detests. If he persists, what was granted to love must be given to fear; her arms are open, while her heart is shut; her prudence should untie with dexterity those same bonds you would have broken. She is without resource, at the mercy of her enemy, if he is incapable of generosity, which is seldom to be met with in him; for if he is sometimes applauded for possessing it, he is never blamed for wanting it.

You will not, doubtless, deny those self-evident propositions. If, however, you have seen me disposing of opinions and events; subjecting those formidable men to my whims and fancies; taking from the one the will, and from the other the power, of annoying me. If I have discovered the secret, according to my roving taste, to detach the one, and reject the other, those dethroned tyrants becoming my slaves; if in the midst of those frequent revolutions, my reputation has been still preserved unsullied; should you not from thence have concluded, that, born to revenge my sex and command yours, I found out means unknown to any that went before me.

Ah, keep your advice and your fears for those infatuated women, who call themselves sentimental; whose exalted imaginations would make one believe, that Nature had placed their senses in their heads; who, having never reflected, blend incessantly the lover with love; who, possessed with that ridiculous illusion, believe that he alone with whom they have sought pleasure is the sole trustee of it, and, true to enthusiasm, have the same respect and faith for the priest that is due to the Divinity only.

Reserve your fears for those who, more vain than prudent, do not know when to consent or break off.

But tremble for those active, yet idle women, whom you call *sentimental*, on whom love so easily and powerfully takes possession; who feel the necessity of being taken up with it, even when they don't enjoy it; and, giving themselves up without reserve to the fermentation of their ideas, bring forth those soft but dangerous letters, and do not dread confiding in the object that causes them these proofs of their weakness; imprudent creatures! who in their actual lover cannot see their future enemy.

But what have I to do in common with those inconsiderate women? When have you seen me depart from the rules I have laid down to myself, and abandon my own principles? I say, my own principles, and I speak it with energy, for they are not like those of other women, dealt out by chance, received without scrutiny, and followed through custom; they are the proofs of my profound reflections; I have given them existence, and I can call them my own work.

Introduced into the world whilst yet a girl, I was devoted by my situation to silence and inaction; this time I made use of for reflection and observation. Looked upon as thoughtless and heedless, paying little attention to the discourses that were held out to me, I carefully laid up those that were meant to be concealed from me.

This useful curiosity served me in the double capacity of instruction and dissimulation. Being often obliged to hide the objects of my attention from the eyes of those who surrounded me, I endeavoured to guide my own at my will. I then learnt to take up at pleasure that dissipated air which you have so often praised. Encouraged by those first successes, I endeavoured to regulate in the same manner the different motions of my person. Did I feel any chagrin, I endeavoured to put on an air of serenity, and even an affected cheerfulness; carried my zeal so far, that I used to put myself to voluntary pain; and tried my temper, by seeming to express a satisfaction; laboured with the same care and trouble to repress the sudden tumult of unexpected joy. It is thus that I gained that ascendancy over my countenance which has so often astonished you.

I was yet very young and unconcerned, but still reflected. My thoughts were my own, and I was exasperated to have them either surprised or drawn from me against my will. Provided with such arms, I immediately began to try their utility. Not satisfied with the closeness of my character, I amused myself with assuming different ones. Confident of my actions, I studied my words; I regulated the one and the other according to circumstances, and sometimes according to whim. From that moment I became selfish; and no longer showed any desire, but what I thought useful to me.

This labour had so far fixed my attention on the characters of the physiognomy, and the expression of the countenance, that I acquired the penetrating glance, which experience, however, has taught me not to place an entire confidence in, but which has so seldom deceived me.

I had scarce attained my fifteenth year, when I was mistress of those talents to which the greatest part of our female politicians owe their reputation, and had only attained the first rudiments of the science I was so anxious to acquire.

You may well imagine, that like all other young girls, I wanted to be acquainted with love and pleasure: but never having been in a convent, having no confidant, and being moreover strictly watched by a vigilant mother, I had only vague ideas. Nature even, which certainly I have had since every reason to be satisfied with, had not yet given me any indication. I may say, she silently wrought to perfect her work. My head alone fermented. I did not wish for enjoyment; I wanted knowledge: my strong propensity for instruction suggested the means.

I was sensible, the only man I could apply to on this occasion without danger was my confessor. As soon as I was determined, I got the better of my bashfulness. I accused myself of a fault I had not committed, and declared I had done *all that women do*. Those were the exact words: but when I spoke thus, I really had no idea of what I expressed. My expectations were neither entirely satisfied, nor altogether disappointed; the dread of discovering myself prevented my information: but the good father made the crime so heinous, that I concluded the pleasure must be excessive; and the desire of tasting it succeeded that of knowing it.

I don't know how far this desire might have carried me; being then totally unexperienced, the first opportunity would have probably ruined me: but fortunately a few days after my mother informed me that I was to be married. Immediately the certainty of coming to the knowledge of every thing stifled my curiosity, and I came a virgin to Mr. de Merteuil's arms.

I waited with unconcern the period that was to resolve my doubts; and I had occasion for reflection, to assume a little fear and embarrassment. This first night, which generally fills the mind with so much joy or apprehension, offered me only an opportunity of experience, pleasure, and pain. I observed every thing with the utmost exactitude, and those different sensations furnished matter for reflection.

This kind of study soon began to be pleasing: but faithful to my principles, and knowing, as it were, by instinct, that no one ought to be less in my confidence than my husband, I determined, for no other reason than because I had my feeling, to appear to him impassible. This affected coldness laid the foundation for that blind confidence which he ever after placed in me: and in consequence of more reflection, I threw in an air of dissipation over my behaviour, to which my youth gave a sanction; and I never appeared more childish than when I praised him most profusely.

Yet, I must own, at first I suffered myself to be hurried away by the bustle of the world, and gave myself up entirely to its most trifling dissipations. After a few months M. de Merteuil having brought me to his dreary country house, to avoid the dulness of a rural life, I again resumed my studies; and being surrounded by people whose inferiority sheltered me from suspicion, I gave myself a loose in order to improve my experience. It was then I was ascertained that love, which is represented as the first cause of all our pleasure, is at most but the pretence.

M. de Merteuil's sickness interrupted those pleasing occupations. I was obliged to accompany him to town, where he went for advice. He died a short time after, as you know; and though, to take all in all, I had no reason to complain of him, nevertheless I was very sensibly affected with the liberty my widowhood gave me, which had so pleasing a prospect.

My mother imagined that I would go into a convent, or would go back to live with her: I refused both one and the other: the only sacrifice I made to decency was to return to the country, where I had yet some observations to make.

I strengthened them by reading, but don't imagine that it was all of that kind you suppose: I studied my morals in romances, my opinions amongst the philosophers, and even sought amongst our most severe moralists, what was required of us. — Thus I was ascertained of what one might do, how one ought to think, and the character one should assume. Thus fixed on those three objects, the last only offered some difficulties in the execution: I hoped to conquer them; I ruminated on the means.

I began to be disgusted with my rustic pleasures; they were not sufficiently variegated for my active mind, and felt the necessity of coquetry to reconcile me to love; not really to be sensible of it, but to feign it, and inspire it in others. In vain I have been told, and had read, that this passion was not to be feigned. I saw clearly, that to acquire it, it was sufficient to blend the spirit of an author with the talent of a comedian. I practised those two characters, and perhaps with some success; but, instead of courting the vain applause of the theatre, I determined to turn what so many others sacrificed to vanity, to my own happiness.

A year was spent in those different employments. My mourning being expired, I returned to town with my grand projects, but did not expect the first obstacle which fell in my way.

The austere retreat and long solitude I bad been accustomed to, had given me such an air of prudery as frightened our prettiest fellows, and left me a prey to a crowd of tiresome gallants, who all made pretensions to my person; the difficulty was, not to refuse them; but several of those refusals were not agreeable to my family: I lost in those domestic broils the time which I flattered myself to make so charming a use. I was obliged then to recall the one, and disperse the others, to be guilty of some frivolities, and to take the same pains to hurt my reputation that I had taken to preserve it. In this I easily succeeded, as you may very well imagine; but, not being swayed by any passion, I only did what I judged necessary, and dealt out prudently some little acts of volatility.

As soon as I had accomplished my aim, I stopped short, gave the credit of my reformation to some women, who not having any pretensions to beauty or attractions, wrapt themselves up in merit and virtue. This resolution was of great importance, and turned out better than I could have expected; those grateful duennas became my apologists, and their blind zeal for what they called their own work, was carried to such a length, that upon the least conversation that was held about me, the whole prude party exclaimed shame and scandal! The same means acquired me also the good opinion of our women of talents, who, convinced that I did not pursue the same objects they did, chose me for the subject of their praise, whenever they asserted they did not scandalize every body.

However, my former conduct brought back the lovers; to keep the balance even between them and my new female friends, I exhibited myself as a woman not averse to love, but difficult, and whom the excess of delicacy rendered superior to love.

Then I began to display upon the grand theatre the talents I had acquired: my first care was to acquire the name of invincible; in order to obtain it, the men who were not pleasing to me were the only ones whose addresses I seemed to accept. I employed them usefully in procuring me the honours of resistance, whilst I gave myself up without dread to the favoured lover; but my assumed timidity never permitted him to appear with me in public company, whose attention was always thus drawn off to the unfortunate lover.

You know how expeditious I am in my decisions; this proceeds from my observation, that it is always the preparatory steps which betray women's secrets. Let one do what they will, the *ton* is never the same before as after success. This difference does not escape the attentive observer; and I have found it always less dangerous to be mistaken in my choice, than to suffer myself to be seen through; I moreover gain by this conduct, to remove probabilities on which only a judgment may be formed.

Those precautions, and that of never corresponding, to give any proof of my defeat, may appear satisfactory; however, I never thought them sufficient. Examining my own heart, I studied that of others; then I found, there is no person whatever who has not a secret that it is important should not be revealed; an established truth of which antiquity seems to have been more sensible than we are, and of which, perhaps, the history of Samson may have been an ingenious emblem. Like another Dalilah, I always employed my power in discovering this important secret. Ah! how many of our modern Samsons do I not hold by the hair under my scissars! Those I have no dread of; they are the only ones that I sometimes take a pleasure in mortifying. More pliant with others, I endeavour to render them fickle, to avoid appearing inconstant myself. A feigned friendship, an apparent confidence, some generous dealings, the flattering idea that each was possessed with, of being my only lover, has secured discretion; in short, when all those means have failed, I have known how to stifle beforehand, (foreseeing my rapture), under the cloak of ridicule and calumny, the credit those dangerous men might obtain.

What I now tell you, you have often seen me put in practice; and yet you call my prudence in question! Don't you recollect, when you first began your courtship to me? I never was more flattered; I sighed for you before I saw you. Captivated by your reputation, you seemed to be wanting to my glory; I burned with the desire of encountering you face to face; it was the only one of my inclinations that ever took a moment's ascendancy over me; yet, had you been inclined to ruin me, what means had you in your power? Idle conversations that leave no traces after them, that your reputation even would have rendered suspicious, and a set of facts without probability, the sincere recital of which would have had the appearance of a romance badly assimilated. It is true, you have since been in possession of all my secrets; but you are sensible how our interests are united, and which of us two ought to be taxed with imprudence.[1]

Since I am in the humour of giving you an account of myself, I will do it with the utmost exactitude. — I think I hear you say I'm at least at the mercy of my chambermaid! Truly, if she is not in the secret of my sentiments, she is at least in that of my actions. When you spoke to me on this subject formerly, I only answered you, I was sure of her; the proof this answer was then sufficient to make you easy, is, you have since confided in her, and for your own account; but now Prevan gives you umbrage, that your head is turned, I doubt much you'll not take my word: you must, then, be edified.

First, this girl is my foster-sister; this tie, which appears nothing to us, has a great influence with people of her condition: moreover, I am in possession of her secrets; she is the victim of a love intrigue, and would have been ruined if I had not saved her. Her parents, armed at all points with sentiments of honour, wanted to have her shut up: they applied to me about it; I instantly saw how useful their resentment might be to me, and seconded their intentions; solicited the order from court, which I obtained; then suddenly, preferring clemency, brought her parents round, employing my credit with the old minister of state, and prevailed on them to depute me the trustee in this business, to stop or demand the execution of it, according as I should think the behaviour of the girl would deserve. She knows, then, her fate rests in my hands; and if, which is impossible, those powerful motives would not prevent, is it not evident, that her conduct being laid open, and her punishment authenticated, it would soon wipe away all credit to her tale?

Add to all these precautions, which I call fundamental ones, a thousand others, either local or eventual, that reflection and habitude would produce, if needful, the detail of which would be too minute, but the practice very important, and which you must take the trouble to collect in the whole of my conduct, if you want to arrive at the knowledge of them.

But to pretend that I, who have taken so much pains, should not receive any benefit, after having raised myself so much above other women by my assiduous labours; — that I should consent to creep, like them, between imprudence and timidity; but, above all, I should dread a man so far as to find my salvation only in flight. No, Viscount; I must conquer or perish. As to Prevan, I must and will have him. He will tell, you say: but he shall not tell. This, in a few words, is our romance.

Sept. 20, 17 — .

[1] Hereafter will be seen, in the 152d Letter, not Mr. de Valmont's secret, but pretty nearly of what kind it was; and the reader will perceive, that we could throw no more light on that subject.

LETTER LXXII.

CECILIA VOLANGES *to the* CHEVALIER DANCENY.

My God! what trouble your letter gives me! I had great reason, to be sure, to be impatient to receive it. I expected to have received some consolation, and am now more afflicted than ever. I could not help crying when I read it. But that is not what I reproach you with; for I have often cried already upon your account, without giving me so much trouble: but now the case is altered.

What is it, then, you mean to say? That your love is now a torment to you; that you can't live any longer thus, nor bear to be so circumstanced? What! will you cease loving me, because it is not quite so easy to see me as formerly? Don't think I am happier than you; on the contrary: but I love you the more notwithstanding. If Mr. de Valmont has not wrote to you, it is not my fault. I could not prevail on him; because I have never been alone with him; we have agreed never to speak to one another before company; and all upon your account, that he may the sooner do what you would have him. I don't say, but what I wish it as well as you; and you ought to be very sure of it: but what would you have me do? If you think it is so easy, find out the way; it is what I wish for as much as you do.

Do you think it so pleasing to be scolded every day by mamma? She who before never said any thing to me, now it is worse than if I was in a convent. I used to be consoled thinking it was for you; even sometimes, I was very glad of it. Now I perceive you are vexed without my giving any occasion for it. I am more melancholy than for any thing that has happened till now.

Nothing can be more difficult than to receive your letters; so that if Mr. de Valmont was not so complaisant and dexterous as he is, I should not know what to do; and it is still more difficult to write to you. In the morning I dare not, because my mamma is always near me, and comes every moment into my chamber. Sometimes I can do it in the afternoon, under pretence of singing or playing on the harp. I must stop at the end of every line, that they may hear me play. Fortunately my chambermaid falls asleep sometimes at night, and I tell her I can go to bed very well alone; that she may go, and leave me the candle; I am sometimes obliged to hide behind the curtain, that no one may see the light, and listen; for, on the least noise, I hide every thing in my bed, lest any one should come. I wish you were only here to see: you would be convinced one must have a great affection to do all this. In short, you may depend I do every thing in my power.

I can't help telling you I love you, and will always love you. I never told you so with more sincerity, yet you are angry. You assure me, however, before I told you so, that it would be enough to make you happy; you can't deny it, for it is in your letters: although I have them no longer, I remember it as well as when I used to read them every day; and because we are now absent, you have altered your mind; but this absence will not last for ever, perhaps. Good God! how unhappy I am; and you are the cause of it all.

Now I think of it, about your letters; I hope you have kept all those that mamma took from me, and that she sent you back. Surely the time will come, when I shan't be so closely watched as I am at present, and you will give them to me again. How happy shall I be, when I can keep them always, without any one prying into them. — Now, I return them back to Mr. de Valmont, as it would otherwise be running too great a risk, and yet I never return any but it gives me a great deal of trouble.

Adieu, my dear friend! I love you with all my heart, and I will love you all my life. I hope now you will not be vexed any more; if I was sure of it, I would not be so myself. Write to me as soon as you can, for I find that until then I shall be always uneasy.

From the Castle of − − , *Sept.* 21, 17 − .

LETTER LXXXIII.

VISCOUNT DE VALMONT, *to the* Presidente DE TOURVEL.

For heaven's sake, Madam, let us renew the conversation so unfortunately interrupted, that I may convince you how different I am from the odious picture that has been drawn of me, and may, at least, enjoy that amiable confidence you placed in me. How many charms do you not add to virtue! How you embellish and make us cherish virtuous sentiments! It is there you are truly enchanting; that is the strongest of all seductions; it is the only one which is truly respectable and powerful.

It is enough to see you, to wish to please you; and to converse with you, to augment this wish: but he that has the happiness to know you, who can sometimes read your mind, soon gives way to a more noble enthusiasm, and, struck with veneration as with love — in your person adores the image of all the virtues. Formed, perhaps, more than any other, to cherish and admire them, but led away by some errors that had fatally drawn me from virtue, it is you have brought me back, who have again made me feel all its charms. Would you impute, then, to criminality this new affection? Will you blame your own work? Would you reproach yourself the interest you ought to take in it? — How can you dread so virtuous a sentiment, and what happiness can be greater than to experience it?

My affection frightens you. You think it too violent, too immoderate; qualify it, then, by a softer passion. Do not reject the obedience I offer you, which I now swear never to withdraw myself from, and in which I shall be ever virtuously employed. What sacrifice would be painful when your heart could dispense the reward? Where is the man so unthinking as not to know how to enjoy the privations he imposes on himself; who would not prefer a word or a look which should be granted him, to all the enjoyments he could steal or surprise? And yet you have believed me to be such a man, and have dreaded me. Ah! why is not your happiness dependent on me? How pleasingly should I be avenged in making you happy! But the influence of barren friendship will not produce it; it is love alone can realize it.

This word alarms you; and, pray, why? A tender attachment, a stronger union, congenial thoughts, the same happiness as the same sorrows; what is there in this that is foreign to you? Yet such is love; such is, at least, the passion you have inspired, and which I feel. It is it that calculates without interest, and rates the actions according to their merit, and not their value, the inexhaustible treasure of sensitive souls; every thing becomes precious formed for it or by it.

Those striking truths, so easy to put in practice, what have they in them frightful? What fears can a man of sensibility occasion you, to whom love will never permit any other happiness than yours. It is now the only vow I make. I would sacrifice every thing to fulfil it, except the sentiment it inspires, which, if you even consent to admit, you shall regulate at will. But let us not suffer it to part us, when it ought to reunite us, if the friendship you have offered me is not a futile word. If, as you told me yesterday, it is the softest sentiment your soul is capable of, let it stipulate between us; I shall not challenge its decree: but in erecting it the judge of love, let it, at least, consent to hear its defence. To refuse to admit it would be unjust, which is not the characteristic of friendship.

A second conversation will not be attended with more inconvenience than the first; chance may furnish the opportunity; you might even appoint the time. I will readily believe I am wrong: but would you not rather recall me by reason, than to combat my opinion? And do you doubt my docility? If I had not been interrupted, perhaps I had already been brought over to your opinion; for your power over me knows no bounds.

I will acknowledge, that this invincible power to which I have surrendered, without daring to examine the irresistible charm that gives you the ascendancy over my thoughts and actions, often alarms me; and, perhaps, this conversation that I now solicit may be formidable to me. Perhaps, after being bound down by my promises, I shall see myself reduced to consume with a flame which I well feel can never be extinguished, without even daring to implore your assistance. Ah! for heaven's sake, Madam, do not abuse your power over me: but if it will make you happier, if I shall appear more worthy of you, how much will my pains be softened by those consoling ideas! Yes, I feel it. Again to converse with you, is furnishing you with stronger arms against me: it is submitting myself entirely to your will. It is easier to make a defence against your letters; it is true, they are your sentiments: but you are not present to give them their full force; yet the pleasure of hearing you induces me to defy the danger; at least, I shall have the happiness of thinking I have done every thing for you even against myself, and my sacrifices will become a homage; too happy, in being able to convince you in a thousand shapes, as I feel it, in a thousand ways, that without self-exception, you are, and always will be, the dearest object of my heart.

Sept. 23, 17 —.

LETTER LXXXIV.

VISCOUNT DE VALMONT *to* CECILIA VOLANGES.

You saw how we were disappointed yesterday. I could not find an opportunity to deliver you the letter I had the whole day; and I don't know whether I shall be more successful this day. I am afraid of hurting you by my over zeal; and should never forgive myself, if by my imprudence you should suffer; that would make my friend distracted, and you miserable. Yet I am not insensible to a lover's impatience. I feel how painful it is in your situation to experience delay in the only consolation you are capable of receiving at this time. By dint of thinking on means to remove obstacles, I have found one that will be pretty easy if you will but give your assistance.

I think I remarked, the key of your chamber door, that opens into the gallery, hangs always upon your mamma's chimney-piece. Every thing would become easy, if we were once in possession of that key; but if it is not practicable, I can procure another exactly similar, which will answer the purpose: it will be sufficient I should have the key for an hour or two. You can easily find an opportunity of taking it; and that it may not be missed, you have one belonging to me, which resembles it pretty much, and the difference won't be perceived unless it is tried, which I don't think will be attempted. You must only take care to tie a blue ribband to it, like the one that is to your own.

You must endeavour to get this key to-morrow or the next day at breakfast, because it will be then easier to give it me, and it may be put in its place again in the evening, which would be the time your mamma might take notice of it. I can return it to you at dinner, if we act properly.

You know, when we go from the saloon to the dining room, Madame de Rosemonde always comes last; I will give her my hand; and all you have to do will be to quit your tapestry frame slowly, or let something fall, so that you make stay a little behind; then you will be able to take the key, which I will hold behind me: but you must not neglect, as soon as you have taken it, to join my old aunt; and make her some compliments. If you should accidentally let the key fall, don't be disconcerted; I will pretend it is myself, and I'll answer for all.

The small confidence your mamma shows you, and the moroseness of her behaviour, authorises this little deceit: but it is, moreover, the only means to continue to receive Danceny's letters, and to send him yours. Every other is too dangerous, and might irretrievably ruin you both; and my prudent friendship would reproach me for ever, if I was to attempt any other.

When I am once master of the key, there will be still some other precautions to be taken against the noise the door and lock may make, but them are easily removed. You will find, under the same clothes-press where I left your paper some oil and a feather. You sometimes go into your room alone, and you must take that opportunity to oil the lock and the hinges; the only thing you have to take care of is, that no drops may fall on the floor, which might discover you. You must also take care to wait till night comes, because if you manage this business dexterously, as I know you are capable of, nothing will appear in the morning.

If, however, any thing should be perceived, don't hesitate to say it was the servant that rubs the furniture; in that case, perhaps, it would be necessary to tell the time and the conversation that passed: as, that he takes this precaution against rust for all the locks that are not constantly used; for you must be sensible it would not be very probable that you should be a witness of it without asking the reason. Those are little details that aid probability, and probability makes lies of no consequence; as it takes away all curiosity to verify them.

After you have read this letter once, I beg you to read it again, and imprint it well in your memory; for first one must understand well what one has to do, and then, again, that you should be certain I have omitted nothing. As I am little used to employ artifice or cunning for my own occasion, nothing but the strong friendship that I have for Danceny, and my compassion for you, could determine me to make use of those innocent methods. I hate every thing that has the appearance of deceit; that is my character: but your misfortunes so sensibly affect me, I would attempt everything to soften them.

You may believe, when once this communication is established between us, it will be much easier for me to procure you a meeting with Danceny, which he has so much at heart; but yet don't mention all this to him, as it would only increase his impatience, and the time is not entirely come to satisfy it. You ought rather, I think, to calm than to irritate it; but that I leave to your own delicacy. Adieu, my pretty pupil; for now you are my pupil. Love your tutor a little: but, above all, be very tractable, and you will find the benefit of it. I am employed in endeavouring to make you happy; which, I promise you, will add much to my own.

Sept. 24, 17—.

LETTER LXXXV.

MARCHIONESS DE MERTEUIL *to* VISCOUNT DE VALMONT.

At length you will be satisfied, and do me justice; no longer blend me with the rest of womankind: I have at last put an end to my adventure with Prevan, and you shall judge which of the two has a right to boast The recital will not be so amusing as the action; neither would it be just, whilst you have done nothing but argue well or ill on this matter, you should enjoy as much pleasure as me, who employed my time and care in this business.

But if you have any great affair in hand, any enterprise wherein this dangerous rival is your competitor, return; he has left you a clear stage, at least for some time; and perhaps will never recover the blow I have given him.

What a happy man you are, to have me for a friend! I am your good genius. You languish in absence from the beauty that possesses your heart; I speak the word, and instantly you are with her: you wish to be revenged of a mischievous woman: I point out the place where you are to strike, and deliver her up to you: again, to set aside a formidable competitor, you still invoke me, and I grant your petition. Upon my word, if you don't employ the remainder of your days in demonstrating your gratitude, you are a base man: but to return to my adventure, and its origin. The rendezvous given out so loud at coming out of the opera[1] was heard, as I expected. Prevan was there, and when the Marechale told him obligingly, that she was happy to see him, twice running, on her public day, he took care to reply, that since Tuesday he had got rid of a thousand appointments, to have it in his power to wait upon her this evening; *a word to the wise:* however, as I was determined to be certain whether or not I was the true object of this flattering eagerness, I was determined to oblige my new admirer, to make a choice between me and his reigning passion. I declared I would not play, and he made a thousand pretences not to play: thus my first triumph was over Lansquenet.

I engrossed the bishop of — — for my conversation; chose him on account of his relationship with the hero of the adventure, for whom I wished to smooth the way to make his approaches: was, moreover, glad to have a respectable witness, who could upon occasion answer for my conduct and conversation: this arrangement succeeded.

After the customary vague chat, Prevan having soon made himself master of the conversation, engaged, upon different subjects, to endeavour to find out that which was most agreeable to me. The sentimental I rejected, as not worthy of credit. I stopped, by my serious air, his gaiety, which seemed too volatile for an opening: then he returned to delicate friendship; and this was the subject that engaged us.

The bishop did not come down to supper; Prevan gave me his hand, and consequently placed himself at table by me: I must be just; he kept up our private conversation with great address, as if he was only taken up with the general conversation, to which he seemed all attention. At the dessert, a new piece was mentioned that was to be played the Monday following at the French Comedy. — I expressed some regret at not being provided with a box; he offered me his, which I refused, as usual: to which he replied, with great good humour, that I did not understand him, for, certainly, he would not offer his lodge to a person he did not know; he only meant to inform me that Madame la Marechale had the disposal of it; she acquiesced to this piece of humour, and I accepted the invitation. Being returned to the saloon, he begged, as you may suppose, a seat in this box; and as the Marechale, who treats him very familiarly, promised it to him if he behaved himself well, he took the opportunity of one of those double entendre conversations, for which you so profusely praise him, and throwing himself at her knees as a naughty child, under pretence of begging her advice and opinion, he said a great many tender and flattering things, which it was easy for me to apply to myself. Many of the company not having returned to play after supper, the conversation became more general and less interesting, but our eyes spoke a great deal — I should say his, for mine had one language only, that of surprise; he must have imagined that I was astonished, and amazingly taken up with the prodigious impression he had made on me. I believe I left him pretty well satisfied; and I was no less contented myself.

The Monday following I went to the French Comedy, as was agreed: notwithstanding your literary curiosity, I cannot give you any account of the representation, and can only tell you, that Prevan has an admirable talent for flattery, and that the piece was hooted. I was somewhat troubled to see an evening so near an end, from which I promis'd myself so much pleasure, and, in order to prolong it, I requested the Marechale to sup with me, which gave me an opportunity to invite the lovely flatterer; he only begged time to disengage himself with the Countesses de P— —.[2] This name raised my indignation; I saw plainly he was beginning to make them his confidants; I called to mind your prudent advice, and determined — — to pursue the adventure, as I was certain it would cure him of this dangerous indiscretion.

Being a stranger in my company, which was that night very small, he paid me the usual compliments, and when we went to supper, offered me his hand — I was wicked enough, when I accepted it, to affect a light tremor, and, as I walked, to cast my eyes downwards, accompanied with a difficulty of respiration — assumed the appearance of foreseeing my defeat, and to dread my conqueror; he instantly remarked it, and the traitor immediately changed his tone and behaviour: he was polite before, but now became all tenderness; — not but the conversation was pretty much the same, — the circumstances required it; but his look was not so lively, yet more flattering; the tone of his voice was softer; his smile was not that of art but satisfaction; and his discourse gradually falling from his sallies, wit gave way to delicacy. Pray, good Sir, what could you have done more?

On my side, I began to grow thoughtful to such a degree that it was taken notice of; and when I was reproached with it, I had the address to defend myself so awkwardly, and to cast a quick, timid, and disconcerted glance at Prevan, to make him imagine that all my fear was lest he should guess at the cause of my confusion.

After supper, I took the opportunity, whilst the good Marechale was telling one of those stories she had repeated a hundred times before, to place myself upon my sofa, in that kind of lassitude which a tender reverie brings on. I was not sorry Prevan should see me thus; and he really did me the honour of a most particular, attention. You may very well imagine my timid eyes did not dare lift themselves up to my conqueror, but being directed towards him in a more humble manner, they soon informed me I had obtained my end: but still it was necessary to persuade him I also shared it, and as the Marechale said it was time to retire, I exclaimed in a soft and tender tone, "Oh, good God, I was so happy there!" However, I rose; but before we parted, I asked her how she intended to dispose of herself, to have an opportunity of saying, I intended to stay at home the day after to-morrow; on which we all parted.

Then I sat down to reflect; I had no doubt but Prevan would improve the kind of rendezvous I had just given, that he would come time enough to find me alone, and the attack would be carried on with spirit; but I was certain that, reputation apart, he would not behave with that kind of familiarity which no well-bred person ever permits himself, only with intriguing or unexperienced women; and I did not doubt of my success, if he once let slip the word love, or if he even made any pretension to draw it from me.

How convenient it is to be connected with you men of principle! Sometimes the quarrels of lovers disconcert through timidity, or embarrass by its violent transports; it is a kind of fever which has its hot and cold fits, and sometimes varies its symptoms; but your regular progressions are easily seen through; the first salutation, the deportment, the *ton*, the conversation, I knew all the evening before: I shall not, then, give you an account of the conversation, which you will readily conceive; only observe, that in my feigned defence I helped him all in my power; embarrassments to give him time to speak, bad arguments to be discussed, fears and diffidence to bring on protestations, the perpetual requisition from him, *I beg but one word,* that silence on my part which only seemed to make him wish for it more; and besides all this a hand often squeezed, always drawn back, and never refused; thus a whole day would have passed, and we should have passed another in this frivolity, perhaps would have been still engaged in the same, if we had not heard a coach coming into my court. This happy mischance made his solicitations more pressing, and when I found myself safe from all surprise, after having breathed a long sigh, I granted the precious word. Soon after company came in.

Prevan requested to visit me the morning following, to which I consented; being careful of myself, I ordered my waiting maid to stay during the whole time of this visit in my bed chamber, from whence you know, one may see every thing that passes in my dressing room. Our conversation was easy, and both having the same desires, we were soon agreed; it was necessary to get rid of this troublesome spectator; that was where I waited for him.

Then giving him an account of my domestic life, I easily persuaded him we should never find a favourable opportunity, and he must look upon it a kind of miracle that which he had yesterday, and was attended with such dangerous consequences as might expose me, as there was every instant company coming into the saloon. I did not fail to add, those were long established customs in my family, which, until then, had never been varied, and at the same time insisted on the impossibility of altering them, as they would expose me to the reflections of my servants. He endeavoured to affect grief, to be out of humour, to tell me I had very little love: you may guess what an impression that made on me. Being determined to strike the decisive blow, I called tears to my assistance. It was the real scene in Zara, *You weep*. The ascendant he thought he had gained over me, and the hope he conceived of ruining me in his own way, supplied him with all the love of Orosmane.

This theatrical scene being over, we returned to the settling our measures. No probability of success in the day, our thoughts were taken up with the night; but my porter was an insurmountable obstacle, and I could not agree to any attempt to corrupt him: he then proposed the small door of my garden; that I had foreseen. I pretended a dog there, that was quiet and silent in the day-time, but a mere devil at night. The facility with which I gave into all his schemes served to encourage him, and he soon proposed the most ridiculous expedient, which was the one I accepted.

First, he assured me his domestic was as secret as himself; there he did not deceive me, for one was as secret as the other: I was to give a public supper, he would be of the party, would take his opportunity to slip out alone, his dextrous confidant would call his carriage, open the door, and he, instead of getting in, would slip aside; thus, having disappeared to every body, yet being in my house, the question was, how he should get into my apartment? I must own, that at first my embarrassment was to find out reasons against the project, to have the appearance of destroying it. He answered them by proofs; nothing was more common than this method, he had often made use of it; it was even the one he practised most, as being the least dangerous.

Being convinced by those unanswerable authorities, I candidly owned I had a back-stairs that led very near to my private closet; I could leave the key in the door, and he possibly might shut himself up in it, to wait there without any danger till my women were retired; then, to give more probability to my consent, the moment afterwards I refused, then again consented, only upon condition of the most perfect submission and good behaviour. To sum up all, I wanted to prove my affection, but not to satisfy his.

His departure in the morning, which I had forgot to mention, was settled to be through the little gate in the garden; as he was to go off by day-light, the Cerberus would not speak a word; not a soul passed at that hour, and my people were all to be in a profound sleep. If you are astonished at this heap of nonsense, you must forget our situation: what business had we for better arguments? All that he required was, that the business should be known, and I was very certain it never should: the day after was fixed for the execution.

Observe, here is an affair settled, and no one has ever yet seen Prevan in my company; he offers his box for a new piece, I accept of a place in it; I invite this woman to supper during the performance, in Prevan's presence; I can scarcely dispense proposing to him to make one; he accepts my offer; two days afterwards makes me a ceremonial visit;—he comes, it is true, to visit me the day following, in the morning; but besides, as the morning visits are no longer exceptionable, it belongs to me to judge of this, and I account it trifling.

The fatal day being come, the day on which I was to lose my virtue and reputation, I gave my instructions to my faithful Victoire, and she executed them to admiration.

When evening came, I had a good deal of company; Prevan was announced; I received him with singular politeness, a proof of my slender acquaintance with him; I placed him with the Marechale's party, as it was in her company I had first been acquainted with him: the evening produced nothing but a little note which the discreet lover found means to convey to me, and was burned, according to custom: he informed me, I might depend upon him; it was embellished with all the parasitical phrases of love, happiness, &c., which are never wanting upon such occasions.

At midnight, the parties being all finished, I proposed a short macedoine.[3] In this project I first had in view to favour Prevan's evasion, and at the same time to make it remarkable, which could not fail to happen, considering his reputation as a gamester; I was also glad, if there should hereafter be occasion, it might be remembered I was left alone. The game lasted longer than I had imagined; the devil tempted me; I gave way to my desire, to console the impatient prisoner. I was thus proceeding to my ruin, when I reflected, if I once surrendered, I should abandon the power of keeping him within the necessary bounds of decency for my projects: I had strength enough to resist, and returned not in a very good humour to my place at this abominable game; at last it was finished, and every one departed: I rung for my women, undressed myself expeditiously, and sent them away.

Only think now, Viscount, you see me in my light robe, approaching with a circumspect timid pace, and trembling hand, opening the door to my conqueror. The moment he perceived me, he flew like lightning. What shall I say? I was overcome, totally overcome, before I could speak a word to stop him or defend myself. Afterwards he wanted to take a more commodious situation, and more adapted to our circumstances. He cursed his dress as an obstacle to his complete bliss. He would engage with equal arms; but my extreme timidity opposed his desire, and my tender caresses did not give him time. He was employed in other matters.

His rights were doubled; his pretensions revived: then "Harkee," said I, "so far you have a tolerable pretty story for the two Countesses de P— —, and a thousand others: but I have a great curiosity to know how you will relate the end of this adventure." Then ringing with all my strength, I had my turn, my action was quicker than his speech. He scarcely stammered out a few words, when I heard Victoire calling all my people that she had kept together in her apartment, as I had ordered her; then assuming the tone of a queen, and raising my voice, "Walk out, Sir," said I, "and never dare appear again in my presence." On which all my servants crowded in.

Poor Prevan was distracted, and imagined murder was intended, when in reality it was nothing but a joke, seized his sword; he was mistaken, for my valet-de-chambre, a resolute lusty fellow, grasped him round the body, and soon brought him down. I own, I was very much terrified, ordered them not to use him ill, but let him retire quietly, only to take care he was put out of the house. My servants obeyed my orders: there was a great bustle among them; they were enraged to the highest degree, any one should dare to insult *their virtuous mistress*; they all accompanied the unfortunate Chevalier, with all the noise and scandal I could wish. Victoire alone remained with me, and we repaired the disorder the bed had suffered.

My people returned tumultuously; and I, *still in great emotion*, desired to know by what good fortune they happened to be all up. Victoire said, she had given a supper to two of her friends; that they had sat up in her apartment; and, in short, every thing as had been agreed on. I thanked then all, desired them to retire, directing one of them to go immediately for my physician. I thought I was authorised to guard against the effects of this *dreadful shock*; this was the surest means to give it currency, as well as celebrity.

He came, pitied me much, and prescribed repose. I moreover ordered Victoire to go about the neighbourhood in the morning early to spread the news.

Every thing succeeded so well, that before noon, as soon as my doors were open, my devout neighbour was at my bed's head, to know the truth and the circumstances of this horrible adventure. I was obliged to lament with her a whole hour the corruption of the age. Soon after, I received the enclosed note from the Marechale, and before five, to my great astonishment, M — — [4] waited on me, to make his excuses, as he said, that an officer of his corps should be guilty of such an offence. He was informed of it at dinner at the Marechale's, and immediately sent an order to Prevan, putting him under arrest. I requested he might be forgiven, which he refused. I thought, as an accomplice, I should also be punished, and kept within doors; I ordered my gate to be shut, and to let every one know I was indisposed.

It is to this solitude you are indebted for so long a letter. I shall write one to Madame de Volanges, which she will certainly read publicly, where you will see this transaction as it must be related.

I forgot to tell you, that Belleroche is outrageous, and absolutely determined to fight Prevan. Poor fellow! But I shall have time to cool his brain. In the mean time, I will go to repose my own, which is much fatigued by writing. Adieu, Viscount!

Sept. 25, 17 — .

[1] See Letter the 74th.
[2] See Letter the 70th.
[3] Several persons, perhaps, do not know that a macedoine is a collection of games at hazard, in which each person who cuts the cards has a right to choose when he holds the hand: it is one of the inventions of the age.
[4] The commandant of the corps in which Prevan served.

LETTER LXXXVI.

The Marechale DE — — *to the* MARCHIONESS DE MERTEUIL.

(*Enclosed in the former.*)

My good God! what is this I learn, my dear Madam? Is it possible that little Prevan should be guilty of such an abominable action to you! What is one not exposed to! We can be no longer safe in our own houses! Upon my word, these events are a consolation to age; I shall never forgive myself, as I have been partly the cause of your receiving such a monster into your house; I assure you, if what I hear is true, he shall never more set foot in mine: it is what every one must do that has any sentiments of honour, if they act properly.

I have been informed you was very ill, and have been very uneasy about your state of health; I beg you will let me hear from you; or if you are not able to write, pray let one of your women inform me how you are. A word will be sufficient to relieve my anxiety. I should have been with you this morning; but my doctor will not allow me to miss a day from my bath.

I must go this morning to Versailles on my nephew's business.

Farewell, dear Madam! Depend upon my sincerest friendship.

Paris, Sept. 25, 17 — .

LETTER LXXXVII.

The MARCHIONESS DE MERTEUIL *to* MADAME DE VOLANGES.

My dear and worthy friend, I write this in bed. The most disagreeable accident, and the most impossible to be foreseen, has, by the violent shock and chagrin it has occasioned, given me a fit of illness; not that I have any thing to reproach myself with: but it is always painful to a virtuous woman, who would preserve the modesty of her sex, to have the eyes of the public fixed on her, and I would give the world to have avoided this unhappy adventure. I do not yet know but I shall go to the country until it is blown over. The matter is thus:

I met at the Marechale de — —'s a Mr. Prevan, who you certainly know by name, and was no otherwise known to me; meeting him accidentally at her house, I thought myself safe in looking upon him as good company; his person is tolerable, and he is not deficient in wit; chance, and being tired at play, left me the only woman in company with him and the bishop of — —. Whilst all the others were engaged at lansquenet, we chatted together until supper. At table a new piece was mentioned, which gave him an opportunity of offering his box to the Marechale, who accepted of it; it was agreed I should attend her: this appointment was for Monday last at the French Comedy. As the Marechale was to sup with me after the performance, I proposed to this gentleman to accompany her; he accordingly came. Two days after he paid me a visit, which passed in the usual conversation; not a single word of any thing remarkable; the day following he again visited me in the morning, which, as it was something extraordinary, I thought it was better, instead of making him sensible, by my manner of receiving him, to politely inform him we were not yet on so intimate a footing as he seemed to think; for this reason I sent him that same day a ceremonious invitation to a supper which I gave the day before yesterday. I did not speak four words to him during the whole evening, and he retired as soon as his party was finished. So far you will agree, nothing had the air of an intrigue. After play was over, we made a macedoine, which lasted till two o'clock, and then I went to bed.

My women were gone a full half-hour, when I heard a noise in my apartment. I drew my curtain in a great fright, and saw a man coming in from my closet-door. I shrieked out, and recognised, by my watch light, this Mr. Prevan, who, with a most inconceivable effrontery, bid me not be alarmed, that he would clear up the mystery of his conduct, and requested me not to make any noise. Thus saying, he lighted a bougie. I was frightened to such a degree, that I could not speak a word; his easy and tranquil air petrified me still more: but he had not spoke two words, before I perceived what this pretended mystery was, and my only answer, as you may well believe, was to ring my bell.

By good fortune, my servants, who had been making merry with one of my women, were not gone to bed. My waiting woman, when near my room, heard me speaking very loud, was frightened, and called all my people. Judge you what a scandal! They were enraged; I thought my valet-de-chambre would have killed Prevan. I must own, at that time I was very glad to have such a powerful assistance: but on reflection, I would rather my waiting woman alone had come; she would have been sufficient, and I should, perhaps, have avoided all this noise which afflicts me.

The tumult awoke all the neighbours; the people talked, and since yesterday the news has spread all over Paris. Monsieur de Prevan is a prisoner, by order of the commandant of his corps, who had the politeness to call on me to make an apology. This imprisonment will augment the noise, but I have not been able to prevent it. The court and city have been at my gate, which is shut to every body. The few persons I have admitted have assured me, every one does me justice, and the public resentment is very high against Monsieur de Prevan; he certainly deserves it: but that does not wipe away this disagreeable occurrence.

Moreover, this man has certainly some friends, and who knows what such friends may invent to my prejudice? Good God! how unhappy a young woman is! When she has even sheltered herself against slander, it is not sufficient, she must also silence calumny.

I beg you will let me know what you would have done, and what you would do in my situation, with your opinion. It has always been from you I received the gentlest and most prudent consolations: it is still from you I wish to receive them. Adieu, my dear, good friend! You know the sentiments that attach me to you for ever. I embrace your amiable daughter, and am, &c.

Paris, Dec.. 26, 17—.

END OF THE SECOND VOLUME.

DANGEROUS

CONNECTIONS:

OR,

LETTERS

COLLECTED IN A SOCIETY,

AND

PUBLISHED FOR THE INSTRUCTION OF

OTHER SOCIETIES.

---

*By M. C**** de L ***.*

I have observed the Manners of the Times, and have wrote those Letters.

J.J. Rousseau. Pref. to the New Eloise.

VOL. III.

LONDON:

Printed for T. HOOKHAM,

At his Circulating Library, New Bond Street Corner of Bruton Street.

M.DCC.LXXXIV.

LETTER LXXXVIII.

CECILIA VOLANGES *to the* VISCOUNT DE VALMONT.

Although I have the greatest pleasure in receiving the Chevalier Danceny's letters, and I wish as ardently as he does, we might see each other without interruption, yet I dare not venture to do what you propose. First, I think it too dangerous; the key you desire I should put in the place of the other resembles it pretty much, it is true: but still there is some difference, and mama is so exceedingly watchful, that nothing escapes her; besides, though it has not been used since we came here, an accident might happen, and if it was missed, I should be ruined for ever. Moreover, it would be very wrong to have a double key; that would be too much: it is true, you would take the management of it yourself; but yet if it should come to be known, all the reproach would fall on me, as it would be done for me; not that there is any difficulty in the matter, and I twice had a mind to take it, but something came over me, and I was seized with such a tremor, my resolution failed me. I believe, then, we had better remain as we are.

If you will be so good to continue your friendship as you have done hitherto, you will always find an opportunity to deliver me a letter. Even the last I should have had very readily, had it not been for the accident of your turning about so suddenly. I am very sensible, you cannot be always taken up with those matters as I am: but I would rather have a little patience than run such risks. I am certain Mr. Danceny would be of the same opinion: for whenever he wanted any thing I was not inclined to, he instantly gave it up.

You will find, Sir, with this letter, your own, Mr. Danceny's, and your key. I am, nevertheless, extremely obliged to you for your kindness, which I entreat you to continue to me. I am, indeed, very miserable, and should be much more so, were it not for you: but she is my mother, and I must have patience; and provided Mr. Danceny will always love me, and you do not desert me, I may yet, perhaps, be happy.

I have the honour to be, with the utmost gratitude, Sir, your most humble and obedient servant.

Sept. 26, 17—.

LETTER LXXXIX.

The VISCOUNT DE VALMONT *to the* CHEVALIER DANCENY.

If your affairs do not go on quite so rapidly as you wish, my dear friend, it is not altogether my fault. I have many obstacles to encounter here. Madame de Volanges' vigilance and severity are not the only ones; your young friend also throws some in my way. Whether it proceeds from coldness, or timidity, she will not always do what I advise her; and yet I think I should know better than she what is proper to be done.

I had proposed an easy, commodious, and safe way of delivering your letters to her, and even to smooth the way of the interviews you wish for so much; but I have not been able to determine her to make use of it. This gives me the more concern, as I can't think of any other means of bringing you together; and I am even incessantly terrified at the danger we all three are exposed to on account of your correspondence; you may then very well imagine, I do not choose to risk myself, nor expose you both to it.

Still it would give me the greatest uneasiness, that your little friend's want of confidence in me should deprive me of the pleasure of being useful to you; I think you would do well to write to her on the subject. Act as you think proper; you are to determine; for it is not enough that we serve our friends: we must serve them in the manner the most pleasing to themselves. It might be also one other means of ascertaining the degree of her affection for you; for the woman who retains a will of her own, does not love to that degree she ought. Not that I have any suspicion of her constancy: but she is very young; she is in great awe of her mother, who you already know to be your enemy; therefore it might be dangerous to suffer her to wain her mind from you: however, I would not have you make yourself in the least uneasy, as it is the solicitude of friendship only, and not any diffidence whatever, that makes me so explicit.

I must break off, as I have some important matters of my own to attend. I am not so far advanced as you are: but my passion is as ardent; that is my consolation. And was I to be unsuccessful in my own, it would be a pleasure to think, my time has been well employed if I can be useful in yours. Adieu, my dear friend!

Castle of — —, Sept. 26, 17 —.

LETTER XC.

The Presidente DE TOURVEL *to the* VISCOUNT DE VALMONT.

I much wish, Sir, this letter may not give you uneasiness; or, if it should, I hope it will be alleviated by that which I confess I now experience in writing to you. You should, I think, by this time be sufficiently acquainted with my sentiments, to be assured I would not willingly afflict you; and flatter myself, you are incapable of making me for ever miserable. I beseech you, then, by the tender friendship I have professed, and those softer sentiments, and more sincere than any you have for me, let us no longer see one another. Leave me; and until then, let us avoid particularly those dangerous conversations, when by an unaccountable attraction I am lost in attending to what I ought not to listen to, and forget what I intend to say.

When you joined company with me in the park yesterday, I fully intended telling you what I am now about to write. What was the consequence? Why to be totally engaged on a subject to which I ought never to listen: your love. For heaven's sake! depart from me. Fear not that absence should alter my sentiments for you; for how can I possibly overcome them, when I am no longer able to contend with them. You see I confess my weakness, and I dread less to own it than I do to yield to it: but the command I have lost over my mind, I will still preserve over my actions; this I am determined on, were it at the expence of life.

Alas! the time is not very distant, that I imagined myself proof against such temptations. I felicitated myself on it, I fear, too much; I was, perhaps, too vain of it; and Heaven has punished, and cruelly punished, that pride: but all-merciful, even in the hour in which it strikes us, it warns me again before an utter fall; and I should be doubly guilty, if, being sensible of my weakness, I should abandon my prudence.

You have often told me, you would not desire a happiness purchased at the expence of my tears. Let us no longer talk of happiness; let me, at least, regain some degree of tranquillity.

In acceding to my request, what fresh claims will you not acquire over my heart, and those founded upon virtue! How I shall enjoy my gratitude! I shall owe to you the happiness of entertaining, without any remorse, a sentiment of the most delicious kind. Now, on the contrary, startled at my sentiments and my thoughts, I am equally afraid of occupying my mind either with you or myself. The very idea of you terrifies me. When I cannot fly from it, I combat it. I do not banish it, but repulse it.

Is it not better for us to terminate this state of trouble and anxiety? You, whose tender heart has even in the midst of errors remained the friend of virtue, you will attend to my distressed situation; you will not reject my prayer. A milder but as tender an attachment will succeed these violent agitations. Then regaining my existence through your beneficence, I will cherish that existence, and will say in the joy of my heart, the calm I now feel I owe to my friend.

By submitting to some slight privations, which I do not impose upon you, but entreat you to yield to, will you think a termination of my sufferings too dearly purchased? Ah! if to render you happy, there was only my own consent that I should be unhappy, you may rely on it, I should not hesitate a moment: but to become criminal! no, my friend, I shall prefer a thousand deaths.

Even now, assailed by shame, and on the eve of remorse, I dread all others and myself equally. I blush when in any circle, and feel a horror when in solitude. I no longer lead any but a life of grief. I can only re-establish my tranquillity by your consent; my most laudable resolutions are insufficient to afford me security. I have formed the resolution I have just mentioned no longer than yesterday, and yet have passed the last night in tears.

Behold your friend, her whom you love, confounded, and supplicating you for the preservation of her repose and her innocence. Oh, heaven! would she ever but through your means have been reduced to make such humiliating entreaties! I, however, do not reproach you with any thing. I feel too sensibly, from the experience of myself, how difficult it is to resist so over-ruling a sentiment. A lamentation such as mine ought not to be deemed a murmur. Do, from generosity what I do from duty; and to all the sentiments you have inspired me with, I shall add that of eternal gratitude. Adieu, adieu, Sir!

From — —, Sept. 27, 17 —.

LETTER XCI.

VISCOUNT DE VALMONT *to the* Presidente DE TOURVEL.

Plunged into consternation as I am by your letter, how shall I answer it, Madam? Doubtless, if the alternative is your unhappiness or mine, it is my duty to sacrifice myself, and I do not hesitate to do it: but concerns so interesting, merit, I think, full discussion and elucidation; and how shall we arrive at that, if we are no longer to see or speak to one another.

What! whilst the most tender sentiments unite us, shall a vain terror be able to separate us, perhaps, for ever! Shall tender friendship and ardent love in vain endeavour to assert their rights, and their voices remain unattended to! And why? what is this very urgent danger which threatens you? Ah! believe me, such fears, and fears taken up so lightly, are in themselves sufficiently powerful motives for your considering yourself in a state of security.

Permit me to tell you, I can here trace again the unfavourable impressions which have been made upon you with regard to me. No woman trembles at the man she esteems. No woman banishes him in a marked manner, whom she has thought worthy of some degree of friendship. It is the dangerous man who is feared and fled.

And yet, was there ever a person more respectful and submissive than I? You must perceive it. Guarded in my language, I no longer permit myself those appellations so sweet, so dear to my heart, and which that heart unceasingly applies to you secretly. It is no longer the faithful and unfortunate lover receiving the advice and consolation of a tender and feeling female friend. I am in the situation of the accused before his judge, of the slave before his lord. These new titles certainly impose on me duties: I bind myself to fulfil them all. Hear me, and if you condemn me, I subscribe to my sentence and depart. I will go farther. Do you prefer that despotism which decides without a hearing? Do you feel boldness enough to commit an act of injustice? Give your orders; you shall be obeyed.

But let me have this sentence or order from your mouth. But why? You will tell me in your turn. Ah! if you put such a question, you are a stranger to love and to my heart. Is it nothing to see you? I repeat it again. Even when you shall strike despair to my soul, perhaps a consoling glance will prevent its sinking. In a word; if I must renounce love and friendship, the only props of my existence, at least you will behold your works, and I shall engage your compassion. Though I should not even deserve this small favour, I think I submit to pay dearly enough for it, to give me hopes of obtaining it. What, you are about to banish me from you! You can consent, then, that we should become utter strangers to one another! What do I say? It is the wish of your heart; and whilst you assure me that my absence shall not prejudice me in your sentiments, you only hasten my departure, in order more securely to effect their destruction, which you begin even now, by talking of substituting gratitude in their place. Thus you offer me only that sentiment which a stranger would inspire you with for a slight service; that kind of sentiment which you would feel for an enemy desisting from premeditated injury; and you expect my heart to be content with this. Interrogate your own. If a lover, a friend, should ever come to talk to you of gratitude, would you not say to him with indignation, Withdraw, you are a worthless man?

I shall here stop, and repeat my requests of your indulgence. Pardon the expressions of grief of which you are the cause; they shall not interfere with my perfect submission: but I conjure you in turn, in the name of those tender sentiments which you yourself resort to with me, refuse not to hear; and from mere compassion for the aggravated distress you have plunged me in, defer not the moment in which you will condescend to hear me. Adieu, Madam!

From — —, Sept. 7, 17—, at night.

LETTER XCII.

CHEVALIER DANCENY *to the* VISCOUNT DE VALMONT.

Your letter, my dear friend, has overwhelmed me with sorrow. Heavens! Is it possible Cecilia no longer loves her Danceny! Yes, I plainly see it through the veil your friendship has thrown over it. You wished to prepare me for this mortal stab; I thank you for your care: but a lover it not thus to be deceived; he anticipates his concerns; he is not to learn his fate, he presages it. I have no longer any doubt of mine. I entreat you to inform me, without evasion, from whence your suspicions arise, and what confirms them; the most minute trifles are important. Recollect particularly her expressions. A word may alter a phrase, or bear a double meaning. You may have mistaken her.

Alas, I endeavour still to flatter myself. What did she say? Has she any thing to reproach me with? Does she not attempt to excuse herself? I might have foreseen this alteration by all the difficulties she has lately started. Love admits no obstacles.

What am I to do? What would you advise me to? Is it then impossible to see her? Absence is such a dreadful, such a fatal—and she refuses the means you proposed to see me! You don't, however, tell me what it was; if it really was dangerous, she is convinced I would not have her run a great risk: however, I am satisfied of your prudence, and pay no regard to any other consideration.

What will now become of me? How shall I write to her? If I hint my suspicions, she will probably be grieved; and should they be ill grounded, how shall I ever forgive myself for having given her cause for affliction? If I conceal them, it is deceiving her, and I cannot dissemble it.

Oh! could she but know what I suffer, my distress would move her, for she is tender, has a most excellent heart, and I have a thousand proofs of her affection. Too much timidity, some distress, she is young, and her mother treats her so severely. I will write to her; yet I will contain myself, and will only beg of her to leave the management of every thing to you. If she should even still refuse, she cannot at least be angry with me, and perhaps she may consent.

I beg ten thousand pardons, my dear friend, both for her and myself. Give me leave to assure you, she is very sensible of the trouble you have had, and is exceedingly grateful. It is not distrust, it is merely timidity. Have a little compassion for her weakness, the highest attribute of friendship. Yours to me is inestimable, and I am really at a loss how to express my gratitude. Adieu! I am just going to write to her.

All my fears return on me. I could not have believed yesterday, when it would have been my greatest happiness, that I should now experience so much distress in writing to her.

Adieu, my dear friend! continue your friendship, and compassionate me.
Paris, Sept. 27, 17—.

LETTER XCIII.

CHEVALIER DANCENY *to* CECILIA VOLANGES.

I cannot conceal my affliction at hearing from Valmont how much you still distrust him. You know he is my friend, and the only person who can give us an opportunity of seeing each other: I fondly imagined this would have been a sufficient recommendation, but am very sorry to find I am mistaken. May I, however, hope to know your reasons? There are, perhaps, some obstacles that prevent you; I cannot, however, without your aid, guess at this mysterious conduct. I dare not entertain any suspicion of your affection, neither would you deceive mine. Ah, Cecilia!

It is, then, past a doubt, that you have refused *an easy, commodious, and safe way*[1] of seeing me. And is it thus I am beloved? Has so short an absence altered your sentiments? — Why, then, deceive me? Why tell me you still love me, and even still more? Has your mama, by destroying your affection for me, also destroyed your candour? — If, however, she has not left you destitute of compassion, you will feel for the pangs you occasion me, which death cannot even equal.

Tell me, then, have I for ever lost your heart? Am I totally forgotten? I know not when you will hear my complaints, nor when they will be answered. Valmont's friendship had secured our correspondence, but you rejected it; you thought it troublesome; it was too frequent. Never more will I confide in love or in promises. Who is to be believed, when Cecilia deceives me?

Am I no longer, then, your beloved Danceny? No, that is not possible; you deceive your own heart. A transitory apprehension, a momentary gloom, causes my present distress, which love will soon dispel: is it not so, my adorable Cecilia? Yes, it is, and I am much to blame for accusing you. How happy shall I be to discover my error, and repair it by soothing apologies and never-ending love.

Cecilia, lovely Cecilia, take pity on me; consent to see me; form the plan yourself: this is the consequence of absence; fears, doubts, and perhaps coolness. One single glance, a word only, and we shall be happy. But why mention happiness? Mine is, perhaps, at an end, and that for ever. Tortured with apprehensions, suspended between doubts and fears, I cannot form a resolution. My existence depends on love and sufferings: You alone, my Cecilia, are the arbitress of my fate; you alone can decide on my happiness or misery.

Paris, Sept. 27, 17—.

[1] Danceny does not know the way; he only repeats Valmont's expression.

LETTER XCIV.

CECILIA VOLANGES *to the* CHEVALIER DANCENY.

I cannot conceive a word of your letter, — — it gives me much uneasiness. What, then, has M. de Valmont wrote to you? Can you think I no longer love you? Perhaps it would be much better for me if it was otherwise, for I should not be so tormented as I am; it is really hard, that, loving as I do, you should always think me wrong; and instead of receiving consolation in my afflictions, the cause of all my troubles should proceed from you. You imagine I deceive and misrepresent matters to you. Upon my word you have a good opinion of me: But even suppose it the case, what would it avail me? Certainly, if I ceas'd loving you, all my friends would be glad of it; but it is my misfortune I cannot, and must love a man who is not in the least obliged to me.

What have I done, then, to put you so much out of temper? I was afraid to take a key, lest my mama should discover it, and bring more trouble on you and me; moreover, I did not think it right. How did I know whether I was acting right or wrong, as you knew nothing of the matter, and it was Mr. Valmont only that mentioned it? Now that I know you would wish me to do it, I will take it to-morrow; then, I suppose, you will be satisfied — Mr. de Valmont may be your friend, for ought I know, but I think I love you at well as he does, at least; and yet he is always right, and I am wrong. — I assure you, I am very angry; however, that gives you no great uneasiness, as you know I am soon pacified: when I have the key, I can see you whenever I please: if you behave in this manner, though, I will not wish for it; I can better bear my own troubles than those you bring on me.

We might be happy still, only for the little disagreeable occurrences thrown in our way; if I was my own mistress, you would have no reason to complain: But, if you will not believe me, we shall always be very miserable; yet it shall not be my fault. I hope we shall soon see each other, and then shall have no reason to be so tormented as we are now.

Could I have foreseen all this, the key should have been in my possession; but, indeed, I thought I was doing right. Do not be angry with me, I beg of you. Don't afflict yourself any more, and love me as much as I love you; then I shall be happy. Adieu, my dear friend.

From the castle of — —, *Sept.* 28, 17—.

LETTER XCV.

CECILIA VOLANGES *to the* VISCOUNT DE VALMONT.

SIR,

I beg you will return me the key you gave me to put in the place of the other; since it must be so, I must agree to it.

I don't know why you should write to Mr. Danceny, I did not love him: I don't think I ever gave you any reason to say so; it has given us both a great deal of uneasiness: — I know you have a friendship for him, therefore should not fret him nor me neither. I should be much obliged to you if, when you write to him next, you would assure him of the contrary; for he reposes his confidence in you: nothing gives me so much trouble as not to be believed when I say a thing.

As to the key, you may make yourself perfectly easy; I remember all you wrote me very well; but if you have your letter still by you, and will give it to me at the same time, I assure you I shall take particular notice of it. If you contrive to give it me to-morrow as we go to dinner, I would give you the other key the day after at breakfast, and you could return it to me in the same way you did the first. Pray do not defer it any longer, as we ought not to give Mama an opportunity to discover it.

When you have once got possession of the key, you will be so good to make use of it to take my letters; and by this means Mr. Danceny will oftener hear from me, which will be much more convenient than at present. I was a good deal frightened at first, which I hope you will be so good to excuse; and that you will, nevertheless, continue your friendship as heretofore: you may depend on my gratitude.

I have the honour to be, SIR, Your most obedient Humble Servant.
Sept. 28, 17—.

LETTER XCVI.

VISCOUNT DE VALMONT *to the* MARCHIONESS DE MERTEUIL.

I dare say, you have been in daily expectation of my compliments and eulogiums on your adventure; I even make no doubt but my long silence may have put you a little out of temper: But to sum up all, I will freely own I have ever thought, that when one had nothing but praise to offer a woman, he might safely trust to herself, and employ his time on other matters. Yet I must thank you for my share in it, and congratulate you on your own. I will even, for this once, to make you perfectly happy, agree you have much surpassed my expectations. And now let us see, whether, on my side, I have not partly fulfilled yours.

Madame de Tourvel is not the subject we are now on; her slow proceedings do not meet your approbation; you like to hear of business done; long-spun scenes disgust you; but I never before experienced the pleasure I do now in those pretended delays.

Yes, I enjoy it; to see this prudent woman, entangled imperceptibly in a path from whence she cannot return; whose rapid and dangerous declivity hurries her on against her will, and forces her to follow me—then, frightened at the danger, would, but cannot stop;—her anxiety and wariness make her steps slow, but still they must succeed each other. Sometimes, not daring to view the danger, she shuts her eyes, and abandons herself to my care. New dreads often reanimate her efforts; and, in her grievous fright, she again endeavours to return, wastes her strength to climb painfully a short space; and soon, by a magic power, finds herself nearer the danger she vainly endeavoured to fly. Then, having no other guide or support but me, without thinking any longer of reproaching me with her inevitable fall, she implores me to protract it. Fervent prayers, humble supplications, all that terrified mortals offer up to the Divinity, I receive from her; and you would have me be deaf to her vows, to destroy the worship she renders me, and employ the power she invokes to support her, in hurling her into destruction. Let me at least have time to contemplate this affecting struggle between love and virtue.

Is not this, then, the exhibition you fly to at the theatre with so much avidity, and applaud with so much ardour? And do you imagine it can be less endearing in realizing it?—The sentiments of a pure and tender heart, which dreads the happiness it wishes, and ceases not to defend itself when it even ceases to resist, you enthusiastically admire: And pray, is the ruling principle of this great work to be rejected?

Yet, those are the delicious enjoyments this celestial woman daily offers me, and you reproach me for relishing them. Alas! the time will come too soon when, degraded by her fall, I shall view her with as much indifference as another.

But I wander; for, speaking of her, I forget that I did not intend even to mention her. An unknown power impels me, and incessantly recalls her to me when I am even injuring her: let me banish this dangerous idea, be myself again, and entertain you with a more agreeable adventure. Your late pupil, now become mine, shall be the subject; and now, I hope, you'll again know your friend.

Having, for a few days past, been more gently treated by my charming devotee, and consequently more disengaged, I observed the little Volanges was really handsome; and that if it was ridiculous in Danceny to be in love with her, it would be no less so in me not to embrace a dissipation that my solitude called for. I even thought it an act of justice, to repay myself for the trouble I had had with her: I recollected, also, that you offered her to me before Danceny had any pretensions to her; and thought myself well grounded in asserting certain rights, which he claimed only from my refusal and abdication. The engaging mien of the little creature, her pretty mouth, her childish air, even her awkwardness, strengthened those sage reflections. I determined to act conformably, and success has crown'd the enterprise. I think I see you all impatience to know how I supplanted the cherished lover, the seducing arts fit to be employed for such a tender age, and so unexperienced: spare yourself the trouble, for I employed none.—Whilst you, managing with dexterity the arms of your sex, triumph by artifice, I, in a manly way, subdue by authority,—sure of my prey, if I can close with it. I had no occasion for dissimulation, but to get it within my reach, and that I made use of scarcely deserves the name.

I took the advantage of the first letter Danceny wrote to his fair one, and, after having made the signal agreed on, instead of employing my address to deliver it, I contriv'd obstacles to prevent it; and, feigning a share in the impatience this excited, pointed out the remedy after causing the evil.

The young thing is lodged in an apartment that opens into the gallery, and the mother, very properly, keeps the key. Nothing, then, was wanting but to get possession of the key, and nothing more easy in the execution: I asked for it for two hours, only to have another made by it: then correspondence, interviews, nocturnal rendezvous, all were convenient and safe: but, would you believe it, the timid child was frightened, and refused. Any other would have been driven to despair: to me it was a more poignant pleasure. I wrote to Danceny, complaining of this denial; and was so successful, that the thoughtless youth urged, nay even exacted of his timid mistress, that she should agree to my request, and give herself up to my discretion.

I must own myself well pleased to change my character, and that the young man should do for me what he expected I was to do for him. This idea enhanc'd the value of the adventure; and, as soon as I got possession of the delicious key, I lost no time: — it was last night.

When I was assured all were at rest in the Castle, taking my dark lantern, and in a proper toilette for the hour and circumstance, I paid my first visit to your pupil. Every thing had been prepared (and that by herself) to prevent noise: she was in her first sleep, so that I was by her bed side without awaking her. I was at first tempted to go on farther, and make every thing pass for a dream; but dreading the effects of a surprise, and the consequences naturally attendant, I chose to awake the pretty sleeper cautiously, which I effected without the alarm I dreaded.

After having calmed her first fears, as I did not come there to chat, I ventured to take some liberties: they did not, certainly, inform her in the convent, to how many different dangers timid innocence is exposed, and all that she had to take care of to guard against a surprise; for, using all her strength to prevent a kiss, which was only a false attack, she left all the rest defenceless: how was it possible to resist the temptation? — I then changed my attack, and immediately took possession of the post. At that instant we had both like to be undone; the little girl, scared, was in earnest going to cry out; happily, her voice was stifled with her tears: she flung herself, also, on the string of the bell, but I held her arm opportunely.

"What are you about? (then said I) Will you ruin yourself for ever? Do you think you will be able to persuade any one that I am here without your consent? Who but yourself could supply me the means of getting in? — And this key that I had from you, which I could not have from any one else, will you take it upon you to tell the use it was designed for?" — This short speech did not calm either grief or anger, but it brought on submission. I don't know whether I had the tone of eloquence, but certain I am I had not the action: one hand employed for strength, the other for love, what orator could pretend to gracefulness in such a situation? If you conceive it right, you must own, at least, it was very favourable for the attack: but I know nothing; and, as you say, the simplest creature, a boarding school girl, would lead me like a child.

She was in the utmost affliction, but felt the necessity of coming to some resolution, and entering into a composition. Being inexorable to prayers, she proceeded to offers: you think, perhaps. I sold this important post very dear; by no means; I promised every thing for a kiss; however, the kiss taken, I did not keep my word; my reasons were good: it had not been agreed whether it should be given or taken; by dint of bargaining we agreed on a second, and that was to be received; then guiding her trembling arms round me, and pressing her with one of mine more amorously, the soft kiss was not only received, but perfectly received in such a manner, that love could not have done it better. — So much plain dealing deserved to be rewarded, and I immediately granted the request: the hand was withdrawn, but, I don't know by what accident, I found myself in its place. You now suppose me very alert, and in great haste, don't you? — Not in the least; I have already told you I delight in delays: when one is once certain of coming to the end of the journey, what occasion for haste?

Seriously, I was glad, for once, to observe the power of opportunity; and it was here divested of all foreign aid. She had, however, love to combat with; and love, supported by modesty and shame, strengthened by the bad humour I had put her in. There was nothing in my favour but opportunity; — it was there, always ready, always present, and love absent.

To be certain in my observations, I was so mischievous to employ no more force than what could be easily combated: only, if my charming enemy, abusing my condescension, attempted to escape me, I kept her in awe, by the same dread whose happy effects I had already experienced. — At length the tender, lovely girl, without farther trouble, first complied, and then consented: not but that, after the first moment, reproaches and tears returned together — I can't tell whether true or feigned; but, as it always happens, they ceased as soon as I began to give fresh cause for them. At last, from weakness to reproach, and from reproach to weakness, we separated, perfectly satisfied with each other, and equally agreed for the rendezvous this night.

I retired to my apartment at the dawn of day, quite exhausted with fatigue and sleep; yet I sacrificed one and the other to my inclination to be at breakfast in the morning. I am passionately fond of the next day's exhibition. You cannot conceive any thing like this. It was a confusion in the countenance, a difficulty in the walk, dejected eyes so swelled, and the round visage so lengthened, nothing could be so grotesque; and the mother, for the first time, alarmed at this sudden alteration, seemed to show a deal of affection for her; and the Presidente also, who seemed to be much concerned for her. As to her cares, they are only lent; for the day will come, and it is not far off, when they may be returned to her.

Adieu, my lovely friend!

Oct. 1, 17—.

LETTER XCVII.

CECILIA VOLANGES *to the* MARCHIONESS DE MERTEUIL.

Ah, Madam! I am the most miserable creature on earth; my affliction is very great, indeed. To whom shall I fly for consolation? or who will give me advice in my distress? Mr. de Valmont and Danceny—the very name of Danceny distracts me—How shall I begin? How shall I tell you?—I don't know how to go about it; my heart is full—I must, however, disburthen myself to some one: and you are the only person in whom I can or dare confide; you have been so kind to me. But I am no longer worthy of your friendship; I will even say, I do not wish for it. Every one here has been uneasy about me, and they only augmented my grief; I am so convinced I am unworthy of it. Rather scold me, abuse me, for I am guilty; yet save me from ruin. If you do not compassionate and advise me, I shall expire of grief.

I must tell you then—my hand shakes so, I can hardly hold the pen, and I am as red as scarlet; but it is the blush of shame. Well, I will bear it, as the first punishment of my crime. I will relate the whole.

I must tell you that Mr. Valmont, who has always hitherto delivered me Mr. Danceny's letters, on a sudden discovered so much difficulty in it, that he would have the key of my chamber. I assure you, I was very much against it: but he wrote to Danceny about it; and Danceny also insisted on it. It gives me so much pain to refuse him any thing, especially since our absence, which makes him so unhappy, that I consented; not in the least suspecting what would be the consequence.

Yesterday Mr. Valmont made use of this key to get into my chamber while I was asleep. I so little expected such a visit, that I was greatly frightened at waking: but as he spoke to me instantly, I knew him, and did not cry out; as I immediately thought he came to bring me a letter from Danceny. No such thing. He wanted to kiss me directly; and while I was struggling, he contrived to do what I would not have suffered for the whole world. But he would have a kiss first; which I was forced to comply with: for what could I do? I endeavoured to call out; but, besides that I could not, he told me, that if any one should come he would throw all the fault on me; which, indeed, was very easy to be done on account of the key. After that, he did not go away any more. Then he would have a second kiss; and I don't know how that was, but it gave me a strange perturbation; and after that it was still worse. At last, after—but you must excuse me from telling the rest; for I am as unhappy as it is possible. But what I reproach myself most for, and that I can't help mentioning, is, I am afraid I did not make as much resistance as I could. I can't tell how it was, for certainly I don't love Mr. Valmont, but on the contrary; yet there were some moments that I was as if I lov'd him—however, you may well think I always said no: but I was sensible I did not do as I said; and it was as if in spite of me; and I was, moreover, in great trouble. If it is always so hard to defend one's self, one must be very well used to it. Mr. de Valmont speaks to one in such a way, that one does not know how to answer him: and would you believe it, when he went away I was vexed; and yet I was silly enough to consent to his coming again this night: that afflicts me more than all the rest.

Notwithstanding, I promise you I will prevent him from coming. He was hardly gone, but I found I did very wrong to promise him, and I cried all the rest of the time. My greatest trouble is about Danceny. Every time I think of him, my tears almost choke me, and I am always thinking of him—and even now you may see the effect, for the paper is wet with my tears. I shall never be able to get the better of it, if it was only on his account. I was quite exhausted, and yet I could not close my eyes. When I got up, and looked in the glass, I was enough to frighten one, I was so altered.

Mama perceived it as soon as I appeared, and asked me, what was the matter with me? I burst out crying immediately. I thought she would have chid me, and maybe that would not have been so distressing to me; however, it was quite otherwise; she spoke to me with great mildness, which I did not deserve. She desired I would not afflict myself so; but she did not know the cause of my distress; and that I should make myself sick. I often wish I was dead. I could hold out no longer. I flung myself in her arms, sobbing, and told her, "Ah, mama! your daughter is very unhappy." Mama could no longer contain herself, and wept a little. All this increased my sorrow. Fortunately she did not ask the reason; for if she had, I should not known what to say.

I entreat you, dear Madam, to write to me as soon as possible, and inform me how I am to act; for I have no power to think of any thing, my affliction is so great. Please to enclose your letter to Mr. Valmont: but if you write to him at the same time, I entreat you not to mention a word of this.

I have the honour to be, with great friendship, Madam, your most humble and obedient servant.

I dare not sign this letter.

Oct. 1, 17—.

LETTER XCVIII.

MADAME DE VOLANGES *to the* MARCHIONESS DE MERTEUIL.

A few days ago you applied to me, my charming friend, for advice and consolation; it is now my turn, and I am to make the same request you made to me for myself. I am really in great affliction, and fear I have not taken the proper steps to avoid my present sorrow.

My uneasiness is on account of my daughter. Since our departure, I observed she was always dejected and melancholy; that I expected, and assumed a severity of behaviour which I judged necessary; flattering myself, that absence and dissipation would soon banish an affection, which I viewed as a childish error, rather than a deep-rooted passion; but I am disappointed in my expectations, and observe she gives way more and more to a dangerous dejection. I am seriously alarmed for her health. These few days past, particularly, there is a visible alteration in her; and yesterday she affected me very much, and alarmed us all.

The strongest proof I have of her being sensibly affected, is because I find that awe she always stood in of me is greatly diminished. Yesterday morning, on my only asking her if she was indisposed, she flung herself in my arms, saying, she was very unhappy, and sobbed and cried piteously. You can't conceive my grief; my eyes filled immediately; I had scarcely time to turn about, to prevent her seeing me. Fortunately, I had the prudence not to ask her any questions, and she did not venture to say any thing more; nevertheless, I am confident it is this unhappy passion disturbs her.

What resolution to take, if it should last, I know not. Shall I be the cause of my child's unhappiness? Shall the most delicate sensations of the mind, tenderness and constancy, be employed against her? Is this the duty of a mother? Were I even to stifle the natural inclination that induces us to seek our children's happiness; should I call that weakness, which I am persuaded is the first, the most sacred duty? Should I force her inclinations, am I not answerable for the dreadful consequences that may ensue? What abuse of my maternal authority would it not be to place my daughter between guilt and misery!

My dear friend, I will not imitate what I have so often condemned. I was certainly authorised to choose for my daughter; in that, I only assisted her with my experience: I did not mean to use it as a right; I only fulfilled a duty, which I should have counteracted, had I disposed of her in contempt of an inclination which I could not prevent, the extent and duration of which neither she or I can foresee. No; she shall never marry Gercourt and love Danceny; I will much rather expose my authority than her virtue.

I am, then, of opinion, it will be the most prudent way to recall my promise to M. de Gercourt. You have my reasons which, I think, stronger than my promise. I will go farther; for as matters are circumstanced, by fulfilling my engagement I should in reality violate it: for if I am bound to keep my daughter's secret from M. de Gercourt, I am also bound not to abuse the ignorance I leave him in, and to act for him, as I believe he would act himself, was he better informed. Should I, then, injuriously deceive him, when he reposes his confidence in me, and, whilst he honours me with the title of mother, deceive him in the choice he makes for his children? Those reflections, so just in themselves, and which I cannot withstand, give me more uneasiness than I can express.

In contrast to the misfortunes I dread, I picture to myself my daughter happy in the choice her heart has made, fulfilling her duties with pleasure; my son-in-law, equally satisfied, daily congratulating himself on his choice; each enjoying the other's happiness, and both uniting to augment mine. Should, then, the prospect of so charming a futurity be sacrificed to vain motives? And what are those that restrain me? Interest only. Where is, then, the advantage of my daughter being born to a large fortune, if she is to be nevertheless the slave to that fortune? I will allow, that M. de Gercourt is, perhaps, a better match than I could have expected for my daughter; I will even own, I was much pleased when he made her his choice: but Danceny is of as good a family as he, and is nothing inferior to him in personal accomplishments; he has, moreover, the advantage over M. de Gercourt of loving and being beloved. He is not rich, it's true; but my daughter is rich enough for both. Ah! Why should I deprive her the pleasure of making the fortune of the man she loves? Those matches of convenience, as they are called, where certainly every thing is convenient except inclination and disposition, are they not the most fruitful source of those scandalous rumours which are become so frequent? I would much rather defer matters a little. I shall have an opportunity to study my daughter's disposition, which as yet I am a stranger to. I have resolution enough to give her some temporary uneasiness, in order to make her enjoy some temporary happiness: but I will not risk making her miserable for ever.

Thus, my dear friend, I have related to you my afflictions, on which I beg your advice. Those severe subjects are a contrast to your amiable gaiety, and seem not at all adapted to your age; but your good sense outstrips your years. Your friendship will also aid your prudence; and I am confident, both will gratify the maternal anxiety that implores them.

Adieu, my dear friend! never doubt the sincerity of my sentiments.

Castle of — —, Oct. 2, 17—.

LETTER XCIX.

VISCOUNT DE VALMONT *to the* MARCHIONESS DE MERTEUIL.

Trifling events still, my dear friend; nothing of consequence; no action; scenes only; therefore arm yourself with patience: you must take a large dose; for whilst my Presidente goes such a slow pace, your pupil slides back, which is much worse: but I am of that happy temper, I can divert myself with all this nonsense. I really begin to be very comfortable here; and can assure you, I have not experienced a tedious moment in my old aunt's melancholy castle. What could I wish for more than what I have, enjoyments, privations, hope, and incertitude? What more is to be had on a grand theatre? Why spectators. Ah! a little patience, they will not be wanting. If they do not see me at work, they shall at least see my work completed; they will then have nothing to do but to admire and applaud: for they shall applaud. I can this instant with certainty foretell the moment of my austere devotee's fall. I this night assisted at the last agonies of her virtue; soft weakness has replaced it. I have fixed its epocha, at farthest, to our next interview: you will call this pride. He announces his victory before he has gained it! Softly; be calm! To give you a proof of my modesty, I will give you the history of my defeat.

Upon my word, your little pupil is a most ridiculous being. She is really a child, and should be treated as one; it would be of service to enjoin her a little penance. Would you believe it? after what passed between us the day before yesterday, after the amicable manner in which we parted yesterday morning, I found her door locked on the inside when I came at night, as was agreed. What do you think of that? Those childish tricks are passable on the eve; but on the morrow is it not ridiculous? I did not, however, laugh at first; for never did I feel the ascendancy of my character more hurt. I went to this rendezvous without any incitement for pleasure, and merely through decency; my own bed, which I much wanted at that time, was preferable to any other, and I parted from it with some reluctance; yet when I met this obstacle I was all on fire to surmount it: I was humbled, to be sported with by a child. I was obliged to retire in very bad humour, fully resolved to have nothing more to do with this silly girl, or her matters. I immediately wrote her a note, which I intended giving her this day, wherein I appreciated her as she deserved: but night bringing good counsel, as is said, I reflected this morning, that not having here a choice of dissipations, it was better to keep this, and suppressed my note. Since I have reflected on it, I can't reconcile it to myself to have had the idea of putting an end to an adventure before I had it in my power to ruin the heroine. What lengths will not a first emotion carry us to! Happy are those, my dear friend, who, like you, never accustom themselves to give way to it. I have deferred my revenge; and this sacrifice I make to your designs on Gercourt.

Now my wrath is subsided, I only see the ridiculousness of your pupil's behaviour. I should be fond to know what she expects to gain by it; for my part, I am at a loss: if it should be to make a defence, she is rather late. She must explain this enigma to me one day or other, for I must be satisfied. It is only, perhaps, that she was fatigued; and really that may be the case, for certainly she does not yet know that the shafts of love, like the lance of Achilles, carry with them the remedy for the wounds they give. But no: I will engage by her little mien all day, that there is something like repentance; a something like virtue—virtue, indeed!—she is a pretty creature to pretend to virtue! Ah! she must leave that to the only woman who was truly born for it, knows how to embellish it, and make it revered. Your pardon, my dear friend: but this very evening it was that the scene between Madame de Tourvel and me happened, of which I am about giving you an account, and which has still left me in great emotion. It is not without some violence I endeavour to dissipate the impression it has left on me; it is even to assist it, I sit down to write to you: you must make some allowance for this first impulse.

For some days past Madame de Tourvel and I have been agreed about our sentiments, and we no longer dispute on any thing but words. It was always, *her friendship* that answered *my love:* but this conventional language made no alteration in the meaning of things. Had we even still remained so, I should not have gone on, perhaps, with so much dispatch, but with no less certainty. There was no longer any thought of putting me from hence, as was at first mentioned; and as to our daily conversations, if I am solicitous to offer opportunities, she takes care not to let them slip.

It is usually in our walks our rendezvous occur; the bad weather we had all day left no room for hope; I was much disappointed at it, and did not foresee how much it was in my favour. Not being able to walk, after dinner they sat down to cards; as I seldom play, and was not wanted, I retired to my room, with no other design than to wait till the party was over. I was returning to join the company, when the charming woman, who was going into her apartment, whether through weakness or imprudence, said in a soft manner, "Where are you going? There is no one in the saloon." That was sufficient, you may believe, for me to endeavour to go in with her. I found less reluctance than expected: it's true, I had the precaution to begin the conversation at the door on indifferent matters; but we were scarcely settled when I began the true one, and I spoke *of my love to my friend.* "Oh," says she, "let us not speak of that here;" and trembled. Poor woman! she sees herself going.

Yet she was in the wrong to have had any terrors. For some time past being certain of success one day or other, and seeing her employ so much exertion in useless struggles, I resolved to reserve mine, and wait without effort her surrender from lassitude. You already know I must have a complete triumph, and that I will not be indebted to opportunity. It was even after the formation of this plan, and in order to be pressing without engaging too far, I reverted to the word love, so obstinately resisted. Being assured my ardour was not questioned, I assumed a milder strain. This refusal no longer vexed me, it only afflicted me; my tender friend should give me some consolations. As she consoled me, one hand remained in mine, the lovely body rested on my arm, and we were exceeding close together. You must have certainly remarked, how much in such a situation, as the defence abates, the demands and refusals draw nearer; how the head turns aside, the looks cast down, whilst the conversation, always pronounced in a weak tone, becomes scarce and interrupted. Those precious symptoms announce, in an unequivocal manner, the consent of the mind, but rarely has it reached the senses. I even think it always dangerous to attempt any enterprise of consequence; because this state of abandonment being always accompanied with the softest pleasure, cannot be disturbed without ruffling the temper, which infallibly decides in favour of the defence.

But in the present case, prudence was so much more necessary, as I had every thing to dread from the forgetfulness of the danger this abandonment would occasion to my tender pensive devotee; and the avowal I solicited I did not even require to be pronounced; a look would suffice; a single glance would crown my happiness.

My charming friend, those lovely eyes then were raised on me, that celestial mouth even pronounced—"Well; yes, I—" in an instant the look was extinct, the voice failed, and this adorable woman dropped in my arms. I had scarcely time to receive her, when disengaging herself with a convulsive force and wild look, her hands raised to heaven, she exclaimed, "God—Oh, my God, save me!" and instantly, as quick as lightning, was on her knees ten paces from me. I could hear her almost suffocating. I came forward to assist her: but seizing my hands, which she bathed with her tears, sometimes embracing my knees, "Yes it is you," said she, "it is you will save me; you do not wish my death; leave me; save me; leave me; for God's sake! leave me:" and those incoherent expressions were brought out with most affecting sobs; yet still she held me so strong I could not get from her; however, making an effort, I rais'd her in my arms: instantly her tears ceas'd; she could not speak, her joints stiffened, and violent convulsions succeeded this storm.

I must own, I was exceedingly moved, and believe I should have complied with her request, if the circumstances had not even obliged me to it. But this much is certain; after having given her some assistance, I left her, as she desired; and I am well pleased with myself for it. I have already received almost my reward.

I expected, as on the first day of my declaration, I should not see her any more for the evening; but she came down to the saloon about eight, and only told the company she had been much indisposed: her countenance was dejected, her voice weak, her deportment composed, but her look mild, and often fixed on me.—As she declined playing, I was obliged to take her seat, and she placed herself beside me. During supper she remained alone in the saloon. At our return, I thought I perceived she had been crying: to be satisfied, I told her I was afraid she still felt some uneasiness from her disorder, to which she obligingly answered, "Her disorder would not go so quickly as it came." At last, when we retired, I gave her my hand, and at the door of her apartment, she very forcibly squeez'd mine: it is true, this motion seemed to me to be involuntary; so much the better; it is a stronger proof of my power.

I am confident she is now happy to have gone such a length; all expences are paid; nothing now remains but enjoyment. Perhaps now, whilst I am writing to you, she is possessed with the soft idea; but, if she should even be engaged in a new scheme of defence, you and I know how such projects end. Now let me ask you, can things be put off longer than our next interview? I expect there will be some forms to be settled; but, the first difficulties surmounted, do those austere prudes know where to stop? Their affections are real explosions; resistance gives them strength; my untractable devotee would run after me, if I ceas'd running after her.

At length, my lovely friend, I shall soon call on you for the performance of your promise; you undoubtedly remember our agreement after my success; this trifling infidelity to your Chevalier.—Are you ready? I wish for it as passionately as if I had never known you. However, knowing you is, perhaps, a stronger motive for wishing for it.

I am just, and no galant.[1]

It shall be the first infidelity I shall commit against my solemn conquest; and, I promise you, I will embrace the first pretence to be absent from her four and twenty hours: that shall be her punishment for having kept me so long distant from her: It is now more than two months I have been taken up with this adventure: ay, two months and three days, including to-morrow, as it will not be really consummated until then. This brings to my memory, that Mademoiselle B— — held out three complete months. I am pleased to find sheer coquetry can make a longer defence than austere virtue.

Adieu, charmer! I must leave off, for it is very late. This letter has led me farther than I intended; but, as I send to Paris to-morrow, I would not miss the opportunity of letting you partake a day sooner of your friend's good success.

Oct. 2, 17—, at Night.

[1] Voltaire's comedy of Nanine.

LETTER C.

The VISCOUNT DE VALMONT *to the* MARCHIONESS DE MERTEUIL.

My dear friend! I am betrayed, bubbled, ruined; I am enraged beyond expression: Madame de Tourvel is gone off. She is gone, and I knew nothing of it! I was not in the way to oppose her, to reproach her with her base treachery! Do not imagine I should have let her go quietly; she should have staid, had I been even obliged to have used force. Fool as I was! I slept peaceably, wrapped in a credulous security! I slept whilst the thunder struck me! I cannot conceive the meaning of this abrupt departure; I will for ever renounce the knowledge of women.

When I recall the transactions of yesterday!—or rather the evening—the melting look, the tender voice, the squeezing the hand—all the while planning her flight.—Oh! woman, woman! complain, then, if you are deceived! Yes, every kind of treachery that is employed against you is a robbery committed on you.

With what rapture shall I be revenged! I shall again meet this perfidious woman; I will resume my power over her. If love has been sufficient to furnish the means, what is it not capable of when assisted with revenge? I shall again see her at my knees, trembling, and bath'd in tears! calling on me for pity with her deceitful voice; and I will have none for her.

What is she now doing? What can she think of? Perhaps applauding herself for having deceived me; and, true to the genius of her sex, enjoys that pleasure in the highest degree. What her boasted virtue could not effect, deceit has accomplished without a struggle; it was her disingenuity I should have dreaded.—Then, to be obliged to stifle my resentment; to be obliged to affect a tender sorrow, when my heart is possessed with rage. Reduced to supplicate a rebellious woman, who has withdrawn herself from my obedience! Ought I then be so much humbled? And by whom? By a weak woman, who was never accustomed to resist! What avails my having possession of her heart, having inflamed it with the whole fire of love, having raised her feelings even to intoxication; if, calm in her retreat, she can now be prouder of her flight than I of my victories? And must I bear this? My dear friend, you will not believe it; you will not, surely, have such a humiliating opinion of me!

What fatality attaches me to this woman? Are there not a hundred others who wish I would pay attention to them, and eagerly accept it? If even none were so enchanting, the charms of variety, the allurements of new conquests, the splendour of the number; do not they afford a plentiful harvest of soft pleasures? Why, then, do I run madding after this one that flies me, and neglect those that offer? I am at a loss to account for it, but so it is. — There is no happiness, no repose for me, until I possess this woman, whom I love and hate with equal rage. I shall not be able to support my fate until I have disposed of hers: then, tranquil and satiated, I shall behold her a prey to the ravages I now experience, and will raise a thousand others; hope and fear, diffidence and security, all evils the offspring of hatred, all the gifts that love can bestow, shall alternately engross her heart at my will. The time will come — — But what labours have I not yet to encounter? — How near was I yesterday, and how distant to-day! How am I to regain the ground I have lost? I dare not undertake any one step: to come to some resolution I should be calm, and my blood boils in my veins.

The calm serenity with which every one replies to my demands on this extraordinary, on this uncommon event, and its cause, adds to my torments. — No one knows the reason: none seem to give themselves the least uneasiness about it; it scarcely would have been mentioned, could I have started any other subject. I flew to Madame de Rosemonde the moment I heard the news, who replied, with the natural indifference of old age, it was the consequence of the indisposition Madame de Tourvel had suffered yesterday: she dreaded a fit of illness, and wished to be at home; a resolution she did not think proper to oppose, as she would have done on a similar occasion; as if the contrast was applicable, — between her who should think of nothing but futurity, and the other, who is the delight and torment of my life.

Madame de Volanges, who I had suspected at first of being an accomplice, seems dissatisfied for not having been consulted on this occasion. I must own I am very well pleased she has been disappointed of the pleasure of prejudicing me; which is still a stronger proof she has not the confidence of this woman so much as I dreaded: that is an enemy the less. How would she have exulted, did she know she fled from me! How intolerable her pride, had it been the consequence of her advice! To what an immensity would her importance have been raised! Good God! how I detest her! — Yes, I will renew my connection with the daughter, and initiate her in her business: I believe I shall stay here some time; I am at present inclined to this measure, in the tumult of reflections that crowd on me.

Don't you, really now, think, after so extraordinary a proceeding, my ungrateful fair one should dread me? If she imagines I shall pursue her, she will not fail to prevent my admission; and, I can assure you, I am as little inclined to permit her such a custom, as to bear such an insult. I had much rather she should be told I remain here; I will even strenuously press her to return again: then, when she is fully convinced I am far from her, I will suddenly come to her house, and abide the effect of my scheme. — That it may have its full force, it must not be hurried; still I will not answer for my impatience; twenty times this day was I tempted to call for my horses. I will contain myself, however, and wait your answer here; I only request, my lovely friend, you will not let me wait long for it.

What hurts me most is to be ignorant of what happens: my fellow, who is at Paris, has a claim on her waiting maid; he may be serviceable; I send him money, and his instructions. Permit me to include both in this letter, and request to have them delivered into his hand by some of your servants: this precaution is the more necessary, as the scoundrel has a trick of never receiving any letters I write him on business he finds troublesome; and, at this period, he does not seem to be quite so enraptured with his girl as I could wish him.

Adieu, my lovely friend! If a happy thought should strike you, or any means of bringing me speedily to action, lose not a moment. I have often experienced your friendship; I forcibly experience it now, for I am more serene since I sat down to write. I speak, at least, to one who comprehends me, not to the inanimate beings with whom I vegetate since this morning. On my word, the more I proceed, the more I am inclined to think we are the only couple worth any thing in this life.

Oct. 3, 17—.

LETTER CI.

The VISCOUNT DE VALMONT to AZOLAN, his Huntsman.

(Enclosed in the foregoing.)

You must be a stupid fellow, indeed, to set out this morning, and not have known that Madame de Tourvel was going away also; or, if you knew it, not to have given me notice. To what purpose is it, then, you spend my money, if you only get drunk with the men, and loiter your time in courting the waiting maids, if you do not give me better information of what is going forward?—This is entirely owing to your negligence; therefore, I now give you notice, if such another happens in this business, it shall be the last you will be guilty of in my service.

You must inform me of every thing that happens at Madame de Tourvel's, relative to her health; whether she sleeps well; whether she is melancholy or cheerful; if she goes abroad often, and where; if she sees much company, and who goes there; how she passes her time; whether she is out of temper with her women, particularly the one that was with her here; how she employs her time when alone; if, when she reads, she is composed, or stops to muse; and the same when she writes. Remember, also, to make a friend of whoever carries the letters to the post office: often do that business for him; and, when he accepts it, send away only those you think of no consequence, and send me the rest, especially those for Madame de Volanges, if there should be any.

Settle your matters so as to be still the favourite of Julia. If she has another, as you thought, bring her to consent to share her favours; and do not be so ridiculous as to give yourself airs of jealousy: you will be only circumstanced as your superiors; but, if your rival should be troublesome, or if you perceive he takes up too much of Julia's time in the day, so that she should not be so often with her mistress, to observe her, you must, by some means or other, drive him away, or pick a quarrel with him; do not be afraid of the consequences,—I will support you: above all, leave the house as little as possible; for it is by assiduity only you can make your observations with certainty. If, by chance, any of the servants should be discharged, offer yourself in their room, as if no longer in my service: in such case, you must say you left me to get into a more quiet and regular service. Endeavour, as much as possible, to be hired; I shall, notwithstanding, keep you still in mine during the time; and you will be as you was before at the Duchess of — —, and Madame de Tourvel will also reward you in the end.

If you was zealous and skilful, those instructions should be sufficient: but, to assist one and the other, I send you some money: the enclosed bill on my steward entitles you to call on him for twenty-five louis, for I suppose you have no money. You will make use of as much as is necessary, to prevail on Julia to settle a correspondence with me; the remainder to treat the servants: let it be as often as you can in the porter's lodge, that he may like to see you. However, do not forget, it is your services I mean to pay, and not your pleasures.

Accustom Julia, betimes, to observe and report every thing, even what she may think the most trifling; it is better she should write ten useless lines, than omit a material one; and what often appears a matter of indifference, is quite otherwise. As I must be instantly informed, if any thing should happen you think of consequence after you receive this letter, send off Philip directly on the message horse, to fix himself at − −, and remain there until farther orders; it will be a stage in case of necessity; but, for common correspondence, the post will be sufficient.

Take great care not to lose this letter; read it over every day; not only not to forget any thing, but also to be certain you have it. Do, in a few words every thing you ought, now I honour you with my confidence. You very well know, if I am satisfied with your conduct, you shall be satisfied with me.

Oct. 3. 17 −.

LETTER CII.

The Presidente DE TOURVEL *to* MADAME DE ROSEMONDE.

You will be very much surprised, dear Madam, to learn I quitted your house so precipitately: this proceeding will, doubtless, appear very extraordinary; but how will your astonishment be increased, when you shall know my reasons! You will perhaps imagine, when I confide them to you, I have not paid proper attention to the respect the necessary tranquility of your age commands; that I am insensible to the sentiments of veneration you are so justly entitled to from me. Ah! forgive me, Madam! my heart is oppressed; it seeks to pour out its distress into the friendly bosom of prudence and mildness: − where could it find it but with you? Look upon me as your child; take a maternal compassion on me; I implore it; my sentiments for you may give me a claim to it.

The time is fled, when, wholly possessed with those laudable ideas, I knew not these I now experience, which ravage the soul, and deprive me of the power of resistance, whilst they impose its necessity! Ah! this fatal visit has undone me!

What can I say? − I love, − yes, I love to distraction! Alas! this fatal word, which now I write for the first time, − this word, so often solicited but never granted, my life should now expiate to let him hear who has inspired it; yet I must ever refuse! He will remain doubtful of the sentiments I feel for him. − I am miserable! − Oh, that he could as readily read my heart as rule it! I should suffer less if he but knew what I endure; but even you, my venerable friend, can have but a faint idea of my sufferings.

I shall in a few minutes fly him, and load him with affliction. He will think me near him, and I shall be far from him. — At the usual hour of seeing him every day, I shall be in places unknown to him, and where he cannot come: every thing is prepared full in my view, and all announce my unhappy flight: all is ready but me! — and the more my heart recoils, the more I am convinced of the necessity of submitting to my fate. — I must submit; it is better to die than live in guilt: already I feel my criminality; modesty only is preserved, but virtue is vanished: — what yet is left me, I must acknowledge, is due to his generosity. Intoxicated with pleasure, seeing and listening to him, enraptured in his arms, and the greatest of all extacy, that of making him happy, I was diverted of strength or power; scarce any left to struggle, but none to resist; I shuddered at my danger, but had not power to fly: — he saw my sufferings, and had compassion on me. — Must I not cherish him to whom I owe more than life!

Had that been my only care, remaining with him, do not imagine I should ever have thought of going! for what is life without him? Happy should I have been to die for him! But, condemned to be the cause of his misery and my own, without daring to complain, or console him; to be daily exposed to struggle, not only against him, but also against myself; to employ my cares to bring him to anguish, when I would devote my days to make him happy: such a life is worse than a thousand deaths; yet this is to be my fate: I will still resolutely bear up against it. And do you, who I have chosen for a mother, receive my solemn vow to observe it.

Receive also another, of never concealing any of my actions from you. I beseech you to accept it. I demand it as a necessary aid to my conduct. I shall be engaged to relate you all; I shall think myself in your presence; your virtue will assist my weakness. I will never consent to shame in your sight; and by means of this powerful restraint, whilst I cherish the indulgent friend, the confidant of my weakness, I shall reverence my tutelar angel that guards me from shame.

It is experiencing it too fatally, to be compelled to this requisition. Oh, the unhappy effect of presumptuous confidence! Why did I not oppose sooner this growing inclination? Why did I flatter myself with being able to conquer it at my pleasure? Senseless wretch! Little did I know the power of love! Ah! had I struggled against it with more care, it would not have overpowered me. This sudden departure would have been unnecessary; or, even being compelled to this painful step, I might not have been forced to break a connection, which might have been less frequent. But to lose all at once, and for ever! — Oh, my dear friend! — I forget myself, and again wander in criminal wishes. Let us part; and, at least, let me expiate by my sacrifice those involuntary injuries.

Adieu, most respectable friend! Love me as a daughter; adopt me as one; and be assured, notwithstanding my weakness, I would rather die than be unworthy that name.

Oct. 3, 17 — , One in the morning.

LETTER CIII.

MADAME DE ROSEMONDE *to the* Presidente DE TOURVEL.

I was more afflicted, my lovely dear, at your departure, than surprised at the cause; long experience, and my concern for you, had sufficiently informed me the state of your heart; and to sum up all, you have told me almost nothing in your letter but what I feared. Was I to depend on it for information, I should still be ignorant who it is you love; for in speaking of *him* all the time, you never once mention his name. It was not necessary; too well I know who it is. This I remark only, because I recollect, it always has been the language of love. I see things are the same as they were formerly.

I little imagined my thoughts would ever be called back to things so foreign to my age, and so much out of my memory. Since yesterday, however, my mind has been much taken up with it, in order to find out something that may be useful to you. What can I then do, but admire and pity you? I am charmed with your proceeding; yet terrified because you thought it indispensable; and when things have gone so far, it is a difficult matter to avoid those our hearts are continually drawing us towards.

However, you must not be discouraged; nothing is impossible to such a virtuous mind; and were you ever to yield, (which God forbid!) you will at least, my lovely dear, have the consolation of having resisted with all your might; moreover, what human wisdom cannot accomplish, the divine grace operates when it pleases. You are, perhaps, now at the eve of your deliverance; and your virtue, which has been tried in those dreadful conflicts, will arise more pure and refined. The strength which forsakes you to-day, you must hope for to-morrow. Do not, however, depend on it; use it only as an incentive to encourage you to employ all your own.

Leaving to Providence the care of assisting you in a danger where I can bring no prevention, I reserve to myself that of supporting and consoling you as much as in my power. I cannot relieve your troubles, but I will share them. On those conditions I will accept your confidence. I know your heart wants to be disburthened; I offer you my own; age has not so far frozen it, as to leave it insensible to friendship: you will always find it open to receive you. This is a poor relief to your distress, but you shall not, however, weep alone; and when this unhappy passion overpowers you, and obliges you to speak, it will be better it should be with me than *him.* Now I speak as you do; and I believe between us both we shall not be able to name him, but we understand each other.

I do not know whether I do right in telling you he appeared amazingly affected as your sudden departure; it would, perhaps, be better not to mention it: but I am not fond of that prudence that afflicts one's friends. I am obliged to stop short on that subject; for the weakness of my sight and a trembling hand will not indulge long letters, when I am under the necessity of writing them myself.

Adieu, my lovely dear! Adieu, my amiable child! I adopt you freely as a daughter. You have every accomplishment to fill a mother's heart with pride and pleasure.

Oct. 3, 17 — .

LETTER CIV.

The MARCHIONESS DE MERTEUIL to MADAME DE VOLANGES.

It was with some difficulty, my dear worthy friend, I could suppress an impulse of pride on reading your letter. You honour me, then, with your full confidence; you even condescend to ask my advice. I should be completely happy if I merited this favourable opinion; or, that it did not proceed from the prepossession of your friendship. Whatever may be the motive, it is so flattering, that having obtained it, I shall endeavour more ardently to deserve it. I shall then, but without presuming to advise, tell you freely my thoughts. I own I am diffident of them, as they differ from yours; yet, when you have my reasons, you will then judge, and if they should not meet with your approbation, I declare beforehand I submit. I shall, at least, be so prudent as not to think myself wiser than you. However, for this once, if my opinion should have the preference, you will find the cause in the facility of maternal fondness. With you we must look for so laudable an inclination, and readily recognize it in the measure you are inclined to embrace. Thus if you sometimes err, it is always on the side of virtue.

When we are to decide on the lot of others, but more especially, when the question is to fix it by a sacred and indissoluble band, such as marriage, prudence, I think, ought to take place of all other considerations. It is then an equally wise and tender mother should, as you well observe, *assist her daughter with her own experience.* I ask then, how is she to attain it, but by making a distinction between what is pleasing and what convenient.

Would it not be debasing maternal authority, nay even annihilating it, to make it subservient to a frivolous inclination, whose illusive power is felt only by those that dread it, and immediately vanishes when contemptuously treated? For my part, I must own I never believed in those irresistible, impetuous passions, which one would imagine the world has adopted, as an universal excuse for their irregularities. I cannot conceive how a passion, that one moment creates, and the next destroys, can overpower the unalterable principles of chastity, decency and modesty; nor how a woman, that has relinquished them, can be justified by a pretended passion, no more than a robber for a thirst for money, or a murderer for a desire of revenge. Where is the person who has not had their struggles? I have been always persuaded, inclination was sufficient for resistance, and experience has confirmed my opinion. Of what estimation would virtue be, without the obligations it imposes? Its worship are our sacrifices, its reward in our hearts. Those incontestable truths can be denied only by those whose interest it is to forget them; and who being already contaminated, hope to carry on the illusion, and justify their bad conduct by worse reasoning.

But is this to be apprehended from an innocent timid child; from a child of yours, whose pure and modest education is strengthened by a happy disposition? Still it is to this apprehension, which I will venture to call very humiliating for your daughter, you would give up an advantageous match your prudence had provided. I have a great friendship for Danceny; and you know for some time past I have seldom seen M. de Gercourt: but my friendship for the one, nor my indifference for the other, can prevent me from observing the immense difference between the two matches.

As to birth, I agree with you, they are on an equality: but the one is deficient in fortune, and the other's is such as, exclusive of blood, is sufficient to raise him to the highest employments. I acknowledge, happiness may be independent of fortune; but we must also own it a very necessary ingredient. You say, Mademoiselle de Volanges is rich enough for both; yet sixty thousand livres per annum, which she is to possess, will not be too much for one who bears the name of Danceny, to furnish and keep up a house suitable to it. These are not Madame de Sévigné's days. Luxury absorbs every thing; we blame, yet imitate it; and our superfluities end in depriving us of necessaries. As to personal accomplishments, which you with great reason dwell much on, certainly on that point M. de Gercourt is irreproachable, which he has already proved. I am fond of thinking, and really believe Danceny is not his inferior; but are we so certain of it? It is true, hitherto he appears untainted with the follies of the age, and notwithstanding the ton of the day, he shows a taste for good company, which inclines one to judge favourably of him. Yet who knows whether this apparent discretion is not the result of the mediocrity of his income? To be a gamester or a libertine, money must be had; or if there should be a tincture of knavery or epicurism, one may be fond of the defects, and still dread their excess. There are thousands who are admitted into good company because they have no other employment.

I do not say, God forbid I should! that I believe such things of him: yet there is some danger; and if the event should not answer your expectations, how you would reproach yourself! What reply could you make to your daughter, who would probably say, "Mother, I was young and unexperienced; I was even led astray by an error excusable at my age: Providence, which had foreseen my incapacity, had given me a prudent mother to preserve me. How is it then, that laying your discretion aside, you have consented to make me unhappy? Was I to choose a husband, I who knew nothing of a married state? If even I was determined on it, should you not have opposed it? But I never was possessed with that foolish self will. Determined to obey you, I waited with respectful veneration your choice. Did I ever swerve from my submission? Yet now I suffer the afflictions due to rebellious children only. Your weakness has been my ruin." Perhaps her respect might stifle those complaints: but your maternal love would discover them; and your daughter's tears, though concealed, would still overwhelm your heart.

Where then will you seek consolation? Will it be in this ridiculous passion, against which you should have guarded her, by which you even suffer yourself to be seduced?

Perhaps I may, my dear friend, conceive too strong a prejudice against this attachment: I view it in a formidable light, even in case of a marriage. Not that I disapprove a decent and pure intention should embellish the matrimonial bands, to soften in some measure the obligations it requires: but he is not the man appointed to tie them; it is not an illusory moment that ought to regulate our choice for life: for to choose well, we ought to compare; how then is it possible, when our imaginations are engrossed by a sole object; when that object cannot even be investigated, as we are plunged in intoxication and blindness? I have often, I assure you, fallen in with women attacked by this dangerous disorder; some of them I have been in confidence with: hear them speak, their lovers were in every degree all perfection; but those perfections were confined to their imaginations only. Their exalted ideas dress at pleasure those they prefer; they dream of nothing but excellence and virtue; it is the drapery of an angel often worn by an abject model: be him as he may, they have no sooner adorned him, than, dupes to their own labour, they fall down and adore him.

Your daughter, then, does not love Danceny, or, she is fascinated by this same illusion; and if they mutually love, they both experience the same. Thus your reason for uniting them is reduced to a certainty that they do not know each other, but also, that they never can know each other. I think I hear you say, "Can M. de Gercourt and my daughter know each other better?" No, certainly; but at least they do not mistake themselves; they are not sufficiently acquainted together. What then happens between a couple that I suppose decent? Why they study to please, observe, seek, and find out soon what inclinations or desires they must relinquish, for their mutual tranquillity. Those small self denials give but little uneasiness, as they are foreseen, and are reciprocal; they are soon converted into mutual good will; and custom, which ever strengthens all inclinations it does not destroy, gradually leads to that sincere friendship, that tender confidence, which, when united with esteem, forms, I think, the true solid happiness of the married state.

The illusions of love, I will allow, are more engaging; but don't we well know they are not so lasting? And what dangers does not their destruction bring on! Then the most trivial faults become shocking and intolerable, being contrasted with the ideas of perfection which had seduced us. Each then thinks the other is only altered, and they themselves of as much worth as in the first instant the error took its rise. They are astonished they can no longer create the charm they experienced; they are humbled; vanity is hurt, the mind is soured, injuries augmented, which bring on peevishness, and is succeeded by hatred; thus frivolous pleasures are repaid by long misfortunes.

I have now given you, my dear friend, my thoughts on this subject. I do not insist on them, only lay them before you:—you are to decide. Should you persist in your opinion, I shall only beg to know the reasons that combat mine. I shall be happy to be set right by you, and, above all, to be made easy on the fate of that lovely child, whose happiness I so ardently wish, not only for my particular friendship for her, but also for that which unites me to you for ever.

Paris, Oct. 4, 17—.

LETTER CV.

The MARCHIONESS DE MERTEUIL *to* CECILIA VOLANGES.

Well, my dear little creature, you are very much vexed and ashamed; and this same Valmont is a wicked man, is he not? How is all this? He dared behave to you as he would to the woman he loved best! He has taught you what you was going mad to know! Upon my word, such proceedings are unpardonable. And you, like a good girl, would have kept your chastity for your lover, who would not attempt it; you cherish the torments of love only, but not its pleasures. Why this is charming; and you will make a conspicuous figure in a romance. Love, misfortunes, and virtue in abundance! Lord! what a deal of fine things! In the midst of this brilliant train, it is true, one may have nothing to do, but they may repay themselves.

How the poor little thing is to be pitied! her eyes were sunk the next morning! What will you say, then, when your lover's will be so? My dear angel, you will not be always so; all men are not Valmonts: and again; not dare lift up your eyes! Oh, there you was very right; every one would have read your adventure in them. Believe me, however, if it was so, our women and our young ladies even would assume more modest countenances.

Notwithstanding the praises you perceive I am obliged to give you, yet you must agree you failed in your master piece, which was to tell all to your mama. You had begun so well; you had flung yourself in her arms; you sobbed and cried. What a pathetic scene! What a pity you did not complete it! Your tender mama, overjoyed, and to assist your virtue, would have shut you up in a convent for life; and there you might have loved Danceny as much as you pleased, without a rival, and without any sin; you might be afflicted at your leisure; Valmont would not certainly have come to trouble your affliction with his naughty amusements.

But seriously, is it possible to be so childish, and turned of fifteen, as you are! You are much in the right to say, you are scarcely worthy my care; yet I wish to be your friend: you want one with the mother you have, and the husband she intends for you; but if you do not improve more, what can one make of you? What can be hoped, if what gives girls sense and understanding, deprives you of them.

If you could once bring yourself to reflect for a moment, you would soon discover, you would rather congratulate yourself than grieve: but you are ashamed; and that hurts you. Compose yourself; the shame that follows love is like the pain; you suffer it but once. It may be feigned afterwards, but is never felt: and yet the pleasure remains, and you will own that is of consequence. I think I can even pick out among your nonsense, you lay some stress on it. Come, be honest; that uneasiness that prevented *you from doing as you said*; that made you find it *so difficult to struggle*; that made you, as it were, *vexed*, when Valmont went away; was it shame or pleasure occasioned it? And *his manner of speaking, to which one did not know how to answer*, did it not proceed from *his manner of doing*? Ah, little girl! you tell a lie to your friend; that's not right: but enough of that.

What above every thing to any one else is nothing more than pleasure, in your situation is real happiness. Being so circumstanced with a mother, whose affection is of so much importance, and a lover whom you wish ever to enjoy, can you not plainly see the only means to unite successfully those opposite interests is to bring in a third? Drawn off by this new adventure, whilst you will seem to your mama to sacrifice submissively to her will, a passion that was not agreeable to her, you will establish with your lover the honour of having made a fine resistance. Assuring him constantly of your affections, you must not grant him the convincing proofs. Those refusals, which are so trifling in your situation, he will not fail to attribute to virtue; he may, perhaps, repine, but his love will increase; and to enjoy the double merit of sacrificing to the one your affection, and to the other only to resist its force, it will cost nothing more than the enjoyment of its delights. How many women have lost their reputation, who would have anxiously preserved it, had they such a field.

Does not this scheme appear the most feasible as well as the most delightful to you? Do you know what you have got by the one you have taken? Your mama attributed your immoderate grief to your increase of love, and was so enraged, that she only waited to be convinced, in order to punish you. I have just received a letter from her. She will attempt every method to extract the avowal from yourself. She writes me, she may, perhaps, even go so far as to propose Danceny to you for a husband, and this only to make you speak out. If, seduced by this affectation of tenderness, you should open your heart, she would shut you up for a long time, perhaps, for ever, to deplore at leisure your blind credulity.

This scheme she intends to execute against you must be counteracted by another. Begin, then, to be more cheerful, to make her believe you do not think so much of Danceny. She will be the more easily prevailed on to believe it, as it is the usual effect of absence; and she will be the more pleased with you, as she will applaud herself for her prudence which suggested the method. If she should still have her doubts, should persist in sounding you, and should come to mention matrimony, abide, like a prudent girl, in your absolute submission for you risk nothing; as to a husband, one is always as good as another; the most troublesome is not more so than a mother.

When your mama is once better pleased, she will have you married; then, being more free in your proceedings, you can, if you please, quit Valmont to have Danceny, or even keep both; for observe, Danceny is agreeable, it is true, but he is one of those men one can have when they please, and as often as they please; so you may be easy as to him. — Not so with Valmont; it is dangerous to quit him, and difficult to keep him; one must be very skilful, or very tractable: if you could, however, attach him as a friend, you would be happy indeed. He would elevate you to the first rank among the modish women; that is the way to gain consistency in life, and not sit blushing and crying as if your nuns had made you eat your dinner on your knees.

If you are prudent, you will then endeavour to make it up with Valmont, who must be very angry with you: as you must learn to repair your folly, do not be afraid to make him some advances; you will soon learn, that although the men make the first to us, we are always obliged to make the second. You will have a pretence for it, for you must not keep this letter; and I require you will deliver it to Valmont as soon as you have read it. Do not forget to seal it again, however, before you give it: for, in the first place, I want to leave the whole merit of this proceeding to yourself, that it should not carry the appearance of an advice; moreover, I do not know any one I have so much friendship for, as to write as I do to you.

Adieu! my charming angel! follow my advice, and let me know how it succeeds.

P. S. Now I think on't, I had like to forget — A word more — Take a little more care in your style of writing; you always write so like a child; I know from whence it proceeds; you always write as you think, but do not study what you ought to say: that may do very well between you and me, who should not have any secrets from one another; but with every one else, particularly with your lover, it looks so foolish. You must observe, when you write to any one, it is for them, and not for yourself: you must endeavour, then, to write to please them, and not give them your thoughts.

Adieu! my heart! I embrace you, instead of being angry, in hopes you will be more rational.

Paris, Oct. 4, 17 — .

LETTER CVI.

The MARCHIONESS DE MERTEUIL *to the* VISCOUNT DE VALMONT.

Admirable, my dear Viscount! now I love you to distraction; after the first of your two letters, I might well expect the second, which did not much surprise me; although you were so proud of your future success as to solicit the reward, and ask me if I was ready, I foresaw there was no necessity for all that expedition. Yes, upon honour, perusing the recital of your tender scene, that had *affected you so much*; and reflecting on your modesty, worthy the most glorious days of chivalry, I exclaimed, "The opportunity is lost!" How could it be otherwise? What would you have a poor woman do, who surrenders, and will not be accepted? Why, faith, in such a circumstance, appearances must be saved, and that is only what your Presidente has done. For my part, I very well know, the step she has taken has its effect, and intend to follow the example on the first serious occasion that offers; but I swear, if whoever I take this trouble for does not make a better use of it than you have done, he may certainly renounce me for ever.

Thus are you reduced, positively, to a mere nothing! by two women, one of which was fixed for the next day, and the other wished for nothing so much! Well, you will be apt to think I boast, and say it is easy to prophecy after the event; but I swear I expected it; for you really have no genius for your profession; you barely know what you have learned; you have no invention; when circumstances do not assist your formalities of custom, and you are obliged to go out of the common road, you stop short like a school-boy; to sum up all, a childishness on the one hand, a return of prudery on the other, because they are not every day experienced, are enough to disconcert you; you neither know how to remedy or prevent them. Ah, Viscount! Viscount! you teach me not to judge men by their success, and we must soon say of you, "he was brave such a day." When you commit blunder on blunder, why then you fly to me—One would imagine I have nothing else to do but retrieve your follies: it is certainly work enough for any one person.

However, as to those two adventures; the one was undertaken contrary to my inclination;—the other, as you have paid some attention to my wishes, I take on myself.

Read first the enclosed letter, then give it to the little Volanges; it is more than sufficient to recall her; but I beg you will pay some attention to this child; let us join together to make her the greatest curse and affliction of her mother and Gercourt: there is no danger in giving her large doses; I see plainly the little thing will not be frightened; and, our scheme once completed, she may act as she pleases.

I shall be totally unconcerned about her. I had some thoughts of making her a subaltern intriguer, to take her to play the second parts under me; but I perceive she has no genius; she has a kind of foolish openness that has not given way to the specific you administered, which, however, seldom fails; and, in my opinion, it is the most dangerous disorder a woman can possibly have; it marks, more than any thing, a weakness of temper, which opposes every thing, and which is almost always incurable; so that our time would be lost in forming this little girl for intrigue, as, at best, she never will be more than a comeatable woman. I don't know any thing so insipid, as that stupid facility, that makes a woman compliant without knowing why or wherefore; only because she is attacked, and knows not how to resist; those sort of women are absolutely mere machines. You will say, that is all we want; and that is sufficient for our purpose. Be it so: but it must not be forgot, that every one soon becomes acquainted with the springs and contrivers of those machines; so that to use this one, without bad consequences, we must lose no time, stop when necessary, and afterwards break it. We shall not be at a loss to get rid of her, and Gercourt will be ready to cloister her when we please. When he can no longer doubt his disaster, when it will be public and notorious, what matters it us if he revenges himself, provided he is inconsolable? What I say of the husband, I dare say you think the same of the mother; therefore look it as done.

This measure, which I conceive to be the best, attracted my thoughts, made me resolve to lead on the young thing briskly, as you will perceive by my letter; it is also of the utmost consequence not to leave any thing in her possession that may commit us, which I beg you will attend to. This precaution observed, I take the morality on myself; the remainder is in your department; however, if we should hereafter find she improves, we shall always have time to alter our plan; which had like to have been the case, and that we should one time or other have been employed at what we are now about; but at all events our labour will not be lost.

I must, however, tell you, mine had like to be destroyed; and Gercourt's good fortune had nearly overpowered my prudence. Madame de Volanges, in a fit of maternal fondness, was on the point of giving away her daughter to Danceny; from thence proceeded the remarkable tenderness you observed the *next morning*. This would have been still one of your master strokes. Fortunately the tender parent consulted me about it; and I expect my answer will give her a disrelish to it. I said so much in praise of virtue, and wheedled her so well, that I am sure she will be pleased with my reasons.

I am sorry I had not time to take a copy of my letter, for your edification, on the austerity of my morals. You would there see how contemptible I hold those women of depraved principles who have lovers. Nothing so commodious, as to be a rigourist in convention; it only hurts others, and gives us no uneasiness. Moreover, I am informed the good lady has had her little foibles, as well as others, in her younger days. I was not sorry to humble her conscience, at least, which was some consolation for the praises I was obliged to give her against my own. It was thus, in the same letter, the idea of hurting Gercourt inspired me the resolution to speak well of him.

Adieu, Viscount! I approve much of your plan of remaining where you are for some time. I have no means for expediting your march: but I recommend you should employ your time with our pupil. As to myself, notwithstanding your polite summons, you find you must still wait, and you will agree with me it is not my fault.

Paris, Oct. 4, 17—.

LETTER CVII.

AZOLAN *to the* VISCOUNT DE VALMONT.

Sir,

On receipt of your orders, I immediately waited on Mr. Bertrand, your honour's steward, who paid me twenty-five louis d'ors, as your honour had ordered. I asked him for two more for Philip, who was to set off immediately, as your honour had ordered, and who had no money; but your steward would not give them, as he said he had not any order from your honour to that purpose; so I was obliged to give them to myself, and which your honour will be pleased to observe.

Philip set out last night. I recommended it to him strongly not to leave the inn, that you may find him when necessary.

I went immediately after to Madame the Presidente's, to see Mademoiselle Julie: but she was abroad, and I could only speak to La Fleure, from whom I could not get any intelligence, because he has been always abroad since his return only at meal times. It is the second that has always attended table, and your honour knows I had no acquaintance with him: but I began to-day.

I returned this morning to Mademoiselle Julie, and she seemed very glad to see me. I asked her concerning the reason of her mistress returning to town; she told me, she knew nothing of it, and I believe she spoke truth. I scolded her, because she did not tell me of their going away, and she declared she knew nothing of it till her mistress was going to bed; so she was obliged to sit up to settle every thing, and the poor girl had but two hours rest. She did not leave her mistress till past one; and she left her writing.

In the morning Madame de Tourvel left a letter with the housekeeper. Mademoiselle Julie does not know for who: but imagined it was for your honour, but your honour said nothing of it to me. During the whole journey Madame had a great cloak over her, which hid her entirely; but Mademoiselle Julie thinks she cried very often. She did not speak a word during the whole journey, and she would not stop at − −,[1] as she did in coming; which was not very agreeable to Mademoiselle Julie, who had not breakfasted: but, as I said, masters will be masters.

When they came to town, Madame went to bed for two hours. When she got up, she sent for the porter, and gave him orders not to admit any one. She did not make any toilette. She sat down to dinner, but only tasted a little soup, and went away directly. Her coffee was brought to her apartment. Mademoiselle Julie went in at the same time. She found her mistress settling some papers in her desk, and she could perceive they were letters. I would lay a wager they were your honour's; and of the three she received the same evening, there was one she had before her late the same night. I am very certain it was one from your honour: but why should she come away that way, that astonishes me; but certainly your honour knows, and it is no business of mine.

Madame the Presidente went to the library in the evening, and took two books, which she carried into her dressing room: but Mademoiselle Julie declares she did not read a quarter of an hour the whole day, and that she did nothing but read the letter, muse, and lean on her arm. As I thought your honour would be glad to know what books they were, and that Mademoiselle Julie did not know, I made an excuse to go and see the library to-day: there is no void but for two books; one is the second volume of Christian Thoughts, and the other the first book of a work entitled Clarissa. I write as it was before me; your honour will certainly know what it is.

Last night Madame had no supper, only took tea. This morning she rung early, and ordered her carriage immediately, and went before nine to mass at the Fenillant's. She wanted to go to confession, but her confessor was not in the way, and will not return for eight or ten days. I thought it necessary to inform your honour of this. She then came home, breakfasted, and sat down to write, and stayed at it till near one o'clock. I then found an opportunity of doing what your honour wished most for, for I carried the letters to the post office. There was none for Madame de Volanges; but I send your honour one for Monsieur the President; I thought that might be the most necessary. There was one also for Madame de Rosemonde; but I thought your honour might see that whenever you had a mind, and I let it go. Besides, your honour will know all, as Madame the Presidente has wrote to him. Hereafter I can have all your honour pleases; for it is Mademoiselle Julie that almost always gives them to the servants, and she has promised me, that out of friendship to me as well as for your honour, she will do every thing I would have her. She would not even take the money I offered her; but I dare say your honour will make her some small present; and if it is your pleasure, and that you think proper, I shall soon know what will please her.

I hope your honour will not think me negligent in your service. I have it much at heart to be clear of the reproaches made me. It was my zeal for your honour's service was the reason of my not knowing Madame the Presidente's departure, because your honour ordered me to set out at three in the morning, which hindered me from seeing Mademoiselle Julie at night as usual, as I went to sleep with the ostler, that I might not disturb the people in the castle.

As to what your honour says, I am often in want of money, it is because I always love to be decent, as your honour may see; besides, one must keep up the honour of the livery they wear. I know very well I ought to save something for a rainy day; but I depend entirely on your honour's generosity, who has been so good a master.

As to what your honour desires, of my entering into Madame de Tourvel's service, and still remaining in yours, I hope your honour will not require it; it was quite different at the Duchess's, for I certainly cannot stoop to wear a livery, and a lawyer's livery, after having been your honour's huntsman. As for all the rest, your honour may dispose as you please of him, who is, with the greatest respect and affection, his most humble and obedient servant,

Roux Azolan, *huntsman.*
Paris, Oct. 5, at night.

[1] The same village, half way on the roads.

LETTER CVIII.

The Presidente DE TOURVEL *to* MADAME DE ROSEMONDE.

My dear indulgent mother, what obligations do I not lay under to you! what comfort have I not received from your letter! I have read it over and over; I cannot lay it down; to it I owe the few moments of ease I have had since my departure. Your bounty, your virtue, your prudence can, then, compassionate my weakness. You pity my misfortunes. Ah! could you but be sensible of them—they are frightful. I imagined I had experienced the pangs of love; but the most excruciating, which must be felt to have any idea of it, is to be separated from the beloved object, for ever separated!—The anguish that sinks me to-day will again return to-morrow, the next day, all my life! Great God! I am yet but young, what a length of sufferings!

To be the cause of one's own misery; to tear one's heart with their own hands; and during those insupportable torments, to know one can put a period to them with a word, and that word to be criminal! — Alas, my dear friend! —

When I took the painful resolution to banish myself from him, I was flattered with the hope that absence would increase my strength and resolution. How fatally am I deceived! They seem to have totally abandoned me. I had more to struggle with, it's true: but in my resistance I was not deprived of all resource; I could sometimes see him; often even not daring to look on him, I was sensible his eyes were fixed on me, they seemed to cheer my heart. But now in my dismal solitude, separated from all my heart held dear, lonely with my misfortunes, every moment of my painful existence is marked with tears, nothing to soften their bitterness, no consolation to mingle with my sacrifices; and those I have already made, render those I still must make more sorrowful.

Even yesterday, how forcibly did I experience this! Among the letters brought me, there was one from him, which I distinguished from among the rest before they were delivered. I trembled — I rose involuntarily — scarce could conceal my emotion; and yet that state was not unpleasing. Soon after left alone, this deceitful pleasure fled, and left one more sacrifice to be made: for how could I open this letter, which I was impatient to read? Strange fatality! that the few consolations which offer are so many new privations to me; which are still made more intolerable by the idea that M. de Valmont shares them.

It is out at last; that name that incessantly possesses me, that I had so much pain to write: the kind of reproach you gave me, has been truly alarming — I beseech you will be persuaded, no false shame has altered my confidence in you; — then why should I be afraid to name him? Ah! I am ashamed of my sentiments, but not of him who causes them. Where is there another so worthy to inspire them? Yet I can't account why that name does not naturally flow from my pen; and even now, I could not write it without some pause: but to return to him. You write me, he appeared *amazingly affected at my departure*. What did he say then? What did he do? Did he talk of returning to Paris? I beg you will put him off it, if you possibly can. If he does me justice, he ought not to be angry with me for this step: but he must be sensible it is an irreversible resolution. One of my greatest tortures is to be ignorant of his thoughts. I still have his letter there — but you will certainly agree with me, I ought not to open it.

It is only through you, my most indulgent friend, I shall not be entirely separated from him. I will not abuse your goodness. I know well you must not write long letters: but you will not refuse a few words to your child, to assist her resolution, and console her. Adieu, my most respectable friend!

Paris, Oct. 5, 17 — .

LETTER CIX.

CECILIA VOLANGES *to the* MARCHIONESS DE MERTEUIL.

Dear Madam, I did not deliver the letter you did me the honour to write me until this day to M. de Valmont. I kept it four days, often under great apprehensions lest it should be discovered; but concealed it carefully; and when a fit of dulness seized me, I locked myself up to read it again. I begin to think what I imagined so great a misfortune, is a trifling thing; I own there is a deal of pleasure in it; so that I begin to be tolerably easy. Nothing now gives me any trouble, but the idea of Danceny; I am often, that I do not think of him at all, and I believe it is because M. de Valmont is so engaging. I made it up with him two days ago; which was not at all difficult; for before I had scarcely spoke, he said, if I had any thing to tell him, he would come to my room at night if it was agreeable to me. As soon as he came, he was as good humoured as if I had not done any thing to vex him. He did not scold me till afterwards, and then very gently, but in such a manner—just as you used to do; which convinces me, he loves me very much.

I cannot remember all the comical stories he told me, which I should never have believed, particularly about mama. I would be much obliged to you, if you would let me know if it is all true. I could not refrain from laughing; once I was ready to burst out, which frightened us both; for mama would have heard me, and then what would become of me! she would have infallibly shut me up in the convent.

I must be prudent; and, as M. de Valmont says he would not run the risk of a discovery for all the world, we have agreed, hereafter he will only come, open the door, and we will go to his chamber. There will be no danger then; I was there last night: whilst I am writing to you, I expect him. Now, Madam, I hope you will not be angry with me. There is still something in your letter that surprises me a good deal; that is, in regard to Danceny and M. de Valmont when I am married. I think you told me at the opera, when once I was married, I should love no one but my husband, and I must even forget Danceny: may be I did not understand you right; and I would much rather it was otherwise, because I should not then be so much afraid of being married. I shall even wish for it, as I shall have the more liberty. I hope then matters may be so settled, that I shall have Danceny only to think of. I know very well I shall never be truly happy but with him; for the thoughts of him constantly disturb me; I have no peace but when I do not think of him, and that is not in my power; as soon as he comes in my head, I grow melancholy.

My greatest consolation is, you promise me Danceny will love me the more for it: are you very sure of it? You would not deceive me, I know; however, it is very whimsical that it should be Danceny I love, and that M. de Valmont—but, as you say, may be it is all for the better. I do not well understand what you mention about my writing. Danceny likes my letters very well: I must not say any thing to him, I know, about what passes between M. de Valmont and me—you need not be uneasy about that.

Mama has not spoke yet about marriage; but when she does, since it is to ensnare me, I promise you I will know how to tell a lie.

Adieu, my dear friend; I am very much obliged to you; I assure you I shall never forget your friendship: I must conclude, for it is almost one, and M. de Valmont will be here soon.
Oct. 10, 17—.

LETTER CX.

VISCOUNT DE VALMONT *to the* MARCHIONESS DE MERTEUIL.

Ye heavenly powers! I have a soul formed for sorrow; grant me one for bliss.[1]. I think it is the tender Saint Preux, who thus expresses himself: more equally divided than he, I at once am possessed of both. I am, my dear friend, at once very happy and very miserable; since you are entirely in my confidence, I will relate my pains and pleasures.

My ungrateful devotee still perseveres in her inflexibility; she has returned me four letters unopened—not four neither, for guessing that after the first, it would be followed by another, I resolved not to lose my time thus, to make my mournful complaints as common-place without a date, and since the second post, it is always the same letter goes and comes, I only change the cover. If my fair one ends as fair ones generally do, and will relent, at least through fatigue; she will at length keep it: then will be the time to renew the correspondence; you may guess this new method hurts my intelligence.—I have, however discovered the fickle woman has changed her confidant; I am certain at least since her leaving the castle, she has not wrote to M. de Volanges; but has twice wrote to old Rosemonde. As she has not said any thing of it to us, and does not even mention her *dear fair one*, who she was incessantly talking of, I concluded she is appointed successor: I conjecture the necessity of talking of me on the one hand, and the shame of again assuming with Madame de Volanges, a subject so long disavowed, have produced this grand revolution: I am apprehensive I shall lose by the change; for the older women grow, the more morose and severe they are: the first would have said every thing evil of me, but the other will say more of the evils of love; and the sensible prude is more afraid of the passion than the Person. The only method to be informed is, as you will observe, to put a stop to the clandestine trade; I have already given my huntsman ample directions, and am hourly in expectation; until then, chance rules all. For these last eight days I have run over all manner of known methods, as also those of romances and secret memoirs, and cannot find a precedent neither for the circumstances of the adventure, or character of the heroine. The difficulty does not lie in getting into her house, even at night, or even to set her asleep as in Clarissa, but after two months of care and trouble, to be obliged to recur to such strange methods; follow the track others have left, and triumph without glory!—No, she shall not have *the pleasure of vice and the honour of virtue.*[2] It is not enough to possess her, she shall give herself up: to compass this, I must not only get in to her house, with her consent; find her alone, and inclined to listen to me; above all, blind her on her danger, for if she perceives it, she will overcome it or perish. The more convinced I am what is necessary to be done, the greater I find the difficulties in the execution; were you again to ridicule me, I will confess my embarrassment increases the more I think of it.

I really believe I should have gone mad, were it not for the pleasing distraction our pupil gives me; my recreations with her are an antidote to melancholy.

Would you believe it was three whole days before your letter had any effect on the little terrified creature? Thus one false idea is capable of destroying the best disposition.

At length on Saturday she came about, began to mutter a few words, in such a low tone, and so inarticulate, with shame no doubt, it was almost impossible to understand her: her blushes, however, declared the business; until then, I assumed a consequential air, but soon softened by so pleasing a repentance, I condescended to promise the pretty penitent, to go to her at night; this favour was accepted with all the gratitude due to so great a kindness.

As I never lose sight of your schemes or my own, I resolved not to neglect this opportunity of coming at the intrinsic value of this child, also to accelerate her education. To be more at liberty to prosecute this business, it was necessary to change the place of rendezvous, for as there is only a closet which separates her room from that of her mother's, she could not think herself sufficiently safe to indulge at her ease: I was determined then to contrive *innocently*, some noise which should frighten her, and make her resolve in future to accept a place of more safety, but she saved me the trouble.

The little thing laughs much, and to keep up her spirits, I took it in my head between the acts, to tell her some scandalous adventures that occurred to me; to give them a greater relish, and fix her attention the more, I put them all to her mother's account, who I loaded with vice and folly. My design in this, was to encourage my timid scholar, and inspire her with a most despicable opinion of her mother. I have always observed, that if this method was not always necessary for the seduction of a young girl, it is indispensable, even the most efficacious, to vitiate her; for she who has no respect for her mother, will never have any for herself: this moral truth, which I think so useful, I am glad to illustrate by an example to corroborate the precept. But your pupil, who did not dream of the moral, was every moment ready to burst with laughing, and once had like to have broke out. I had no difficulty to persuade her she made a great noise; I seemed much alarmed, so did she: that it might make the impression more forcible, I did not suffer pleasure to make its appearance again, but left her three hours sooner than usual, after having agreed to meet the next night in my chamber. I have already received her twice: in this short interval, the scholar is almost as learned as the master: yes, upon my word I have taught her every thing as far as the compliances: I have concealed nothing but the precautions.

Being thus engaged all night, I sleep the greatest part of the day; and as, in the present state of the castle, I have nothing to attract me, I scarcely appear an hour in the day in the saloon. To-day I have taken the resolution to eat in my room — shall only leave it now and then for a short walk: those oddities will be imputed to my health; I have declared I was *devoured with spleen*; I have also talked of a little fever; it will be sufficient to speak in a weak and languid voice to make that go down; and for an alteration in my countenance, rely on your pupil, *love will provide for it*.[3] My leisure hours are taken up with the means of regaining the advantages I have lost over my ingrate, in competing a catechism of debauchery for the use of my scholar, wherein I call every thing by its technical name; I anticipate my joy on the very affecting conversation it will furnish between Gercourt and she the first night after their marriage. Nothing can be more diverting than the ingenuousness with which she expresses what little she knows of this language; she does not think people ought to speak otherwise; this is really enchanting; this contrast of simple candour, with the style of barefaced impudence, has its effect; and I do not know how it is, but of late nothing pleases me but oddities.

I give too much way perhaps to this, as I commit my time and health; but I hope my feigned sickness may, besides saving me the disagreeable tediousness of the saloon, be of service with my austere devotee, whole ferocious virtue is still allied to tender sensibility! I make no doubt she is by this time informed of this great event, and I have a strong desire to know how she takes it, as I would venture to lay a wager she will take the honour of it to herself; I shall regulate the state of my health according to the impression it makes on her. Now, my charming friend, you have my whole story: I wish to have more interesting news for you; and I hope you will be persuaded, that I reckon on the reward I expect from you as a great share in the pleasure I promise myself.

Oct. 11, 17 — .

[1] New Heloise.
[2] New Heloise.
[3] Regnard's Amorous Follies.

LETTER CXI.

COUNT GERCOURT *to* MADAME DE VOLANGES.

Every thing in this country, Madam, has the most pacific appearance, and we daily expect orders to return to France. I hope you have not the least doubt of my eagerness for this return, to complete my union with Mademoiselle de Volanges and you. Yet the Duke of — —, my cousin, to whom you know I am under so many obligations, has just informed me of his recall from Naples. He writes me, his intention to come by Rome, and take in his way that part of Italy he has not seen. He requests I should accompany him on this journey, which will be of six weeks or two months. I will not conceal from you, it would be very agreeable to me to embrace this opportunity. For when once married, I shall not readily undertake any journeys but those the service will require; perhaps, it would be also more convenient to postpone the ceremony until winter, as all my relations will not be in Paris until then, particularly the Marquis de — —, to whom I am indebted for the hope of being allied to you. Notwithstanding those considerations, my resolutions on this matter shall be entirely governed by yours; and if you are not perfectly satisfied with this proposal, I instantly renounce mine. I only request you will do me the favour to inform me of your intentions. I shall wait your answer here, which will regulate my conduct.

I am, with great respect, and every sentiment due from a son,
your most humble servant,
Count de Gercourt.
Bastia, Oct. 10, 17 — .

LETTER CXII.

MADAME DE ROSEMONDE *to the* Presidente DE TOURVEL.

(*Dictated only.*)

This instant, my lovely dear, I received your letter of the 11th,[1] and the mild reproaches it contains. You must confess you intended to make many more; if you had not recollected my title of mother, you would have given me a scolding. That would have been very unjust. It was my hope and wish, to have been able to answer you myself, which made me defer it daily; yet, after all, you see I am obliged to employ my waiting woman's hand, to do me that office. The abominable rheumatism has again seized me; it has this time taken its residence in my right arm, so I am absolutely deprived of its use. This is the consequence of such a young blooming creature's having old friends; they suffer from our disorders.

As soon as my pains will give me any relief, assure yourself I will have a long chat with you. In the mean time I must acquaint you, I received both your letters. If it was possible, they would have redoubled my friendship for you; and that I shall never cease taking a lively share in every thing that concerns you.

My nephew is also a little indisposed; but it is not of any consequence, and need not give any uneasiness. It is a slight indisposition, which seems to affect his temper more than his health. We scarcely ever see him now.

His retreat, and your departure, will not much enliven our little circle. The little Volanges has an immense deal of chat, and yawns all day, as if she would swallow you; for these few days especially, she does us the honour to fall into a profound sleep every evening.

Adieu, my lovely dear! I am ever your sincere friend, your mama, your sister even, if my great age would allow me the title. I am, in few words, most tenderly attached to you.

Signed, Adelaide, *for Madame de* Rosemonde.

From the castle of − −, Oct. 14, 17−.

[1] This letter was never found.

LETTER CXIII.

MARCHIONESS DE MERTEUIL *to the* VISCOUNT DE VALMONT.

I think it time to inform you, Viscount, the world begin to talk of you. Your absence from Paris is remarked, and the cause guessed. I was yesterday at a public supper, which was very numerous; where it was positively asserted, you was detained in a village by an unfortunate romantic amour. Joy was instantly visible on the countenance of all those envious of your successes, and of all the women you have neglected. Believe me, you should not suffer such dangerous reports to gain ground, and should immediately return to destroy them by your presence.

Remember, if you once lose the reputation of irresistible, you will soon more readily find resistance; your rivals will lose the respect they had for you, and will dare you; for is there one amongst them who does not think himself more powerful than virtue? But, above all, remember, among the number of women you have held up to public view, all those you have not had, will attempt to undeceive the public, whilst the others will use every means to abuse it. To sum up all, you must expect to be rated, perhaps, as much beneath your value, as you have hitherto been above it.

Return then, Viscount, and no longer sacrifice your reputation to a puerile whim. You have done all we wanted with the little Volanges; and as for your Presidente, it is not very probable you will do your business with her at ten leagues distance. Do you imagine she will go after you? Perhaps she no longer thinks of you, or thinks of you only to felicitate herself for having humbled you. But here you would find some opportunity of appearing with eclat, and you really want it. If even you should continue obstinate in your ridiculous adventure, I can't see how your return would hurt you — on the contrary.

For if your Presidente *adores you,* as you have so often told me, but never yet proved, her only consolation, her sole pleasure, ought now to be to speak of you, to know what you do, what you say, what you think, even the most trifling matter about you. Those wretched fooleries are of some consequence, according to the privations that are experienced. They are the crumbs falling from the table of the rich man, which he despises; but which the poor one collects with avidity, and feeds on. So the poor Presidente at present receives those crumbs; and the more she has of them, she will be less greedy for the rest. Moreover, as you know her confidant, there is no doubt but every letter contains a little exhortation to corroborate her prudence, and strengthen her virtue. Why will you then leave resources to the one for her defence, and power to the other to hurt you.

Not that I am in the least of your opinion on the loss you think you sustain by the change of confidant; for M. de Volanges detests you, and hatred is always more ingenious and clear sighted than friendship. Your old aunt's virtue will never permit her to slander her dear nephew, for virtue has its foibles. Again, your fears lead you into an error. It is not true, that *the older women grow, the more morose and severe they are.* It is from forty to fifty that grief for faded beauties rage, to be forced to abandon pretensions and pleasures to which the mind is still attached, make almost all women peevish and ridiculous. It is necessary they should have this long interval to prepare for this great sacrifice: but when it is once completed, they divide into two classes.

The most numerous, which are those who never possessed any thing but youth and beauty, fall into a weak apathy, from which they never recover but for play and a few practical devotions; that class is always tiresome, often morose, sometimes marplots, but rarely mischievous. It is not easy to determine whether those women are or are not severe; without ideas, or in a manner without existence, they repeat indifferently, and without comprehending, every thing they hear; and are, as to themselves, *non entities.*

The other class, much more uncommon, but truly valuable, are those of good disposition, who having cultivated their minds, can create themselves an existence, when nature fails; and can, when the embellishments of the outward figure are useless, place them to their minds. Those women have most commonly a sound judgment, and a mind replete with solidity, good humour, and kindness. — They replace the seducing charms with attractive goodness and cheerfulness, whose charms increase with their years. Thus they may be said in some shape to renew their age, by gaining the affections of the youthful part of society. But far from being what you call *morose and severe;* the habits of indulgence, the long reflections on human nature, but especially the remembrance of youth, by which alone they have a relish for life, would rather make them too condescending.

I can aver, having always cultivated an intimacy with old women, of whose good opinion I saw early the advantage, I have known several who I frequented as much from inclination as interest. I shall stop here; for I dread you should fall in love with your old aunt, you are so apt to be inflamed suddenly and morally, and bury yourself with her in the tomb you have so long dwelt in.

But to return. Although you seem enraptured with your little scholar, I fancy she has no share in your projects. You found her ready to your hand, and took her: be it so. But that cannot be called taste. It is not even, properly speaking, an enjoyment; you possess her person only. Not to mention her heart, which I suppose does not give you the least uneasiness, you don't even engage her imagination. I cannot tell whether you have observed it, but I have a proof of it in the last letter she wrote me: I send it you, that you may be convinced. Observe, always when she mentions you, it is *M. de Valmont*; all her ideas, even those you raise, terminate in Danceny; she does not call him Monsieur, but plain Danceny. Thus she distinguishes him from all others: and even giving herself up to you, she familiarises herself only with him. If such a conquest has any thing *bewitching*, if the pleasures you receive are so *attaching*, you are certainly modest, and not difficult to please. Keep her; I agree to it; it is even a part of my scheme: but I really think it should not discompose you in the least. You should also have some ascendant over her, and not suffer her to draw near Danceny, until he is a little worn out of her memory.

Before I think of your coming to me, I must tell you this pretended sickness is an exploded common trick. On my word, Viscount, you lack invention! I am also guilty of repetitions sometimes, as you shall hear: but I endeavour to amuse by the circumstances; and success justifies me. I am going to attempt another adventure. I will agree, it has not the merit of difficulty; but it will be a distraction at least, for time lies very heavy on my hands.

I cannot account for the reason, but since Prevan's affair, Belleroche is become insupportable to me. He has redoubled his attention, tenderness, and *veneration*, to so violent a degree, I can hold out no longer. His wrath at the time was pleasant enough; but it was necessary to check it, otherwise I must have committed myself; there was no making him listen to reason. I resolved to show him more affection, to bring him round more easily; he has taken it so seriously, that ever since he puts me out of all patience with his eternal charms. I moreover take notice of his insulting confidence, for he really looks on me as his property. I am really humbled. He holds me cheap, indeed, if he thinks himself capable of fixing me. He had the assurance to tell me lately, I never should have loved any other but him. Then, indeed, I lost all patience, and was obliged to call my prudence in aid, not to undeceive him instantly, by telling how matters stood. He is certainly a pretty fellow, to aspire to an exclusive right! I will allow, he is well made, and a tolerable person: but take him all in all, he is only a manœuverer in love. The time is come, we must part.

I have endeavoured at it this fortnight past. I have, by turns, treated him with coolness, capriciousness, bad humour, quarrelled even; all in vain: the tenacious creature will not quit his hold. I must, then, use some violence; for this purpose I take him with me to the country. We set out the day after to-morrow. We shall only have some people of no consequence, and not very discerning, and shall be almost as much at liberty as if we were alone. There I shall so overload him with love and fondness, we shall so live for each other only, that he will wish to see the end of this journey, which is now his greatest bliss, more than I shall; and if he does not return more tired of me than I shall be of him, I consent you may say, you know more of the matter than I do.

The pretence for this retreat is, I want seriously to employ my time in preparing for my great law suit, that is to be decided the beginning of winter, which pleases me much; for it is really very disagreeable to have one's fortune in suspense. Not that I am uneasy about the issue; for, first, I have right on my side, as all my lawyers assure me; — if it even was not the case, I should be very unskilful, indeed, if I could not gain a suit against minors of tender years, and their old guardian: however, as nothing must be omitted in a business of such consequence, I shall have two lawyers with me. Will not this be a sprightly jaunt? If I gain my cause, and lose Belleroche, I shall not regret the time.

Now, Viscount, I will give you a hundred guesses before you name his successor; I forget though, you never guess any thing — Why, Danceny. You are astonished; for I am not yet reduced to the education of children. This one, however, deserves an exception in his favour. He has the graces of youth, but not its frivolousness. His reserve in a circle is well adapted to banish all manner of suspicion, and he is the more amiable when in a tête-à-tête; not that I yet have had one with him on my own account. I am only his confidant: but under this mask of friendship, I think I see a strong inclination for me, and I already feel a violent one for him. It would be pity so much wit and delicacy should be sacrificed and stupified with that little idiot Volanges. I hope he deceives himself in thinking he loves her; she is so far from deserving him. Not that I have the least tincture of jealousy: but it would be murder; and I wish to save Danceny. I therefore beg, Viscount, you will use your endeavours that he may not come near his Cecilia, as he has got the disagreeable custom of calling her. A first liking has always an inconceivable power. If he was now to see her, I could not be certain of any thing, especially during my absence. At my return, I shall take every thing on myself, and will answer for the success.

I had some notion of taking the young man with me; but sacrificed my inclination to my usual prudence: moreover, I mould have been apprehensive he might make some observations on Belleroche and me; an idea even of such a thing would distract me; as I wish to offer myself immaculate to his imagination: such as one should be to be worthy of him.

Paris, Oct. 15, 17 — .

LETTER CXIV.

The Presidente DE TOURVEL *to* MADAME DE ROSEMONDE.

My dear friend, my uneasiness for the state of your health is so great, I cannot forbear writing to you. Without knowing whether you will be able to answer me, I cannot avoid interrogating you. M. de Valmont's state, which you tell me *is not dangerous*, does not, however, dispel my apprehensions so much as it does yours. It is no novelty that melancholy and distaste for company should be symptoms of an approaching disease; bodily disorders, as well as those of the mind, incline us to solitude; and we often load those with ill temper, whose disorder we ought to compassionate.

I think he ought, at least, consult with some one. How happens it, that being yourself indisposed, you have not a physician? Mine, who I sent for this morning, and whom, for I will not conceal it from you, I consulted indirectly, is of opinion, that with persons of naturally an active disposition, this kind of sudden apathy should by no means be neglected. He told me, moreover, disorders will not give way to remedies, when they have been neglected in the beginning. Why then run such a hazard with one so dear to you?

It adds greatly to my uneasiness, I have not had any news of him these four days. Good God! I beg you will not deceive me on his state! Why is it he has left off writing to me so suddenly? If it was only the effect of my obstinacy in returning his letters, I believe he would have taken the resolution sooner. Without having, however, any faith in forebodings, for these few days I have been in a most melancholy situation. I fear I am on the eve of some great misfortune. You cannot imagine, and I am ashamed to tell you, how much I regret not receiving those letters which I refused to read. I was certain he at least thought of me, and saw something that came from his hands. I did not open them, but I wept over them: my tears were softer, and flowed with more ease; they only partly dissipated the habitual oppression I experience since my return. I conjure you, my most respectable friend, to write to me yourself as soon as you can; in the mean time, pray indulge me every day in hearing from you, and of him.

I now perceive, I have scarcely said a word to you: but you know my sentiments, my unreserved attachment, my tender gratitude, for your sincere friendship. You will forgive my distress, my painful anguish, for dreading evils of which I am, perhaps, the cause. Merciful God! this desponding idea pursues me and wrings my heart. This misfortune only was wanting. I know I am born to experience them all.

Adieu, my dear friend! love me, pity me. Shall I hear from you this day?
Paris, Oct. 16, 17—.

LETTER CXV.

The VISCOUNT DE VALMONT *to the* MARCHIONESS DE MERTEUIL.

It is a most unaccountable thing, my charming friend, when we are at a remote distance, we cannot so readily understand each other. Whilst I was near you, we always had the same sentiments, and viewed every object in the same light; because I am now about three months absent, we are no longer of the same opinion on any thing. Which of us is in the wrong? You certainly will not hesitate in your answer: but I, more wise, or more polite, will not decide. I shall only reply to your letter, and continue to lay my conduct open.

First, accept my thanks for the intelligence of the reports flying about me; that does not make me uneasy: I think soon I shall be furnished with materials to silence them all. Have a little patience; I shall again appear more celebrated than ever, and more worthy of you.

I expect even they will give me credit for the affair of the little Volanges, which you affect to treat as such a trifle: as if there was no merit in carrying in one night a young girl from a favoured lover; to make use of her after as much as one chooses, even as their own property, and without any farther trouble; to obtain from her what one dare not even require from girls whose vocation it is; and all this without in the least disturbing her tender affection; without making her inconstant, or even false; for certainly I don't engage her imagination. So that after my fancy is at an end, I will deliver her into her lover's arms, without, as I may say, her having taken notice of any thing. Pray is that so common an exploit? Yet believe, when she is gone from under my tuition, the principles I have instilled into her will nevertheless display themselves; and I prophesy, the timid scholar will take a flight that will do honour to her master.

If, however, they like heroics better, I will show my Presidente; this model cited for every virtue, respected even by our greatest libertines; insomuch, they had given up the idea of attacking her. I will show her, forgetting duty and virtue, sacrificing her reputation and two years prudence to run after the happiness of pleasing me; intoxicated with love; sufficiently recompensed for so many sacrifices by a word, a look, which yet she will not always obtain. I will do more, I will even abandon her; and if I know this woman, I shall not have a successor; she will resist the necessity of consolation; the habitude of pleasure; even the thirst for revenge: she shall have existed for me only; and let her career be long or short, I alone will have opened and shut the barrier; when once I rise to this triumph, I will tell my rivals, "that is my exploit, search the world for such an example."

You ask me whence proceeds this excessive confidence? Why, for eight days past, I am my fair one's confidant; she does not tell me her secrets, but I come at them; two of her letters have given me sufficient information; the rest I will only read out of curiosity. I now absolutely want nothing to crown my success but admittance, my measures are taken; I shall immediately execute them. I think you are curious; but to punish you for not believing my intentions, you shall not know them; you really in earnest deserve I should withdraw my confidence from you, at least, for this adventure; were it not for the tender reward you have attached to its success, I would not mention it again. You see I am vexed; however, in hopes of your amendment, I will be satisfied with this slight reprimand, and my indulgent mind for a moment, forgetting my grand project, shall employ itself on yours.

You are then in the country, dull as sentiment, and sorrowful as fidelity; and poor Belleroche, not satisfied with making him drink the waters of oblivion, you will also put him to the torture; how does he like it? Does he bear the nausea of love well? I would rather than a great deal he should become more attached to you; I am curious to learn what more efficacious remedy you would use; I really pity you, to have been obliged to have recourse to that. Never did I make love but once methodically; I certainly had a strong motive, as it was with the Countess de — —; and twenty times in her arms have I been tempted to tell her, "Madam, I renounce the place I solicit, and permit me to quit that I occupy." Of all the women I have had, she is the only one of whom I take pleasure in speaking ill. Your motive, I must own, is truly ridiculous, and you was right in thinking I should not guess the successor: — What, then, is it for Danceny you have taken all this trouble? Ah, my dear friend, let him alone to adore *his virtuous Cecilia*, and do not commit yourself in this children's play; leave the scholars to be formed by good old women, or play with the pensioners at pretty innocent games. What, would you instruct a novice who neither knows how to take or leave you, for whom you must do every thing? I tell you seriously, I disapprove your choice; and let it be ever so secret, it will humble you in my mind, and your own conscience. You say you have taken a great liking to him; for shame! you certainly deceive yourself. I think I have discovered the cause of your error; this fine disgust for Belleroche happened at a time of scarcity, and Paris not offering any choice, your lively ideas fixed on the first object they met; but remember, at your return you may choose among a thousand; and if you dread the inaction you risk falling into in deferring your choice, I offer myself for your amusement at your leisure hours. From this time until your arrival, my great affairs will be determined one way or other; certainly neither the little Volanges, nor the Presidente even, will employ me so much, but I may devote myself to you as much as you wish; perhaps even before that time, I may have delivered the little one into the hands of her discreet lover. Say what you please, which I don't agree to, that it is not an *attaching* enjoyment, as I intended she should ever retain an idea of me superior to all the rest of mankind, I assumed such a tone with her as I could not support long without prejudice to my health; and from this moment I am no longer hers only for family duty. You don't understand me; I mean I wait a second period to confirm my hopes, and give me full assurance I have amply succeeded in my scheme. Yes, my dear friend, I have already a first indication that my scholar's husband will not die without posterity, and the chief of the house of Gercourt will be a younger brother of that of Valmont. But let me finish to my own liking this business which I undertook at your request: remember if you make Danceny inconstant, you deprive the adventure of its poignancy. Consider also, in offering myself to you, I have a right to a preference.

I depend so much upon it, I was not afraid to counteract your designs in even assisting to increase the tender passion of the discreet lover, for the first and worthy object of his choice. Having yesterday found your pupil writing to him, and disturbed her in this pleasing task, for another still more pleasing: I afterwards desired to see the letter; as it was too cold and constrained, I made her sensible it was not thus she should console her lover, and made her write another which I dictated; where, imitating her nonsense as well as I could, I endeavoured to feed the young man's passion by more certain hopes; the little, creature was overjoyed, she said, to find she wrote so well, and hereafter I should hold the correspondence. What have I not done for this Danceny! I have been at once his friend, his confidant, his rival, and his mistress; even at this instant, I am endeavouring to save him from your dangerous toils: ay, dangerous; for to possess, and then lose you, is purchasing a moment's happiness with an eternity of regret.

Adieu, my lovely friend! muster up resolution to dispatch Belleroche as soon as possible; think no more of Danceny; and prepare to again find and return me the delicious pleasures of our first connection.

Oct. 19, 17—.

P. S. I congratulate you on the approaching decision of your great cause; I should be very happy this event should occur during my reign.

LETTER CXVI.

CHEVALIER DANCENY *to* CECILIA VOLANGES.

Madame de Merteuil set out this morning for the country; thus am I deprived, my charming Cecilia; of my only remaining consolation in your absence, of conversing of you with our mutual friend: she has given me leave for some time past to distinguish her by that title; I accepted it the more eagerly, as it has something the appearance of drawing me nearer to you; she is a most amiable woman, and knows how to add the most attractive charms to friendship:—It would seem as if this pleasing sensation was embellished and strengthened in her the more, for what she refuses to love. You cannot imagine how much she loves you; how pleased she is to hear me speak of you: it is this certainly that attaches me so much to her. What happiness, to exist only for you both! to make such sudden transitions from the ecstasy of love, to the charms of friendship; to devote my life to it; to be in some measure the point of re-union to your reciprocal attachment; to be convinced the happiness of the one is also that of the other.

You cannot, my charming Cecilia, love this adorable woman too much: add to my attachment for her, by sharing it with me. Now I experience the charms of friendship, I wish you also to taste them; I think no enjoyment complete you do not partake of: Yes, my dear Cecilia, I wish to inspire you with all the tender sentiments; that every idea should convey happiness to you; and would still think I returned you only a portion of the felicity I have received from you.

Alas! those enchanting dreams are only the pleasing fancies of imagination, and reality only offers me mortifying privations. I now plainly see I must give up the flattering hope of seeing you in the country: my sole consolation is endeavouring to be persuaded you cannot accomplish it, and you do not choose to afflict me more by informing me of it; twice already have I lamented this disappointment, and received no reply:—Ah! Cecilia, I really believe you love me with your whole soul, but your heart is not so ardent as mine. If the obstacles were left to me to be removed, or my own interests to be managed instead of yours, I would soon convince you nothing was impossible to love. You do not inform me even when this cruel absence is to be at an end: here surely I can see you; your enchanting looks would revive my sorrowful heart which is almost totally depressed: forgive, my dear Cecilia, my fears, they are not suspicious; I place implicit faith in your love, in your constancy; I should be too miserable, had I any doubts; but so many obstacles still renewed—I am, my dear, very much dejected:— Madame de Merteuil's departure has renewed all my sorrows.

Adieu, my dear Cecilia, adieu!—Remember your lover is in affliction, and you only can make him happy.

Paris, Oct. 17, 17—.

LETTER CXVII.

CECILIA VOLANGES *to the* CHEVALIER DANCENY.

(Dictated by Valmont.)

Do you think my dear friend there is any necessity to be angry with me to make me melancholy, when I know you to be in affliction; and do you think I have not my share of sufferings as well as you? I even partake of those I am obliged to give you; and still you are unjust. I see plainly what puts you out of temper; it is because I was silent to the two requisitions you made to me here; do you think an answer to it is so easy to give? Do you think I do not know what you want is not right? And if I am so distressed to refuse you at such a distance, how would it be if you was here? Then again I must be afflicted all my life for giving you a moments consolation.

I hide nothing from you, I give you my reasons, you may judge for yourself; I should perhaps have done what you wish, had it not been for what I wrote you, that M. de Gercourt, who is the cause of all our trouble, will not come so soon; and as mama is greatly pleased with me now, I caress her as much as possible; who knows what I may bring her to: if we could be happy without having any thing to reproach myself with, surely it would be much better. If I am to believe what I have often heard, that men, when they have loved their wives before marriage, do not love them so much after; the dread of that restrains me more than any thing:— Are you not sure of my heart, and will there not be always time enough.

I promise you, if I cannot avoid marrying M. de Gercourt, who I already hate without knowing him, nothing shall prevent me from being yours as much as I can, even before any thing, as I do not mind being loved by any but you:—you will see if I act wrong it shall not be my fault; the rest is indifferent to me, provided you promise to love me always as much as you do now:—but until then let me be as I am; and do not ask a thing I have good reasons not to do, and am vexed to refuse you.

I would likewise be very glad M. de Valmont would not be so pressing on your account, which only makes me more unhappy: he is your very good friend I assure you; he does every thing as you would do yourself; but adieu, my dear friend! it was late when I began to write, and spent a good part of the night at it. I am going to bed to retrieve the time I lost. I embrace you; but do not scold me any more.

Castle of − − , *Oct.* 18, 17 − .

LETTER CXVIII.

CHEVALIER DANCENY *to the* MARCHIONESS DE MERTEUIL.

If I am to credit my almanack, my charming friend, you are absent only two days; but my heart tells me it is an age. According to your own doctrine then, the heart must always be believed. It is time you should return: surely your affairs should be finished by this time. How can I be any way concerned in the success of you law suit, as I must suffer by your absence? I am now much inclined to scold; and it is really hard, being so ripe for bad humour, I dare not give way to it.

Is it not a species of infidelity, to leave your friend, after having accustomed him not to be able to exist out of your presence? Your lawyers will even find it difficult to defend so bad a cause: besides, those gentlemen generally make use of arguments which are not valid answers to sentiments.

You have given me so many for this journey, that I am sick of them, and will pay no farther attention to them, were they even to persuade me to forget you. Yet that would not be so unreasonable, nor so difficult, as you may imagine: it would be only laying aside the habit of always thinking of you; for nothing here, I can assure you, would ever recall you to my memory.

Our prettiest women, those even called the most amiable, are so inferior to you, that they could give but a very faint idea indeed. I even think, that, with all their practised looks, the more one might at first think that they resembled you, the more striking the difference would afterwards appear. In vain do they use their utmost exertions; they always fail being you; and that precisely constitutes the charm. Unfortunately, when the days are so long, and one is unoccupied, reveries, ideal projects, and chimeras, fill the brain; the mind acquires a degree of elevation. We are intent on ornamenting our productions; we collect together every thing that can please; we arrive at length at perfection; and when we are there, the portrait brings us back to the original, and one is quite astonished to see that you were the only object of all these turns of the mind. Even at this moment I am the dupe of pretty much the same sort of error. You fancy, perhaps, that it was in order to employ myself on your subject, that I resolved to write to you—not at all: it was in order to direct my attention a little from you. I have a hundred things to tell you, of which you were not the object, and which, nevertheless, you very well know concern me nearly; and yet it is from these things my attention is led away. Since when, then, do the charms of Friendship dissipate those of Love? If I considered it narrowly, perhaps I should have to reproach myself—but hush! Let us forget that small fault, lest we relapse into it; and let even my best female friend be in ignorance of it.

Why are you absent? Why not here to give me an answer? To recall me if I should stray? To talk to me of my Cecilia? To add, if possible, to the happiness I experience in loving her, by the additionally charming idea that it is your friend I love? Yes, I avow the love she inspires me, is become more precious. Since you have been kind enough to become the confidant of it, I feel so great a pleasure in opening my heart to you, in interesting yours in my sentiments, in depositing them there without reserve! I think them the more dear to me in proportion as you condescend to hear them; that I look at you, and say to myself, It is in her that all my happiness is centered. I have nothing new to inform you of as to my situation. The last letter I received from her increases, and gives a degree of security to my hopes; though she still brings a delay to them, yet her motives are so tender and honourable, that I can neither blame her, nor complain of it. Perhaps this is obscure to you; but why are you not here? Though we can say every thing to a friend, every thing cannot be written. The secrets of love especially, are so delicate, that one ought not to let them go in that way, relying on honour. If they are sometimes permitted to go abroad, they never should be permitted to go out of sight; they ought even to be watched back to their new asylum. Return, then my adorable friend; you see your return is necessary: forget, then, the *thousand reasons* that detain you where you are, or teach me to live where you are not.

I have the honour to be, &c.
Paris, Oct. 16, 17 — .

LETTER CXIX.

MADAME DE ROSEMONDE *to the* Presidente DE TOURVEL.

Although, still suffering much pain, my lovely dear, I endeavour to write to you myself, in order to tell you what interests you so much. My nephew still preserves his misanthropy: he sends every day regularly to enquire about my health; but has never come once in person, although I requested it; so that we see no more of him than if he was at Paris. This morning, however, I met him, when least expected: it was in my chapel, where I came down for the first time since my painful disorder. They inform me, for four days past he goes there regularly every morning to mass. God grant it may last.

When I entered, he congratulated me very affectionately on my recovery. As mass was beginning, we broke off the conversation, expecting to renew it afterwards: he disappeared before I could join him again. I will not conceal from you, he is something altered; but, my lovely dear, do not make me repent my confidence in your good sense, by your too great uneasiness; and be assured I would rather afflict than deceive you.

If my nephew continues to treat me so severely, I am resolved, when I am something better, to visit him in his chamber, and endeavour to dive into the cause of this extraordinary madness, in which you certainly have some share. The result of my observations you shall be informed. I must leave off, not being able to stir my fingers. If Adelaide knew I had been writing, she would be very much vexed. Adieu, my lovely dear!
Castle of — — , *Oct.* 20, 17 — .

LETTER CXX.

VISCOUNT DE VALMONT *to* FATHER ANSELMUS,

(Of the Feuillant Convent, St. Honoré Street.)

Not having the honour of being known to you, Sir, but thoroughly acquainted with the well-placed confidence Madame the Presidente de Tourvel reposes in you, I think I may address myself to you without being guilty of indiscretion, to obtain an essential piece of service, truly worthy your holy ministry, wherein Madame de Tourvel's advantage is equally concerned with mine.

Having in my possession some papers of consequence that concern her nearly, and should not be entrusted to any person, which I neither ought or will deliver but into her own hands. Being deprived of the means of informing her of this resolution, for reasons which you may probably have learned from her, but which I do not think myself at liberty to acquaint you with, she determined to refuse corresponding with me; a determination which I do not now in the least blame, as she could not foresee events, so unexpected, and which required the supernatural power, that one is forced to acknowledge for their completion. Therefore I request, Sir, you will be so good to inform her of my new resolves, and ask, in my name, a particular interview, where I may in some measure repair the injuries I have been guilty of by my apologies; and, as the last sacrifice, annihilate, in her presence, the only remaining impressions of an error or crime, which made me culpable towards her.

It cannot be until after this preliminary expiation, I shall dare, at your knees, make the humiliating, avowal of my long bad conduct, and implore your mediation, for a still more important, and, unhappily, a much more difficult reconciliation. May I hope, Sir, you will not refuse me your assistance in a business so necessary and so important; and that you will vouchsafe to aid my weakness, and guide my steps in this new path, which I ardently wish to follow, and to which, with shame, I own myself an utter stranger.

I wait your answer with the impatience of repentance that wishes to reform; and beg you will believe me to be, with as much gratitude as veneration,

Your most humble, &c.

P. S. I authorise you, Sir, if you think proper, to communicate this letter entirely to Madame de Tourvel, who I shall make it my duty to respect during the rest of my days, and whom I shall never cease to revere, as the instrument heaven has been pleased to use to bring me back to virtue, by the striking example of her own.

Castle of — —, Oct. 22, 17—.

LETTER CXXI.

The MARCHIONESS DE MERTEUIL *to* CHEVALIER DANCENY.

I received your letter, my very young friend, and must scold you before you receive my thanks for it; farther I warn you, if you do not amend, you shall not have any answer from me. Leave, then, that wheedling style, which is but mere cant, when it is not the expression of love. Is it the style of friendship? No, my dear friend; each sentiment has its peculiar language suitable to it; and to use another, is to disguise the thought we should express. I am well aware our silly women do not understand what is said to them, unless it is translated in some shape into this fashionable nonsense: but I imagined you would have distinguished me from them. I am really hurt, and, perhaps, more than I ought, you should imbibe such an opinion of me.

You will find in my letter what is wanting in yours, frankness and simplicity. As I shall say, it would give me infinite pleasure to see you, and am grieved to have only those about me who stupify me instead of those that give me pleasure; but you translate this same phrase thus: *Teach me to live where you are absent*; thus, suppose you was with your mistress, you could not live was I absent. What a misfortune! And these women *that always fail being me!* You will find, perhaps, that wanting also to your Cecilia! This, however, is the style which, by the abuse now made of it, is beneath the nonsense of compliment, and becomes a mere precedent, to which no more attention is paid than to your most humble servant.

My dear friend, when you write to me, let it be to express your thoughts and feelings, and do not stuff your letter with phrases, which I shall find, without your assistance, well or ill told in the first romance of the day. I hope you will not be displeased at what I now say, if even you should discover some peevishness in it; for it must not be denied I am a little so at present. To avoid even the shadow of the defect with which I reproach you, you must not be told, perhaps, this peevishness is not a little increased by the distance I am from you. And I am inclined to think, all things considered, you are more eligible than a law suit and two lawyers, and, perhaps, even the *attentive* Belleroche.

Observe, instead of being afflicted at my absence, you should be highly gratified; for I never before paid you so handsome a compliment. Your example influences me; I shall be apt to wheedle. No; I will retain my sincerity: it alone assures you of my tender friendship, and the interesting things it inspires. Is it not very pleasing to have a young friend, whose inclinations lead him elsewhere? However, that is not the system of the generality of women, but it is mine. I always thought the pleasure greater, and more satisfactory, in a sentiment where there is no apprehension. Don't you think I have assumed the character of confidant for you tolerably soon: but you choose your mistress so young, that, for the first time, I begin to think I grow old. You are certainly right, thus to prepare yourself for a long career of constancy; and I sincerely wish it may be reciprocal.

You do right to cherish the *tender and honourable motives*, which you say *retard your hopes*. A long defence is the only merit of those who do not always resist; and I should think it unpardonable in any other but a child, like the little Volanges, not to fly a danger, of which she has had sufficient warning by the confession she made of her love. You men have no idea of virtue, and what the sacrifice of it costs a woman; but if she is capable of reasoning, she should know, that independent of the fault she commits, a single weakness is one of the greatest misfortunes; and I cannot conceive how any can fall, if they have a moment for reflection.

Do not attempt to combat this idea: it principally attaches me to you. You will save me from the dangers of love; and although I have hitherto guarded myself against them without your assistance, yet I consent to be grateful, and shall love you more and the better for it.

On which, my dear chevalier, I pray God to have you in his holy keeping.
Castle of — —, Oct. 22, 17—.

LETTER CXXII.

MADAME DE ROSEMONDE *to the* Presidente DE TOURVEL.

I flattered myself, my lovely daughter, to have been able to calm your uneasiness; with grief, however, I am forced still to increase it; yet be pacified, my nephew is not in any dangerous way. I cannot even say he is really sick. Still there is something very extraordinary in his disorder, which is incomprehensible. I left his chamber with sensations of grief, and even of terror, which I blame myself for imparting to you, and still cannot conceal. I will give you an account of the transaction. You may depend on its veracity; Were I to live eighty years more, I should never forget this melancholy scene.

I went this morning to see my nephew. He was writing, surrounded with a heap of papers, which appeared to be the object of his employment. He was so deeply engaged, I was in the middle of the room before he looked about to see who came in. As soon as he perceived me, I observed, as he rose, he endeavoured to compose his countenance, and perhaps it was that made me pay more attention to it. He was undressed, and without powder; but his countenance pale, wan, and very much altered; his look, which used to be so gay and lively, was melancholy and dejected: and, between ourselves, I would not for any consideration you had seen him thus, for his whole deportment was very affecting, and the most apt to inspire that tender compassion, which is one of the most dangerous snares of love.

Although struck with those remarks, yet I began a conversation as if I had not taken notice of any thing. First, I enquired about his health; and without saying it was very good, he did not complain of its being bad. I then began to lament his recluseness, which had something the appearance of a disordered fancy, and endeavoured to mingle a little sprightliness with my reprimand: but he replied in an affecting tone; "I confess it is another error, which shall be repaired with the rest." His looks more than his reply, disconcerted my cheerfulness; and I told him, he took up a little friendly reproach in too serious a manner.

We then began to chat on indifferent matters. A little while after he told me, an affair, *the greatest affair of his whole life*, would, perhaps, soon call him back to Paris. I was afraid to guess at it, my lovely dear; and lest this beginning should lead to a confidence I did not wish, asked him no questions, but only replied, a little dissipation might put him in better health; saying, at this time I would not press him, as loving my friends for their own sake. At this so simple a speech, he squeezed my hands, and with a vehemence I can't express, "Yes, my dear aunt," said he, "love a nephew who respects and cherishes you, and, as you say, love him for his own sake. Do not be afflicted at his happiness, and do not disturb with any sorrow, the eternal tranquillity he soon hopes to enjoy. Repeat once more, you love me, you forgive me; yes, you will forgive me; I know the goodness of your heart: but can I hope for the same indulgence from those I have so grievously offended?" Then leaned down towards me, as I believe to conceal some marks of grief, which, however, the tone of his voice betrayed.

Inexpressibly affected, I rose suddenly; and he, no doubt, observed my affright, for instantly composing himself, he replied, "Your pardon, Madam, I perceive I am wandering in spite of me. I beg you will remember my profound respect, and forget my expressions. I shall not omit waiting on you before my departure to renew them." This last sentence seemed to imply a wish, I should terminate my visit; I accordingly retired.

I am lost in reflection, as to his meaning. What can this affair be, *the greatest of his whole life?* On what account should he ask my pardon? From whence could that involuntary melting proceed whilst he was speaking? I have since put myself those questions a thousand times, without being able to solve them. I can't even discover any thing relative to you; yet, as the eyes of love are more penetrating than those of friendship, I would not conceal any thing from you that passed between my nephew and me.

This is the fourth time I have sat down to write this long letter, which I should yet have made longer, but for the fatigue I undergo. Adieu, my lovely dear!

Castle of — —, Oct. 25, 17—.

LETTER CXXIII.

FATHER ANSELMUS *to the* VISCOUNT DE VALMONT.

I received, Monsieur Viscount, the letter you did me the honour to write to me, and yesterday, as you requested, waited on the person mentioned. I laid before her the motives and intentions that induced you to this measure. Although very determined to pursue the prudent resolution she at first took, yet on the remonstrances I made, that by a refusal she might incur the danger of throwing an obstacle in the way of your conversion and in a manner oppose the designs of all-merciful Providence, she consented to receive your visit, on condition nevertheless, it shall be the last; and has desired me to inform you, she should be at home on Thursday next, the 28th. If this day should not be convenient for you, please to inform her, and appoint some other; your letter will be received.

Give me leave to recommend to you, Sir, to avoid delays, unless for very cogent reasons, that you may as soon as possible give yourself up entirely to the laudable dispositions you express. Remember, whoever is silent to the calls of divine grace, exposes himself to have it withdrawn; that if the divine bounty is infinite, the dispensation of it is regulated by justice; and the time may come, when the God of mercy may be changed to a God of vengeance.

If you continue to honour me with your confidence, be assured all my care shall be devoted to you the instant you require it. Let my business be ever so great, the most important shall ever be to fulfil the duties of the holy ministry, to which I am particularly devoted; and the most valuable part of my life, that wherein I see my weak endeavours crowned with the benediction of the Most High. We are weak sinners, and cannot do any thing of ourselves! but the God that now calls you is omnipotent; and we shall equally owe to his goodness; you the desire of being reunited to him, and I the means of conducting you. It is with his divine assistance, I hope soon to convince you, that religion only can give even in this world that solid and durable happiness, which is vainly sought in the blindness of human passions. I have the honour to be, with great respect, &c.

Paris, Oct. 25, 17—.

LETTER CXXIV.

The Presidente DE TOURVEL *to* MADAME DE ROSEMONDE.

The astonishment in which I am thrown, Madam, at the news I received yesterday, will not, however, make me forget the satisfaction it ought to give you, therefore I am in haste to impart it. M. de Valmont's thoughts are no longer taken up with me or his love; he wishes nothing more ardently, than to repair, by a more edifying life, the faults, or rather the errors of his youth. This great event was announced to me by Father Anselmus, whom he addressed to be his director in future, and to treat with me of an interview, the principal design of which is, I imagine, to return my letters, which he has kept hitherto, notwithstanding my requisitions.

I cannot undoubtedly but applaud this happy change, and congratulate myself, if, as he says, I have any way contributed to it. But why should I have been the instrument, and that at the expence of my repose for life? Could not M. de Valmont's happiness be completed but by my misfortune? Oh! forgive me this complaint, my most indulgent friend! I know it does not belong to mortals to fathom the decrees of heaven. Whilst I am incessantly and vainly imploring strength to overcome my unfortunate passion, it is prodigal of its favour to him who does not sue for it, and leaves me helpless a prey to my weakness.

Let me stifle those guilty murmurs. Did not the prodigal son at his return, find more grace with his father, than the one who never had been absent? What account can we demand of him who owes us nothing? And were it possible we could have any pretensions in the sight of God, what could mine be? Should I boast of a modesty, for which I am only indebted to Valmont? It was he saved me; and shall I dare complain of suffering for him? No, my sufferings shall be dear to me, if his happiness is purchased at their expence. Doubtless, in his turn he should come back to our common father. The almighty hand that formed him should cherish its own work. He did not create that charming being to be reprobated. It is me should bear the pain of my daring imprudence. Should I not have reflected, since I was forbid loving him, I should not indulge myself in gazing on him.

My fault or misfortune is to have rejected this truth too long. You, my dear and worthy friend, will be my witness, I submitted to this sacrifice as soon as I discovered the necessity of it: but to render it complete, there wanted the circumstance of M. de Valmont not taking any share in it. Shall I confess to you, this is the idea that at present torments me most? Intolerable pride! which alleviates the evils we endure, by a consciousness of those woes we cause to others! But I will conquer this rebellious heart. I will accustom it to humiliation.

This, motive exclusive of all other considerations, made me at last consent to receive next Thursday, M. de Valmont's painful visit;—he will then tell me he no longer knows me; that the feeble, transitory impression I had made on him exists, no longer! He will look upon me without any emotion, whilst the dread of revealing mine will cast my eyes down. Even those very letters which he so long refused to my repeated solicitations, I shall receive from his indifference; he will return them as useless trifles he no longer cares for; and my trembling hand will receive this shameful trust from a tranquil steady one; last he will depart!—Depart for ever!—My eyes which will follow him, will not see his return to me.

Am I then reserved for all this humiliation? Let me at least make it useful by being penetrated with a sense of my weakness.—Those letters he will no longer keep, I will lay up with care:—I will impose on myself the shame of daily reading them until my tears have defaced the last letter—and his, I will destroy, as infected with the dangerous poison which has tainted my soul.—What then is love, which makes us regret even the danger it exposes us to, and dread feeling it, even when we can no longer inspire it? Let me fly this destructive passion, which leaves no choice between shame and misery, and often reunites them:—let prudence then replace virtue.

How distant is this Thursday still! Why can't I instantly consummate this sorrowful sacrifice, and forget at once the cause and the object? This visit importunes me; I repent having promised it—what occasion to see me again—what are we now to each other? If he has offended me, I forgive him—I even congratulate him on his reformation; I praise him for it; I do more, I will follow his example; and, seduced by the same errors, his example shall reform me. But why, when his resolution is to fly me, why begin by seeking me? The one that is in most danger, ought they not to forget the other? Doubtless they ought; and that shall hereafter be my sole care.

With your permission, my amiable friend, it shall be with you I will undertake this difficult task; if I should want assistance, or perhaps consolation, I will not receive it from any other—you alone understand and can speak to my heart:—Your endearing friendship will fill up my existence;—nothing will be difficult to second your cares:—I shall be indebted to you for my tranquillity, my happiness, my virtue; and the fruits of your goodness will be to have at length made made me deserving of it.

I believe I have gone very much astray in this letter, at least I think so, from the perturbed state I have been in during the whole time:—If there is a sentiment which ought to make me blush, cover it with your indulgent friendship; I submit entirely to it; I have not a wish to hide from you any emotion of my heart.

Adieu, my most respectable friend! I hope to be able in a few days to announce that of my arrival.

Paris, Oct. 25, 17—.

END OF THE THIRD VOLUME.

DANGEROUS

CONNECTIONS:

OR,

LETTERS

COLLECTED IN A SOCIETY,

AND

PUBLISHED FOR THE INSTRUCTION OF

OTHER SOCIETIES.

By M. C**** de L***.

I have observed the Manners of the Times, and have wrote those Letters.

J.J. Rousseau. Pref. to the New Eloise.

VOL. IV.

LONDON:

Printed for T. HOOKHAM,

At his Circulating Library, New Bond Street Corner of Bruton Street.

M.DCC.LXXXIV.

LETTER CXXV.

VISCOUNT DE VALMONT *to the* MARCHIONESS DE MERTEUIL.

At last this haughty woman is conquered, who dared think she could resist me. — She is mine — totally mine. — She has nothing left to grant since yesterday.

My happiness is so great I cannot appreciate it, but am astonished at the unknown charm I feel: — Is it possible virtue can augment a woman's value even at the time of her weakness? — Avaunt such puerile ideas — don't we every day meet resistance more or less feigned at the first conquest? Yet I never experienced the charm I mean; it is not love — for although I have had fits of weakness with this amazing woman, which very much resembled that pusillanimous passion, I ever subdued them and returned to my first rules — if even the scene of yesterday should have led me farther than I intended; had I partook for a moment of the intoxication I raised, that transitory illusion would have been now evaporated, yet still the same charm remains — I own I should be pleased to indulge it, if it did not give me some uneasiness: — At my age must I then be mastered like a school-boy by an unknown and involuntary sentiment? — I must first oppose and then examine it.

Perhaps I already see into the cause — the idea pleases me — I wish it may be true.

Among the multitude of women with whom I have played the part of a lover, I never met any who were not as well inclined to surrender as I was to persuade them — I used even to call those *prudes* who met me but halfway, in contrast to so many others, whose provoking defence is intended as a cloak to their first advances.

But here I found an unfavourable prepossession against me, afterwards confirmed on the report and advice of a penetrating woman who hated me; a natural, excessive timidity, fortified with genuine modesty; a strong attachment to virtue under the powerful direction of religion, and who had already been married two years — an unsullied character — the result of those causes, which all tended to screen her from my solicitations.

It is not any way similar to my former adventures: — a mere capitulation more or less advantageous, which is easier to be acquired than to be vain of; but this is a complete victory, purchased by a hard campaign, and decided by skilful manœuvres, therefore it is not at all surprising, this success, solely my own acquisition, should be dear to me; and the increase of pleasure I experienced in my triumph, which I still feel, is no more than the soft impression of a sentiment of glory. I indulge this thought, as it saves me the humiliation of harbouring the idea of my being dependent on the very slave I have brought under subjection, as well as the disagreeable thoughts of not having within myself the plenitude of my happiness, or that the power of calling it forth into energy and making me fully enjoy it, should be revived for this or that woman exclusively of any other.

Those judicious reflections shall regulate my conduct on this important occasion and you may depend, I shall never suffer myself to be so captivated, but that I may at pleasure break those new bands: — Already I begin to talk of a rapture, and have not yet informed you how I acquired the powers — proceed and you will see to what dangers wisdom exposes itself endeavouring to assist folly — I studied my conversation and the answers to them with so much attention, I hope to be able to give you both with the utmost exactitude.

You will observe by the annexed copies of letters,[1] what kind of mediator I fixed on to gain me admittance with my fair one, with what zeal the holy man exercised himself to reunite us; I must tell you also, I learned from an intercepted letter, according to custom, the dread the humiliation of being left, had a little disconcerted the austere devotee's prudence, and stuffed her head and heart with ideas and sentiments which, though destitute of common sense, were nevertheless interesting — After these preliminaries necessary to be related, yesterday, Thursday the 28th, the day appointed by my ingrate, I presented myself as a timid and repentant slave, to retire a successful conqueror.

It was six in the evening when I came to the fair recluse; for since her return, her gates were shut against every one. She endeavoured to rise when I was announced; but her trembling knees being unable to support her, she was obliged to sit down immediately. The servant who had showed me in, having something to do in the apartment, she seemed impatient. This interval was taken up with the usual compliments. Not to lose a moment of so precious an opportunity, I examined the room carefully, and fixed my eye on the intended spot for my victory. I could have chose a more commodious one; for there was a sopha in the room: but I observed directly opposite to it a picture of the husband; and I own I was afraid with so strange a woman, a single glance, which accidentally she might cast on that side, would in an instant have destroyed a work of so much care. At last we were alone, and I entered on the business.

After relating in few words, I supposed Father Anselmus had informed her the motive of my visit, I lamented the rigorous treatment I received, and dwelt particularly on the *contempt* that had been shown. She made an apology, as I expected, and you also: but I grounded the proof on the diffidence and dread I had infused; on the scandalous flight in consequence of it, the refusal to answer my letters, or even receive them, &c. &c. As she was beginning a justification, which would have been very easy, I thought proper to interrupt her; and to compensate for this abrupt behaviour, I immediately threw in a flattery. "If such charms," said I, "have made so deep an impression on my heart, so many virtues have made as great a one on my mind. Seduced by the desire of imitating them, I had the vanity to think myself worthy of them. I do not reproach you for thinking otherwise; but I punish myself for my error." As she preserved a silent perplexity I went on. "I wish, Madam, to be justified in your sight, or obtain your pardon for all the wrongs you suppose me to have been guilty of; that I may, at least, terminate in tranquillity a life which is no longer supportable since you refuse to embellish it."

To this, however, she endeavoured to reply. "My duty would not permit me."—The difficulty to finish the fib which duty required, did not allow her to end the sentence. I replied in the most tender strain, "Is it true, then, it was me you fled from?—this retreat was necessary—and that you should put me from you—It must be so—and for ever—I should—" It is unnecessary to tell you, during this short dialogue, the tender prude's voice was oppressed, and she did not raise her eyes.

I thought it was time to animate this languishing scene; and rising in a pet, — "Your resolution, Madam," said I, "has given me back mine. We will part; and part forever: you will have leisure to congratulate yourself on your work." Surprised with this reproaching tone, she should have replied — "The resolution you have taken," said she — "Is only the effect of despair," I replied with passion. "It is your pleasure I should be miserable — you shall have the full extent of your wish. I wish you to be happy." Here the voice began to announce a strong emotion: then falling at her knees, in the dramatic style, I exclaimed, "Ah, cruel woman! Can there be happiness for me that you do not partake? How then shall I find it, when absent from you? Oh, never, never!" — I own, in abandoning myself thus, I depended much on the assistance of tears; but, whether for want of disposition, or, perhaps, only the continual, painful attention my mind was engaged in, I could not weep. Fortunately I recollected, all means are equally good to subdue a woman; and it would be sufficient to astonish her by a grand movement, to make a deep and favourable impression. I therefore made terror supply the place of absent sensibility; changing only my tone, but still preserving my posture, I continued, "Yes, at your feet I swear I will die or possess you." As I pronounced those last words our eyes met. I don't know what the timid woman saw, or thought she saw, in mine; but she rose with a terrified countenance, and escaped from my arms, which surrounded her waist: it it is true, I did not attempt to hold her; for I have often observed, those scenes of despair became ridiculous when pushed with too much vivacity or lengthened out, and left no resource but what was really tragic, of which I had not the least idea. Whilst she fled from me, I added in a low disastrous tone, but so that she might hear, "Well then, death."

I rose silently, and casting a wild look on her, as if by chance, nevertheless observed her unsteady deportment, her quick respiration, her contracted muscles, her trembling, half-raised arms; every thing gave me sufficient evidence, the effect was such as I wished to produce: but as in love nothing can be brought to issue at a distance, and we were pretty far asunder, it was necessary to draw nearer. To attain which, I assumed, as soon as possible, an apparent tranquillity, proper to calm the effects of this violent agitation, without weakening the impression. My transition was:—"I am very miserable. I only wished to live for your happiness, and I have disturbed it:"—then with a composed but constrained air;—"Forgive me, Madam; little used to the rage of passions, I do not know how to suppress their violence. If I am wrong in giving way to them, I beg you will remember it shall be the last time. Compose yourself; I entreat you compose yourself." During this long discourse, I drew near insensibly. "If you wish I should be calm," replied the terrified fair, "do you then be calm." "I will then, I promise you," said I; and in a weaker tone, "If the effort is great, it ought not at least to be long: but I came to return your letters. I request you will take them. This afflicting sacrifice is the only one remaining; let me have nothing to weaken my resolution." Then drawing from my pocket the precious collection—"Here is the deceitful deposit of your friendship: it made this life supportable; take it back, and give the signal that is to separate us for ever." Here the timid lover gave way to her tender grief—"But, M. de Valmont, what is the matter? What do you mean? Is not your proceeding to-day your own voluntary act? Is it not the result of your own reflections? And is it not they have approved this necessary step, in compliance with my duty?" I replied, "Well, this step decides mine."—"And what is that?"—"The only one that can put an end to my sufferings, by parting me from you."—"But answer me what is it."—Then pressing her in my arms without any opposition, and observing from the neglect of decency, how strong and powerful her emotions were, I exclaimed, "Adorable woman! you can't conceive the love you inspire. You will never know how much you was adored, and how much dearer this passion was than my existence. May all your days be fortunate and peaceful! May they be decorated with that happiness you have deprived me of! At least, repay this sincere wish with one sigh, one tear; and be assured, the last sacrifice I make will not be the most painful to my heart. Adieu!"

Whilst I spoke, I felt her heart throb violently; her countenance altered; her tears almost suffocated her. Then I resolved to feign retreat: but she held me strongly.—"No, hear what I have to say," said she, eagerly. I answered, "Let me go."—"You shall hear me."—"I must fly from you; I must."—"No," she exclaimed; then sunk, or rather swooned in my arms. I was still doubtful of so happy an issue, seemed much terrified, and still led, or rather carried her to the place I had marked out for the field of glory. She did not recover herself until she was submitted, and given up to her happy conqueror.

So far, my lovely friend, you will perceive a methodical neatness, which I am sure will give you pleasure. You will also observe, I did not swerve in the least from the true principles of this war, which we have often remarked bore so near a resemblance to the other. Rank me, then, with the Turennes or the Fredericks. I forced the enemy to fight who was temporising. By skilful manœuvres, gained the advantage of the ground and dispositions; contrived to lull the enemy into security, to come up with him more easily in his retreat; struck him with terror before we engaged. I left nothing to chance; only a great advantage, in case of success; or a certainty of resources, in case of a defeat. Finally, the action did not begin till I had secured a retreat, by which I might cover and preserve all my former conquests. What more could be done? But I begin to fear I have enervated myself, as Hannibal did with the delights of Capua.

I expected so great an event would not pass over without the customary tears and grief. First I observed somewhat more of confusion and recollection than is usual, which I attributed to her state of prudery. Without paying much attention to those slight differences, which I imagined merely local, I followed the beaten road of consolation; fully persuaded, as commonly happens, the sensations would fly to the assistance of sentiment, that one act would prevail more than all my speeches, which I did not, however, neglect: but I met with a resistance really tremendous: less for its excess, than the form under which it appeared. Only think of a woman sitting stiff and motionless, with unalterable features; seeming divested of the faculties of thinking, hearing, or understanding, from whose eyes tears flowed without effort. Such was M. de Tourvel during my conversation. If I endeavoured to recall her attention by a caress, or even the most innocent gesture, terror immediately followed this apparent apathy, accompanied with suffocation, convulsions, sobs, and shrieks by intervals, but without a word articulated. Those fits returned several times, and always stronger; the last was even so violent, I was much frightened, and thought I had gained a fruitless victory. I returned to the usual common-place phrases—"What do you then regret you have made me the happiest man on earth?" At those words this adorable woman turned to me; her countenance, although still a little wild, had yet recovered its celestial expression. "The happiest?" said she.—You may guess my reply. "You are happy, then?"—I renewed my protestations. "Have I made you happy?"—I added praises, and every thing tender. Whilst I was speaking, all her members were stilled; she fell back softly in her chair, giving up a hand I ventured to take. "This idea relieves and consoles me," said she.

You well believe, being thus brought back in the right road, I quitted it no more; it certainly was the best, and, perhaps, the only one. When I made a second attempt, I met some resistance; what had happened before made me more circumspect: but having called on my idea of happiness for assistance, I soon experienced its favourable influence. "You are right," replied the tender creature, "I can support my existence no longer than it contributes to your happiness. I devote myself entirely to you. From this moment I give myself up to you. You shall no more experience regret or refusal from me." Thus with artless or sublime candour did she deliver her person and charms, increasing my happiness by sharing it. The intoxication was complete and reciprocal: for the first time mine survived the pleasure. I quitted her arms, only to throw myself at her feet, and swear eternal love. To own the truth, I spoke as I thought. Even after we parted, I could not shake off the idea; and I found it necessary to make extraordinary efforts to divert my attention from her.

I wish you were now here, to counterpoise the charm of the action by the reward: but I hope I shall not lose by waiting; for I look on the happy arrangement I proposed in my last letter as a settled point between us. You see I dispatch business as I promised: my affairs will be so forward, I shall be able to give you some part of my time. Quickly get rid, then, of the stupid Belleroche, and leave the whining Danceny to be engrossed solely by me. How is your time taken up in the country? You don't even answer my letters. Do you know, I have a great mind to scold you? Only prosperity is apt to make us indulgent. Besides, I can't forget ranging myself again under your banner. I must submit to your little whim. Remember, however, the new lover will not surrender any of the ancient rights of the friend.

Adieu, as formerly!—Adieu, my angel! I send you the softest kisses of love.

P. S. Poor Prevan, at the end of his month's imprisonment, was obliged to quit his corps; it is public all over Paris. Upon my word he is cruelly treated, and your success is complete.

Paris, Oct. 29, 17—.

[1] Letters cxx and cxxii.

MADAME DE ROSEMONDE *to the* Presidente DE TOURVEL.

I would have answered your letter sooner, my dear child, if the fatigue of my last had not brought on a return of my disorder, which has deprived me ever since of the use of my arm. I was very anxious to thank you for the good news you gave me of my nephew, and not less to congratulate you sincerely on your own account. Here the interposition of Providence is visible, that touching the heart of the one has also saved the other. Yes, my lovely dear! the Almighty, who sent you this trial, has assisted you in the moment your strength was exhausted; and notwithstanding your little murmurings, I think you have great reason to return him your unfeigned thanks: not but I believe you would have been very glad to have been the first in this resolution, and that Valmont's should have been the consequence of it; I even think, humanly speaking, the dignity of our sex would have been better preserved, and we are not fond of giving up any of our rights. But what are these considerations to those more important objects! We seldom hear a person saved from shipwreck complain, the means were not in his option.

You will soon experience, my dear child, the afflictions you dreaded so much will grow lighter of themselves, and even were they to last for ever in their full force, you will be sensible they are easier to bear than the remorse of guilt or self-contempt. It would have been useless to talk to you before with this apparent severity: love is an independent passion, that prudence may make us avoid, but cannot conquer, which when once it has taken root, must die its own natural death, or of absolute despair. This last being your case, gives me the resolution and the right to tell you freely my sentiments. It is cruel to frighten a sick person that is despaired of, to whom palliatives only and consolations should be administered: but it is the part of wisdom to remind those on the recovery, of the dangers they escaped, to assist them with necessary prudence and submission to the advice they stand in need of. As you have chose me for your physician, in that character I address you, and tell you, the little inconveniencies you feel at present, which may require, perhaps, some remedies, are nothing in comparison of the dreadful disorder whose cure is now certain. Then, as your friend, as the friend of a virtuous and reasonable woman, give me leave to add, this passion you have subdued, so unhappy in itself, became infinitely more so in its object. If I am to believe what I am told, my nephew, who I must own I love even to a degree of weakness, unites many laudable qualities to a great many attractions, is very dangerous to the women, blameable in his behaviour towards them, and piques himself as much on exposing as seducing them. I really believe you would have converted him. Sure never was any one so worthy; however, so many others flattered themselves in the same manner, whose hopes were frustrated, that I am overjoyed to find you are not reduced to that resource.

Reflect now, my dear woman, that instead of so many dangers as you would have had to go through, you will have, besides the testimony of a good conscience and your own peace, the satisfaction of being the cause of Valmont's reformation. I own, I think it in a great measure owing to your resolute defence, and that a moment's weakness on your part would have left my nephew in lasting disorders. I love to indulge this way of thinking, and wish you to do the same; you will find it consoling; it will be an additional reason for me to love you the more.

I shall expect you in a few days, my dear child, as you promised. You will once more find serenity and happiness where you lost them. Come and rejoice with your tender mother, that you have so happily kept your word to do nothing unworthy yourself or her.

Castle of — —, Oct. 30, 17—.

LETTER CXXVII.

The MARCHIONESS DE MERTEUIL *to the* VISCOUNT DE VALMONT.

It was not for want of time, that I did not answer your letter of the 19th, Viscount, but plainly because it put me out of temper, and did not contain a single syllable of common sense. I thought it then the best way to leave it in oblivion—but since you seem fond of this production, and the sublime ideas it contains, that you construe my silence into consent, it is necessary you should have my opinion explicitly.

I may have heretofore formed the design of singly performing the functions of a whole seraglio; but it never entered my head to become only a part of one; this I thought you knew, now, that you cannot plead ignorance, you may readily conceive how ridiculous your proposition must appear to me. Should I sacrifice an inclination, and a new one, for you? And in what manner, pray? Why, waiting for my turn, like a submissive slave, the sublime favours of your *highness.* When, for example, you was inclined to relax for a moment from *that unknown charm* that the *adorable, the celestial* M. de Tourvel only had made you feel;—or when you dread to risk with the *engaging Cecilia,* the superior idea you wished her to preserve for you;—then condescending to stoop to me, you will seek pleasures less violent, but of not much consequence, and your inestimable bounty, though scarce, must fill the measure of my felicity. Certainly you stand high in your own opinion; and my modesty nor my glass have yet prevailed on me to think I am sunk so low. This may be owing to my wrong way of thinking; but I beg you will be persuaded I have more imaginations of the same kind.

One especially, which is, that *Danceny, the school-boy, the whiner,* totally taken up with me, sacrificing, without making a merit of it, his first love, even before it was enjoyed, and loving me to that excess that is usual with those at his age, may contribute more to my happiness and pleasure than you—I will even take the liberty to add, that if I had the inclination to give him a partner, it should not be you, at least now.

Perhaps you'll ask me why? Probably I should be at a loss for a reason; for the same whim that would give you the preference, might also exclude you. However, politeness requires I should inform you of my motive—I think you must make too many sacrifices; and instead of being grateful, as you certainly would expect, I should be inclined to think you still owed me more—You must therefore be sensible, our manner of thinking being so opposite, we can by no means unite: I fear it will be some time, nay a great while, before I change my opinion.

When that happens, I promise to give you notice:—Until then, let me advise you to take some other measures, and keep your kisses for those to whom they will be more agreeable.

You say *adieu, as formerly!* but formerly, if I remember, you set a greater value on me than to appoint me entirely to the third characters; and was content to wait until I answered in the affirmative, before you was certain of my consent: don't be angry then, if instead of saying adieu, as formerly, I say adieu, as at present.

Your servant, Viscount.
The castle of — —, Oct. 31, 17 —.

LETTER CXXVIII.

The Presidente DE TOURVEL *to* MADAME DE ROSEMONDE.

I did not receive, until yesterday, Madam, your dilatory answer — it would instantly have put an end to my existence if I had any left; but M. de Valmont is now in possession of it: you see I do not conceal any thing from you; if you no longer think me worthy your friendship, I dread the loss of it less than to impose on you; to tell you all in all, I was placed by M. de Valmont, between his death and happiness — I chose the latter — I neither boast nor accuse myself; I relate the fact plainly as it is.

You will readily perceive, after this, what kind of impression your letter, and the truths it contains, must have made on me. Do not, however, imagine, it could give birth to any repining, or ever make me alter my sentiments or conduct; not that I am exempt from some torturing moments; but when my heart is rent, and I dread not being any longer able to bear my torments, I say to myself, Valmont is happy; and at this idea my miseries vanish; all is converted into joy.

It is to your nephew, then, I have devoted myself; it is for his sake I am undone; he is now the centre of my thoughts, sentiments, and actions. Whilst my life can contribute to his happiness, I shall cherish it; I shall think it fortunate; if he should hereafter think otherwise, he shall never hear from me either complaint or reproach. I have already ventured to fix my eyes on this fatal period, and my resolution is taken.

You will now perceive how little I am affected with the dread you seem to entertain, that M. de Valmont, will one day or other defame me — Before that happens, he must lose the affection he has for me; that once lost, of what signification will vain reproaches be which I shall never hear? He alone will judge me, as I will have lived for him, and him only; and my memory will repose in him; and if he will be obliged to acknowledge I loved him, I shall be justified sufficiently.

Now, Madam, you read my heart — I preferred the misfortune of being deprived of your esteem by my candour, to that of making myself unworthy of it by the baseness of a lie. I thought I owed this entire confidence to your former goodness; the addition of a word would, perhaps, give room to suspect I should be vain enough yet to depend on it; far from it: I will do myself justice, by giving up all pretensions to it.

I am with great respect, Madam, your most humble and most obedient servant.
Paris, Nov. 1, 17 —.

LETTER CXXIX.

VISCOUNT DE VALMONT *to the* MARCHIONESS DE MERTEUIL.

Whence arises, my charming friend, this strain of acrimony and ridicule which runs through your last letter? What crime have I unintentionally committed which puts you so much out of temper? You reproach me with presuming on your consent before I had obtained it—-I imagined, however, what might appear like presumption in any one else, would, between you and me, be only the effect of confidence. I would be glad to know how long has this sentiment been detrimental to friendship or love? Uniting hope with desire, I only complied with that natural impulse, which makes us wish to draw as near as possible to the happiness we are in pursuit of—and you have mistaken that for vanity, which is nothing more than ardour. I know very well, in such cases, custom has introduced a respectful apprehension; but you also know, it is only a kind of form, a mere precedent; and I imagined myself authorised to believe those trifling niceties no longer necessary between us.

I even think this free and open method much preferable to insipid flattery, which so often love nauseates, when it is grounded on an old connection. Moreover, perhaps the preference I give this method proceeds from the happiness it recalls to my memory—this gives me more uneasiness that you should take it in another light. However, this is the only thing that I am culpable in—for I cannot believe you can seriously imagine, that the woman exists who I would prefer to you; and still less, that I should estimate you so little as you feign to believe. You say, you have consulted your glass on this occasion, and you do not find yourself sunk so low—I believe it; and that only proves your glass to be true—but should you not rather from thence concluded that certainly that was not my opinion.

In vain I seek the cause of this strange idea—however, I suspect it is more or less dependent on the praises I lavished on other women—at least, this I infer, from the affectation of quoting the epithets, *adorable, celestial, attaching,* which I used, speaking of Madam de Tourvel, and the little Volanges: but you are not to be told, those words, which are oftener the effect of chance than reflection, express more the situation one happens to be in at the time, than the value one sets upon the person. If at the time I was affected with the one or the other, I nevertheless rapturously wished for you—If I gave you an eminent preference over both, as I would not renew our first connection without breaking off the two others, I do not think there is such great reason for reproaches.

I shall not find it more difficult to exculpate myself from the charge of the *unknown charm,* which, it seems, shocks you not a little; for being unknown, it does not follow that it is stronger—What can equal the delights you alone can always embellish with novelty and bliss? I only wished to convey to you an idea, it was a kind I never before experienced; but without pretending to give it any rank; and added, what I again repeat, whatever it be, I will overcome it: and shall exert myself more zealously if I can in this trifling affair, to have one homage more to offer to you.

As to the little Cecilia, it is useless to mention her: you have not forgot it was at your instance I took charge of this child; and only wait your orders to be rid of her. I may have made some remarks on her bloom and innocence; and for a moment thought her *engaging,* because one is always more or less pleased with their work; but she has not, in any shape, consistency to fix the attention.

Now, my lovely friend, I appeal to your justice, your first attachment to me, the long and sincere friendship, the unbounded confidence which have linked us together—have I deserved the severe manner in which you have treated me? But how easy can you make me amends when you please! Speak but the word, and you will see whether all the charms, all the attachments will keep me here, not a day, but even a minute; I will fly to your feet—into your arms—and will prove a thousand times, and in a thousand ways, that you are, you ever will be, the only mistress of my heart.

Adieu, my lovely friend! I wait your answer impatiently.

Paris, Nov. 3, 17—.

LETTER CXXX.

MADAME DE ROSEMONDE, *to the* Presidente DE TOURVEL.

Why, my lovely dear, will you no longer be my daughter? Why do you seem to announce that our correspondence is to cease?[1] Is it to punish me for not guessing at what was improbable; or do you suspect me of creating you affliction designedly? I know your heart too well, to imagine you would entertain such an opinion of mine.—The distress your letter plunges me in is much less on my own account than yours. Oh! my young friend, with grief I tell you, you are too worthy of being beloved ever to be happy in love—Where is there a truly delicate and sensible woman, who has not met unhappiness where she expected bliss? Do men know how to rate the women they possess?

Not but many of them are virtuous in their addresses and constant in their affections—but even among those, how few that know how to put themselves in unison with our hearts. I do not imagine, my dear child, their affection is like ours—They experience the same transport often with more violence, but they are strangers to that uneasy officiousness, that delicate solicitude, that produces in us those continual tender cares, whose sole aim is the beloved object—Man enjoys the happiness he feels, woman that she gives.

This difference, so essential, and so seldom observed, influences in a very sensible manner, the totality of their respective conduct. The pleasure of the one is to gratify desires; but that of the other is to create them. To know to please, is in man the means of success; and in woman it is success itself.

And do not imagine, the exceptions, be they more or less numerous, that may be quoted, can be successfully opposed to those general truths, which the voice of the public has guaranteed, with the only distinction as to men of infidelity from inconstancy; a distinction of which they avail themselves, and of which they should be ashamed; which never has been adopted by any of our sex but those of abandoned characters, who are a scandal to us, and to whom all methods are acceptable which they think may deliver them from the painful sensation of their own meanness.

I thought, my lovely dear, those reflections might be of use to you, in order to oppose the chimerical ideas of perfect happiness, with which love never fails to amuse our imagination. Deceitful hope! to which we are still attached, even when we find ourselves under the necessity of abandoning it—whose loss multiplies and irritates our already too real sorrows, inseparable from an ardent passion—This task of alleviating your troubles, or diminishing their number, is the only one I will or can now fulfil—In disorders which are without remedy, no other advice can be given, than as to the regimen to be observed—The only thing I wish you to remember is, that to pity is not to blame a patient. Alas! who are we, that we dare blame one another? Let us leave the right of judging to the searcher of hearts; and I will even venture to believe, that in his paternal sight, a crowd of virtues, may compensate a single weakness.

But I conjure you above all things, my dear friend, to guard against violent resolutions, which are less the effects of fortitude than despondency: do not forget, that although you have made another possessor of your existence (to use your own expression) you had it not in your power to deprive your friends of the share they were before possessed of, and which they will always claim.

Adieu, my dear child! Think sometimes on your tender mother; and be assured you always will be, above every thing, the dearest object of her thoughts.

Castle of — —, Nov. 4, 17—.

[1] See Letter cxxviii.

LETTER CXXXI.

The MARCHIONESS DE MERTEUIL *to the* VISCOUNT DE VALMONT.

Very well, Viscount; come, I am better pleased with you than I was before: now let us converse in a friendly manner, and I hope to convince you, the scheme you propose would be the highest act of folly in us both.

Have you never observed that pleasure, which is the *primum mobile* of the union of the sexes, is not sufficient to form a connection between them? and that if desire, which brings them together, precedes it, it is nevertheless followed by disgust, which repels it—This is a law of nature, that love alone can alter; and pray, can we have this same love at will? It is then necessary it should be always ready, which would have been very troublesome had it not been discovered, it is sufficient if it exists on one side: by this means the difficulty is lessened by half, even without apparent prejudice; for the one enjoys the happiness of loving, the other of pleasing—not perhaps in altogether so lively a manner, but that is compensated by deceit, which makes the balance, and then all is right.

But say, Viscount, which of us two will undertake to deceive the other? You know the story of the two sharpers who discovered each other at play—"We must not prejudice ourselves," said they; "let us club for the cards, and leave off." Let us follow this prudent advice, nor lose time together, which we may so usefully employ elsewhere.

To convince you that I consult your interest as much as my own, and that I am not actuated either by ill humour or capriciousness, I will not refuse your reward—I am very sensible one night will be sufficient; and do not in the least doubt, we shall know how to make it so pleasing, the morning will come with regret—but let us not forget, this regret is necessary to happiness; although the illusion may be enchanting, nor flatter ourselves it can be durable.

You see I fulfil my promise in my turn, and even before you perform the conditions stipulated—for I was to have had your celestial prude's first letter. Whether you do not choose to part with it, or that you have forgot the conditions of a bargain that is not so interesting to you as you would have me think, I have not received any thing; and I am much mistaken, or the tender devotee must have wrote a great deal; for how can she employ her time alone? she certainly has not sense enough for dissipation? If I was inclined, then, I have room to make you some little reproaches, which I shall pass over in silence, in consideration of the petulance I perhaps showed in my last letter.

Nothing more remains, now, Viscount, but to make you a request, and it is as much for you as myself; that is, to defer the time, which perhaps I wish for as much as you, but which I think may be put off until my return to town. On the one hand, it would be very inconvenient here; and on the other, it would be running too great a risk; for a little jealousy would fix me with the dismal Belleroche, who no longer holds but by a thread. He is already struggling to love me; we are at present so critically circumstanced, I blend as much malice as prudence in the caresses I lavish on him; at the same time you will observe, it would not be a sacrifice worthy of you—A reciprocal infidelity will add power to the charm.

Do you know I regret sometimes we are reduced to those resources — At the time we loved each other, for I believe it was love, I was happy — and you, Viscount — but why engage our thoughts on a happiness that can never return? No, say what you will, it is impossible — First, I should require sacrifices that you could not or would not make; that probably I do not deserve. Again, how is it possible to fix you? Oh, no; I will not even think of it; and notwithstanding the pleasure I now have in writing to you, I prefer quitting you abruptly. Adieu, Viscount.

Castle of — —, *Nov. 6, 17* — .

LETTER CXXXII.

The Presidente DE TOURVEL *to* MADAME DE ROSEMONDE.

Deeply impressed, Madam, with your goodness, to which I would entirely abandon myself, if I was not restrained from accepting by the dread of profaning it. Why, convinced of its inestimable value, must I know myself no longer worthy of it? Let me, at least, attempt to testify my gratitude. I shall admire, above all, the lenity of virtue, which views weakness with the eye of compassion; whose powerful charm preserves its forcible but mild authority over hearts, even by the side of the charm of love.

Can I still be worthy a friendship, which is no longer useful to my happiness? I must say the same of your advice. I feel its force, but cannot follow it. How is it possible to discredit perfect happiness, when I experience it this moment? If men are such as you describe them, they must be shunned, they are hateful: but where is the resemblance between Valmont and them? If, in common with them, he has that violence of passion you call transport, is it not restrained by delicacy? My dear friend, you talk of sharing my troubles; take a part, then, in my happiness; to love I am indebted for it, and how immensely does the object raise its value! You love your nephew, you say, perhaps, with fondness: ah! if you knew him as I do, you would idolize him, and yet even less than he deserves. He has undoubtedly been led astray by some errors; he does not conceal it; but who like him ever knew what was love? What can I say more? He feels it as he inspires it. You will think this is *one of the chimerical ideas with which love never fails to abuse our imagination:* but in my case, why should he be more tender, more earnest, when he has nothing farther to obtain? I will own, I formerly thought I observed an air of reflection and reserve, which seldom left him, and which often, contrary to my inclination, recalled to me the false and cruel impressions that were given me of him; but since he has abandoned himself without constraint to the emotions of his heart, he seems to guess at all my desires. Who knows but we were born for each other? If this happiness was not reserved for me to be necessary to his! — Ah! if it be an illusion, let me die before it ends. — No, I must live to cherish, to adore him. Why should he cease loving me? What woman on earth could he make happier than me? And I experience it by myself, this happiness that he has given rise to, is the only and the strongest tie. It is this delicious sentiment that exalts and purifies love, and becomes truly worthy a tender and generous mind, such as Valmont's.

Adieu, my dear, my respectable, my indulgent friend! Vainly should I think of continuing my letter. This is the hour he promised to come, and every idea flies before him. Your pardon. But you wish me happiness; it is now so great I can scarce support it.

Paris, Nov. 7, 17 —.

LETTER CXXXIII.

The VISCOUNT DE VALMONT *to the* MARCHIONESS DE MERTEUIL.

What, then, my charming friend, are those sacrifices you think I would not make to your pleasure? Let me only know them; and if I hesitate to offer them to you, I give you leave to refuse the homage. What opinion have you of late conceived of me, when even favourably inclined, you doubt my sentiments or inclinations? Sacrifices that I would not or could not make! So you think I am in love, subdued! The value I set on the success, you suspect is attached to the person. Ah! thank heaven, I am not yet reduced to that, and I offer to prove it. I will prove it, if even it should be at Madame de Tourvel's expence. Certainly after that you cannot have a doubt remaining.

I may, I believe, without committing myself, give up some time to a woman, who, at least, has the merit of being of a cast rarely met. The dead season, perhaps, when this adventure took its rise, was another reason to give myself totally up to it; even now that the grand current of company scarcely begins to flow, it is not surprising my time is almost entirely taken up with her. I beg you will also recollect, it is scarce eight days I enjoy the fruits of three months labour. I have often indulged longer with what has not been so valuable, and had not cost me so much; and yet you never from thence drew any conclusions against me.

Shall I tell you the real cause of my assiduity? It is this. She is naturally of a timid disposition; at first she doubted incessantly of her happiness, which was sufficient to disturb it; so that I but just begin to observe how far my power extends in this kind. This I was curious to know, and the occasions are not so readily offered as one may think.

In the first place, pleasure is nothing but mere pleasure with a great number of women, and never any thing else; with them, whatever titles they think proper to adorn us with, we are never but factors, simple commissioners, whose activity is all their merit, and among whom he who performs most is always esteemed the best.

In another class, the most numerous now-a-days, the celebrity of the lover, the pleasure of carrying him from a rival, the dread of a reprisal again, totally engage the women. Thus we are concerned more or less in this kind of happiness which they enjoy; but it depends more on circumstances than on the person: it comes to them by us, and not from us.

It was then necessary to find a woman of delicacy and sensation to make my observations on, whose sole concern should be love, and in that passion be absorbed by the lover; whose emotions, disdaining the common track, should fly from the heart to the senses; who I have viewed, (I don't mean the first day) rise from the bed of delight all in tears, and the instant after recover voluptuousness by a word that touched her soul. She must also have united that natural candour, which habitude had made insurmountable, and would not suffer her to dissemble the least sentiment of her heart. You must agree with me, such women are scarce; and I am confident, if I had not met this one, I never should have found another.

Therefore it is not at all surprising she should have fascinated me longer than another; and if the time I spend makes her happy, perfectly happy, why should I refuse it, especially when it is so agreeable to me? But because the mind is engaged, must the heart be enslaved? Certainly not. And the value I set on this adventure will not prevent my engaging in others, or even sacrificing this to some more agreeable one.

I am even so much at liberty, that I have not neglected the little Volanges, to whom I am so little attached. Her mother brings her to town in three days, and I have secured my communication since yesterday; a little money to the porter, a few soft speeches to the waiting maid, did the business. Would you believe it? Danceny never thought of this simple method. Where, then, is the boasted ingenuity of love? Quite the contrary; it stupifies its votaries. Shall I not, then, know how to preserve myself from it? Be not uneasy, in a few days I shall divide the impression, perhaps rather too strong, it made on me, and weaken it; if one will not do, I will increase them.

Nevertheless, I shall be ready to give up the young pensioner to her discreet lover, when you think proper. I can't see you have any longer reason to oppose it. I freely consent to render poor Danceny this signal service: upon my word, it is but trifling, for all those he has done for me. He is now in the greatest anxiety to know whether he will be admitted at Madame de Volanges's. I keep him as easy as possible, by promising some how or other to gratify him one of those days; in the mean time, I take upon me to carry on the correspondence, which he intends to resume on his Cecilia's arrival. I have already six of his letters, and shall have one or two more before the happy day. This lad must have very little to do.

However, let us leave this childish couple, and come to our own business, that I may be entirely engaged with the pleasing hope your letter has given me. Do you doubt of fixing me yours? If you do, I shall not forgive you. Have I ever been inconstant? Our bands have been loosened, but never broken; our pretended rupture was an error only of the imagination; our sentiments, our interests, are still the same. Like the traveller who returned undeceived, I found out, as he did, I quitted happiness to run after hope.[1] The more strange lands I saw, the more I I loved my country. No longer oppose the idea, or sentiment rather, that brings you back to me. After having tried all manner of pleasures in our different excursions, let us sit down and enjoy the happiness of knowing, that none is equal to what we have experienced, and that we shall again find more delicious.

Adieu, my lovely friend! I consent to wait your return; however, hasten it as much as possible, and do not forget how much I wish for it.

Paris, Nov. 8, 17—.

[1] Du Belloi's tragedy of the Siege of Calais.

LETTER CXXXIV.

MARCHIONESS DE MERTEUIL *to the* VISCOUNT DE VALMONT.

Upon my word, Viscount, you are exactly like the children, before whom one cannot speak a word, nor show a thing but they must have it immediately. Because I just mention an idea that came into my head, which I even told you I was not fixed on, you abuse my intention, and want to tie me down, at the time I endeavour to forget it, and force me in a manner to share your thoughtless desires. Are you not very ungenerous to make me bear the whole burthen of prudential care? I must again repeat, and it frequently occurs to me, the method you propose is impossible. When you would even throw in all the generosity you mention, do you imagine I am divested of my delicacies, and I would accept sacrifices prejudicial to your happiness?

My dear Viscount, you certainly deceive yourself in the sentiment that attaches you to M. de Tourvel. It is love, or such a passion never had existence. You deny it in a hundred shapes; but you prove it in a thousand. What means, for example, the subterfuge you use against yourself, for I believe you sincere with me, that makes you relate so circumstantially the desire you can neither conceal nor combat, of keeping this woman? Would not one imagine, you never had made any other happy, perfectly happy? Ah! if you doubt it, your memory is very bad: but that is not the case. To speak plainly, your heart imposes on your understanding, and pays it off with bad arguments: but I, who am so strongly interested not to be deceived, am not so easily blinded.

Thus, as I remarked, your politeness made you carefully suppress every word you thought would displease me, I could not help observing, perhaps, without taking notice of it; nevertheless you preserved the same ideas. It is no longer the adorable, the celestial Madame de Tourvel, but *an astonishing woman, a delicate sentimental woman,* even to the exclusion of all others; *a wonderful woman,* such *as a second could not be found.* The same way with your unknown charm, which is not *the strongest.* Well; be it so: but since you never found it out till then, it is much to be apprehended you will never meet it again; the loss would be irreparable. Those, Viscount, are sure symptoms of love, or we must renounce the hope of ever finding it. You may be assured I am not out of temper now; and have made a promise, I will not be so any more: I foresee it might become a dangerous snare. Take my word for it, we had better remain as we are, in friendship. Be thankful for my resolution in defending myself; for sometimes one must have it, not to take a step that may be attended with bad consequences.

It is only to persuade you to be of my opinion, I answer the demand you make, on the sacrifices I would exact, and you could not make. I designedly use the word exact, because immediately you will think me too exacting—so much the better: far from being angry with your refusal, I shall thank you for it. Observe, I will not dissemble with you; perhaps I have occasion for it.

First I would exact—take notice of the cruelty! that this same rare, this astonishing Madame de Tourvel, should be no more to you than any other woman; that is, a mere woman: for you must not deceive yourself; this charm, that you believe is found in others, exists in us, and it is love only embellishes the beloved object so much. What I now require, although so impossible for you to grant, you would not hesitate to promise, nay, even to swear; but I own I would not believe you the more. I could not be convinced, but by the whole tenor of your conduct.

That is not all; I should be whimsical, perhaps; the sacrifice you so politely offer me of the little Cecilia, does not give me the least uneasiness: on the contrary, I should require you to continue this toilsome duty until farther orders. Whether I should like thus to abuse my power, or whether more indulgent, or more reasonable, it would satisfy me to dispose of your sentiments without thwarting your pleasures. I would, however, be obeyed, and my commands would be very severe.

Certainly I should think myself obliged to thank you, and, who knows? perhaps to reward you. As for instance, I might shorten an absence, which would be insupportable to me. I should at length see you again, Viscount; and see you again—How?—Remember this is only a conversation, a plain narrative of an impossible scheme. I must not be the only one to forget it.

I must tell you my lawsuit begins to make me a little uneasy. I was determined to know exactly what my pretensions were. My lawyers have quoted me some laws, and a great many *authorities*, as they call them; but I can't perceive so much reason and justice in them. I am almost afraid I did wrong to refuse the compromise; however, I begin to be encouraged, when I consider my attorney is skilful, my lawyer eloquent, and the plaintiff handsome. If those reasons were to be no longer valid, the course of business must be altered; then what would become of the respect for old customs? This lawsuit is actually the only thing keeps me here. That of Belleroche is finished; the indictment quashed, each party to bear their own costs: he even is regretting not to be at the ball to-night; the regret of a man out of employment. I shall let him free at my return to town. In making this grievous sacrifice, I am consoled by the generosity he finds in it.

Adieu, Viscount! write to me often. The particulars of your amusements will make me amends partly for the dulness I suffer.

Castle of — —, Nov. 11, 17—.

LETTER CXXXV.

The Presidente DE TOURVEL *to* MADAME DE ROSEMONDE.

I am now endeavouring to write to you, and know not whether I shall be able. Gracious God!—excessive happiness prevented my continuing my last letter; now despair overwhelms me, and leaves me only strength sufficient to tell my sorrows, and deprives me of the power of expressing them.—Valmont—Valmont no longer loves me! He never loved me! Love does not depart thus. He deceived me, he betrayed me, he insults me! I suffer every kind of misfortune and humiliation; and all proceed from him.

Do not think it a mere suspicion. I was far from having any. I have not even the consolation of a doubt: I saw it. What can he say in his justification?—But what matters it to him? He will not attempt it even.—Unhappy wretch! What avail thy reproaches and thy tears? He is not concerned about thee.

It is, then, too true, he has made me a sacrifice; he has even exposed me—and to whom?—To a vile creature.—But what do I say? Ah! I have no right to despise her. She has not broke through any ties; she is not so culpable as I am. Oh! what grief can equal that which is followed by remorse! I feel my torments increase. Adieu, my dear friend! though I am unworthy your compassion, still you will have some left for me, if you can form an idea of my sufferings.

I have just read over my letter, and perceive it gives you no information. I will endeavour to muster up resolution to relate this cruel event. It was yesterday, I was to sup abroad for the first time since my return. Valmont came to me at five; he never appeared so endearing: he did not seem pleased with my intention of going abroad; I immediately resolved to stay at home. In two hours after, his air and tone changed visibly on a sudden. I don't know any thing escaped me to displease him; however, he pretended to recollect business that obliged him to leave me, and went away; not without expressing a tender concern, which I then thought very sincere.

Being left alone, I resolved to fulfil my first engagement, as I was at liberty. I finished my toilet, and got in my carriage. Unfortunately my coachman drove by the opera, and my carriage was stopped in the crowd coming up. I perceived at a little distance before mine, and the range next to me, Valmont's carriage: my heart instantly palpitated, but not with fear; and my only wish was, that my carriage should get forward: instead of which, his was obliged to back close to mine. I immediately looked out; but what was my astonishment to see beside him a well-known courtezan! I drew back, as you may believe; I had seen enough to wound my heart: but what you will scarcely credit is, this same girl, being probably in his confidence, did not turn her eyes from me, and with repeated peals of laughter stared me out of countenance.

Notwithstanding my abject state, I suffered myself to be carried to the house where I was to sup. I found it impossible to stay there long; every instant I was ready to faint, and could not refrain from tears.

At my return I wrote to M. de Valmont, and sent my letter immediately; he was not at home. Being determined at all events to be relieved from this miserable state, or have it confirmed for ever, I sent the servant back, with orders to wait: before twelve he came home, telling me the coachman was returned, and had informed him, his master would not be home for the night. This morning I thought it would be better to request he would give up my letters, and beg of him never to see me more. I have given orders accordingly, but certainly they were useless. It is now near twelve; he has not yet appeared, nor have I received a line from him.

Now, my dear friend, I have nothing farther to add. You are informed of every thing, and you know my heart. My only hope is, I shall not long trouble your tender friendship.
Paris, Nov. 15, 17—.

LETTER CXXXVI.

The Presidente DE TOURVEL *to the* VISCOUNT DE VALMONT.

Certainly, Sir, after what passed yesterday, you do not expect I should see you again, and you as certainly do not desire it. The intention of this note, then, is not so much to require you never to come near me more, as to call on you for my letters, which ought not to have existed. If they could at any time have been interesting, as proofs of the infatuation you had occasioned, they must be, now that is dissipated, indifferent to you, as they were only proofs of a sentiment you have destroyed.

I own, I was very wrong in placing a confidence in you, of which so many before me have been victims; I accuse no one but myself: but I never thought I deserved to be exposed by you to contempt and insult. I imagined, that making a sacrifice of every thing, and giving up for you my pretensions to the esteem of others, as also my own, I might have expected not to be treated by you with more severity than by the public, whose opinion always makes an immense difference between the weak and the depraved. Those are the only wrongs I shall mention. I shall be silent on those of love, as your heart would not understand mine. Farewell, Sir!

Paris, Nov. 15, 17 — .

LETTER CXXXVII.

VISCOUNT DE VALMONT *to the* Presidente DE TOURVEL.

This instant only have I received your letter, Madam. I could not read it without shuddering, and have scarcely strength to answer it. What a horrible opinion have you, then, conceived of me! Doubtless, I have my faults, and such as I shall never forgive myself, if even you should hide them with your indulgence. But how distant from my thoughts are those you reproach me! Who, me insult you! Me make you contemptible, at a time when I reverence as much as cherish you! when you raised my vanity by thinking me worthy of you! Appearances have deceived you. I will not deny they make against me: but had you not sufficient within your own heart to contend against them? Did it not revolt at the idea of having a cause of complaint against me? Yet you believed it! Thus you not only thought me capable of this atrocious frenzy, but even dreaded you had exposed yourself to it by your indulgence. Ah! if you think yourself so much degraded by your love, I must be very despicable in your sight. Oppressed by the painful sense of this idea, I lose the time I should employ in destroying it, endeavouring to repel it. I will confess all: another consideration still prevents me. Must I go back to facts I would wish to forget for ever, and recall your attention and my own to errors I shall ever repent; the cause of which I cannot yet conceive, which fill me with mortification and despair. If I excite your anger by accusing myself, the means of revenge will not be out of your reach; it will be sufficient to abandon me to my own remorse.

Yet the first cause of this unhappy event is, the all-powerful charm I feel in being with you: it was it made me too long forget an important business that could not be put off. I stayed with you so long, I did not find the person at home I wanted to see; I expected to have met her at the opera, where I was also disappointed. Emily, who I met there, and knew at a time when I was a stranger to you and love, Emily had not her carriage, and requested I would set her down at a little distance from thence; I consented, as a matter of no consequence. It was then I met you. I was instantly seized with the apprehension you would think me guilty.

The dread of afflicting or displeasing you is so powerful, it is impossible for me to conceal it, and was soon perceived. I will even own, it induced me to prevail on this girl not to show herself; this precaution, the result of delicacy, was unfavourable to love: but she, like the rest of her tribe, accustomed to the abuse of her usurped power, would not let slip so splendid an opportunity. The more she observed my embarrassment increase, the more she affected to show herself; and her ridiculous mirth, which I blush to think you could for a moment imagine yourself to be the object, had no other foundation than the cruel anxiety I felt, which proceeded from my love and respect.

So far, doubtless, I am more unfortunate than guilty. Those crimes being thus done away, I am clear of reproach. In vain, however, are you silent on those of love, which I must break through, as it concerns me so much.

Not but, in my confusion for this unaccountable misconduct, which I cannot without great grief recall to my remembrance; yet I am so sensible of my error, I would patiently bear the punishment, wait my pardon from time, from my excessive love, and my repentance; only what I yet have to say concerns your delicacy.

Do not think I seek a pretence to excuse or palliate my fault; I confess my guilt: but I do not acknowledge, nor ever will, this humiliating error can be a crime of love. For where is the analogy between a surprise of the sensations, a moment of inadvertency, which is soon replaced by shame and regret, and an immaculate sentiment, which delicate souls are only capable of, supported by esteem, and of which happiness is the fruit? Ah! do not thus profane love; or, rather, do not profane yourself, by uniting in the same point of view what never can be blended. Leave to despicable and degraded women the dread of a rivalship, and experience the torments of a cruel and humiliating jealousy; but turn your eyes from objects that would sully them: and pure as the Divinity, punish the offence without feeling it.

What punishment can you inflict on me will be more sorrowful than what I already feel—that can be comparable to the grief of having incurred your displeasure—to the despair of giving you affliction—to the unsufferable idea of being unworthy of you? Your mind is taken up with punishing, whilst I languish for consolation; not that I deserve it, but only that I am in want of it, and that it is you alone can console me.

If on a sudden, forgetful of our mutual love as of my happiness, you will abandon me to perpetual sorrow, I shall not dispute your right—strike: but should you incline to indulgence, and again recall those tender sentiments that united our hearts; that voluptuousness of soul, ever renewing, ever increasing; those delightful days we passed together; all the felicities that love only can give; you will, perhaps, prefer the power of renewing to that of destroying them. What shall I say? I have lost all, and lost it by my own folly: but still all may be retrieved by your goodness. You are now to decide. I shall add but one word more. Yesterday you swore my happiness was certain whilst it depended on you. Ah! will you this day, then, Madam, give me up to everlasting despair?

Paris, Nov. 15, 17—.

LETTER CXXXVIII.

VISCOUNT DE VALMONT *to the* MARCHIONESS DE MERTEUIL.

I insist on it, my charming friend, I am not in love; and it is not my fault, if circumstances oblige me to play the character of a lover.—Only consent to return, and you will be able to judge my sincerity—I made my proofs yesterday, and cannot be injured by what happens to-day.

I was with the tender prude, having nothing else to do; for the little Volanges, nothwithstanding her situation, was to spend the night at Madame de V —-'s early ball: the want of business first gave me an inclination to prolong the evening; and I had, with this intention, even required a little sacrifice: it was scarcely granted, than the pleasure I promised myself was disturbed with the idea of this love which you so obstinately will have it, or at least reproach me with being infected; so I determined at once to be certain myself, and convince you, that it was a calumny of your own.

In consequence I took a violent resolution; on a very slight pretence, I took leave, and left my fair one quite surprised, and doubtless more afflicted, while I quietly went to meet Emily at the opera: she can satisfy you, that until morning, when we parted, no regret disturbed our amusements.

Yet there was a pretty large field for uneasiness, if my total indifference had not preserved me: for you must know, I was scarce four houses from the opera, with Emily in my carriage, when that of the austere devotee ranged close beside mine, and a stop which happened, left us near half a quarter of an hour close by each other; we could see one another as plain as at noon day, and there was no means to escape.

That is not all; I took it in my head to tell Emily confidentially, that was the letter-woman. You may recollect, perhaps, that piece of folly, and that Emily was the desk[1]. She did not forget it, and as she laughs immoderately, she was not easy until she had attentively viewed this piece of virtue, as she called her; and with scandalous bursts, such as would even disconcert effrontery.

Still this is not all; the jealous woman sent to my house that same night; I was not at home, but she obstinately sent a second time, with orders to wait my return. I sent my carriage home, as soon as I resolved to spend the night with Emily, without any other orders to my coachman, than to return this morning. When he got home he found the messenger, whom he informed I was not to return that night. You may guess the effect of this news, and that at my return, I found my discharge announced with all the dignity the circumstance required.

Thus, this adventure, which according to your opinion, was never to be determined, could, as you see, have been ended this morning? if it should not, I would not have you think I prize a continuance of it; but I do not think it consistent with my character to be quitted: moreover, I intend to reserve the honour of this sacrifice for you.

I have answered her severe note with a long sentimental epistle; I have given long reasons, and rely on love to make them acceptable. I have already succeeded — I have received a second note, still very rigorous, and which confirms an everlasting rupture, as it ought to be — but the ton is not the same; I must not be seen again; this resolution is announced four times in the most irrevocable manner. From thence I concluded, there was not a moment to be lost in presenting myself: I have already sent my huntsman to secure the porter, and shall follow instantly, to have my pardon sealed: for in crimes of this nature, there is only one form for a general absolution, and that must be executed in each others presence.

Adieu, my charming friend! I fly to achieve this grand event.
Paris, Nov. 15, 17 —.

[1] Letters xlvi and xlvii.

LETTER CXXXIX.

The Presidente DE TOURVEL *to* MADAME DE ROSEMONDE.

How I reproach myself, my dear friend, for having wrote too soon, and said too much of my transitory troubles! I am the cause you at present are afflicted; the chagrin I have given you still continues, and I am happy; yes, every thing is forgot, and I forgive; or rather all is cleared up. Calm and delight succeed this state of grief and anguish; how shall I express the ecstasy of my heart! Valmont is innocent: with so much love there can be no guilt — those heavy offensive crimes with which I loaded him so bitterly, he did not deserve; and although I was right in one single point, yet I was to make reparation for my unjust suspicions.

I will not relate minutely the circumstances of facts or reasonings in his justification — Perhaps even the mind would but badly appreciate them — it is the heart only can feel them. However, were you even to suspect me of weakness, I would call on your judgment in support of my own; you say among men infidelity is not inconstancy.

Not but I am sensible, this opinion, which custom authorises, hurts delicacy: but why should mine complain, when Valmont's suffers more? This same injury which I forget, I do not think he forgives himself; and yet he has immensely repaired this trivial error, by the excess of his love, and my happiness!

My felicity is greater, or I know the value of it better, since my dread of losing him; I can aver to you, if I had strength sufficient to undergo again such cruel chagrins as I have just experienced, I should not think I had purchased my increase of happiness at too high a rate. Oh, my dear mother! scold your unthinking daughter for afflicting you by her precipitation; scold her for having rashly judged him she should ever adore; and knowing her imprudence, see her happy: augment her bliss by partaking it.

Paris, Nov. 15, 17 — .

LETTER CXL.

The VISCOUNT DE VALMONT *to the* MARCHIONESS DE MERTEUIL.

How comes it, my charming friend, I receive no answers from you? I think, however, my last letter deserved one; these three days have I been expecting it, and must still wait! I really am vexed, and shall not relate a syllable of my grand affairs.

Such as the reconciliation had its full effect: that instead of reproaches and dissidence, it produced fresh proofs of affection; that I now actually receive the excuse and satisfaction due to my suspected candour; not a word shall you know — had it not been for the unforeseen event of last night, I should not have wrote to you at all; but as it relates to your pupil, who probably cannot give you any information herself, at least for some time, I have taken upon me to acquaint you with it.

For reasons you may or may not guess, Madame de Tourvel, has not engaged my attention for some days: as those reasons could not exist with the little Volanges, I became more assiduous there. Thanks to the obliging porter, I had no obstacles to surmount; and your pupil and I led a comfortable, regular life — Custom brings on negligence; at first we had not taken proper precautions for our security; we trembled behind the locks: yesterday an incredible absence of mind occasioned the accident I am going to relate; as to myself, fear was my only punishment, but the little girl did not come off so well.

We were not asleep, but reposing in the abandonment consequent to voluptuousness, when on a sudden, we heard the room door open, I instantly seized my sword to defend myself and our pupil; I advanced, and saw no one; but the door was open: as we had a light, I examined all about the room, and did not find a mortal; then I recollected we had forgot our usual precautions, and certainly the door being only pushed or not properly shut, opened of itself.

Returning to my terrified companion to quiet her, I did not find her in the bed; she fell out, or hid herself by the bedside; at length I found her there, stretched senseless on the ground, in strong convulsions — You may judge my embarrassment — However, I brought her to herself, and got her into bed again, but she had hurt herself in the fall, and was not long before she felt its effect.

Pains in the loins, violent cholics, and other symptoms less equivocal, soon informed me her condition — To make her sensible of it, it was necessary to acquaint her with the one she was in before, of which she had not the least suspicion: never any one before her, perhaps, went to work so innocently to get rid of it — she does not lose her time in reflection.

But she lost a great deal in afflicting herself, and I found it necessary to come to some resolution: therefore we agreed I should immediately go to the physician and surgeon of the family, to inform them they would be sent for; I was to make them a confidence of the whole business, under a promise of secrecy — That she should ring for her waiting maid, and should or should not make her a confidence of her situation, as she thought proper; but at all events, send for assistance, and should forbid her from disturbing Madame de Volanges. An attentive delicacy natural to a girl who feared to give her mother uneasiness.

I made my two visits and confessions as expeditiously as I could, and then went home, from whence I have not since stirred. The surgeon, who I knew before, came to me at noon, to give me an account of the state of his patient — I was not mistaken — He hopes, however, it will not be attended with any bad consequences. Provided no accident happens, it will not be discovered in the house; the waiting woman is in the secret; the physician has given the disorder a name, and this affair will be settled as a thousand others have been, unless hereafter it might be useful to us to have it mentioned.

Have you and I mutual interests or no? Your silence makes me dubious of it; I would not even think at all of it, if my inclinations did not lead me on to every method of preserving the hope of it. Adieu, my charming friend! yet in anger.

Paris, Nov. 21, 17 —.

LETTER CXLI.

The MARCHIONESS DE MERTEUIL *to the* VISCOUNT DE VALMONT.

Good God, Viscount! How troublesome you are with your obstinacy! What matters my silence to you? Do you believe it is for want of reasons I am silent? Ah! would to God! But no, it is only because it would be painful to tell them to you.

Speak truth, do you deceive yourself, or do you mean to deceive me? The difference between your discourse and actions, leaves in doubt which I am to give credit to. What shall I say to you then, when I even do not know what to think?

You seem to make a great merit of your last scene with the Presidente; but what does that prove in support of your system, or against mine? I never certainly told you, your love for this woman was so violent as not be capable of deceiving her, or prevent you from enjoying every opportunity that appeared agreeable and easy to you. I never even doubted but it would be equally the same to you, to satisfy, with any other, the first that offered, the desires she would raise. I am not at all surprised, that from a libertinism of mind, which it would be wrong to contend with you, you have once done designedly, what you have a thousand times done occasionally—Don't we well know this is the way of the world, and the practice of you all? and whoever acts otherwise is looked on as a simpleton—I think I don't charge you with this defect.

What I have said, what I have thought, what I still think, is, you are nevertheless in love with your Presidente: not if you will with a pure and tender passion, but of that kind of which you are capable; for example, of that kind which makes you discover in a woman, charms and qualities she has not: which ranks her in a class by herself, and still links you to her even while you insult her—Such, in a word, as a Sultan has for a favourite Sultana; that does not prevent him from often giving the preference to a plain Odalisk. My comparison appears to me the more just, as, like him, you never are the lover or friend of a woman, but always her tyrant or her slave. And I am very certain, you very much humbled and debased yourself very much, to get into favour again with this fine object! Happy in your success, as soon as you think the moment arrived to obtain your pardon, you leave me *for this grand event*.

Even in your last letter, the reason you give for not entertaining me solely with this woman is, because you will not tell me any thing of your *grand affairs*; they are of so much importance, that your silence on that subject is to be my punishment: and after giving me such strong proofs of a decided preference for another, you coolly ask me whether *we have a mutual interest!* Have a care, Viscount; if I once answer you, my answer shall be irrevocable: and to be in suspense, is perhaps saying too much; I will therefore now say no more of that matter.

I have nothing more to say, but to tell you a trifling story; perhaps you will not have leisure to read it, or to give so much attention to it as to understand it properly? At worst, it will be only a tale thrown away.

A man of my acquaintance, like you, was entangled with a woman, who did him very little credit; he had sense enough, at times, to perceive, this adventure would hurt him one time or other—Although he was ashamed of it, yet he had not the resolution to break off—His embarrassment was greater, as he had frequently boasted to his friends, he was entirely at liberty; and was not insensible, the more he apologised, the more the ridicule increased—Thus, he spent his time incessantly in foolery, and constantly saying, *it is not my fault*. This man had a friend, who was one time very near giving him up in his frenzy to indelible ridicule: but yet, being more generous than malicious, or perhaps from some other motive, she resolved, as a last effort, to try a method to be able, at least, with her friend, to say, *it is not my fault*. She therefore sent him, without farther ceremony, the following letter, as a remedy for his disorder.

"One tires of every thing, my angel! It is a law of nature; it is not my fault.

"If, then, I am tired of a connection that has entirely taken me up four long months, it is not my fault.

"If, for example, I had just as much love as you had virtue, and that's saying a great deal, it is not at all surprising that one should end with the other; it is not my fault.

"It follows, then, that for some time past, I have deceived you; but your unmerciful affection in some measure forced me to it! It is not my fault.

"Now a woman I love to distraction, insists I must sacrifice you: it is not my fault.

"I am sensible here is a fine field for reproaches; but if nature has only granted men constancy, whilst it gives obstinacy to women, it is not my fault.

"Take my advice, choose another lover, as I have another mistress — The advice is good; if you think otherwise, it is not my fault.

"Farewell, my angel! I took you with pleasure, I part you without regret; perhaps I shall return to you; it is the way of the world; it is not my fault."

This is not the time to tell you, Viscount, the effect of this last effort, and its consequences; but I promise to give it you in my next letter; you will then receive also my ultimatum on renewing the treaty you propose. Until when, adieu.

Now I think on it, receive my thanks for your particular account of the little Volanges; that article will keep till the day after her wedding, for the scandalous gazette. I condole with you, however, on the loss of your progeny. Good night, Viscount.

Nov. 24, 17 — . Castle of — — .

LETTER CXLII.

VISCOUNT DE VALMONT *to the* MARCHIONESS DE MERTEUIL.

I don't know, my charming friend, whether I have read or understood badly your letter, the little tale you relate, and the epistolary model it contains — But this I must say, the last is an original, and seems very proper to take effect; therefore I only copied it, and sent it without farther ceremony to the celestial Presidente. I did not lose a moment, for the tender epistle was dispatched yesterday evening — I chose to act so; for first, I had promised to write to her; and, moreover, I thought a whole night not too much for her to collect herself, and ruminate on *this grand event*, were you even to reproach me a second time with the expression.

I expected to have sent you back this morning my well-beloved's answer; it is now near twelve, and it is not yet come — I shall wait until five; and if I receive no news by that time, I shall in person seek it, for every thing must be done according to form, and the difficulty is only in this first step.

Now you may believe I am impatient to know the end of your story of that man of your acquaintance, who was so violently suspected of not knowing how to sacrifice a woman upon occasion — Did he not amend, and did not his generous friend forgive him?

I am no less anxious to receive your ultimatum as you call it so politically; but I am curious, above all, to know if you can perceive any impression of love in this last proceeding? Ah! doubtless there is, and a good deal! But for whom? Still I make no pretensions; I expect every thing from your goodness.

Adieu, charmer! I shall not close my letter until two, in hope of adding the wished-for answer.

Two o'clock in the afternoon.

Nothing yet — the time slips away; I can't spare a moment — but surely now you will not refuse the tenderest kisses of love.

Paris, Nov. 27, 17 — .

LETTER CXLIII.

The Presidente DE TOURVEL *to* MADAME DE ROSEMONDE.

The veil is rent, Madam, on which was painted my illusory happiness — The fatal truth is cleared, that leaves me no prospect but an assured and speedy death; and my road is traced between shame and remorse. I will follow it — I will cherish my torments if they will shorten my existence — I send you the letter I received yesterday; it needs no reflections; it contains them all — This is not a time for lamentation — nothing remains but sufferings — I want not pity, I want strength.

Receive, Madame, the only adieu I shall make, and grant my last request: leave me to my fate — forget me totally — do not reckon me among the living. There is a limit in misery, when even friendship augments our sufferings and cannot cure them — When wounds are mortal, all relief is cruel. Every sentiment but despair is foreign to my soul — nothing can now suit me, but the darkness where I am going to bury my shame — There will I weep crimes, if I yet can weep; for since yesterday I have not shed a tear — my withered heart no longer furnishes any.

Adieu, Madame! Do not reply to this — I have taken a solemn oath on this letter never to receive another.

Paris, Nov. 27, 17 —.

LETTER CXLIV.

VISCOUNT DE VALMONT *to the* MARCHIONESS DE MERTEUIL.

Yesterday, at three in the afternoon, being impatient, my lovely friend, at not having any news, I presented myself at the house of the fair abandoned, and was told she was gone out. In this reply I could see nothing more than a refusal to admit me, which neither surprised nor vexed me; I retired, in hope this step would induce so polished a woman to give me an answer. The desire I had to receive one, made me call home about nine, but found nothing. Astonished at this silence, which I did not expect, I sent my huntsman on the enquiry for information, whether the tender fair was dead or dying. At my return, he informed me, Madame de Tourvel had actually gone out at eleven in the morning with her waiting maid; that she ordered her carriage to the convent of — —; that at seven in the evening she had sent her carriage and servants back, sending word they should not expect her home. This is certainly acting with propriety. The convent is the only asylum for a widow; and if she persists in so laudable a resolution, I shall add to all the obligations I already lay under, the celebrity this adventure will now have.

I told you sometime ago, notwithstanding your uneasiness, I would again appear in the world with more brilliant eclat. Let those severe critics now show themselves, who accused me of a romantic passion; let them make a more expeditious and shining rupture: no, let them do more; bid them go offer their consolations — the road is chalked out for them; let them only dare run the career I have gone over entirely, and if any one obtains the least success, I will yield him up the first place: but they shall all experience when I am in earnest; the impression I leave is indelible. This one I affirm will be so. I should even look on all former triumphs as trifles, if I was ever to have a favoured rival.

I own the step she has taken flatters my vanity; yet I am sorry she had so much fortitude to separate from me. There will be no obstacle, then, between us, but of my own formation. If I should be inclined to renew our connection, she, perhaps, would refuse; perhaps not pant for it, not think it the summit of happiness! Is this love? And do you think, my charming friend, I should bear it? Could I not, for example, and would it not be better, endeavour to bring this woman to the point of foreseeing a possibility of a reconciliation, always wished for while there is hope? I could try this course without any consequence, without giving you umbrage. It would be only a mere trial we would make in concert. Even if I should be successful, it would be only an additional means of renewing, at your pleasure, a sacrifice which has seemed agreeable to you. Now, my charming friend, I am yet to receive my reward, and all my vows are for your return. Come, then, speedily to your lover, your pleasures, your friends, and the pursuit of adventures.

That of the little Volanges has had a surprising turn. Yesterday, as my uneasiness would not suffer me to stay long in a place, in my various excursions I called at Madame Volanges's. I found your pupil in the saloon, in the drapery of a sick person, but in full health, fresher, and more interesting. Some of you ladies, in such a case would keep your beds for a month, Oh, rare lasses! Egad, this one has given me a strong inclination to know if the cure be complete.

I had almost forgot to tell you, the little girl's accident had like to have turned your *sentimental* Danceny's brain: at first it was for grief, but now it is with joy. *His Cecilia* was sick. You will agree, the brain must turn with such a misfortune. Three times a day did he send to enquire about her, and never missed every day going himself; at last, he wrote a fine epistle to the mama, begging leave to go and congratulate her on the recovery of so dear an object; Madame de Volanges assented; so that I found the young man established as heretofore, only not quite so familiar. This narrative I had from himself; for I came out with him, and made him prate. You can't conceive what an effect this visit had on him; his joy, his wishes, his transports are inexpressible. As I am fond of grand emotions, I finished him, by telling him, in a few days I hoped to place him much nearer his fair one.

I am determined to give her up to him as soon as I have made my trial. I will devote myself entirely to you; moreover, I don't see it would be worth while your pupil should be my scholar, if she had only a husband to deceive. The *chef d'œuvre* is to deceive the lover! and the first lover too! For I can't reproach myself with even having pronounced the word love.

Adieu, my lovely friend! Return as soon as possible to resume your empire over me, to receive my homage, and give me my reward.

Paris, Nov. 28, 17 — .

LETTER CXLV.

The MARCHIONESS DE MERTEUIL *to the* VISCOUNT DE VALMONT.

Now seriously, Viscount, have you left the Presidente? Did you send her the letter I wrote you for her? You are a charming fellow, indeed, and have surpassed my expectations! I must own, this triumph flatters me more than all those I ever obtained. You will think, perhaps, I estimate this woman very highly, who I depreciated very lately; not in the least: but it is not over her this advantage is gained; it is over you; there lies the jest, and it is really delightful.

Yes, Viscount, you loved Madame de Tourvel much, and you still love her; you love her to distraction: but because I made you ashamed, by way of amusement, you nobly sacrifice her. You would have sacrificed a thousand women rather than be laughed at. To what lengths will not vanity lead us! The wise man was right when he said it was the foe to happiness.

What would become of you now, if it had been only a trick I put upon you? But I am incapable of deceit, and you know it well; and should you even in my turn reduce me to despair and a convent, I will risk it, and surrender to my conqueror. Still, if I do capitulate, upon my word it is from mere frailty; for were I inclined, how many cavils could I not start! and, perhaps, you would deserve them!

I admire, for example, with how much address, or awkwardness rather, you soothingly propose I should let you renew with your Presidente. It would be very convenient, would it not? to take all the merit of this rapture without losing the pleasure of enjoyment! And then this proffered sacrifice, which would no longer be one to you, is offered to be renewed at my pleasure! By this arrangement, the celestial devotee would always think herself the only choice of your heart, whilst I should wrap myself up in the pride of being the preferred rival; we should both be deceived; you would be satisfied: all the rest is of no consequence.

It is much to be lamented, that with such extraordinary talents for projects, you have so few for execution; and that by one inconsiderate step, you put an insurmountable obstacle to what you so much wished.

What! you had, then, an idea of renewing your connection, and yet you copied my letter! You must, then, have thought me awkward indeed! Believe me, Viscount, when a woman strikes at the heart of another, she seldom misses her blow, and the wound is incurable. When I struck this one, or rather directed the blow, I did not forget she was my rival, that you had for a moment preferred her to me, placed me beneath her. If I am deceived in my revenge, I consent to bear the blame; therefore, I agree you may attempt every means; even I invite you to it, and promise you I shall not be angry at your success. I am so easy on this matter, I shall say no more of it: let us talk of something else.

As to the health of the little Volanges, you will be able to give me some positive news at my return. I shall be glad to have some. After that, you will be the best judge whether it will be most convenient to give the little girl up to her lover, or endeavour to be the founder of a new branch of the Valmonts, under the name of Gercourt. This idea pleases me much: but in leaving the choice to yourself, I must yet require you will not come to a definitive resolution until we talk the matter over. It is not putting you off for a long time, for I shall be in Paris immediately. I can't positively say the day; but be assured, as soon as I arrive, you shall be the first informed of it.

Adieu, Viscount! notwithstanding my quarrels, my mischievousness, and my reproaches, I always love you much, and am preparing to prove it. Adieu, till our next meeting.
Castle of — —, Nov. 29, 17 —.

LETTER CXLVI.

The MARCHIONESS DE MERTEUIL *to the* CHEVALIER DANCENY.

At last I set out, my young friend; to-morrow evening I shall be in Paris. The hurry always attending a removal will prevent me from seeing any one. Yet if you should have any pressing confidential business to impart, I shall except you from the general rule: but I except you alone; therefore request my arrival may be a secret. I shall not even inform Valmont of it.

Whoever would have told me, sometime ago, you would have my exclusive confidence, I would not have believed them: but yours drew on mine. I should be inclined to think you had made use of some address, or, perhaps, seduction. That would be wrong, indeed! however, it would not at present be very dangerous; you have other business in hand. When the heroine is on the stage, we seldom take notice of the confidant.

And, indeed, you have not had time to impart your late success to me. When your Cecilia was absent, the days were too short to listen to your plaintive strains. You would have told them to the echo, if I had not been ready to hear them. Since, when she was ill, you even honoured me with a recital of your troubles; you wanted some one to tell them to: but now your love is in Paris, that she is quite recovered, and you sometimes see her, your friends are quite neglected.

I do not blame you in the least, it is a fault of youth; for it is a received truth, that from Alcibiades down to you, young people are unacquainted with friendship but in adversity. Happiness sometimes makes them indiscreet, but never presumptuous. I will say, with Socrates, *I like my friends to come to me when they are unhappy:* but, as a philosopher, he did very well without them if they did not come. I am not quite so wise as he, for I felt your silence with all the weakness of a woman.

However, do not think me too exacting; far from it. The same sentiment that leads me to observe those privations, makes me bear them with fortitude, when they are proofs, or the cause of the happiness of my friends. I shall, therefore, not depend on you for to-morrow evening, only as far as is consistent with love and want of occupation; and I positively forbid you to make me the least sacrifice.

Adieu, Chevalier! it will be an absolute regale to see you again—will you come?
Castle of — —, Nov. 29, 17—.

LETTER CXLVII.

MADAME DE VOLANGES *to* MADAME DE ROSEMONDE.

You will most assuredly be as much afflicted, my dear friend, as I am, when I acquaint you with Madame de Tourvel's state; she has been indisposed since yesterday: she was taken so suddenly, and her disorder is of such an alarming nature, that I am really frightened about it.

A burning fever, an almost constant and violent delirium, a perpetual thirst, are the symptoms. The physicians say, they cannot as yet form their prognostics; and their endeavours are frustrated, as the patient obstinately refuses every kind of remedy: insomuch, that they were obliged to use force to bleed her; and were twice since forced to use the same method, to tie up the bandages, which she tore off in her fits.

You and I, who have seen her, so weak, so timid, so mild, could hardly conceive that four persons scarcely could hold her; and on the least remonstrance she flies out in the greatest rage imaginable: for my part, I fear it is something worse than a raving, and borders on downright madness.

And what happened the day before yesterday adds to my fears.

On that day she came about eleven in the morning to the convent of ---- with her waiting maid. As she was educated in that house, and occasionally came to visit there, she was received as usual, and appeared to every one in good health and very quiet. In about two hours after she asked, whether the room she had, whilst she was a pensioner, was vacant? and being answered in the affirmative, she begged leave to see it; the prioress and some of the nuns accompanied her. She then declared she came back to settle in this room, which, said she, I ought never to have quitted; adding, she would not depart from it *until death:* that was her expression.

At first, they stared at each other: but the first surprise being over, they remonstrated, that, as a married woman, she could not be received without a special permission. That, and a thousand other arguments were unavailable; and from that moment she was obstinate, not only to remain in the convent, but even not to stir from the room. At length, being tired out, they consented, at seven in the evening, she should remain there that night. Her carriage and servants were sent home, and they adjourned until the next day.

I have been assured, during the whole night her appearance and deportment did not exhibit the least wandering symptom; on the contrary, she seemed composed and deliberate; only fell into a profound reverie four or five times, which conversation could not remove; and every time before she recovered from it, she seemed forcibly to squeeze her forehead with both hands: on which one of the nuns asked her if she had a pain in her head; she fixed her eyes on her sometime before she replied, and said, "My disorder is not there." Immediately after she begged to be left alone, and also, that in future they should not put any questions to her.

Every one retired except her waiting maid, who was fortunately obliged to sleep in the same chamber.

According to the girl's account, her mistress was pretty quiet until about eleven at night; then she said she would go to bed: but before she was quite undressed, she walked to and fro in her room with much action and gesture. Julie, who was present at every thing that passed during the day, did not dare say a word, and silently waited near an hour. At length, Madame de Tourvel called her twice on a sudden; she had scarce time to reach her, when her mistress dropped in her arms, saying, "I can hold out no longer." She suffered her to lead her to her bed; but would not take any thing, nor allow her to call for assistance. She ordered her only to leave her some water, and go to bed.

The girl avers, she did not go to sleep till two in the morning, and heard neither disturbance nor complaint. At five she was awoke by her mistress, who spoke in a strong loud tone. She asked, if she wanted any thing; but receiving no answer, she went to Madame de Tourvel's bedside with a light, who did not know her; but breaking off her incoherent discourse, exclaimed violently, "Leave me alone! Let me be left in darkness! It is darkness alone suits me!" I remarked yesterday, she often repeated those expressions.

At last, Julie took this opportunity to go out and call for assistance, which Madame de Tourvel refused with the greatest fury and madness. These fits have often returned since.

The distress the whole convent was thrown in, induced the Prioress to send for me yesterday morning at seven, when it was not yet day. I went immediately. When I was announced to Madame de Tourvel, she seemed to come to herself, and said, "Ah! yes, let her come in." She fixed her eyes on me when I came near her bed, and seizing my hand suddenly, she squeezed it, saying, in a strong, melancholy tone, "I die for not having taken your advice;" and immediately covering her eyes, she resumed her delirium of "Leave me alone," &c. and lost all reason.

Those discourses, and some others that fell from her in her delirium, make me apprehend this dreadful disorder has still a more cruel cause; but let us respect the secrets of our friend, and pity her misfortune.

All yesterday was equally stormy, either fits of frightful deliriousness, or lethargic faintness, the only time when she takes or gives any rest. I did not leave her bed's head until nine at night, and am going again this morning for the day.

I will not certainly abandon our unhappy friend: but her obstinacy in refusing all help and assistance is very distressing.

I enclose you the journal of last night, which I have just received, and which, as you will see, brings but little consolation. I will take care to send them you regularly.

Adieu, my worthy friend! I am going to visit our poor friend. My daughter, who is perfectly recovered, presents her compliments to you.

Paris, Nov. 29, 17—.

LETTER CXLVIII.

The CHEVALIER DANCENY *to the* MARCHIONESS DE MERTEUIL.

O you, whom I love! O thou, whom I adore! O you, with whom my happiness hath commenced! O thou, who hast completed it! Compassionate friend! tender mistress! why does the reflection that you are a prey to grief come to disturb my charmed mind? Ah, Madam! resume your calmness; it is the duty of friendship to make this entreaty. O my heart's only object! be happy; it is the prayer of love.

What reproaches have you to make to yourself? Believe me, your extraordinary delicacy misleads you. The regret it occasions you, the injuries it charges me with, are equally imaginary; and I feel within my heart, that there has been between us no other seducer than love. No longer dread, then, to yield to those sentiments you inspire, or to partake of a flame you have kindled. What! would we have had more reason to boast of purity in our connection, if it had taken more time to form? Undoubtedly not. That is the characteristic of seduction, which, never acting unless by projects, is able to regulate its progress and means, and foresees events at a great distance: but true love does not permit that kind of meditation and reflection; it diverts us from thought with occupying us wholly with sentiments. Its empire is never more powerful than when unknown; and it is in obscurity and silence that it steals upon us, and binds us in chains equally impossible to be perceived or to be broken.

Thus, even yesterday, notwithstanding the lively emotions which the idea of your return caused in me, in defiance of the extreme pleasure I felt on seeing you, I nevertheless thought myself led and called upon by serene friendship alone, or rather entirely absorbed by the sweet sentiments of my heart, I concerned myself very little in tracing either their cause or origin. Like me, my dear friend, you experienced, though unconscious of it, that all-powerful charm, which gave up our whole souls to the rapturous impression of tenderness, and neither of us recognised it to be love, till after the intoxication that deity plunged us into.

But that very circumstance is our exculpation, instead of our guilt. No, you did not betray the rights of friendship, nor have I abused your confidence. We both, it is true, were ignorant of our sentiments; but we only underwent the delusion, without any efforts to give birth to it: and far from complaining of it, let us only think of the happiness it procured us, without disturbing it by unjust reproaches; let our only endeavours be to farther augment it, by the pleasures of confidence and entire security. O, my friend! how dear these hopes are to my heart! Yes, henceforward freed from all fears, and wholly occupied by love, you will participate of my desires, of my transports, of the sweet delirium of my senses, of the intoxication of my soul, and each moment of our happy days shall be marked by a new enjoyment.

Adieu, thou whom I adore! I shall see thee this evening; but shall I find you alone? I hardly dare to hope it. Ah! you do not desire it as much as I!

Paris, Dec. 1, 17—.

LETTER CXLIX.

MADAME DE VOLANGES *to* MADAME DE ROSEMONDE.

I was in hopes almost all day yesterday, to have been able to give you, my worthy friend, this morning, a more favourable account of our dear patient; but since last night, that hope is utterly destroyed. A matter seemingly of very little importance, but which, in its consequences, proves to be a very unhappy one, has made the case at least as grievous as before, if not worse.

I should not have had any comprehension of this sudden change, if I had not received yesterday the entire confidence of our unhappy friend. As she did not conceal from me that you also are acquainted with all her misfortunes, I can inform you every thing without reserve of her unhappy situation.

Yesterday morning, on my arrival at the convent, I was informed she had been asleep about three hours; and that sleep, so profound and so easy, I for some time was apprehensive was lethargic—Some time after she awoke, and opened the curtains of the bed herself.

At first she looked at us all with great surprise, and as I rose to go to her, she knew me, called me by my name, and begged I would come near her. She did not give me time to ask her any questions, but desired to know where she was; what we were doing there; if she was sick; and why she was not in her own house? I imagined at first, it was another frenzy, only more gentle than the former: but I soon perceived she understood my replies perfectly; and she had recovered her reason, but not her memory.

She questioned me very minutely on every thing that happened to her since she came to the convent, which she did not remember. I gave her a faithful account, only concealing what I thought might frighten her too much: and when I asked how she was, she replied she did not then feel any pain: but was much tormented during her sleep, and found herself fatigued. I advised her to keep quiet, and say little: then I partly closed the curtains, and sat down by the side of her bed: some broth was then proposed, which she agreed to take, and liked it very well.

She continued thus about half an hour, and only spoke to thank me for my care of her, which she did with that graceful ease you know is so natural to her; afterwards she was for some time quite silent, which she broke at length, saying, "O yes, I now remember my coming here;" and a minute after, exclaimed grievously, "My dear friend, have pity on me! My miseries are all returning on me." I was then coming towards her, she grasped my hand, and leaning her head against it, "Great God!" said she, "cannot I then die!" Her expression more than her words melted me into tears; she perceived it by my voice, and said, "you pity me then; ah, if you but knew!" — Then breaking off: "Let us be alone, and I will tell you all."

I believe I already wrote to you I had some suspicions, which I was apprehensive would be the topic of this conversation that I foresaw would be tedious and melancholy, and might probably be very detrimental to the present state of our unhappy friend. I endeavoured to dissuade her from it, by urging the necessity of repose; she however, insisted, and I was obliged to acquiesce.

As soon as we were alone, she acquainted me with every thing you already know, therefore unnecessary to be repeated.

At last, relating the cruel manner in which she was sacrificed, she added, "I was very certain it would be my death, and I was resolved — but it is impossible to survive my shame and grief." I attempted to contend against this depression, or rather despair, with motives of a religious nature, always hitherto so powerful in her mind; but I was soon convinced I was not equal to this solemn function, and I determined to propose calling in Father Anselmus, in whom I knew she reposes great confidence. She consented, and even appeared much to desire it — He was sent for, and came immediately: he stayed a long time with her, and said, going away, if the physicians were of the same opinion he was, the ceremony of the sacraments he thought might be postponed until the day following.

This was about three in the afternoon, and our friend was pretty quiet until five, so that we all began to conceive some hope; but unfortunately a letter was then brought for her; when it was offered to her, she replied at first she would not receive any, and no one pressed it; but from that time she seemed more disturbed. Soon after she asked from whom the letter came? — It had no post-mark — Who brought it? — No one knew — From what place did the messenger say it came? — The portress was not informed. She remained silent some time after; then again began to speak; but her discourse was so incoherent, we were soon convinced the frenzy was returned.

However there was a quiet interval afterwards, until at last she desired the letter should be given to her. The moment she cast her eyes on it, she exclaimed, "Good God! from him!" and then in a strong and oppressed tone of voice, "Take it, take it." She instantly ordered the curtains of her bed to be closed, and desired no one should come near her; but we were all soon obliged to come round her: the frenzy returned with more violence than ever, accompanied with most dreadful convulsions — Those shocking incidents continued the whole evening; and the account I received this morning, informs me, the night has been no less turbulent. On the whole, I am astonished she has held out so long in the condition she is: and I will not conceal from you, that I have very little, if any, hope of her recovery.

I suppose this unfortunate letter is from M. de Valmont — What! can he still dare to write to her! Forgive me, my dear friend; I must put a stop to my reflections — It is, however, a most cruel case, to see a woman make so wretched an end, who has, until now, lived so happy, and was so worthy being so.

Paris, Dec. 2, 17 —.

CHEVALIER DANCENY *to the* MARCHIONESS DE MERTEUIL.

In expectation of the happiness of seeing you, I indulge myself, my tender friend, in the pleasure of writing to you; and thus by occupying myself with you, I dispel the gloom that otherwise would be occasioned by your absence. To delineate to you my sentiments, to recall yours to my mind, is a true enjoyment to my heart; and thus even the time of privation affords me a thousand ideas precious to my love — Yet, if I am to believe you, I shall not obtain any answer from you, even this letter shall be the last, and we shall abandon a correspondence which, according to you, is dangerous, *and of which we have no need* — Certainly I shall believe you if you persist; for what can you desire that does not of course become my desire? But before you ultimately decide upon it, will you not permit a slight conversation on the subject.

Of the head of danger you are the only judge — I can frame no calculation of it — and I shall confine myself to requesting you would look to your own safety, for I can have no tranquillity while you are disquieted — As to this object, it is not we two that are but one, it is thou that art us both.

As to the matter of necessity, we can have but one thought; and if we differ in opinion, it can only rise from a want of proper explanation, or from not understanding one another. I shall therefore state to you what I think is my sensation.

Without doubt a letter appears very unnecessary when we can see one another freely — What could it say that a word, or look, or even silence itself, could not express? A hundred times before, this appeared to me so clear, that in the very moment that you spoke to me of not writing any more, that idea my mind immediately adopted — It was a restraint upon it perhaps, but did not affect it — Thus, when I have offered a kiss upon your bosom, and found a ribband or piece of gauze in my way, I only turn it aside, and have not the least sentiment of an obstacle.

But since we have separated, and you are no longer there, this idea of correspondence by letters has returned to torment me — What is the reason, I have said to myself, of this additional privation? Why is it, because we are at some distance, we have nothing more to say to each other? Suppose that a fortunate concurrence of circumstances should bring us together for a day, shall we then employ in conversation the time that ought to be wholly dedicated to enjoyment, which letters between us would prevent? I say enjoyment, my dear friend; for with you the very moments of repose furnish, too, a delicious enjoyment; in a word, whenever such a happy opportunity offers, the conclusion is still separation; and one is so solitary, it is then a letter becomes truly precious: if not read, it is sure to be the only object that employs the eye. Ah! there can be no doubt, but one may look at a letter without reading it; as I think that I even could have some pleasure at night by barely touching your portrait.

Your portrait have I said? but a letter is the portrait of the soul; it has not, like a cold image, that degree of stagnation so opposite to love; it yields to all our actions by turns; it becomes animated, gives us enjoyment, and sinks into repose — All your sentiments are precious to me; and will you deprive me of the means of becoming possessed of them?

Are you quite sure that a desire to write to me will never torment you? If in the midst of your solitude your heart should be too much compressed or desolated; if a joyous emotion should pass to your soul; if an involuntary sadness should disturb it for a moment, it would not then be in the bosom of your friend that you would pour out your happiness or distress; you would then have a sensation he should not share; and you would punish him to wander in solitude and distrust far from you. My friend, my dearest friend! you are to pronounce — I have only proposed to myself to discuss the question with you, and not to over-rule you — I have only offered you reasons — I dare hope I should have stood on stronger ground if I had proceeded to entreaties — I shall endeavour, then, if you should persist, not to be afflicted; I shall use my efforts to tell myself what you would have wrote to me; but you would tell it better than I, and I should have a much higher gratification in hearing it from you.

Adieu, my charming friend! The hour approaches at last, when I shall be able to see you: I fly from you with the more haste, in order the sooner to meet you again.

Paris, Dec. 3, 17—.

LETTER CLI.

The VISCOUNT DE VALMONT *to the* MARCHIONESS DE MERTEUIL.

Surely, Marchioness, you do not take me to be such a novice, to imagine I could be duped in the tête-à-tête which I found you in this afternoon; or by the *astonishing chance* that led Danceny to your house! Not but your well-practised countenance wonderfully assumed a calm serenity of expression; or that you, by the most trifling word, betrayed, which sometimes happens, the least disorder or uneasiness. I will even allow your submissive looks served you eminently; and could they have made themselves as well credited as readily understood, far from having or harbouring the least suspicion, I should not at all have doubted the great vexation this *troublesome trio* gave you. But to display to greater advantage those extraordinary talents, to ensure the success you promised yourself, to carry on the deception you intended, you should have formed your inexperienced lover with more care.

Since you have begun to educate youth, you should teach your pupils not to blush or be disconcerted at a little raillery; not to deny so warmly for one woman, the same charge which they so faintly excuse themselves in for all others; teach them also to learn to hear encomiums on their mistress, without enhancing them.

And if you permit them to fix their looks on you in the circle, let them be taught to disguise that glance of enjoyment which is so easy to discover, and which they so unskilfully blend with the glance of love — Then you will be able to exhibit them in your public exercises, and their behaviour will not do any prejudice to their sage institutrix. Even myself, happy to be able to contribute to your celebrity, will compose and publish the exercises to be performed in this new college.

But I am astonished, I must own, that you should have undertaken to treat me as a school-boy. O! with any other woman, what pleasure I should have in being revenged! How transcendent it would be to that she should think to deprive me of! Yes, it is for you alone I condescend to give preference to satisfaction rather than revenge: and do not think I am restrained by the least doubt or uncertainty — I know all.

You have been in Paris now four days, and each day Danceny has been with you, and you have not admitted any one but him—even this day your door was still close; and had your porter's assurance been equal to his mistress's, I should not have seen you: yet you wrote me I might depend on being the first informed of your arrival. Of that same arrival, the particular day of which could not be ascertained, although you was writing to me the eve of your departure—Can you deny those facts, or will you attempt to excuse them? They are both equally impossible; and still I keep my temper! Acknowledge here your power; be satisfied to have experienced it, but do not any longer abuse it. We know each other, Marchioness; that should be sufficient.

To-morrow you are to be out for the day you told me; be it so, if you really go out, and you think I shall know it: but you will be home in the evening; we shall not have too much time until the next day to settle our difficult reconciliation. Let me know, then, if it will be at your house, *or yonder*, we shall make our numerous reciprocal expiations. But no more of Danceny; your wrong head had filled itself with his idea, and I am willing to overlook this delirium of your fancy; but remember, from this moment, that what was only a whim, would become a decided preference. I am not tempered for such an humiliation, neither do I expect to receive it from you.

I even expect this sacrifice will be but trifling to you—If it should be a little troublesome, I think, however, I have set you a tolerable example! A sensible and lovely woman, who existed for me only, who, perhaps, at this instant, is expiring with love and grief, may well be worth a young scholar, who, if you will, wants neither wit or accomplishments, but is deficient in consistency.

Adieu, Marchioness! I say nothing of my sentiments for you; all I can do at present is not to scrutinize my heart. I wait your answer. Remember, the easier it is for you to make me forget the injury you have done me, the more a denial, even the least delay, would engrave it in indelible characters on my heart.

Paris, Dec. 3, 17—.

LETTER CLII.

The MARCHIONESS DE MERTEUIL *to the* VISCOUNT DE VALMONT.

Take care, Viscount; have a little more regard for my extreme timidity. How do you think I can support the unsufferable idea of your indignation; but especially that I do not sink under the terror of your vengeance? particularly as you know, if you defamed me, it would be impossible for me to return the compliment. In vain should I babble; your existence would nevertheless be brilliant and peaceful: for what would you have to dread? Only to be under the necessity of retiring if you had an opportunity. But could one not live in a foreign country as well as here? And to sum up all, provided the court of France would let you be quiet in the one you choose to settle in, it would be only changing the field of your victories. After endeavouring to bring you back to your *sang froid* by these moral considerations, let us resume our own affairs.

You do not know, Viscount, the reasons I never married again. It was not, I assure you, for want of several advantageous matches being offered to me; it was solely that no one should have a right to control me. It was not even a dread of not being able to pursue my inclinations, for certainly, at all events, that I should have done: but it would have pained me if any one should even have a right to complain. On the whole, it was that I would not wish to deceive but for my own pleasure, and not through necessity. And behold you write me the most matrimonial letter it is possible to conceive! You tell me of the injuries I have committed, and the favours you have granted! I cannot conceive how it is possible to be indebted to one where nothing is due.

Now for the business. You found Danceny at my house, and you was displeased; be it so: but what conclusion do you draw from thence? Why, that it was the effect of chance, as I told you, or of my inclination, which I did not tell you. In the first instance, your letter is wrong; in the second, ridiculous. It was well worth the trouble of writing! But you are jealous, and jealousy never debates. Well, I will argue for you.

You have a rival, or you have not. If you have a rival, you must please, to obtain the preference over him; and if you have none, you must still please, to avoid having one. In all cases the same invariable conduct must be observed. Why, then, will you torment yourself? — And why torment me? Have you, then, lost the secret of being the most amiable? And are you no longer certain of your success? Come, come, Viscount, you do yourself injustice. But that is not the case, for I will not, even in your mind, have you give yourself so much uneasiness. You wish less for my condescension, than an opportunity of abusing your power. Fie! you are very ungrateful! I think this is tolerably sentimental; and was I to continue any time, this letter might become very tender: but you don't deserve it.

Neither do you deserve I should enter farther in my justification. To punish you for your suspicions, you shall keep them; so that I shall make no reply as to the time of my return, or Danceny's visits. You have taken great trouble to be informed of them, most certainly: and pray what progress have you made by it? I hope you received great pleasure from your enquiries; as to mine, it has not been in the least detrimental to them.

All I can say, then, to your threatening letter is this — it has neither the gift of pleasing, nor power to intimidate me; and that at this present time I am not in the least disposed to grant your request.

And, indeed, to receive you, as you exhibit yourself now, would be a downright act of infidelity: it would not be a renewal with my former lover; it would be taking a new one, many degrees inferior to him. I have not so soon forgot the first, to be deceived. The Valmont I loved was a charming fellow. I will even own, I never met a more amiable man. I beg, Viscount, if you find him, to bring him to me, he will be always well received.

Acquaint him, however, that it cannot by any means be either to-day or to-morrow. His Menæchmus has done him some harm, and was I in too much haste, I should dread a deception; or, perhaps, I have given my word to Danceny for those two days: moreover, your letter informs me you do not jest; when one breaks their word, therefore, you see you must wait.

That is, however, of very little consequence, as you can always be revenged on your rival. He will not treat your mistress worse than you will his; and after all, is not one woman as good as another? These are your own principles. Even she who should be *tender and sensible, who existed only for you, who was dying of love and grief,* would nevertheless be sacrificed to the first whim, or the dread of being ridiculed for a moment; and yet you would have one constrain themselves! Ah! that is not reasonable.

Adieu, Viscount! become once more amiable. It is the utmost of my wishes to find you charming as ever. When I am certain of it, I engage to prove it to you—indeed, I am too good natured.

Paris, Dec. 4, 17—.

LETTER CLIII.

VISCOUNT DE VALMONT *to the* MARCHIONESS DE MERTEUIL.

I reply to your letter on the instant, and will endeavour to be explicit; which is not an easy matter with you, when you have once determined not to understand.

Many words are not necessary to convince us, each has the power of ruining the other; we have an equal interest to keep fair with one another: that is not the business at present. But between the violent determination of destruction, and doubtless the more eligible one of being still united as hitherto, or of even being more so, by renewing our first attachment; between those two parties, I say, there are a thousand more to be taken. It was not, then, ridiculous to tell you, neither is it to repeat, that from this day I will either be your lover or your enemy.

I am very sensible the choice will give you some uneasiness; that it would be more convenient for you to shuffle. I am also satisfied, you never liked to be confined to yes or no: but you must be sensible, I cannot let you from this small circle, without risking being deceived; and you ought to have foreseen, I would not bear it. You are now to decide. I may leave you the choice, but will not remain in uncertainty.

I only inform you beforehand, I will not be imposed on by your arguments, good or bad; that I will no longer be seduced by any ornamental wheedling with which you might embellish a refusal; and that the hour of frankness is arrived. I wish for nothing more than to set you the example; and I declare with pleasure, I prefer peace and union. If it is necessary to break one or the other, I think I have the right and the means.

Therefore I will add, the least obstacle you make, I shall consider as a declaration of war. You will observe, the answer I demand does not require either long or studied sentences: two words will be sufficient.

Paris, Dec. 4, 17—.

The answer of the Marchioness de Merteuil, wrote at the bottom of this same letter.

War, then.

LETTER CLIV.

MADAME DE VOLANGES *to* MADAME DE ROSEMONDE.

The journal will inform you much better than I can, my dear friend, the melancholy state of our patient. Totally employed in my attendance on her, I have scarce time to write to you, as there are other matters to be attended to as well as her disorder. Here is a specimen of one which most certainly I did not in the least expect. I have received a letter from M. de Valmont, who has been pleased to choose me for a confidant, and even his mediatrix with Madame de Tourvel, to whom he wrote under my cover. I returned the one when I answered the other. I transmit you my answer; and I believe you will be of my opinion, that I neither could or ought to have any thing to do with what he requests. Had I been even inclined to it, our unhappy friend was unable to understand me. Her frenzy is incessant. But what do you think of M. de Valmont's distraction? Is it real, or does he mean to deceive the world to the last?[1]

If he is sincere this time, he may well say, he has made himself happy. I believe he will not be well pleased with my answer: but, I own, every thing that fixes my attention on this unhappy adventure, raises my resentment more and more against the author of it.

Adieu, my dear friend! I must return to my melancholy employment, which becomes more so, by the small prospect there is of success. I need not repeat my sentiments for you.

Paris, Dec. 5, 17—.

[1] Nothing having appeared in this correspondence that could resolve this doubt, we chose to suppress Valmont's letter.

LETTER CLV.

The VISCOUNT DE VALMONT *to the* CHEVALIER DANCENY.

I called on you twice, my dear Chevalier; but since you have thrown off the character of a lover for the man of intrigue, you are very properly invisible: however, your valet assured me you would be at home to-night; that you had ordered him to expect you. I, who am well acquainted with your designs, immediately conjectured it would be but for a short time for fashion's sake, and that you would immediately pursue your victorious career. Go on; I must applaud you: but, perhaps, you will be tempted to alter your course for this night. You are yet acquainted with only half your business; I must let you into the other half, and then you will resolve. Take time, then, to read my letter. It will not dissipate you from your enjoyments; on the contrary, its object is to give you your choice.

If you had opened your mind confidentially to me; if you had told me the part of your secrets you left me to guess at, I should with my zeal, and less awkwardness, have smoothed the path of your progression. But let us set out from this point. Whatever resolution you take would, at worst, be the summit of good fortune to any one else.

You have a rendezvous for to-night: have you not? With a charming woman, whom you adore? For at your age, where is the woman one does not adore for, at least, the first eight days? The field of action should also add greatly to your enjoyment—A delicious little villa, *which was taken for you only*, must embellish voluptuousness with the charms of mysteriousness and liberty. All is agreed on: you are expected; and you are inflamed with desire to be there! All this we both know, though you told me nothing of it. Now I will tell you what you do not know; but you must be told.

Since my return to Paris, I have been taken up with contriving the means of an interview between you and Mademoiselle de Volanges: I promised it; and when I last mentioned it to you, I had reason to expect from your answer, I may say, from your transports, I was exerting myself in your happiness. I could not succeed alone in this difficult undertaking: but after having settled every thing, I left the rest with your young mistress. She found resources in her affection, resources which escaped my experience; after all, to your great misfortune she has succeeded. She told me this evening, for these two days past all obstacles are removed, and your happiness depends on yourself alone.

She flattered herself, also, for those two days, to have been able to send you this news herself, and notwithstanding her mama's absence you would have been admitted: but you never once showed yourself! and I must farther tell you, whether from reason or capriciousness, the little thing did not seem pleased at your want of assiduity. At last she found means to see me, and made me promise to deliver you the enclosed letter as soon as possible. From the eagerness she expressed, I would venture to lay a wager she gives you an assignation this night; however, I promised her, upon honour and friendship, you should have the tender summons in the course of the day, and neither can or will break my word.

Now, young gentleman, how will you behave in this business? Placed between coquetry and love, pleasure and happiness, which will you choose? If I was writing to the Danceny of three months ago, or even the Danceny of a week past, certain of the emotions of his heart, I should be certain of his proceedings: but the Danceny of the day, carried away by women, hunting after intrigue, and, according to custom, a little profligate, will he prefer a timorous young girl, who has nothing but beauty innocence, and love, to the allurements of a common *intriguer?*

For my part, my dear friend, I think, even in your new system, which, I confess, I am not much averse to, circumstances would decide the preference to the lover. First, it is an additional conquest, then the novelty is attracting, and the fear of losing the fruits of your addresses, by neglecting to gather them; for to take it in this point of view, it would really be an opportunity missed, which is not always to be regained, especially in a first weakness: often in this case, a moment of ill humour, a jealous suspicion, even less, may prevent the finest conquest. Sinking virtue will sometimes grasp at a twig; and once escaped, will be on its guard, and not easily surprised.

On the other hand, you hazard nothing; not even a rupture; at most, a little quarrel: then your purchase with a little trouble the pleasure of a reconciliation; for what other resource has a woman you have already enjoyed but compliance? What would she get by severity? The privation of pleasure, without profit, for her glory.

If, as I suppose, you make love your choice, which appears to me, also, that of reason, I think it would be more prudent not to send any apology for the disappointment of the rendezvous; leave her in expectancy; for if you venture to give a reason, she will, perhaps, be tempted to dive into the truth. Women are curious and obstinate. All may be discovered: I myself, you see, am now an example of this truth. But if you let her remain in hope, which will be supported by vanity, it will not be lost until a long time after the proper hour for information is over; then to-morrow you will have time to choose the insurmountable obstacle that detained you: you may have been sick, dead if necessary, or any thing else that has almost made you frantic, and all will be made up.

But which ever side you incline to, I only beg you will inform me; and as I am totally unconcerned, I will always think you have done right. Adieu, my dear friend!

All I have to add is, I regret M. de Tourvel. I am in a state of desperation at being separated from her; and I would lay down one half my life, to devote the other to her. Ah! believe me, there is no felicity but in love.

Paris, Dec. 5, 17—.

LETTER CLVI.

CECILIA VOLANGES *to the* CHEVALIER DANCENY.

(Annexed to the former.)

How happens it, my dear friend, I no longer see you; although I never cease wishing for it? Your inclinations then, are no longer like mine! Ah, it is now I am truly sorrowful! More so, than when we were totally separate. The affliction I was used to receive from others, now proceeds from you, which is more insupportable.

For some days past, mama is never at home, and you know it—I flattered myself you would have taken the opportunity; but you do not at all think of me—I am very unhappy— How often have you told me, I did not love as much as you did—I was certain it was otherwise, and am now convinced. Had you called, you might have seen me; for I am not like you; I think of nothing but how to contrive to see you—You deserve I should not tell you all I have done: but I love you so much, and have so strong a desire to see you, I can't help telling you, and then I shall see if you really love me.

I have secured the porter, and he has promised every time you come no one shall see you; and we may confide in him, for he is a very honest man. There is then no other difficulty to prevent any one in the house seeing you, and that will be very easy to do; it is only to come at night; then there will be no danger at all—for since mama goes out every day, she always goes to bed at eleven; so that we shall have a great deal of time.

The porter told me when you had a mind to come this way, instead of knocking at the door, you need only tap at the window, and he would open the door directly, and then you can readily find the *back-stairs*—As you will not have any light, I will leave my chamber door open, which will give you some little. You must take great care not to make any noise, particularly passing by mama's little door. As to my waiting maid's room, it is of no signification, for she has promised me not to be awake; and she is also a very good girl! When you are going away it will be the same thing—Now we shall see whether you will come.

O, Lord! I don't know why my heart beats so while I am writing to you! Is it the forerunner of any misfortune, or is it the hope of seeing you that makes me thus? This I know, I never loved you so much, and never so much wished to tell you so. Come, then, my dear, dear friend, that I may a thousand times repeat I love you—I adore you, and never will love any but you.

I found a method to inform M. de Valmont I wanted to see him, and had something to say to him; and as he is our very good friend, will come to-morrow certainly. I will beg of him to give you my letter immediately—That I shall expect you to-morrow night, and you will not fail to come, if you have not a mind to make your Cecilia very miserable.

Adieu, my dear friend! I embrace you with all my heart.

Paris, Dec. 4, 17 — .

LETTER CLVII.

The CHEVALIER DANCENY *to the* VISCOUNT DE VALMONT.

Doubt neither the emotions of my heart, or my proceedings, my dear Viscount — Is it possible I could resist a wish of my Cecilia's? Ah! it is she, and she alone, I will ever love! Her openness, her tenderness, have fixed such a spell over me, that nothing can ever efface, although I have been weak enough to suffer a distraction. Imperceptibly, I may say, engaged in another adventure, the remembrance of Cecilia has disturbed me in the tenderest moments; and perhaps my heart never rendered her a more faithful homage, than at the instant I was unfaithful to her. However, my dear friend, let us spare her delicacy, and hide my fault; not to deceive, but only not to afflict her. Cecilia's happiness is the most ardent wish of my heart; and I should never forgive myself a fault which should cost her a tear.

I feel I deserved the banter you pass upon me, relative to what you call my new system: but I beg you will be assured, I am not led by them at this time; I am resolved to prove it to-morrow — I will go and accuse myself even to her who has been the cause and partner of my error — I will tell her; "read my heart; there you will see the tenderest friendship; friendship united to desire so much resembles love! We have both been deceived; but although liable to error, I am incapable of deceit." I know my friend well; she has probity, and is gentle; she will do more than pardon, she will approve my conduct; she has often reproached herself for having betrayed friendship: her delicacy has often alarmed her love: more considerate than me, she will strengthen my mind with those useful apprehensions which I rashly endeavoured to stifle in hers — I shall owe my reformation to her, and my felicity to you. O, my friends! partake my gratitude: the idea of being indebted to you for my happiness, augments its value.

Adieu, my dear Viscount! the excess of my joy does not prevent me from thinking and sharing your troubles. Why can I not serve you? M. de Tourvel still remains inexorable then! It is said she is very ill — May she at once recover health and condescension, and for ever make you happy! They are the vows of friendship; and I dare hope will be granted by love.

I would write some time longer, but time presses, and perhaps Cecilia already expects me.

Paris, Dec. 5, 17 — .

LETTER CLVIII.

The VISCOUNT DE VALMONT *to the* MARCHIONESS DE MERTEUIL.

Well, Marchioness, how are you after the pleasures of last night? Are you not a little fatigued? You must acknowledge Danceny is a charming fellow! That lad is a prodigy! You did not expect such things from him; is it not true? I must do myself justice; such a rival deserved I should be sacrificed to him. Seriously he has a number of good qualities! So much love, so much constancy, so much delicacy! Ah! if ever he loves you as he does his Cecilia, you will have no occasion to dread being rivalled; he has proved it this night. Perhaps through dint of coquetry, another woman may entice him for a short time; a young man hardly knows how to resist incitements; but you see a single word from the beloved object is sufficient to dissipate the illusion; so that there is nothing wanting to complete your happiness, but being that beloved object.

Certainly you will not be mistaken; you have such exquisite feeling it is not to be apprehended: yet the friendship that unites us, as sincere on my side as acknowledged on yours, made me wish you should experience the proof of this night; it is an effort of my zeal—It has succeeded—But no acknowledgements—it is not worth while—nothing more easy.

But to the point; what did it cost me? Why a slight sacrifice, and a little address. I consented to share with the young man the favours of his mistress; but he had as great a right to them as I had, and I was not in the least uneasy about them. The letter the young creature wrote him, I dictated; but it was only to gain a little time, as we could employ it to so much better purpose. What I wrote with it was nothing, almost nothing. Some few friendly reflections to direct the new lover; but upon honour they were useless—To tell the truth, he did not hesitate a moment. Moreover, he is to wait on you to-day to relate all; and it certainly will give you great pleasure! He will tell you, *read my heart,* so he writes me; and you see that I will settle every thing. I hope that in reading what he pleases, you will also perhaps read, that such young lovers are dangerous—and also, that it is better to have me for a friend than an enemy.

Paris, Dec. 6, 17—.

LETTER CLIX.

The MARCHIONESS DE MERTEUIL *to the* VISCOUNT DE VALMONT.

I do not like to have scurvy jests added to bad actions; it is not agreeable to my taste or manner. When I have cause of complaint against a person, I do not ridicule, I do better; I take revenge. However well pleased you may be with yourself now, do not forget it is not the first time you have applauded yourself beforehand; and singular, in the hope of a triumph that would escape from you, at the instant you was congratulating yourself on it. Adieu.

Paris, Dec. 6, 17—.

LETTER CLX.

MADAME DE VOLANGES *to* MADAME DE ROSEMONDE.

I write this from the chamber of your unhappy friend, whose state is pretty much the same: there is to be a consultation held this afternoon, of four physicians—I need not tell you this resource is oftener a proof of the danger than the means of relief.

However, it seems her head is something better since last night—her waiting maid told me this morning, her mistress ordered her to be called about twelve: she desired they should be left alone, and dictated a pretty long letter—Julie adds, while she was folding it, Madame Tourvel was attacked with her delirium, so that the girl did not know who to direct it to. I was at first surprised the letter itself was not sufficient to inform her; but telling me she was afraid of committing a mistake, and that her mistress had ordered her to send it away immediately, I took it upon me to open it.

There I found the enclosed writing, which is certainly not addressed to any body, being addressed to too many—Yet, I believe, our unhappy friend at first intended it for M. de Valmont, but gave way imperceptibly, to her disordered ideas. However, I thought it ought not to be sent to any one—I send it you, as you will see better than I can tell you, the thoughts that engage the head of our patient. Whilst she continues so intensely affected, I shall have very little hopes—the body seldom recovers when the mind is so agitated.

Adieu, my dear and worthy friend! I am happy you are far from the dismal spectacle I have incessantly before my eyes.

Paris, Dec. 6, 17—.

LETTER CLXI.

The Presidente DE TOURVEL.

(*Dictated by her, and wrote by her waiting maid.*)

Cruel and mischievous being! will thou never be tired persecuting me? Is it not enough to have tormented, degraded, abased? Will thou then rob me of the peaceful tomb? In the gloom of this abode, where shame has drove me to bury myself, are my sufferings to have no respite; is hope to be for ever banished? I do not require a favour I am undeserving of: I shall suffer without complaint, if my sufferings do not exceed my strength: but do not make my torments insupportable—Leave me my sorrows, and take away the cruel remembrance of the advantages I have lost. Although thou hast ravished them from me, do not again draw the afflicting picture of them—I was happy and innocent—I gazed on thee and lost my peace—I listened to thee and was guilty—Thou cause of all my crimes, who gave thee authority to punish them?

Where are now the friends to whom I was dear? My misfortunes have frightened them—No one dares come near me—I am oppressed and left without relief—I die and no one weeps over me—I am debarred of every consolation—Pity stops on the brink of the abyss where the criminal plunges—remorse tears my heart, and its cries are not heard.

And thou who I have injured; thou, whose esteem adds to my torment—thou who only hast a right to revenge; why art thou far from me? Come, punish a faithless woman—Let me suffer the tortures I deserve—I should have already bowed to thy vengeance, but wanted courage to inform thee of thy shame; it was not dissimulation, it was respect. Let this letter at least acquaint thee with my repentance. Heaven has taken thy cause in hand, to punish an injury to which thou wast a stranger—It was heaven tied my tongue—It was heaven prevented my design, lest you should pardon a crime it was resolved to punish—It snatched me from thy commiseration, which would have opposed its judgment.

But unmerciful in its vengeance, it delivered me up to him who ruined me; at once to make me suffer for him and by him. In vain I strive to fly from him; still he follows me—he is there; incessantly he besets me—How different from himself! His eyes show nothing but hatred and contempt—His lips utter insult and reproach—His arms surround me only to destroy me—Is there no one will save me from his savage rage?

How! It is he! I am not deceiv'd; it is he I see again—Oh, my lovely friend! receive me in thy tender arms; hide me in thy bosom! It is thee; yes, it is thyself—What fatal illusion deceived me? Ah, how have I suffered during thy absence—Let us part no more: let us never part. Let me breathe—Feel my heart, how it beats! Ah! it is no longer with fear, it is the soft emotion of love; why refuse my tender caresses? Turn thy languishing eyes towards me—What are those bands you want to break? Why those solemn preparations for death? What can thus alter thy countenance? Leave me! I shudder! O, God! This monster again! My dear friends, do not abandon me—You that wanted me to avoid him; help me to resist him—And you more lenient, who promised to soften my sorrows, why do not you come to me? Where are you both? If I must no longer see you, at least answer this letter, let me hear you still love me.

Leave me, then, cruel man! What new transport inspires thee? Art thou afraid a soft sentiment should invade me? thou redoublest my torments—You will force me to hate you—O, how painful is hatred! how it corrodes the heart from whence it is distilled! Why will you persecute me? What can you have more to say to me? Have you not made it impossible for me either to hear or answer you. Farewell.

Paris, Dec. 6, 17—.

LETTER CLXII.

CHEVALIER DANCENY *to the* VISCOUNT DE VALMONT.

I am informed, Sir, of your behaviour towards me—I also know that after having basely sported with me, you have dared to applaud yourself and brag of it—The proof of your treachery I have seen under your hand—I cannot help acknowledging my heart was pierced, and I felt some shame at having myself so much assisted in the odious abuse you made of my blind confidence: still I do not envy you this shameful advantage—I am only curious to know, whether you will equally preserve them all over me—This I shall be informed of, if, as I hope, you will be to-morrow morning, between eight and nine, at the gate of the wood of Vincennes, village of St. Maude. I will take care to provide every thing necessary for the eclaircissement, which remains for me to take with you.

The Chevalier Danceny.
Paris, Dec. 6, at night, 17—.

LETTER CLXIII.

M. BERTRAND *to* MADAME DE ROSEMONDE.

Madam,

It is with the greatest grief I find myself obliged to fulfil my duty, by giving you an intelligence that will cause you so much affliction. Permit me first to recommend the exertion of that pious resignation which every one has so often admired in you, and which alone can support us among the evils of this miserable life.

M. your nephew—Good God! must I afflict so respectable a lady! M. your nephew, had the misfortune to fall this morning in a duel he fought with M. the Chevalier Danceny. I am entirely unacquainted with the cause of the quarrel: but it appears, by the note which I found in M. the Viscount's pocket, and which I have the honour to send you; it appears, I say, he was not the aggressor: and yet heaven permitted him to fall!

I was at M. the Viscount's, waiting for him, at the very time he was brought back to his hotel. You cannot conceive the shock I received, seeing M. your nephew brought in by two of his servants, bathed in blood. He had two thrusts of a sword in his body, and was very weak. M. Danceny was also there, and even wept. Ah! certainly he ought to weep—it is a pretty time to cry when one has been the cause of an irreparable misfortune!

For my part, I could not contain myself; and notwithstanding my insignificancy, I could not help telling him my thoughts. But it was then M. the Viscount showed himself truly great: he commanded me to hold my tongue; and he even took his murderer by the hand, called him his friend, embraced him before us three, and said to us, "I command you to have for this gentleman all the respect that is due to a brave and gallant man." Moreover, he ordered to be given him, in my presence, some very voluminous papers, that I know nothing of, but which I know he set a value on. Then he desired they should be left together for a little while; however, I sent immediately for assistance, as well spiritual as temporal: but, alas! the evil was without remedy. In less than half an hour after, M. the Viscount was insensible. He could only receive the extreme unction; and the ceremony was scarcely over, before he breathed his last.

Great God! when I received in my arms at his birth this precious prop of so illustrious a family, could I ever have thought he would expire in my arms, and that I should deplore his death! A death so sudden, and so unfortunate—my tears flow in spite of me. I ask pardon, Madam, for taking the liberty of mingling my sorrows with yours: but in every station, tenderness and sensibility will operate; and I should be very ungrateful if I did not lament, during my life, a nobleman who was so kind, and placed such a confidence in me.

To-morrow, when the body will be removed, I will order every thing to be sealed, and you may depend on my care entirely in every thing. I need not inform you, Madam, this unhappy event puts an end to the entail, and leaves you entirely at liberty. If I can be of any service, I beg, Madam, you will give me your orders, which will be executed with the greatest zeal and utmost punctuality.

I am, with the most profound respect, Madam, your most humble Bertrand.

Paris, Dec. 7, 17 — .

LETTER CLXIV.

MADAME DE ROSEMONDE *to* M. BERTRAND.

I this instant received your letter, my dear Bertrand, informing me of the shocking event, to which my nephew is become the unhappy victim—yes, undoubtedly, I shall have orders to give you; and it is they only can take off my thoughts a while from this afflicting intelligence.

M. Danceny's challenge, which you sent me, is a convincing proof he was the aggressor; my intention therefore is, you should commence a prosecution in my name: for although my nephew, in compliance with his natural generosity, may have pardoned his enemy, his murderer, I ought to avenge at once his death, religion, and humanity. One cannot excite too much the severity of the laws against those remains of barbarism which still infect our morals; and I do not believe, in such cases, the forgiveness of injuries can be commanded us; therefore I expect you will prosecute this business with all that zeal and activity of which I know you so capable, and which you owe to my nephew's memory.

But first, take care to confer with M. the President — — from me. I do not write to him, as I am so overwhelmed with grief. You will, therefore, apologise for me, and communicate this to him.

Adieu, my dear Bertrand! I am well pleased with your conduct, and thank you for your good inclinations, and am your sincere friend.

Castle of — — , Dec. 8, 17 — .

LETTER CLXV.

MADAME DE VOLANGES *to* MADAME DE ROSEMONDE.

I know you are already informed, my dear and worthy friend, of the loss you have sustained. I know the tender affection you had for M. de Valmont, and I most sincerely partake of the affliction you must endure. I am truly grieved to add new griefs to those you have already experienced: but, alas! nothing now can be done for our unhappy friend but to deplore her fate. We lost her at eleven o'clock last night. By a fatality linked to her fate, and which seemed to baffle all human prudence, this short interval that she survived M. de Valmont was sufficient to inform her of his death, and, as she said herself, not be able to sink under the weight of her miseries until their measure was filled.

You already know, that for these two days she was insensible;—yesterday morning, when her physician came, and we drew near her bed, she did not know either of us, and we could not obtain a word or a sign. We were scarcely returned to the fire, while the physician was relating to me the melancholy event of M. de Valmont's death, but this unhappy woman recovered her reason: whether nature alone produced this revolution, or whether it was occasioned by the frequent repetition of the words, M. de Valmont and death, which may have recalled the only ideas with which her mind had been so long engaged.

Be it what it may, she suddenly drew back the curtain of the bed, exclaiming, "What! What do you say? M. de Valmont dead!" I hoped to make her believe she was mistaken. At first I endeavoured to persuade her she did not hear well: but all in vain; for she insisted the physician should begin the cruel tale again;—on my endeavouring to dissuade her from it, she called me to her, saying, in a low voice, "Why will you deceive me? Was he not already dead to me?" I then was forced to acquiesce.

Our unhappy friend appeared at first to listen to the story with great tranquillity: but she soon interrupted him, saying, "Enough; I know enough:" and immediately ordered her curtains to be closed—When the physician went to perform the duties of his office, she never would suffer him to come near her.

As soon as he was gone, she also sent away her nurse and her waiting maid. When we were alone, she requested I would assist her to kneel on her bed, and support her. Then she remained some time silent;—and without any other expression than her tears, which flowed most abundantly, joining her hands, and raising them towards heaven; "Almighty God!" said she in a weak but fervent tone, "I submit to thy just judgment: but in thy mercy forgive Valmont. Let not my misfortunes, which I acknowledge, be laid to his charge, and I shall bless thy mercy!" I could not avoid, my dear and worthy friend, going into those digressions on a subject I am sensible must renew and aggravate your sorrows, as I am certain this prayer of Madame de Tourvel's will give you much consolation.

After our friend had uttered those few words she fell in my arms; and she was scarcely settled in her bed, when she fainted for a considerable time, and recovered with the usual helps. As soon as she came to herself, she begged I would send for Father Anselmus, saying, "He is the only physician I have now occasion for. I feel my miseries will soon be at end." She complained of a great oppression, and spoke with great difficulty.

Some time after, she ordered her waiting maid to give me a little box, which I send you, that contains papers belonging to her, and charged me to send them to you immediately after her death.[1] Then she conversed about you, of your friendship for her, as much as her situation would permit, and with great tenderness.

Father Anselmus came about four o'clock, and stayed near an hour alone with her. When we returned, her countenance was calm and serene, but it was easily to be seen Father Anselmus had wept a great deal. He remained to assist at the last ceremonies of the church. This solemn and melancholy sight became more so by the contrast of the composed and settled resignation of the sick person, with the silent grief of the venerable confessor, who was dissolved in tears beside her. The afflicting scene became general, and she who we all deplored was the only one unmoved.

The remainder of the day was spent in the usual prayers, which was now and then interrupted by the frequent faintings of the dear woman. At last, about eleven, she seemed more in pain, with great oppression. I put out my hand to feel her arm; she had still strength to place it on her heart; I could no longer feel it beat, and, indeed, our unhappy friend expired instantly.

You may remember, my dear friend, when you last came to town, about a year ago, chatting together about some people whose happiness then appeared to us more or less complete, we indulged ourselves in the thought of this same woman's felicity, whose misfortune we now lament. Such an assemblage of virtues! so many attractions and accomplishments! so sweet, so amiable! a husband she loved, and by whom she was adored! a circle of friends, in whom she delighted, and was the delight! a figure, youth, fortune! so many united advantages are lost by one act of imprudence! O, Providence! how incomprehensible and adorable are thy decrees!—I fear I shall increase your sorrow by giving way to my own, and therefore will no longer dwell on the melancholy theme.

My daughter is a little indisposed. On hearing from me this morning the sudden death of two persons of her acquaintance, she was taken ill, and I ordered her to be put to bed. I hope, however, this slight disorder will not be attended with any bad consequence. At her age they are not accustomed to such chagrines, and they leave a more lively and stronger impression. This active sensibility is certainly a laudable quality. What we daily see ought to make us dread it. Adieu, my dear and worthy friend!

Paris, Dec. 9, 17—.

[1] This box contained all the letters relative to her adventure with M. de Valmont.

LETTER CLXVI.

M. BERTRAND *to* MADAME DE ROSEMONDE.

Madam,

In consequence of the orders you honoured me with, I waited on M. the President de —
—, and communicated your letter to him, informing him at the same time, as you desired, I
should do nothing without his advice. This respectable magistrate commanded me to observe to
you, the prosecution you intended against M. the Chevalier Danceny would equally affect the
memory of Monsieur your nephew, and his honour would necessarily be tainted by the decree
of the court; which would be, doubtless, a very great misfortune. His opinion is, then, that you
do not make any stir about the matter: but, on the contrary, that you should endeavour as much
as possible to prevent the public officers from taking cognisance of this unfortunate business,
which has already made too much noise.

These observations, so replete with wisdom, oblige me to wait your farther orders.

Permit me, Madam, to request, when you honour me with them, you will mention a
word concerning your state of health, which, I dread much, so many crosses have impaired.

I hope you will pardon the liberty I take, as it proceeds from my zeal and attachment.

I am, with great respect, Madam, your, &c.

Paris, Dec. 10, 17—.

LETTER CLXVII.

ANONYMOUS *to the* CHEVALIER DANCENY.

Sir,

I have the honour to inform you, your late affair with M. the Viscount de Valmont was
this morning much talked of among the King's counsel within the bar, and that it is much to be
feared the public officers will commence a prosecution. I thought this notice might be of service,
either to set your friends at work, to stop the bad consequences, or, in case you could not
succeed, to take every precaution for your personal security.

If you would permit me to add a piece of advice, I think you would do well, for some
time at least, not to appear so much in public as you have done for some days—Although the
world generally have great indulgence for those kind of affairs, yet there is a respect due to the
laws which ought to be observed.

This precaution appears to me the more necessary, that I recollect a Madame de
Rosemonde, who, I am told, is M. de Valmont's aunt, intended to prosecute you; if so, the courts
could not refuse her petition: it would perhaps be proper application should be made to this
lady.

Particular reasons prevent me from signing this letter; but I hope, though ignorant from
whom it comes, you will nevertheless do justice to the sentiment that has dictated it.

I have the honour to be, &c.

Paris, Dec. 10, 17 —.

LETTER CLXVIII.

MADAME DE VOLANGES *to* MADAME DE ROSEMONDE.

There are, my dear and worthy friend, the strangest and most sad reports spread here, on account of Madam de Merteuil. I am certainly far from giving any credit to them; and I would venture to lay a wager, they are horrible slanders; but I know too well, how the most improbable wickedness readily gains credit; and how difficult it is to wipe away the impression they leave, not to be alarmed at those, though I think them so easy to be refuted. I wish, especially, they might be stopped in time, and before they spread abroad; but I did not know until late yesterday, the horrible things that are given out; and when I sent this morning to Madame de Merteuil's, she was just then set out for the country for a couple of days — I could not learn where she was gone; her second woman, who I sent for, told me, her mistress had only given her orders to expect her on Thursday next; and none of her servants she left behind her knew any thing. I cannot even think where she can be; as I do not recollect any of her acquaintance who stay so late in the country.

However, you will be able, I hope, to procure for me, between this and her return, some eclaircissements that may be useful to her; for these odious stories are founded on circumstances attendant on the death of M. de Valmont, of which you will probably have been informed, if there be any truth in them; or you can at least readily receive information, which I particularly request you to do — This is what is published, or at least whispered as yet, but will not certainly fail to blaze out more.

It is said the quarrel between M. de Valmont and Chevalier Danceny, is the work of Madame de Merteuil, who deceived them both; and, as it always happens, the rivals began by fighting, and did not come to an eclaircissement until after, which produced a sincere reconciliation: and in order to make M. de Merteuil known to Chevalier Danceny, and also in his own justification, M. de Valmont had added to his intelligence, a heap of letters, forming a regular correspondence which he had kept up with her; in which she relates, in the loosest manner, the most scandalous anecdotes of herself.

It is added, that Danceny in his first rage gave those letters to whoever had a mind to see them; and that now they are all over Paris — Two of them in particular, are quoted[1]; in one of which, she gives a full history of her life and principles, which are said to be the most shocking imaginable — the other contains an entire justification of M. de Prevan, whose story you may recollect, by the proofs it gives, that he did nothing but acquiesce in the most pointed advances M. de Merteuil made him, and the rendezvous agreed on with her.

But I have fortunately the strongest reasons to believe those imputations as false as they are odious. First, we both know that M. de Valmont was not engaged about Madame de Merteuil; and I have all the reason in the world to think, Danceny was as far from thinking of her: so that I think it is demonstrable, that she could not be either the cause or object of the quarrel. Neither can I comprehend what interest M. de Merteuil could have, who is supposed to be combined with M. de Prevan, to act a part which must be very disagreeable, by the noise it would occasion, and might be very dangerous for her, because she would thereby make an irreconcileable enemy of a man who was in possession of a part of her secrets, and who had then many partizans. —Still it is observable, since that adventure, not a single voice has been raised in favour of Prevan, and that even there has not been the least objection made on his side since.

Those reflections would induce me to suspect him to be the author of the reports that are now spread abroad, and to look on those enormities as the work of the revenge and hatred of a man who, finding himself lost in the opinion of the world, hopes, by such means, at least to raise doubts, and perhaps make a useful diversion in his favour; but whatever cause they may proceed from, the best way will be to destroy such abominable tales as soon as possible; they would have dropped of themselves, if it should happen, as is very probable, that M. de Valmont and Danceny did not speak to each other after their unhappy affair, and that there had been no papers given.

Being impatient to be satisfied as to the truth of those facts, I sent this morning to M, Danceny's; he is not in Paris either; his servants told my valet de chambre, he had set out last night, on some advice he had received yesterday, and the place of his residence was a secret; probably he dreads the consequence of his affair; it is only from you then, my dear and worthy friend, I can learn such interesting particulars, that may be necessary for M. de Merteuil—I renew my request, and beg you will send them to me as soon as possible.

P. S. My daughter's indisposition had no bad consequences. She presents her respects.
Paris, Dec. 11, 17—.

[1] Letters lxxxi and lxxxv.

LETTER CLXIX.

The CHEVALIER DANCENY *to* MADAME DE ROSEMONDE.

Madam,
You will perhaps think the step I now take very extraordinary; but I beseech you to hear before you condemn me, and do not look for either audacity or rashness, where there is nothing but respect and confidence. I will not dissemble the injury I have done you; and during my whole life I should never forgive myself, if I could for one moment think it had been possible for me to avoid it; I also beg, Madam, you will be persuaded, although I feel myself exempt from reproach, I am not exempt from sorrow; and I can with the greatest sincerity add, those I have caused you have a great share in those I feel. To believe in those sentiments which I now presume to assure you of, it will be enough you do yourself justice, and know, that without the honour of being known to you, yet I have that of knowing you.

Still whilst I lament the fatality which has caused at once your grief and my misfortune, I am taught to believe, that totally taken up with a thirst for revenge, you sought means to satiate it even in the severity of the laws.

Permit me first to observe on this subject, that here your grief deceives you; for my interest in this circumstance is so intimately linked with M. de Valmont's, that his memory would be involved in the same sentence you would have excited against me. I should then reasonably suppose, Madam, I should rather expect assistance than obstacles from you, in the endeavours I should be obliged to make, that this unhappy event should remain buried in oblivion.

But this resource of complicity, which is equally favourable to the innocent and guilty, is not sufficient to satisfy my delicacy; in wishing to set you aside as a party, I call on you as my judge: the esteem of those I respect is too dear, to suffer me to lose yours without defending it, and I think I am furnished with the means.

For if you will only agree, that revenge is permitted, or rather, that a man owes it to himself, when he is betrayed in his love, in his friendship, and still more, in his confidence. If you agree to this, the wrongs I have done will disappear: I do not ask you to believe what I say; but read, if you have the resolution, the deposit I put into your hands[1]; the number of original letters seem to authenticate those, of which there is only copies. Moreover, I received those letters, as I have the honour to transmit them to you, from M. de Valmont himself. I have not added to them, nor have I taken any from them but two letters, which I thought proper to publish.

The one was necessary to the mutual vengeance of M. de Valmont and myself, to which we had an equal right, and of which he expressly gave me a charge. I moreover thought, it would be doing an essential service to society, to unmask a woman so really dangerous as Madame de Merteuil is, and who, as you see, is the only, the true cause, of what happened between M. de Valmont and me.

A sentiment of justice induced me to publish the second, for the justification of M. de Prevan, whom I scarcely know; but who did not in the least deserve the rigorous treatment he has met, nor the severity of the public opinion, still more formidable, under which he has languished so long, without being able to make any defence.

You will only find copies of those two letters, as I make it a point to keep the originals. I do not think I can put into safer hands a deposit, which, perhaps, I think of consequence to me not to be destroyed, but which I should be ashamed to abuse. I think, confiding those papers to you, Madam, I serve those who are interested, as well as if I returned them to themselves, and I preserve them from the embarrassment of receiving them from me, and of knowing I am no stranger to events, which undoubtedly they wish all the world to be unacquainted with.

I should, however, inform you, the annexed correspondence is only a part of a much more voluminous collection from which M. de Valmont drew it in my presence, and which you will find at the taking off the seals, entitled as I saw, *An open account between the Marchioness de Merteuil and Viscount de Valmont*. On this you will take what measures your prudence will suggest. I am with great respect,

Madam, &c.

P. S. Some advices I have received, and the opinion of some friends, have made me resolve to leave Paris for some time; but the place of my retreat, which is secret to every one, must not be so to you. If you do me the honour of an answer, I beg you will direct it to the commandery of − − by P.−and under cover, to M. the Commander of − −. It is from his house I have the honour to write to you.

Paris, Dec. 12, 17 — .

[1] It is from this correspondence, from that given at the death of M. de Tourvel, and the letters confided to M. Rosemonde, by Madame de Volanges, that the present collection has been compiled; the originals are still existing in the possession of Madame de Rosemonde's heirs.

LETTER CLXX.

MADAME DE VOLANGES *to* MADAME DE ROSEMONDE.

I go, my dear friend, from wonder to wonder, from sorrow to sorrow: one must be a mother to conceive my sufferings all yesterday morning — If my cruel uneasiness has been since alleviated, there still remains a piercing affliction, of which I cannot see the end.

Yesterday, about ten in the morning, surprised at not seeing my daughter, I sent my waiting maid to know what could occasion this delay — She returned instantly much frightened, and frightened me much more, by telling me my daughter was not in her apartment, and that since morning her waiting maid had not seen her. Judge you my situation! I had all my servants called, particularly the porter, who all swore they knew nothing of her, nor gave me any intelligence on this occasion. I went immediately into her apartment; the disorder it was in soon convinced me, she did not go out until morning, but could not discover any thing to clear up my doubts. I examined her drawers, her bureau; found every thing in its place, and all her clothes except the dress she had on when she went out: she did not even take the little money she had.

As she did not know until yesterday all that is said about M. de Merteuil; that she is very much attached to her; so much, that she did nothing but cry all night after — I also recollect she did not know M. de Merteuil was in the country; it struck me she went to see her friend, and that she was so foolish as to go alone: but the time elapsing, and no account of her, recalled all my uneasiness — Every instant increased my anxiety; and burning with impatience for information, I dared not take any step to be informed, lest I should give cause for a rumour, which perhaps I should afterwards wish to hide from all the world. In my life I never suffered so much.

At length, at past two o'clock, I received together a letter from my daughter, and one from the superior of the convent of — — . My daughter's letter only informed me, she was afraid I would oppose the vocation she had to a religious life, which she did not dare mention to me; the rest was only excusing herself for having taken this resolution without my leave, being assured I certainly would not disapprove it, if I knew her motives, which, however, she begged I would not enquire into.

The superior informed me, that seeing a young person come alone, she at first refused to receive her; but having interrogated, and learning who she was, she thought she served me, by giving an asylum to my daughter, not to expose her to run about, which she certainly was determined on doing. The superior offered me, as was reasonable, to give up my daughter, if I required it; inviting me at the same time, not to oppose a vocation she calls so decided.

She writes me also, she could not inform me sooner of this event, by the difficulty she had of prevailing on my daughter to write to me whose intent was, that no one should know where she had retired — What a cruel thing is the unreasonableness of children.

I went immediately to this convent. After having seen the superior, I desired to see my daughter; she came trembling, with some difficulty—I spoke to her before the nuns, and then alone. All I could get out of her with a deal of crying, was, she could not be happy but in a convent; I resolved to give her leave to stay there; but not to be ranked among those who desired admittance as she wanted. I fear M. de Tourvel's and M. de Valmont's deaths have too much affected her young head. Although I respect much a religious vocation, I shall not without sorrow, and even dread, see my daughter embrace this state—I think we have already duties enough to fulfil, without creating ourselves new ones: moreover, it is not at her age we can judge what condition is suitable for us.

What increases my embarrassment, is the speedy return of M. de Gercourt—Must I break off this advantageous match? How then can one contribute to their children's happiness, if our wishes and cares are not sufficient? You would much oblige me to let me know how you would act in my situation; I cannot fix on any thing. There is nothing so dreadful as to decide on the fate of others; and I am equally afraid, on this occasion, of using the severity of a judge, or the weakness of a mother.

I always reproach myself with increasing your griefs, by relating mine; but I know your heart; the consolation you could give others, would be the greatest you could possibly receive.

Adieu, my dear and worthy friend! I expect your two answers with the greatest impatience.

Paris, Dec. 13, 17—.

LETTER CLXXI.

MADAME DE ROSEMONDE *to the* CHEVALIER DANCENY.

The information you have given me, Sir, leaves me no room for any thing but sorrow and silence. One regrets to live, when they hear such horrible actions; one must be ashamed of their sex, when they see a woman capable of such abominations.

I will willingly assist all in my power, Sir, as far as I am concerned, to bury in silence and forgetfulness every thing that could leave any trace or consequence to those melancholy events. I even wish they may never give you any other uneasiness than those inseparable from the unhappy advantage you gained over my nephew. Notwithstanding his faults, which I am forced to confess, I feel I shall never be consoled for his loss: but my everlasting affliction will be the only revenge I shall ever take on you; I leave it to your own heart to value its extent.

Will you permit my age to make a reflection which seldom occurs to yours? which is, if rightly understood what is solid happiness, we should never seek it beyond the bounds prescribed by religion and the laws.

You may be very certain I will faithfully and willingly keep the deposit you have confided to me: but I must require of you to authorise me not to deliver it to any one, not even to yourself, Sir, unless it should be necessary for your justification. I dare believe you will not refuse me this request, and that it is now unnecessary to make you sensible we often sigh for having given way to the most just revenge.

I have not yet done with my requisitions, persuaded as I am of your generosity and delicacy: it would be an act worthy both, to give me up also Mademoiselle de Volanges's letters, which you probably may have preserved, and which, no doubt, are no longer interesting. I know this young creature has used you badly; but I do not think you mean to punish her; and was it only out of respect to yourself, you will not debase an object you loved so much. I have, therefore, no occasion to add, the respect the girl is unworthy of, is well due to the mother, to that respectable woman, who may lay some claim to a reparation from you; for, indeed, whatever colour one may seek to put on a pretended sentimental delicacy, he who first attempts to seduce a virtuous and innocent heart, by that measure becomes the first abettor of its corruption, and should be for ever accountable for the excesses and disorders that are the consequence.

Do not be surprised, Sir, at so much severity from me; it is the strongest proof I can give you of my perfect esteem. You will still acquire an additional right to it, if you acquiesce, as I wish, to the concealing a secret, the publication of which would prejudice yourself, and give a mortal stab to a maternal heart you have already wounded. In a word, Sir, I wish to render this service to my friend; and if I had the least apprehension you would refuse me this consolation, I would desire you to think first, it is the only one you had left me.

I have the honour to be, &c.
Castle of — —, Dec. 15, 17 —.

LETTER CLXXII.

MADAME DE ROSEMONDE *to* MADAME DE VOLANGES.

If I had been obliged to send to Paris, my dear friend, and wait for an answer to the eclaircissements you require concerning Madame de Merteuil, it would not have been possible to give them to you yet; and even then they would be, doubtless, vague and uncertain: but I received some I did not expect, that I had not the least reason to expect, and they are indubitable. O, my dear friend! how greatly you have been deceived in this woman!

I have great reluctance to enter into the particulars of this heap of shocking abominations; but let what will be given out, be assured it will not exceed the truth. I think, my dear friend, you know me sufficiently to take my word, and that you will not require from me any proof. Let it suffice to tell you, there is a multitude of them, which I have now in my possession.

It is not without the greatest trouble I must also make you the same request, not to oblige me to give my motives for the advice you require concerning Mademoiselle de Volanges. I entreat you not to oppose the vocation she shows.

Certainly, no reason whatever should authorise the forcing a person into that state, when there is no call: but it is sometimes a great happiness when there is; and you see your daughter even tells you, if you knew her motives you would not disapprove them. He who inspires us with sentiments, knows better than our vain wisdom can direct, what is suitable to every one; and what is often taken for an act of severity, is an act of his clemency.

Upon the whole, my advice, which I know will afflict you, for which reason you must believe I have reflected well on it, is, that you should leave Mademoiselle de Volanges in the convent, since it is her choice; and that you should rather encourage than counteract the project she has formed; and in expectation of its being put in execution, not to hesitate in breaking off the intended match.

Now that I have fulfilled those painful duties of friendship, and incapable as I am of adding any consolation, the only favour I have to request, my dear friend, is, not to put me any interrogatories on any subject relative to those melancholy events: let us leave them in the oblivion suitable to them; and without seeking useless or afflicting knowledge, submit to the decrees of Providence, confiding in the wisdom of its views whenever it does not permit us to comprehend them. Adieu, my dear friend!

Castle of — —, Dec. 15, 17 —.

LETTER CLXXIII.

MADAME DE VOLANGES *to* MADAME DE ROSEMONDE.

Alas, my dear friend! with what a frightful veil do you cover the fate of my daughter; and seem to dread I should raise it! What can it hide, then, more afflicting to a mother's heart, than those horrible suspicions to which you give me up? The more I consider your friendship, your indulgence, the more my torments are increased. Twenty times since last night, I wanted to be rid of those cruel uncertainties, and to beg you would inform me, without reserve or evasion, and each time shuddered, when I recollected your request not to be interrogated. At length, I have thought on a way which still gives me some hope; and I expect from your friendship, you will not refuse to grant my wish: which is, to inform me if I have nearly understood what you might have to tell me; not to be afraid to acquaint me with all a mother's tenderness can hide, and is not impossible to be repaired. If my miseries exceed those bounds, then I consent to leave the explanation to your silence: here is, then, what I already know, and so far my fears extended.

My daughter showed a liking for Chevalier Danceny, and I was informed, she went so far as to receive letters from him, and even to answer them; but I thought I had prevented this juvenile error from having any dangerous consequence: now that I am in dread of every thing, I conceive it possible my vigilance may have been deceived, and I dread my daughter being seduced may have completed the measure of her follies.

I now recall to mind several circumstances that may strengthen this apprehension. I wrote you, my daughter was taken ill, on the news of M. de Valmont's misfortune; perhaps, the cause of this sensibility was the idea of the dangers M. Danceny was exposed to in this combat. Since when, she wept so much on hearing every thing was said of Madame de Merteuil; perhaps, what I imagined the grief of friendship, was nothing else but the effect of jealousy, or regret at finding her lover faithless. Her last step may, I think, perhaps be explained by the same motive. Some, who have been disgusted with mankind, have imagined they received a call from heaven. In short, supposing those things to be so, and that you are acquainted with them, you may, no doubt, have thought them sufficient to justify the rigorous advice you give me.

And if matters should be so, at the same time I should blame my daughter, I should think myself bound to attempt every method to save her from the torments and dangers of an illusory and transitory vocation. If M. Danceny is not totally divested of every honourable sentiment, he will not surely refuse to repair an injury of which he is the sole author; and I also think, a marriage with my daughter, not to mention her family, would be advantageously flattering to him.

This, my dear and worthy friend, is my last hope; hasten to confirm it, if possible. You may judge how impatient I shall be for an answer, and what a mortal blow your silence would give me.[1]

I was just closing my letter, when a man of my acquaintance came to see me, and related to me a cruel scene Madame de Merteuil had to go through yesterday. As I saw no one for some days, I heard nothing of this affair. I will recite it, as I had it from an eye witness.

Madame de Merteuil, at her return from the country on Thursday, was set down at the Italian comedy, where she had a box; there she was alone; and what must appear to her very extraordinary, not a man came near her during the whole performance. At coming away, she went, according to custom, into the little saloon, which was full of company; instantly a buzzing began, of which probably she did not think herself the object. She observed an empty place on one of the seats, on which she sat down; but all the ladies who were seated on it immediately rose, as if in concert, and left her entirely alone. This so pointed mark of general indignation was applauded by all the men, redoubled the murmurs, which, it is said, were even at last increased to hootings.

That nothing should be wanting to complete her humiliation, unfortunately for her, M. de Prevan, who had not appeared in public since his adventure, made his appearance at that instant. The moment he entered, every one, men and women, surrounded and applauded him; and he was jostled in such a manner, as to be brought directly opposite M. de Merteuil by the company who formed a circle round him. It is asserted, she preserved the appearance of neither seeing or hearing any thing, and that she did not even change countenance; but I am apt to believe this last an exaggeration. However, this truly ignominious situation lasted until her carriage was announced; and at her departure, those scandalous hootings and hissings were again redoubled. It is shocking to be related to this woman. M. de Prevan received a most hearty welcome from all the officers of his corps who were there, and there is not the least doubt but he will be restored soon to his rank.

The same person who gave me this information told me M. de Merteuil was taken the night following with a very violent fever, that was at first imagined to be the effect of the dreadful situation she was in; but last night the small pox declared itself, it is of the confluent kind, and of the worst sort. On my word, I think it would be the greatest happiness if it should carry her off. It is, moreover, reported, this affair will prejudice her most essentially in her depending lawsuit, which is soon to be brought to trial, and in which, it is said, she stood in need of powerful protection.

Adieu, my dear and worthy friend! In all this I see the hand of Providence punishing the wicked: but do not find any consolation for their unhappy victims.

Paris, Dec. 18, 17—.

[1] This letter remained unanswered.

LETTER CLXXIV.

The CHEVALIER DANCENY *to* MADAME DE ROSEMONDE.

You are very right, Madam; most certainly I will not refuse you any thing that depends on me, and on which you are inclined to set a value. The packet I have the honour to send you, contains all Mademoiselle de Volanges' letters. If you will take the trouble to read them, you will be astonished to see so much candour united with such perfidiousness. This is, at least, what has made the strongest impression on my mind, at my last perusal of them.

But it is impossible to avoid being filled with the greatest indignation against M. de Merteuil, when one recollects what horrible pleasure and pains she took to destroy so much innocence and candour.

No, Madam, I am no longer in love. I have not the least spark of a sentiment so unworthily betrayed; and it is not love that puts me on means to justify Mademoiselle de Volanges. Still would not that innocent heart, that soft and easy temper, be moulded to good more readily than it was hurried to evil? What young person, just come out of a convent, without experience, and almost divested of ideas, and bringing with her into the world, as most always happens, an equal share of ignorance of good and evil; what young person could have resisted such culpable artifices more? In order to inspire us with some indulgence, it is sufficient to reflect on how many circumstances, independent of us, is the frightful alternative from delicacy, to the depravity of sentiment. You, then, did me justice, Madam, in believing me incapable of having any idea of revenge, for the injuries I received from Mademoiselle de Volanges, and which, notwithstanding, I felt very sensibly. The sacrifice is great, in being obliged to give over loving her: but the attempt would be too great for me to hate her.

I had no need of reflection to wish every thing that concerns, or that could be prejudicial to her, should ever be kept secret from the world. If I have appeared something dilatory in fulfilling your wishes on this occasion, I believe I may tell you my motive; I wished first to be certain I should not be troubled on my late unhappy affair. At a time when I was soliciting your indulgence, when I even dared to think I had some right to it, I should have dreaded having the least appearance in a manner of purchasing it by this condescension: certain of the purity of my motives, I had, I own, the vanity to wish you could not have the least doubt of them.

I hope you will pardon this delicacy, perhaps too susceptible, to the veneration with which you have inspired me, and to the great value of your esteem.

The same sentiment makes me request as a favour, you will be so obliging to let me know if you think I have fulfilled all the obligations the unhappy circumstances I was in required. Once satisfied on this point, my resolution is taken; I set out for Malta: there I shall with pleasure take and religiously keep vows which will separate me from a world, with which, though young, I have so much reason to be dissatisfied — I will endeavour in a foreign clime, to lose the idea of so many accumulated horrors, whose remembrance can only bring sorrow to my head.

I am with the greatest respect, Madam, &c.

Paris, Dec. 26, 17 — .

LETTER CLXXV.

MADAME DE VOLANGES *to* MADAME DE ROSEMONDE.

At length, my dear and worthy friend, Madame de Merteuil's fate is determined; and it is such, that her greatest enemies are divided between the indignation she deserves, and the compassion she raises. I was right, when I wrote you it would be happy for her to have died of the small pox. She is recovered, it is true, but horribly disfigured; and has lost an eye. You may well imagine, I have not seen her; but I have been informed she is a hideous spectacle.

The Marquis of — — who never loses an opportunity of saying a sarcastical thing, speaking of her yesterday, said, that her disorder had turned her inside out; that now her mind was painted on her countenance. Unfortunately all present thought the remark very just.

Another event adds to her disgraces and her misfortunes: her lawsuit came to a trial the day before yesterday, and she was cast by the unanimous opinion of all the judges; costs of suit, damages, and interest.

All in favour of the minors: so that the little she had exclusive of this suit, is all swallowed, and more too by the expences.

As soon as she was informed of this news, although still ill, she set off post in the night alone — Her people say to-day, that not one of them would accompany her; it is imagined she has taken the road to Holland.

This sudden flight raises the general outcry more than all the rest; as she has carried off all her diamonds, which are a very considerable object; and were a part of her husband's succession; her plate, her jewels, in short every thing she could; and has left behind her debts to the amount of 50,000 livres — it is an actual bankruptcy.

The family are to assemble to-morrow to take some measures with the creditors. Although a very distant relation, I have offered to contribute, but I was not at this meeting, being obliged to assist at a more melancholy ceremony. To-morrow my daughter will put on the habit of novice; I hope you will not forget, my dear friend, my only motive in agreeing to this sacrifice, is the silence you keep with me.

M. Danceny quitted Paris about a fortnight ago; it is said he is gone to Malta, to settle: perhaps it would be yet time enough to prevent him? My dear friend, my daughter was very culpable then! You will undoubtedly excuse a mother being difficult in acquiescing to such a dreadful truth.

What a fatality I am involved in for some time past, and has wounded me in my dearest connections! My daughter and my friend.

Who can refrain being struck with horror at the misfortunes one dangerous connection may cause, and how many sorrows and troubles would be avoided by seriously reflecting on this point! Where is the woman who would not fly the first advances of a seducer? What mother would not tremble to see any other but herself speak to her daughter? But those cool reflections never occur until after the event. And one of the most important and generally acknowledged truths, is stifled and useless in the vortex of our absurd manners.

Farewell, my dear and worthy friend! I now feel, our reason, which is inadequate to prevent misfortunes, is still less to administer consolation[1].

Paris, Jan. 14, 17 — .

[1] Particular reasons and considerations, which we shall always think it our duty to respect, oblige us to stop here.

We cannot at this time give the reader neither the continuation of M. de Volanges' adventures, nor the sinister events which fulfilled the miseries or ended M. de Merteuil's Punishment.

We shall be permitted, perhaps, some time or other, to complete this work, but we cannot pledge ourselves to this: even if we could, we should first think ourselves obliged to consult the taste of the public, who have not the same reasons we have to be concerned in this publication.

FINIS.

Made in the USA
Las Vegas, NV
18 October 2023

79291037R00138